A LESSON IN OBEDIENCE

ALLIE SHANTE

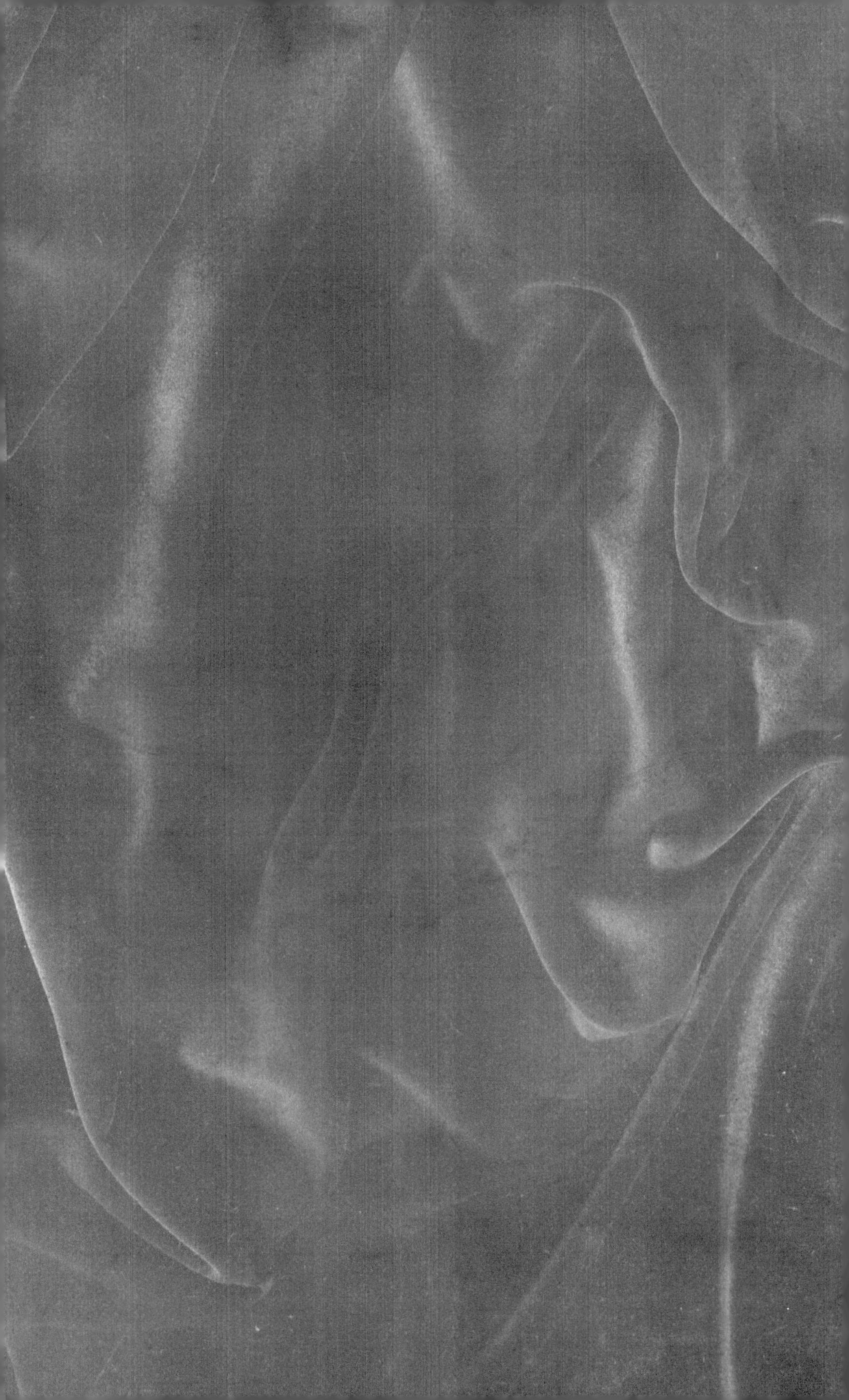

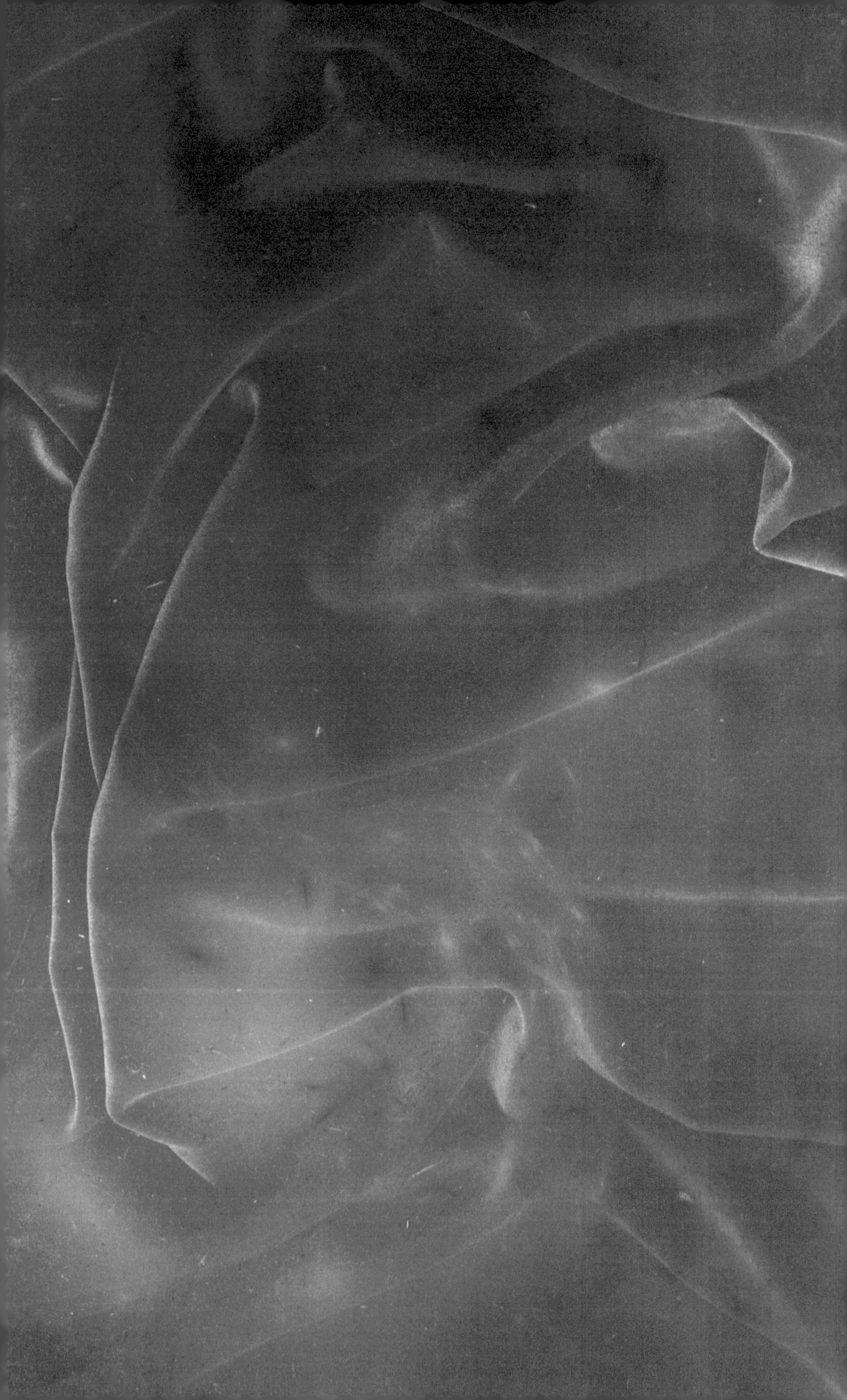

CONTENT WARNING

Parental death, blood/violence, emotional abuse (not by main characters), explicit sexual content, minor animal harm (not by main characters), alcohol, very light degradation, shadow play, explicit language, PTSD, panic attacks

List can also be found at: www.authorallieshante.com

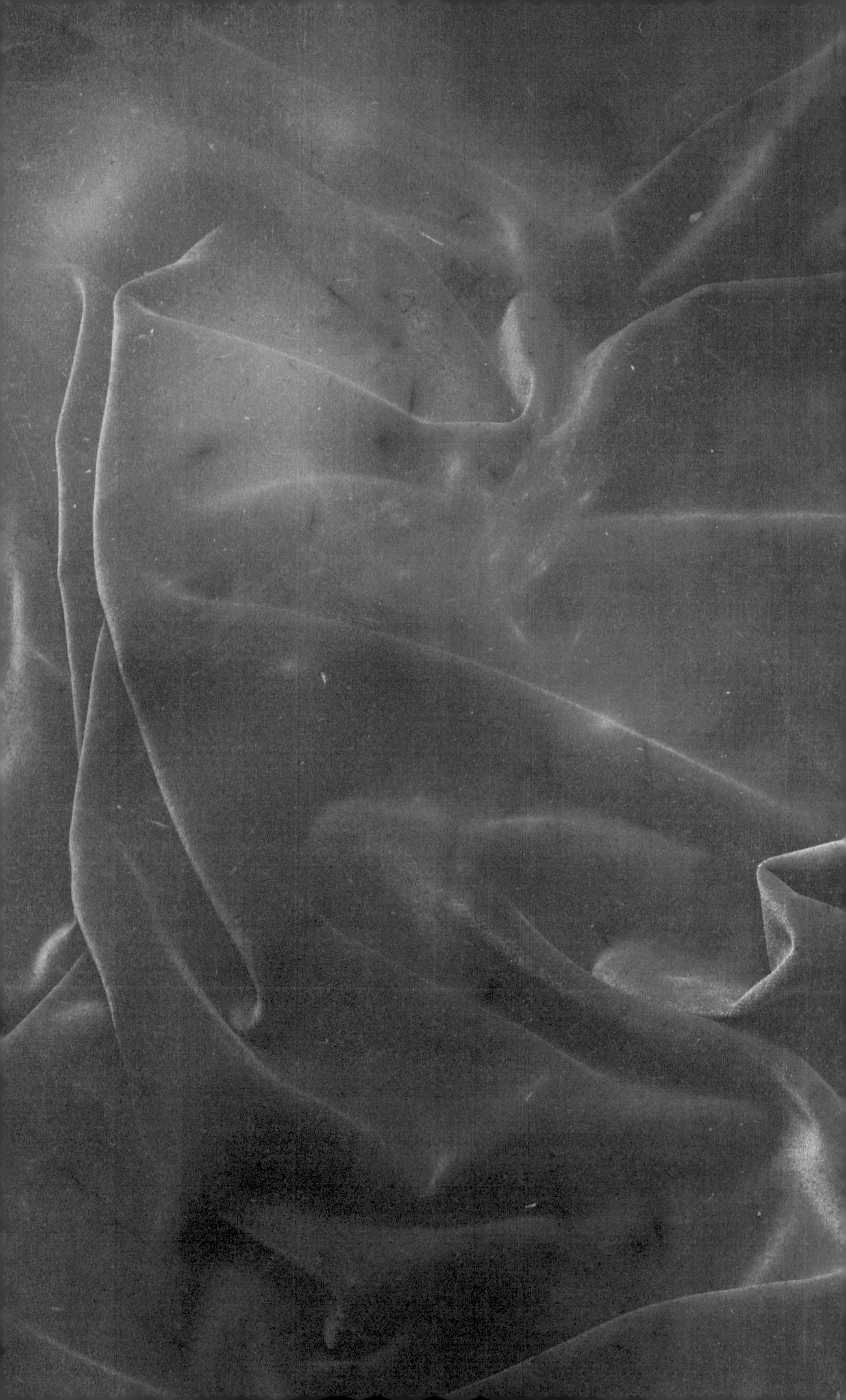

You are a unique result of the events you've experienced, the people you've interacted with, and the temperament you were born with.

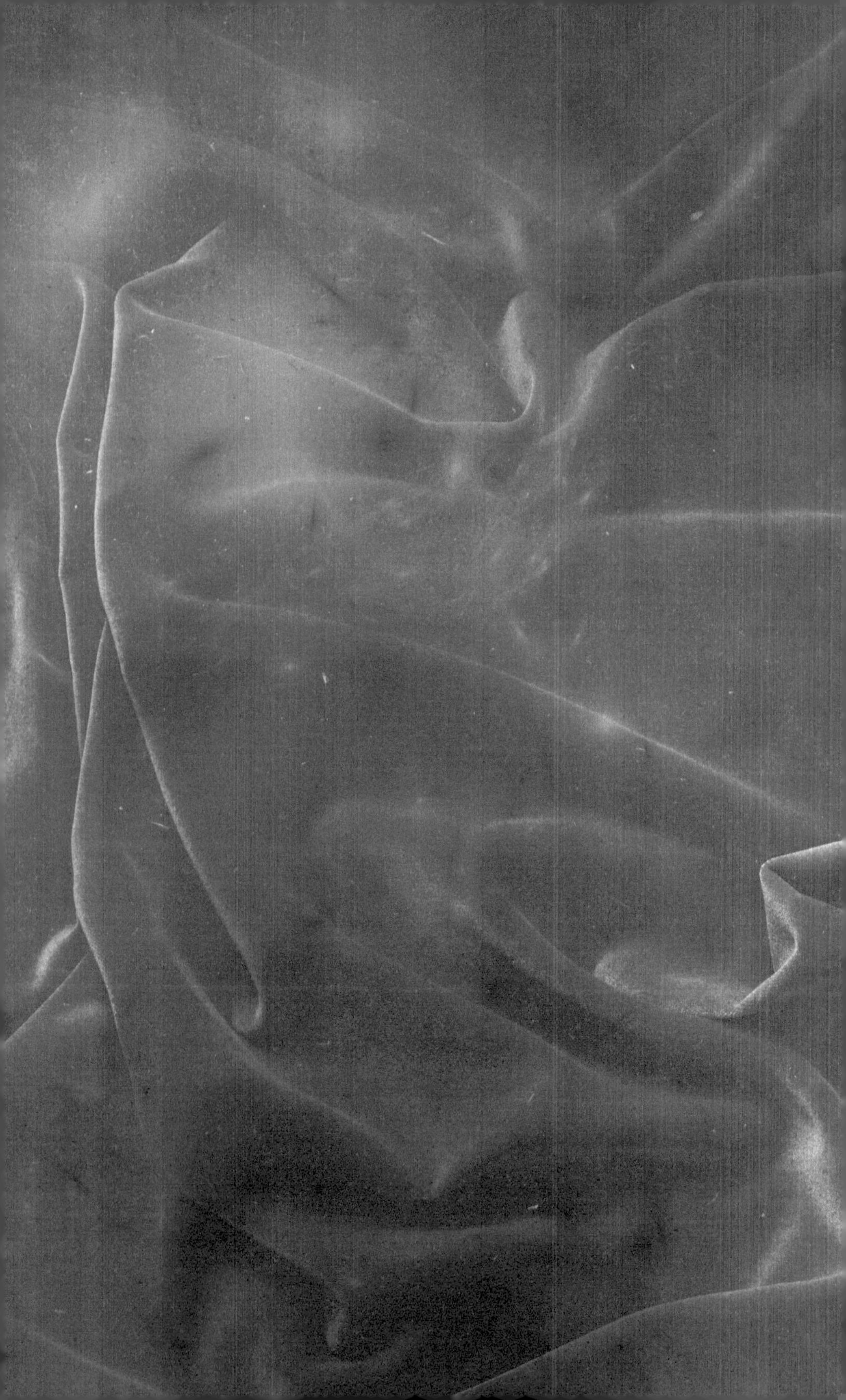

PLAYLIST

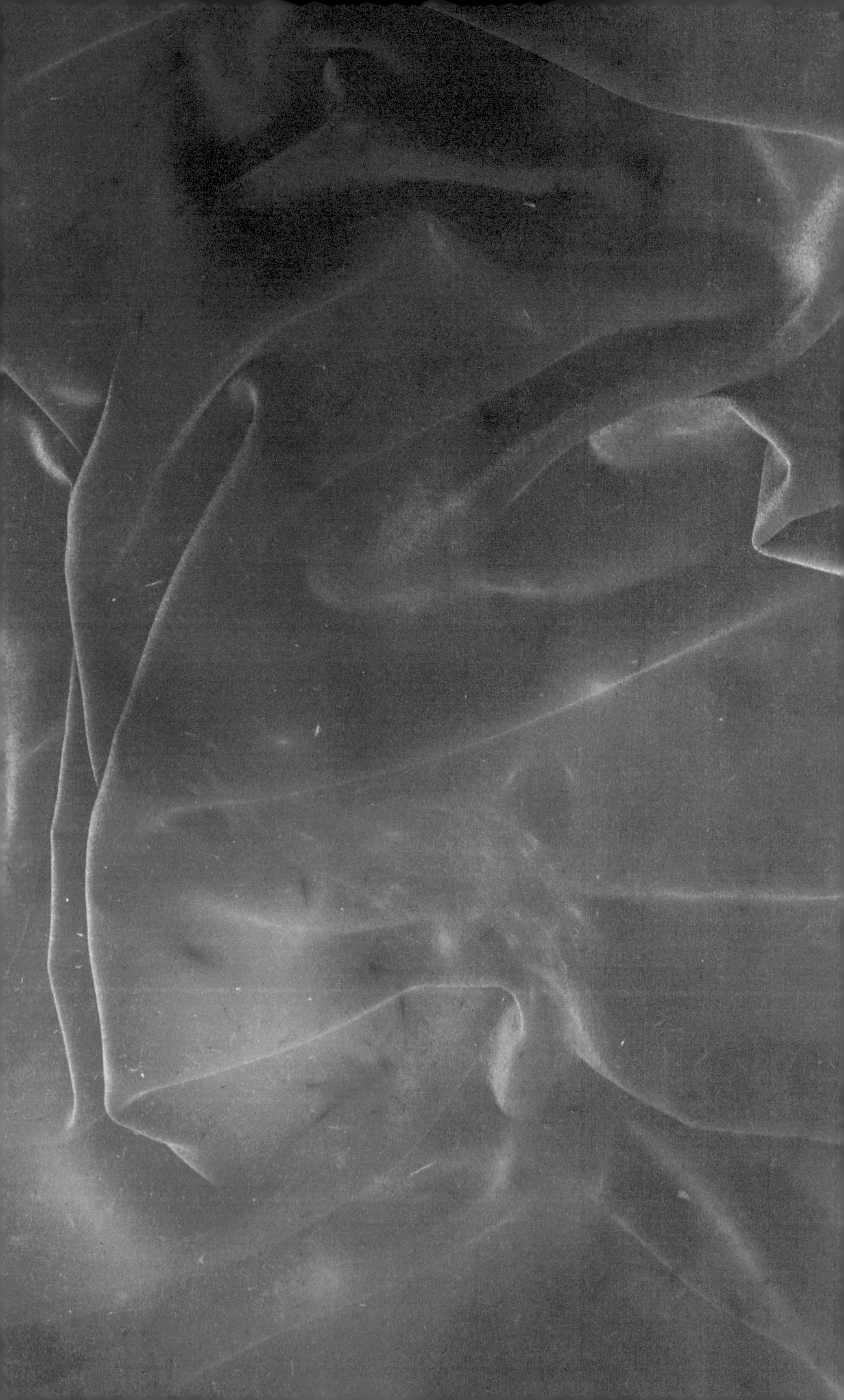

AUTHOR'S NOTE

If you have not read A Lesson in Deceit, I highly recommend going back and reading that first.

I can happily tell you that Beau, Riley's pitbull does make it to the end of the story. Not a spoiler, just a fact.

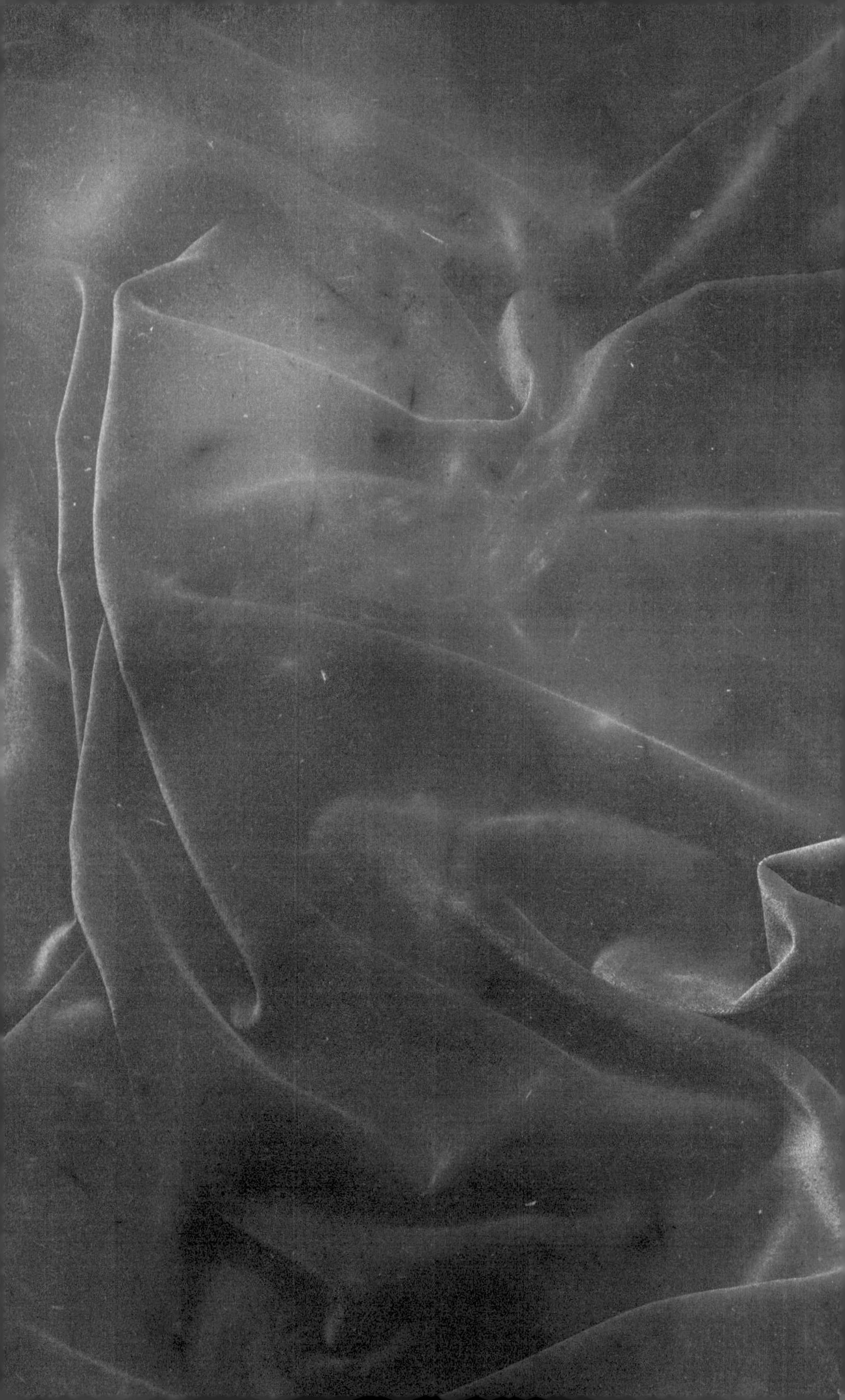

PRONUNCIATION GUIDE

Grayson Ypulong (EE-PULONG)

Corrin (CORE-IN): not CA-REN

Beau (BOW)

Leif (LEAF)

Mystic Riegan (REE-GAN)

SAMIA (SAH- ME- AH)

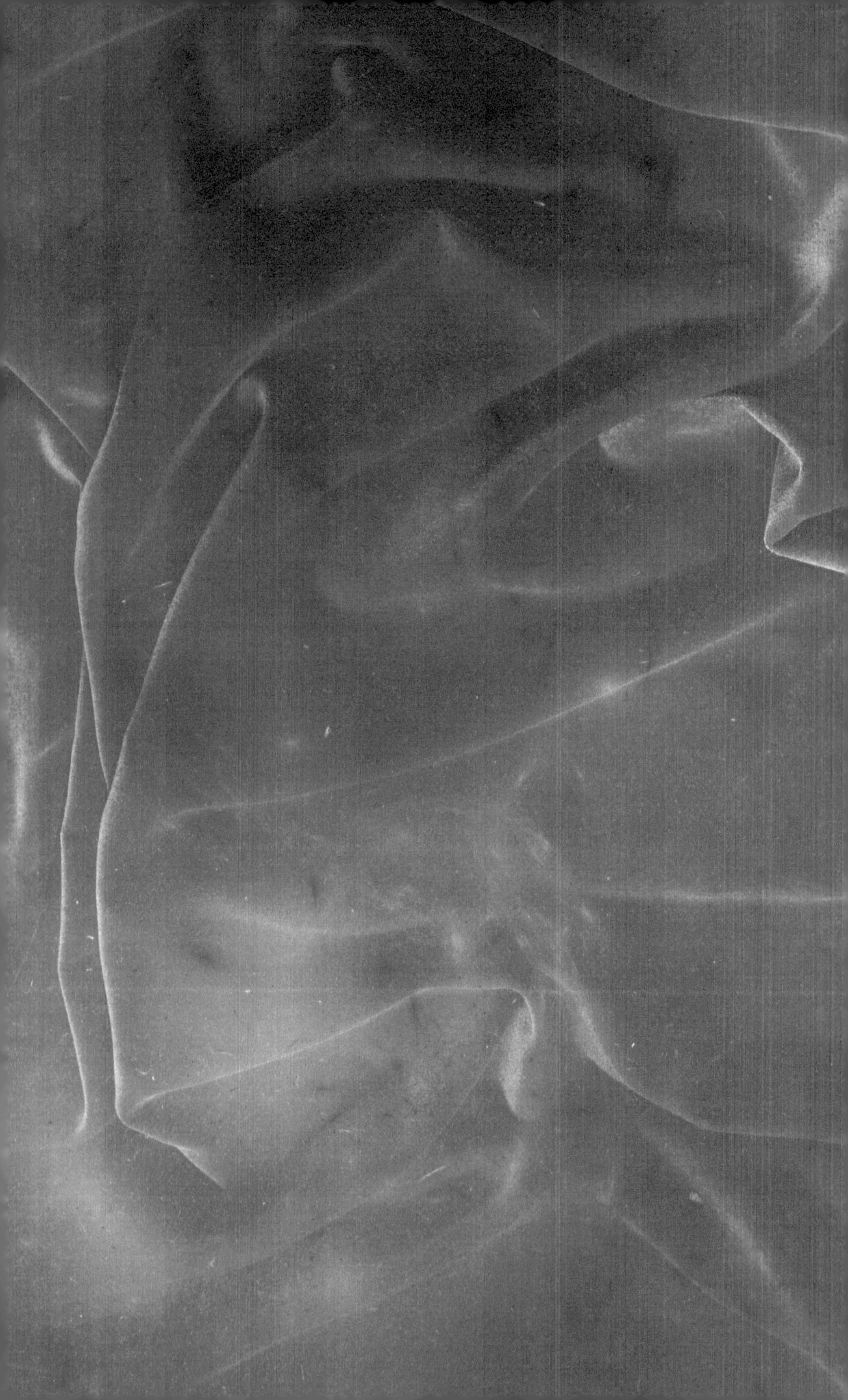

TRANSLATION GUIDE

A Lesson in Obedience has both Spanish and Tagalog phrases throughout, so here is a quick translation guide.

TAGALOG

- *gabi na*: it is late
- *Ang saya ko na nandito ka!*: I'm so happy you're here
- *"Mayasa akong makita ka*: it's nice to see you
- *Ingat ka anak*: stay safe my son
- *Ingat ka*: Take care
- *Hindi mahalaga kung ano man ang tagumpay na iyong narating kung hindi mo naman kayang ipagmalaki kung paano mo ito nakuha*: The achievement doesn't matter if you aren't proud of how you acquired it
- *Di ko gusto kapag na-iistress ka*: I don't like it when you're stressed
- *Huy! Tigilan mo yan!*: Oh stop it, don't be silly
- *Bagay kayo!*: Excellent pairing
- *Anong sinabi mo?*: What did you just say?
- *Sinasabi ko sayo*: I said what I said

- *Anong nangyari?*: What's going on?
- *Pasensya na at pinag alala pa kita:* I am sorry I worried you
- *Syempre anak kita*: Of course, you're my son
- *Syempre:* Of course
- *Oo, okay lang yung unang araw:* Yes, the first day was fine
- *Nakikinig ka pa ba sakin?:* Are you listening to me?
- *Bakit di ka man lang nagsalita?:* Why didn't you say anything?
- *Wag kang magsinungaling:* Stop telling lies
- *Bakit ka nanginginig?:* Why are you shaking?
- *Tumingin ka sa akin:* look at me
- *Nagkamali ako at gumagawa ako ng paraan para maayos ko ang aking mga kasalanan:* I've made some mistakes and I'm trying to fix them
- *Nakakatakot siya,* Dad: He's scary, Dad
- *Anak ka namin:* You're our son
- *Tulungan mo ang girlfriend mo:* Go help your girlfriend
- *Aking sinta:* my love/my darling

SPANISH

- *Ay Dios!:* "Oh my god!
- *Mi amor:* My love
- *No se:* I don't know
- *lobo:* wolf
- *Un perro!:* A dog
- *Hola:* hello
- *Venaqui, mi hermosos bebe:* Come here you beautiful baby
- *Estámos aquí para apoyarte:* we're here to support you
- *Perro:* dog
- *estas loco?!:* are you crazy?
- *Necesitas relajarte:* you just need to relax
- *por un minuto:* for one minute

- *Sabes que eres la cosa más linda del mundo?:* do you know that you are the cutest thing in the world?
- *Amigos! Entren!:* My friends! Come on in!
- *Cálmense, idiotas. No tengo miedo echarlos, por el amor de Dios:* Quiet down, you idiots. I am not afraid to kick you out, for fucks sake
- *Por fin!:* Finally
- *Pajaro:* bird
- *Como suena eso?:* How does that sound?
- *Cabrón:* asshole
- *Guardaespaldas:* bodyguards
- *Buenas noches!:* Good evening

1
RILEY

Chancellor Fowler breathed heavily as he hovered over me, letting his words hit me all at once. There was a sinking feeling in my gut and the air in the room tasted stale as I tried to breath.

"Y-you're what?" I stuttered, finding it hard to swallow.

His previous look of insanity morphed into one of what anyone not in this situation would call a caring expression. His tone was almost soft. "I'm your father, Riley."

"That can't be true! I am not your daughter. You killed the only man who gets to call me that." I spat at him, my eyes flicking over his shoulder to Grayson, whose expression looked confused and defeated. I had no sympathy for his feelings on the matter; I currently had no sympathy for his feelings on *anything*.

Chancellor Fowler chuckled, releasing my arms. My biceps felt hot and I looked down, noticing red handprints that were raised and looked painful to the touch. He casually moved his hand towards my wounds. "I'm truly sorry about that. I never want to hurt you. You're my daughter. I've just missed you, and it frustrates me that you were so misled."

I shot up from the couch and pushed him away from me. Vertigo set in with my sudden movement and I stumbled backwards, colliding with the arm of the couch. I reached out for it, digging my fingernails into the fabric. "You're lying!"

Chancellor Fowler slid his hands down his black jacket and sighed. "I am not. I knew this would be difficult, but this is why I wanted to have a chat. I think it is well within my rights to know my own daughter, my successor."

"Your...your what?" I waved my hands in front of my face, stepping even further away. I swung my head towards Grayson. "Did you know this?!"

Grayson raised his head to look at me as if he just knew I wanted his attention. "Riley, of course not. You really think I would have done any of this—"

Chancellor Fowler tsked. "Don't blame the poor boy. He doesn't matter at the moment, so please refocus on the here and now. We are together and now we can get to know one another."

I took another step back and nearly tripped backwards. I caught myself, looking down at what it was. The bile that had settled in my stomach started to rise again when I saw Marianne's body. I held my hand to my chest and the tears that had stopped minutes ago were back.

Her blonde hair was now soaked in blood and her once lively aura that never faltered was nowhere to be felt or seen. There was so much blood and I noticed shoe marks where I stood, telling me I had stepped in it. I had stepped in my best friend's blood. My best friend who didn't think twice about why I was at Mystic Riegan and just made the best out of a fucked-up situation.

I fell to the floor, letting my jeans get soaked in her blood, reaching out to fan her hair out of her face. It was like I didn't recognize this person lying lifeless in front of me. I ran my knuckle over her cheek and her skin still had some warmth in it, but not much. I tentatively touched where some glass pieces were lodged in her neck and her blood coated my fingers.

My hand shook when I pulled it back. Tears ran down my cheeks, but my breath caught in my throat when a hand gripped my shoulder. I don't know if it was meant to be comforting but it just felt cold. I slowly turned my head up to see Chancellor Fowler with one of his hands in his pockets, looking down at me.

"I am sorry about your friend."

I narrowed my eyes at him. It unnerved me that I was starting to see the resemblance. In the tiny moments that I wasn't just viewing him as a monster, I could see the things that certified our relation to one another. I didn't *want* to believe him, but there were some things I couldn't just decide were false. Resemblance could fuck off. He wasn't my father.

"Fuck off," I said, shrugging roughly so he would quit touching me.

He sighed deeply. "This attitude will get you nowhere. You do understand that, right?"

"My attitude?" I spoke through gritted teeth as I stared down at the lifeless body before me.

Chancellor Fowler cleared his throat. "Yes. Your attitude. Death is a part of life, Riley. You should let this unfortunate event make you stronger. I assure you that you'll need focus and strength..."

I pushed away from the ground and whirled around so I could face him. His eyebrows shot up, surprised. "Unfortunate event?! You are insane! You murdered someone! She was someone I cared about and you think that will be something I can just get past! You think that will make me want to fucking talk to you?!" I shoved my hands against his chest, getting blood on his jacket.

I shoved him again and again. I could hear myself screaming, but it sounded like an echo. I already felt like a shell of my former self. My hands turned to fists and I was ramming them into his chest over and over. Hands folded around my biceps, pulling me back.

"Riley, stop. Please calm down." Grayson's voice was in my ear, pleading.

The voice that could usually soothe me, now only pained me. I quickly turned around, ripping myself away from him. "Don't touch me!"

"Riley, I'm so sorry. I promise you, I knew nothing about this. I was just..." I slapped him across the face before he could finish.

"I. Don't. Care." I could hear the hurt in my voice and the tears were threatening to fall again.

Chancellor Fowler whistled, adjusting his jacket and running his fingertips over the blood stains I'd graced it with. "So feisty. You are your mother's daughter."

I narrowed my eyes at him but said nothing.

"I can forgive your outburst. I may not know you well, but I have a feeling you are eager to know certain things about who you are. I can provide you that insight."

I let out a humorless laugh. "If I say no, are you just going to kill another one of my friends?"

Chancellor Fowler ran a hand through his curls. "I would like to avoid that, but I have no qualms with crossing lines. I never have. You'd be surprised how many people you know who think just like me."

I let my eyes flutter close as I took a deep breath. When I opened them, I glanced over at Grayson, who was looking at me with those deep brown eyes. I quickly looked away and back over to Chancellor Fowler. He gave me an expectant look, but there was no tension anywhere in his body. He would keep me here all day and night until I gave him the time of day.

I wiped my hand across my cheeks, removing any remnants of tears. Without another word, I turned around and made my way over to the couch. I slowly sat down, placing my hands on my knees. I could feel the metal of the dampener ring against my blood-soaked jeans.

"Come shadow wielder, I'll need you when this is over." Chancellor Fowler snapped his fingers, walking around Grayson and sitting on the opposite couch. Grayson perched himself on the arm, avoiding eye contact with me.

I licked my lips, feeling how dry they were. "Were you two married?"

The Chancellor chuckled. "Oh no. I would have married her if she would have stuck around. I would have given her the world." His jaw ticked when he spoke about her.

"Was she aware of your...magic?" I tilted my head to the side.

He nodded. "Jillian loved what I could do. It fascinated her. I let her peek in on coven gatherings and I told her all about my dreams, my plans. Your mother was looking at colleges and I was trying to coax her into applying to Mystic Riegan where we could be together all the time. When I had to take over things changed but I tried to make it better. She was resistant but that was nothing new."

I remained quiet, letting him continue.

"When she told me she was pregnant, I was overjoyed. She was nervous, but I tried to comfort her and let her know she would want for nothing. Our child—you— would have everything."

I ran my palms over the top of my thighs. "Then why would she take me away from you? From all of it?"

"Maybe I had plans she didn't approve of. Maybe she never really loved me. That is a question for your mother. She left me before you were born, hid you away without even so much as a goodbye. You cannot fault me for being upset that she took my child. And then to find out that she shielded you from me..." His expression turned into one of distraught. "It is enough to make any parent go a little insane."

"She wouldn't make that decision without a good reason. My mother doesn't make decisions on a whim. Especially one of that magnitude."

He clucked his tongue, shaking his head. "Of course, you would take her side. She did raise you for all these years."

"She did raise me. Along with my *dad.*"

Chancellor Fowler cracked his neck, shaking out his shoulders. "That man was not your father. He could play house all he wanted, but you are mine. I had a late meeting with Oliver St. James and on my way out I saw Thomas's light on and I hadn't properly met him, so I was going to simply say my hello before I left. He was a nice enough man and we got to talking, but when I heard him mention Jillian's name, I swore it couldn't be the same person. I pressed for more answers and then he started getting antsy and eventually I couldn't take it. That man was assuming my position as your father and it wasn't right, it wasn't fair."

"So, killing him was the only solution?"

"I was angry and perhaps I let my control slip. You would have never come here if I hadn't though. Your necklace was a powerful thing, but we have a familial bond, and you stepped onto a campus that was founded by our family. I was going to feel your presence."

"I've been on this campus before I ever enrolled, how come you never went on your hunt for me then?"

"You had been gone for so long, Riley! I dreamed of the day you would come back. I thought it was wishful thinking, my mind and heart playing tricks on me. Once Thomas was gone, I knew I needed to make every effort to find you again and then well, the pieces just started to fall into place for me. You were right here. Right on campus where you belong." I could see tiny flames lick at his fingertips, but he never let them get any bigger. "Your power will be every bit as strong as mine..."

"She probably knew you were corrupt." I scoffed, my breath coming out harshly. "The smartest thing she ever did was run away from you."

He shrugged. "Clearly it wasn't bad enough for her to come back with that man and think everything would be normal. She really thought that necklace was going to save you from..."

"My necklace," I interrupted him, placing my fingers at my sternum where my necklace should have been.

"Ah, that little trinket. I don't know who did that, but Jillian must have outsourced from somewhere. She was resourceful, clearly. That doesn't matter anymore. You can now take your rightful place in the coven."

I swallowed hard. "The coven? The one you're siphoning powers from?"

"Let's not dwell on the things we can't fix."

"You're taking powers from your coven, your own people. Why would I want to be a part of that?"

Chancellor Fowler sighed, bending his one leg and placing it over the other. "I do it because the coven is mine to uphold, I should get a little something, shouldn't I? The witches are still powerful, still in control. It's simple sharing and no one gets hurt."

"It's stealing! If you are so above them, then why aren't *you* the coven leader? Corrin said..."

He settled back into the couch cushion. "Ah, she's a spirited little witch, your friend. Quite good with potions, yes? Oliver told me about your excursion into Thomas's office." I looked over towards the fire to avoid his eyes. "I'm sure your friend told you about our interim coven leader, she is rather investigative, that one."

"She said that Celica got a new one right after my dad died. Why?"

He cracked his neck again when I said the word *dad*. That really got under his skin. "Everyone has to move on from a job at some point. It was just time."

"That's bullshit!" I accused, prepared to leap off the couch, but a force was holding me back. Chancellor Fowler had a few of his fingers up and it was like I could feel power from them keeping me on the couch.

"Coven leader is just a cute little position that really acts as the face of Celica. I call the shots whether they like it or not. Our family has always taken a place above them all, founding this university and making it what it is. This coven has been around for a long time as you know, and the *leaders* are just a physical presence that the witches can look to. Some members of our family have taken up the mantle as coven leader, while others stepped into the role I now possess."

"In the shadows? A monster hiding as a university Chancellor?"

He smirked at me. "Hate me all you like. You should be happy I care enough not to cause any true harm to my coven members or else that overzealous friend of yours would be in her place." He waved his hand casually towards Marianne's body. I sucked in a breath and peeked over at Grayson, who had been quiet this whole time. "There is no going back now. You've already shown your true self to half the faculty, so I am well within my rights to assume that your file will now be corrected to show that you are a magic wielder. I'll let you get your bearings and then we can announce our family ties, hmm? Celica coven is your home. I will gladly give you the position of coven leader if you'd like, ease you into how things are done."

I placed my hands on the back of my head. "I don't want that. I don't want any of this!"

"These positions of power have been passed down and it's your turn to learn. I didn't have the pleasure of choices, so please don't be so ungrateful. I don't know whether your mother just couldn't handle it or not, but that is of no concern to me any longer. You are here now, and you can't just hide from your lineage. You will hurt people if you can't get your magic under control."

"You don't get to talk about hurting people. You say you want to get to know me, well get this through your head that hurting the people I care about, the people I love will not make me like you. It won't ever make me care about you or acknowledge you as my dad."

Chancellor Fowler hummed, removing his suit jacket and placing it on the back of the couch. "Fine. If you think your resistance will push me away, I would think again." He looked over at Grayson, snapping his fingers to gather his attention. "Take her back."

I shifted so that I could create more distance between Grayson and me. "Take me where?"

Chancellor Fowler made a motion with his hand towards the door to the far right and it swung open. A tall woman with dark black hair quickly walked in, holding a tiny vial of what looked like silver dust. He nodded at her when she gave him a questioning look. "The school will be closed for a day or two, so take that as your time to think about your options. And despite what you think of me, I do love you."

"I don't need to think..."

"Make sure she remains unharmed," Chancellor Fowler patted Grayson on the knee before he stood up. He walked over to me, gripping my hand and yanking my dampener ring off. "When you can't control yourself, you'll be begging for my help." He walked away and I was going to follow after him, but the woman stood in front of me, some of the dust in her palm. She blew it in my face and my vision got blurry.

Marianne's body was becoming distorted and my head felt numb and heavy. Grayson was in front of me now and he moved me so I was laying down, my vision eventually becoming nothing but black.

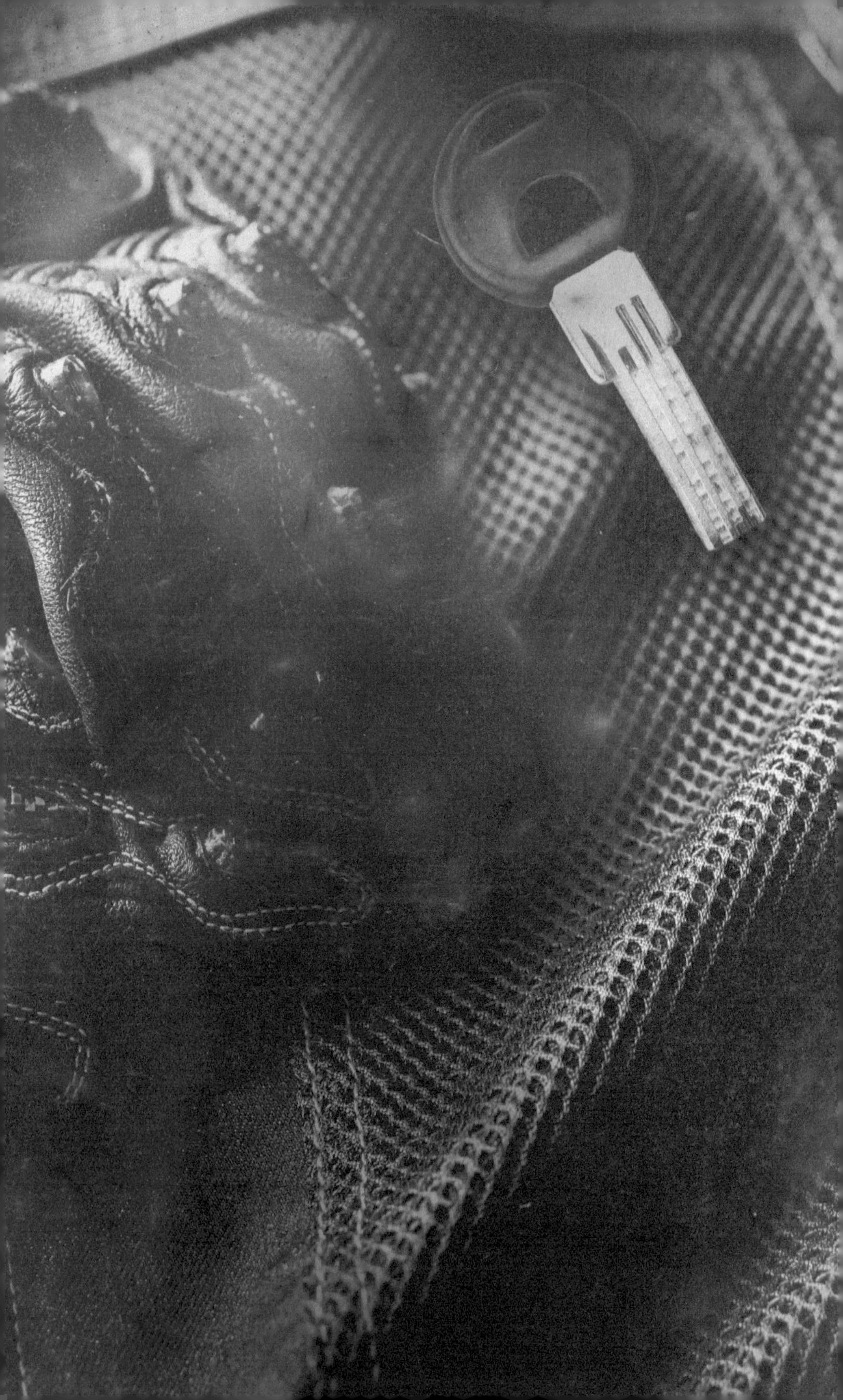

2
RIVER

I ripped my hands through my hair as I looked around the room that was still in a disastrous disarray, but most of the people that had occupied it had fled. I focused my attention back on the space Riley had once been in. I blinked and blinked again as if that would just make her appear.

I couldn't even put my own thoughts together on what had happened. She'd pushed Grayson back out of nowhere, using... magic? The police were here and the fucking fire department. First responders had taken the student that had ripped Riley's necklace off. They would be fine, but the shattered pieces of the ruby gem had me scratching my head. What the fuck was going on?

Grayson had just taken her, removed her from what could have turned into an even worse situation. Although, from the looks of it, I couldn't see it getting any better from where I stood. I started to bend down, noticing a tiny bit of magical residue. Riley was a magic wielder. Since fucking when?

Hands grabbed my shoulders, pulling me back up before I could take a better look. I came face to face with my brother. Asher pulled me off to the side, scrubbing a hand down his face. "What the fuck, River?"

I gave him a surprised look. "What do you mean *what the fuck, River?*"

"I *mean*—" Asher started, looking around us. "—what the fuck was that? Did you know she could do that?"

My eyes widened. "Of course not! I don't even think *she* knew she could either. The look on her face, Asher..."

He huffed out a breath, looking over his shoulder. "Where is she?"

I shook my head, moving away from him and towards the door. "I don't know."

"You don't know!?"

I turned around quickly, pressing my index finger roughly into his chest. "If I knew where she was do you think I would fucking be here right now?" I pulled out my phone, shoving past a few police officers and pushed open the door.

"Have you called Grayson?" Asher was right behind me, nearly on my heels.

I waved my phone over my shoulder. "Already on it." I put my phone to my ear, hearing it ring and ring and ring, eventually going to voicemail. I dialed his number again, listening and waiting. Voicemail again.

"Fuck," I mumbled, switching to text.

RIVER

Let me know when you get this and if Riley is alright. Call me.

Asher rushed past me, his keys jingling in his hand.

"Where are you going?" I asked, jogging to catch up with him.

He scoffed, giving me a small glance over his shoulder. "No. Not me. *We. We* are going to Riley's house."

I grabbed his arm, making him turn around and look at me. "You don't know how to get there. Unless you do, but that would be really odd since you've never fucking been there."

Asher rolled his eyes, which was weird. That was a gesture I hardly even saw him do. He shoved the keys at me. "You're driving."

I pointed towards the closest parking lot. "No, my bike is parked over there. I'm not running all the way to the fucking admin lot for your car. I'll take my bike, and I'll text you the address."

Asher let out a loud groan. "Why are you so difficult?"

"She's my girlfriend, Asher. I don't know why you're so eager to go. We had fun one time and all of a sudden you care?" I started to walk backwards towards the parking lot but stopped to *really* look at him. I didn't have time to dig into his mind, but something told me I didn't have to.

He shook his head, starting to jog in the direction of the admin parking lot.

I tried calling Riley, but her phone went to voicemail as well. I shook my head and quickly got on my motorcycle, hearing the engine rev to life.

I WAS SURPRISED TO SEE ASHER PULLING IN A FEW MINUTES AFTER ME WHEN I got to Riley's house. On my bike, I could swerve around traffic and normally get away with going over the speed limit. I tried to wrap my mind around my brother on the road, cutting people off and intentionally going anywhere near eighty miles per hour.

Asher slammed his car door, walking in step with me as we headed towards the front door. I heard excessive barking and whining from inside. Before we could even attempt to knock, the door swung open and Riley's mom looked at us with wide eyes. Behind her I saw Beau run across the room, his lungs working overtime.

He started to run back the other way, but then he noticed us. The gray pitbull came running at us and I rushed past Mrs. Monroe so I could stop him from escaping out the front door. Beau was strong and I felt his nails dig into my skin. I held him down on the ground, feeling his body shake. He wiggled out of my hold, but Asher closed the door behind him before Beau could attempt another escape.

The dog tilted his head back and howled, running his body into the door and scratching at the paint.

Riley's mom sighed, placing her hands on either side of her head. "Beau, stop it! Calm down!" She clapped her hands loudly, maneuvering herself between the door and Riley's dog. "Stop it!"

Beau backed up and whined. He howled again, turning right and running into the living room.

Asher came over and helped me up. I ran my hand down my pants, watching copious amounts of gray fur fly off my jeans. Mrs. Monroe shook her head, looking over at me. "What are you doing here?" Her voice sounded tired and a little hoarse. I assumed it was due to yelling at Beau.

I glanced over at Asher who raised his eyebrows at me as if to say *well, speak.*

"Is Riley here?" I asked, looking up the staircase and hoping that she was just comfortable in her room. If Beau's temperament was any indication, my hopes would not be met.

Mrs. Monroe narrowed her eyes at me. "No, she's not. Riley sent me a text about that meeting you were going to tonight but told me not to worry about it. She said it had to do with the witches on campus, so I've been in the office all day. I got a call from the next-door neighbor about Beau and rushed home. He's been like this ever since. He nearly knocked me over when I first got home."

Beau's stocky body knocked against the side of my leg when he barreled past me.

"I assumed she would be with you..." Riley's mom let her words fall away.

I shook my head solemnly, taking a step closer to her.

"Where is my daughter, River?"

I opened my mouth to respond, but Asher answered for me. "We don't know. We thought she might be here. At the meeting, something happened—"

Mrs. Monroe placed her hand on her chest, her eyebrows furrowing "Something happened to Riley?" Her breathing was becoming quicker as she gave Asher a curious expression. "Wait, who are you?"

"This is my brother, Asher. He—" I struggled to find the words. "He was at the meeting too. He came as...support." Asher scoffed, moving out of the way when Beau almost took him out from behind his knees. The barking was causing a nasty vibration in my skull and I just needed him to be quiet so I could fucking think.

Riley's mom nodded quickly. "Okay, well, what happened to my daughter? What do you know? You need to tell me what you know so —" She stopped talking when there was a small thud from upstairs.

Asher and I gave each other a look before we headed in that direction. Beau cut us off, sailing up the stairs and straight towards Riley's room. He clawed at the door, attempting to use his teeth to rip at the wood.

"Beau, back off!" Riley's mom yelled, trying to shove the dog away.

I turned the knob, pushing open the door. Beau caused the door to fly open and hit the wall behind it when he rushed into the room, leaping onto the bed. My eyes followed him, and relief washed over me when I saw Riley laying on her bed. Her eyes were closed, but her chest rose and fell letting me know she was alive.

Relief morphed into confusion and dread when I took in her clothes. Blood stained her jeans; her hands and even small bits were on her face. I stepped further into the room, feeling Riley's mom knock against my shoulder as she took in the state of her daughter.

She clasped her hand over her mouth, hurrying over to the side of the bed. She took Riley's hand and then immediately dropped it. "She's burning up."

"Burning up?" Asher asked, tilting his head to the side.

"Her skin is fire." Mrs. Monroe attempted to place the back of her hand on Riley's forehead, but yanked it away, hissing. "What's wrong with her!?" Her voice was full of panic. "Whose blood is that!?" I grabbed her shoulders and pulled her back. I tried to do my own assessment, but a low growl came from next to Riley's body.

Beau had curled his body right next to her with his head on her shoulder. His tail was stiff and standing at attention. He didn't bare all his teeth, but his nose scrunched up with every little growl that left his throat. What was going on with him?

"Hey, buddy. It's just me." I put my hands up, palms out, hoping that he would understand I meant no harm. I would never hurt her.

His ears went back while his large eyes looked down at her. He ran his snout over her cheek and licked her skin.

Wake up. Please wake up.

I blinked when those words entered my mind. I knew what my brother's mind sounded like and that wasn't it. It could have been Riley's mom, but the voice was off. It was almost childlike. I tried to reach out and touch her again, but Beau growled...again. It was as if he needed her to be alright and awake before he let anyone in her personal space, except for her mom.

"From what I can see, she doesn't have any wounds, so I don't think the blood is hers."

Asher scrubbed a hand down his face. "The problem is that it is someone's."

"She wasn't here early. I swear I checked her room. I'm not going crazy! I'm..." Mrs. Monroe looked up at the ceiling as she held her tears at bay. She tentatively sat on the edge of the bed while getting no resistance from Beau. She was careful not to touch her daughter's skin but ran her fingers along her braids. Her body stiffened, her breath catching. "Where's her necklace?"

"Her what?" I asked, squinting.

"Her necklace. The one I gave her when she was twelve. The one her..." she stopped talking, clearing her throat. "Did she have it on when you last saw her?"

I nodded slowly. "She did, but...it got destroyed."

"Destroyed!?" Mrs. Monroe screamed, scrambling off the bed and placing her face in her hands. "That can't happen!"

"Mrs. Monroe, it's a necklace, I hardly think that's the most important thing—" Asher started, getting a glare from Riley's mom when the room started to shake. Tiny vibrations here and there. Various objects around Riley's room began to lift, higher and higher.

"What the fuck?" I said, looking around. The objects started to fly across the room, causing each of us to duck. Different items started to circling through the air, breaking as they hit the wall. Glass from picture frames and clay from random ceramics she'd made when she decided to take that pottery class shattered, leaving remnants all over the floor. The glass from her window shook, cracks developing slowly.

"Is she...doing this!?" Asher yelled, catching a canvas that had flown off the wall before it could do any damage.

"I don't know!" I answered.

"Riley, wake up! Riley stop!" Her mom begged, ducking her head down to avoid any flying objects.

"Get inside her head! Talk to her!" Asher demanded, pointing to my girlfriend.

It sounded ridiculous, but ever since I promised her that I wouldn't read her mind, I had conditioned myself to automatically *not* do it. I almost found myself wanting to argue with him that I couldn't. We needed to stop whatever this was, so I opened my mind to try to dive into hers. Before I could even peel back the layers of her mind, I felt an internal punch to my head.

She had unconsciously kicked me out. I held the side of my head, looking up at Asher and shook my head. "I can't!"

He groaned, giving her his full attention from his place huddled on the ground. I knew that look, he was going to try to infiltrate whatever dream state she might have found herself in. I waited and watched, hearing Beau bark over and over again. Riley's mom reached for her daughter's arm and I could have sworn, smoke bellowed from under her fingers as she touched Riley's skin.

"Fuck!" Asher shouted, shutting his eyes and violently shaking his head. She must have kicked him out too.

Beau whined, getting up quickly and clambering over Riley's body. He laid all his weight on her chest, moving his snout towards her chin. He nuzzled against her neck, licking her. His tail moved rapidly, his whining becoming more incessant.

All at once, anything that was floating in the air came crashing down. The developing cracks in her window stilled and the sound of our breathing was the only thing present in the silence that surrounded us.

Mrs. Monroe tentatively touched her daughter's skin, nodding. "She is still a little warm, but she's okay."

"Okay isn't the word I'd use." Asher helped me off the ground before rubbing his temples.

"Who destroyed her necklace?" Mrs. Monroe questioned, reaching towards Beau and petting his head. If what just happened alarmed her, she didn't let it show. Or maybe it hadn't hit her quite yet. I wasn't sure.

"Just a student. We don't know why. Then she disappeared after..." I looked down at the ground, clearing my throat. "And now she showed up again. Mrs. Monroe, did the necklace have something to do with Riley having magic?"

A sad smile graced her face, but she didn't respond. I wanted to know what she wasn't telling us, so I started to slip into her head, but my attempt was halted when my brother gripped my forearm. He spoke in a low voice only I could hear. "She disappeared after your little shadow wielder friend took her. He brought her here and don't you dare give me some bullshit response in his defense. We need to find him."

I pulled my arm out of his hold. "We will okay, for fucks sake Asher..."

A groggy sound came from Riley's bed and all our eyes turned to look at her. Her fingers twitched and her eyelashes fluttered as she tried to open her eyes. She let out a shallow breath causing Beau to shift himself off her chest; he remained firmly at her side, waiting patiently.

"Riley, honey." Mrs. Monroe grabbed her blood-stained hand, holding it to her chest. Riley turned her head slightly, her eyes widening when she saw her mom.

"Mom?" Her voice was small and laced with concern. She searched around, noticing Beau and then me and Asher. Riley looked down her body, seeing the blood and her body jolted up, backing up into her headboard. She snatched her hand from her mom and attempted to try to rid herself of the blood that soaked her jeans. She lifted her hands up, shaking them and wringing them out as if that would make them clean again.

Beau lifted his paw and swatted at her. She had tears in her eyes. I started to walk over, but Beau snapped his head towards me and gave me a look that told me to back off for now. He lifted his paw again, attempting to move her hands out the way so he could crawl into her lap.

Her breathing slowed and she swallowed, pressing her eyes closed. She touched the top of Beau's head, running her hand down towards his back.

"Riley, we will get you cleaned up, okay? Can you tell us anything that happened, honey?" Her mom spoke in a soothing tone that it even started to ease my racing heart.

Riley nodded, looking up at her mom. She didn't open her mouth to speak though, she just remained quiet.

Asher hadn't looked away from her since she'd woken up. His eyes were trained on her, following nearly every movement she made. I reached into my pocket for my phone. Grayson hadn't messaged me back, so I sent another.

> Call me. I know you took Riley somewhere, but she's back now. Please just explain it to me.

I tried to casually find him in my mind. When I heard his ramblings in my head, I stopped waiting for something to lead me to him. I heard his mind halt and then the sound of his parents echoed in my head. He was at home.

I opened my mouth to alert my brother when Riley's voice grabbed hold of my attention. "I know I'm safe now."

Mrs. Monroe furrowed her brows, trying to reach for her daughter's hand again. "Who are you talking to?"

Riley mirrored her mom's expression. "What do you mean?"

"Riley, I didn't say anything just now. You just spoke as if someone was talking to you."

Riley cocked her head to the side. "I heard *'you're safe now'*, so I was just responding. It was loud and clear, are you telling me you didn't hear someone say that?"

"No, Riley, we didn't. How about we get you cleaned up now..." Her mom tried to be helpful and change the subject.

Her mouth opened slightly as if she was trying to find more words to explain herself, then her eyebrows lifted, and her eyes looked as if she was thinking. "Did you guys hear *that*?"

"Hear what?" Asher sounded frustrated.

"How can you not hear..." With a slowness I didn't think was possible, she looked down at Beau. The pitbull wagged its tail and barked once, his tongue sticking out the side of his mouth. "Oh my god."

The voice I'd heard earlier, that childlike voice that I hadn't recognized. If all of this meant that Riley had magic, that she was some kind of witch, then Beau—was her familiar.

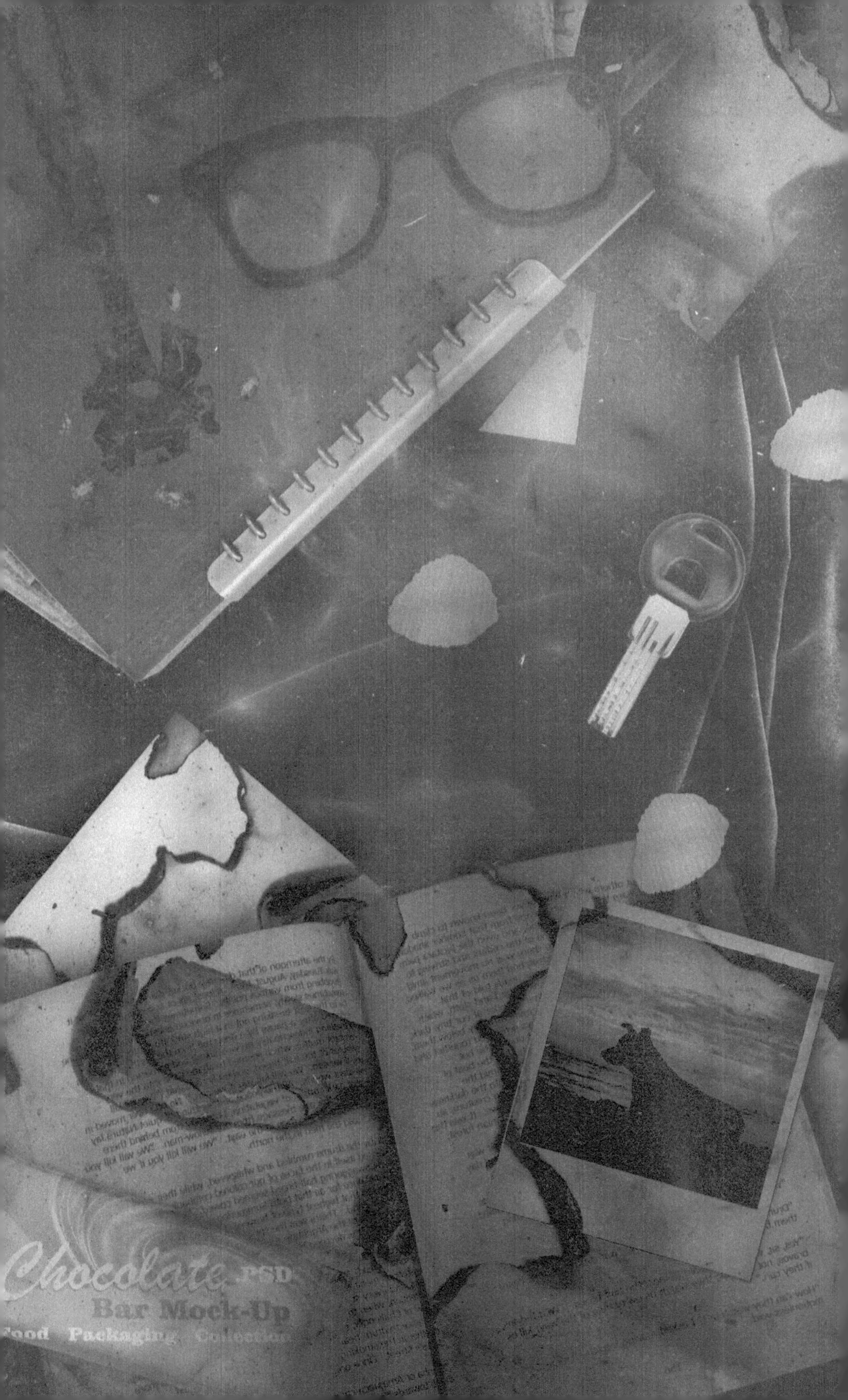
Chocolate PSD
Bar Mock-Up
Packaging

3
RILEY

I heard a voice in my head. It wasn't my own thoughts fumbling inside my mind, but it was one that was playful yet possessive. It gave me a kind of comfort that I'd felt before, but it was stronger this time. I quickly surveyed all the people in the room: my mom, River and oddly enough, fucking Asher.

I focused my gaze on my dog, on my perfect Beau. He gave me a ridiculous lopsided grin that included panting in my face when I realized what was happening. "Oh my god."

"Riley, what's wrong?" My mom's voice went up a few octaves, her tone full of concern.

I took Beau's large face in my hands and smushed his cheeks, forcing him to stare at me. I didn't actually have to force him since he hadn't stopped looking at me. "I—I don't know."

Don't worry, they can't hear me. I am so happy you *finally can, Mom.* I heard in my head. Beau's mouth never moved, but his tail wagged fiercely. He leaned his face further into my hands, catching me by surprise and licking my nose.

I swatted him away, then eyed him skeptically. *So, you can hear everything I'm thinking right now?*

He circled on the bed and sat down so he could look at me straight on. *Sure can. I would appreciate it if you wouldn't scare me like that again.*

"How was I supposed to know Grayson was going to do that?" I realized quickly that I had said that out loud and not in my head. I flinched at the words that had flown out of my mouth.

"Grayson? What does he have to do with any of this? Riley, what the hell is going on?" My mom sounded frustrated but tired. I looked down at the blood that covered my jeans and coated my hands, giving me a less than pleasant reminder of what had transpired.

I was fucking frustrated too. I needed to talk to my mom, but I didn't want to do it with River here, especially since his brother decided to tag along for who knows what reason. I took in my boyfriend and the solemn look in his eye. The mention of Grayson must have made him curious, but something told me he was already suspicious of him long before I woke up.

"Mom, can you start the shower for me? I promise I'll tell you every-thing." My eyes were pleading for her to just do this one thing for me.

Her eyes moved from me to the guys, then back to me. She ran her hand through her mess of curls, shaking her head. "Riley...this is not the time to..."

"Mom." I swung my legs over, so I was sitting on the edge of my bed. "I really don't want to see this blood anymore. I can't see this blood anymore, okay? *Please* do this for me." My voice was on the verge of cracking.

"Honey, you're scaring me." My mom placed her hand softly over her mouth, starting to understand my demand.

"Please Mom." Beau nudged my back, rubbing his face into my spine.

She's worried about you. I nearly tore the house apart because I was a nervous wreck. I heard Beau say. *If I wasn't on the verge of mentally* imploding, I would have laughed at the thought of my dog destroying the house due to my wellbeing.

My mom sighed, breaking her eye contact with me and gazing down at the floor. This was the first time I noticed how much of a mess my room was. It looked like a tornado had come through and swept up anything that wasn't screwed down.

"Fine. You have two minutes." She reached out and stroked my cheek with her knuckles. I really wanted to lean into that motherly touch, but I wanted her to explain things to me before I turned into a heaping mess of tears on her shoulder.

She turned to leave, stepping over debris as she went. Once the door clicked, I sucked in a deep breath. "You know about Grayson, don't you?"

River rubbed the back of his neck. "We know that he swept you up in his shadows after you..."

"After I found out I had powers?" I finished for him.

"We don't know much else besides the fact that he had to be the one who obviously brought you here," Asher continued, adjusting his glasses on his nose.

River took a few tentative steps towards me, his gaze moving over to Beau. The dog blinked, then huffed, nuzzling his face in-between the inside of my arm and my side. River squatted, placing his hand over mine. Before he could speak, Asher chimed in.

"What did Grayson do?" His voice was like venom, like he was genuinely mad at Grayson. It was as if he was frustratingly mad *for* me, rather than for himself.

"You should ask him."

Asher kicked some of the debris away from his feet. "Oh, we plan to."

River sighed, tugging at my hand to get me to look at him. "Riley, whose blood is this?"

My mouth felt dry when I tried to answer. Sweat percolated at the back of my neck and I just wanted all this blood off of me. I wanted *her* blood off of me. I tugged my hand away from him. "That part isn't important."

"Riley, I think it is."

"I don't want to talk about that," I snapped, narrowing my eyes at him.

Asher shook River's shoulder. "We know where he is, so let's go have a talk. She's fine here with her mom."

"She's not fine!" River shouted more to himself than to anyone else, taking a few breaths while looking at the ground. He curled his hand into fists and then uncurled them, finally staring at me with those green eyes I always found so much solace in. They looked a little glassy, like he was begging me to just spew out all I was feeling.

I cupped his chin with my fingers. "Let me talk to my mom, River. I need to figure some shit out before anything else. That's all I'll say." I leaned down, pressing my forehead to his and he lifted himself up a small bit to peck my lips. He straightened up and nodded at his brother.

Asher gave me a once over. "Of all the powers to have, telekinesis isn't the one I'd have thought."

I shrugged, not knowing what to say.

"Or fire," he added.

"Fire?" I inquired, running my hands over my arms and seeing the marks that Chancellor Fowler left. I didn't want to think about having inherited not one but two powers from that man.

Asher nodded towards them. "I'm assuming wherever you went that you accidentally hurt yourself?" I didn't know whether he actually believed that or if he was goading me so that I would fess up about what actually transpired.

I changed the subject. "When you see him, ask him about Chancellor Fowler."

They both gave me a confused look. River reached into his pocket and took out his motorcycle keys. "Chancellor Fowler?"

"Yup."

Asher scratched his trimmed beard. "What does the school chancellor have to do with anything?"

I tucked one of my braids behind my ear, getting up off my bed and repeating myself. This time I said it through gritted teeth. "When. You. See. Him, ask him about Chancellor Fowler." My bedside table rattled and shifted off the ground, luckily it looked like I'd already made a mess with the lamp that had been previously on top of it.

I took a deep breath in, and the table skidded back onto the floor. Beau barked, jumping off the bed and curled against my leg, leaning along the side of my calf.

River gave me a solid nod and half a smile. There was a part of me that knew Grayson would spill the whole truth and that particular part of myself already hurt knowing how River would react. "We'll ask him. Please call me if you need anything."

I nodded absentmindedly while they gave me one last look before heading out the door.

I could hear Beau's heavy breathing on the other side of the bathroom door before I stepped into the shower. The hot water hit my body and I should have felt some sort of instant relief since I was finally getting clean after everything that happened, but I didn't. I watched as the dried blood started to fall off my skin and onto the shower floor. Dark red and pink danced around my feet while I watched it find its way to the drain. Any evidence of Marianne's death was now cleansed from my body, so I should feel better...right?

I took this opportunity to wash my braids, since it had been a minute. I took my shampoo, turned the nozzle at the top and drenched my scalp in it. I massaged the area between my braids, letting my eyes close so I could attempt at some form of relaxation. I let out steady breaths, trying to create nice, pleasing images in my mind. After letting the shampoo sit, I rinsed it out and watched the water clean the product from my hands when a flash of red distorted my vision.

I took a tiny step back, sucking in a sharp breath. I breathed in through my nose and released it out from my mouth, bringing my hand back into the water spewing from the showerhead. Once the stream hit my palm, blood covered my palm, dripping from my fingertips and onto the shower floor. I let out a shriek and stepped away from the water again, feeling something at my feet. I swallowed hard before I looked down seeing blonde hair and I screamed.

I heard Beau scratching at the door, banging his body against the wood.

"Riley! Riley!" I heard my mom shout, her hand about to turn the doorknob.

I slammed my back against the shower wall, closing my eyes hard. "No! Mom, I'm fine. I thought I saw..." I couldn't have this conversation right now. I sniffed, not knowing if the water on my face was from the shower or from the tears that had escaped. The water at my feet started to boil and bubble as if my skin was heating it up. "I'm almost done, okay? I'll be downstairs in a minute."

"Riley, sweetheart..."

"Just let me finish up!" I hadn't meant to scream at her, but I just needed to know she wasn't hovering.

"Okay, honey. I'll make some of that hot chocolate that you like." I waited to hear the door to my bedroom slam. I dipped my head under the showerhead, trying to stifle down my sobs.

Mom... I heard Beau say and it just made me cry harder.

I'm okay, buddy. I didn't know if *he* needed reassurance or if I was talking to myself.

I TOOK THE STAIRS TWO AT A TIME, A COTTON T-SHIRT HOLDING MY WET braids on top of my head and Beau at my heels. I could smell the hot chocolate immediately. I stopped at the threshold of the kitchen, watching her add tiny marshmallows to the mugs. I cleared my throat, causing her to jump a little. She looked over at me, holding up the mugs and nodding towards the couch. I made no move to follow her when she walked past me.

"Was he my real dad?" I asked softly.

Before she made it to the couch, my mom stopped walking. I watched her shoulders stiffen and the air in the entire bottom floor of our house was instantly sucked out with an invisible vacuum. "Riley, what are you talking about?"

I crossed my arms over my chest, hugging my body. "I'm talking about dad. Was I actually his daughter, or was that a lie?"

My mom started walking again, circling around the couch and placing the mugs on the coffee table. When she straightened up, the look she gave me was one full of pain and a tiny bit of regret. "Thomas loved you, honey."

I looked up at the ceiling, needing my tears to stay exactly where they were. I felt Beau lean against my legs, running his snout against my ankle. "Was. He. My. Dad?"

She shook her head. "No, Riley. He wasn't."

I brought my head down and we stood there staring at each other for what felt like hours. I heard the overhead clock in our kitchen ticking and the sound of cars going by outside. It had gotten late and the only light outside was our light above the door outside.

I took a deep breath, walking over to the couch and sitting down. I didn't try to make myself comfortable because I wasn't sure if I was going to have to walk away from this conversation at any moment. I really didn't know how much more I would be able to take tonight.

"Riley..." My mom started grabbing her mug and leaning back against the arm of the couch.

"Did he know who my real father was?" I decided to come at the issue differently than what I had previously planned.

She pressed her lips together, watching as Beau maneuvered himself between the coffee table and the couch. He curled up and rested his head on the ground, closing his eyes. "He did."

"And neither of you thought I should know? Neither of you thought that I should be aware of who my actual father was?" I snatched my mug roughly off the table, watching some of the liquid slosh over the side and onto the wooden coffee table.

She tapped her fingernail on her mug. "Riley, what does this have to do with how you magically ended up in your room, in a coma-like state and covered in blood?"

I could feel my body start to shake from annoyance and the copious amounts of anxiety I was holding in. "It has to do with everything, Mom. He told me that he was my dad. Everything that happened was because I was so fucking important to him, because you hid me away!"

My mom put her mug down, giving me an alarming expression. "Woah, honey, who are you talking about?" Her eyes flicked down to my mug. I heard the bubbling and looked down as well. The hot chocolate was starting to boil and wisps of steam wafted from the top of the mug. The smell of burning chocolate filled my nostrils and I quickly placed the mug back down, noticing how the liquid began to settle down.

I curled my hands into fists, feeling my fingernails dig into my palms. Beau lifted his head, watching me with his big caring eyes. His name tasted vile coming from my lips. "Chancellor Fowler."

My mom's eyebrows turned down. "Chancellor—wait, your school chancellor?"

I nodded.

"Riley, your father never even met the man nor have I, so I'm confused on how he would have any knowledge of anything."

I huffed. "He said you guys were in a relationship. You got pregnant and left him. He wanted you to go to Mystic Riegan and you guys could be some kind of happy family. He said he was so hurt when you just up and disappeared."

My mom brought her hand to her mouth, looking down at the couch. She closed her eyes, muttering what sounded like a quiet stream of the word *no* against her palm. "This wasn't supposed to happen."

"Mom, just be honest with me. *Please.*"

"Erik Lowe."

I raised one of my eyebrows, not understanding.

"Your real father. His name is Erik Lowe."

"Then why did Chancellor Fowler tell me..."

My mom cut me off. "Fowler is his mother's maiden name. He must have taken it on later in life. He was sweet when I met him and I could really see myself having a life with him, but he changed shortly after I told him I was pregnant, maybe he started changing before that.." I didn't interrupt her, so she continued. "I did the only thing I could do. I left. My parents weren't strict; I never gave them a reason to be. I'd explained what I could about Erik and I had always wanted to spend time with the family I had in Oregon, and they let me go. I didn't tell anyone and I knew that if he came around asking, they would find a way to keep me safe.

I didn't know if you would manifest any powers like Erik, so I kept you away. My dad had passed, and my mom was getting sick, so I needed to come back and help them. Time had passed and you were almost two; your grandmother really wanted to meet you."

I couldn't really remember that far back. My earliest memories I had were of me, my mom and my dad celebrating one of my birthdays. That vibrant memory always made me happy, but now all it did was make me more confused.

"After your grandma passed, I was focused on getting an apartment and selling their house. I didn't plan on meeting Thomas, and I never meant to tell him...*everything*. I never expected him to love you as much as he did. I was prepared for it to just be you and me forever.

You just accepted him as your dad and we got married, you grew up carefree and loved. One day about six months before your twelfth birthday you got really frustrated during one of our typical mother-daughter fights and stormed out of the room. I noticed that a few of the items in the kitchen including the knives on the knife block had risen. You stomped up the stairs, slammed your door and then everything fell."

My mouth dropped open in surprise.

"Up until this point you were just—"

"—normal?" I didn't know why I said it with such venom.

"No, Riley. Human. But then again, I guess you never really were."

I touched the empty space at my chest where my necklace used to hang.

"Thomas had just started at Mystic Riegan a year or so before and he tried to reassure me that he could find someone who could help us. I was scared that if you let your powers out, then maybe Erik would take notice. I'd been told by your grandma and many others that he had disappeared for some time and no one had heard from him, but I was scared, Riley. We were all living comfortably and we were happy. I needed a way to subdue your powers, not get rid of them, but just I don't know..."

"I get it, okay." I quickly cut her off.

"If we had known Erik was the chancellor, your father would have never taken a job there. I assumed because of your necklace, you would be perceived as a human. There was no chance of Celica coven recruiting you. Erik's mother never really approved of me and she oversaw the coven in great detail. I assumed Erik would never take the reins from his mother, despite lineage and legacy, they couldn't stand each other. I thought he would have just moved on."

"You *assumed*. You *thought*." I repeated, pushing off the couch and nearly tripping over Beau. He had fallen back asleep and was now on high alert. "You assumed wrong!" I stomped my foot on the ground and my mug went flying across the table, shattering when it hit the ground. "He killed dad because of your fucking assumptions!"

Her eyes went wide. "What?"

"Yes, Mom. He had a nice little chat with dad and your unwanted truth came out. He didn't like that you moved on, that you let someone else take his place, so he punished him for it. He pushed him out a fucking window and that school that he has wrapped around his finger just pretended like it was an accident." My vision started to get a little blurry from the tears that I was keeping at bay. It physically hurt to not let them fall. "He tortured people to find me. He manipulated people I cared about. He—" I choked on my last words. I saw the picture frames from the mantle rise and fly through the air, hitting the wall. The coffee table rattled and started to lift from the ground.

"Riley..." She reached her arm out, holding up her hand as if that would calm me down. "I'm sorry, honey. Is that where you went after that meeting? Did he take you somewhere? Is that where the blood came from?"

I blinked, seeing Beau lift up so that he was standing on his back legs and pawing at me. I tried to get the coffee table to settle down, but the rattling got worse and it started to slam against the floor. The vases my mom had put on corner tables in the room flew past her head. My heart hammered in my chest and I wanted to stop.

He didn't take me anywhere.

"Grayson." His name came out like a plea. It was a plea that didn't matter anymore. A plea no one would hear. "The b-blood. Her b-blood."

"Whose blood? Riley, you have to talk to me, honey." Her words were trying to sound relaxed, but there was a shift in her tone. She was scared for me. I felt Beau's weight again and I teetered back a little.

"Mom—," I started, causing her to get up off the couch and head over to me. I put my hand out willing her to stop. I heard a guttural noise, looking past my hand and seeing my mom open and closing her mouth as she gasped for air. I could see the way her throat was cinched by whatever I was doing. My name was broken and raspy coming from her lips as she tried to breathe.

Beau barked repeatedly and then I felt the full force of his body against mine as he shoved me with his paws against the wall. I heard my mom coughing and rapidly taking in air. She had tears in her eyes. Beau started whining, his ears falling back against his head. I flicked my eyes to my mom and shook my head when she tried to come towards me again.

I ripped the t-shirt off my head, letting my slightly damp braids hit my back. "I-I'm sorry."

"Riley, stop!" My mom yelled at my back when I turned around making a beeline for the front door. I didn't stop to think about where I was going. I just couldn't be here.

I threw the door open with a shaky hand and ran. I heard the heavy pants of Beau following me, but I didn't look back.

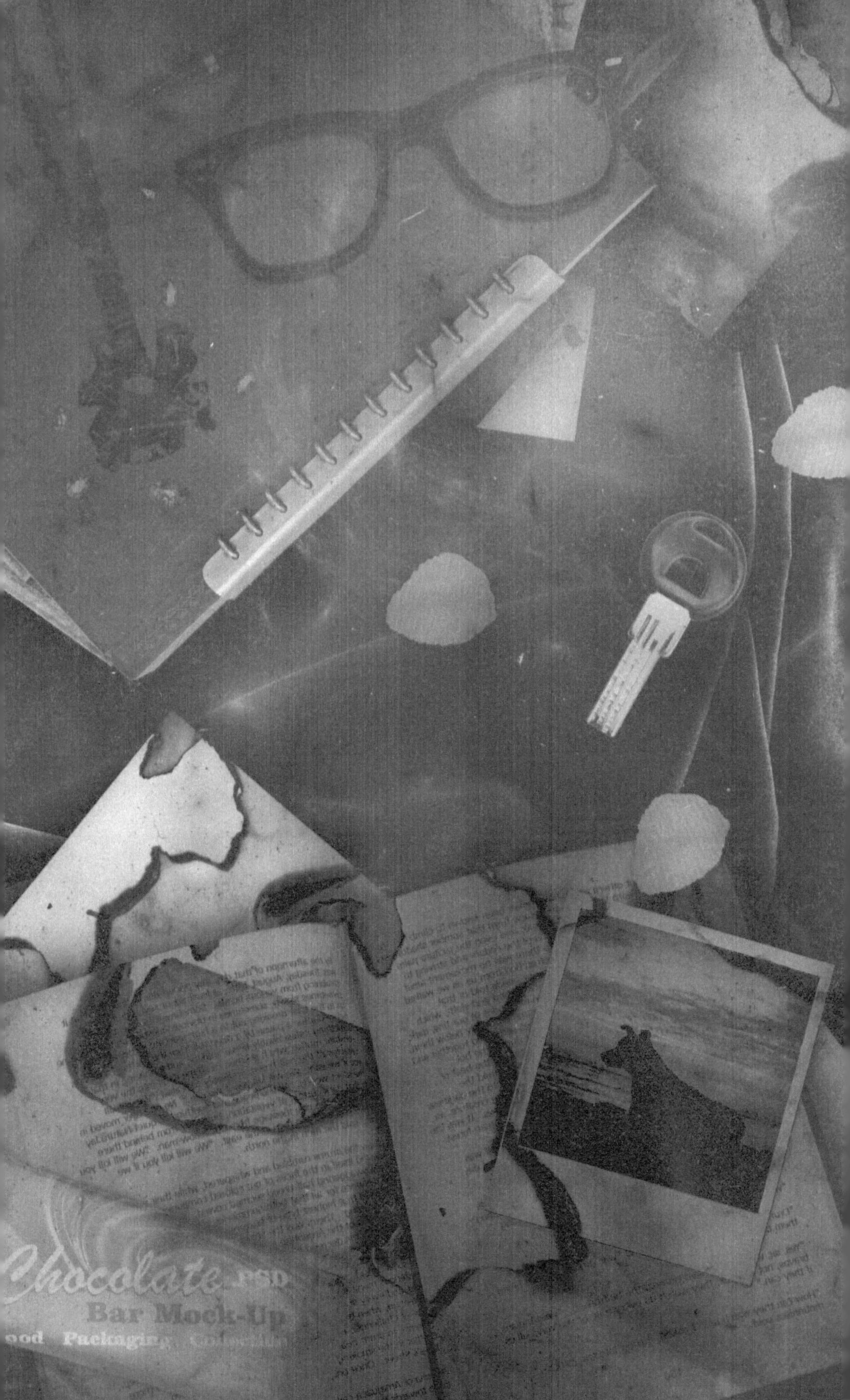
Chocolate PSD
Bar Mock-up
ood Packaging Collection

4
ASHER

My hands hurt from how tight I gripped my steering wheel while I followed River to Grayson's house. When he texted me the address, I'd let out the most obnoxiously loud groan in my car. When River and Grayson met, my brother had just moved into my apartment with me when I was still living in Berkeley. I'd wanted him to finish high school at the same school, so I waited until his senior year to start house hunting somewhere far away from our parents.

Grayson was living in Blyth, a city close by, and they'd somehow struck up a conversation at a fucking football game. Next thing I knew, Grayson was hanging out at our apartment more and more, but I noticed a shift in my brother's demeanor and a difference in the way he carried himself that thankfully caused me to have to worry about him less than I already did. River had always been a confident guy, but I guess I always silently thanked Grayson for making sure my brother knew he could be that way all the time and not just for show.

I hadn't been keeping up with my brother's friends or I would have realized that between the spark of their friendship and now, Grayson—or at least his parents—had moved to fucking Santa Rosa. It was nearly two hours away from San Jose, but River rode that death trap of a motorcycle like a bat out of Hell, so he could cut that down easily. I tried to tell myself to stay calm and remember that speed limits were important, but I found myself not caring. I would pay off any ticket I got.

I rode in silence, not interested in any sort of distraction the radio could provide me. Once the GPS got down to one minute I started to pay more attention to the houses around me. It wasn't a fancy neighborhood, but it was hard to tell anything this late at night. I parked behind my brother, in front of what I assumed was Grayson's driveway.

Lights turned on near the front of the house, likely motion detectors for security reasons. They gave me a better view of the exterior, which had a Spanish style to it. The lights let me see the red terracotta roof and the arched windows. There was a small patio that was lined with succulents that appeared to be thriving.

River knocked on the door, seeming calm despite what I knew was going on in his head. I didn't need mental powers to figure that out. The door opened and a woman who favored Grayson far too much to not be his mother stood before us. Her neutral expression turned into a smile when she saw River. My brother gave her a half smile that I could tell was forced; his eyes flicked over her shoulder, quickly scanning the area behind her.

"River, *gabi na*, what brings you here?" she asked, tucking a piece of her dark hair behind her ear.

"Is Grayson home?"

She nodded, moving aside so we could come in. River was already taking off his shoes and leaving them by the door. Mrs. Ypulong was watching me expectedly, nonverbally telling me to do the same. I took a small look around, the small Jesus figure hanging in the living room catching my attention, along with a few candles that decorated floating shelves that lined the walls. "He came home a few hours ago. I was shocked when he wouldn't eat. He's been quiet for the most part. *Ang saya ko na nandito ka!* He must have called you." She peeked a glance at me.

"I'm his brother." I casually pointed to River. "And I'm a professor at the school."

A man with short hair and a thin frame came from another room and settled beside her. He reached out and patted my brother's arm. "River, *mayasa akong makita ka.* Grayson told us that meeting at the school wasn't anything for us to concern ourselves with; he doesn't really like us driving so far out if we don't have to. He worries too much. Since someone from the school is here…is there something wrong? He said that the business with his scholarship was fixed."

As much as I wanted to shout that there were some things they needed to know about their son, I refrained. "He was right. Nothing to worry about, I just tagged along for the sake of my brother."

River raised his eyebrow for a moment and then rallied. "Yeah, I couldn't meet up with him after the meeting, so I told him to call me when he was settled at home. Can I head up?"

Grayson's parents shooed us up the stairs, which creaked during certain steps. River rapped his knuckles on the door and we waited.

"This is fucking ridiculous," I whispered.

River ignored me. "Grayson, it's me. Can we come in?"

I let out an exasperated sigh. I was usually the more collected one, but right now, his friendly approach was irritating the fuck out of me. I shoved him out of the way and turned the doorknob, throwing the door open.

Grayson was sitting on his bed, his knees pressed to his chest. He had his head down and if I hadn't noticed the way his fingers flexed, wrapped around the front of his legs, I would have assumed he was asleep. Shadows wafted off of him, swirling around his body. River moved around me while I closed the door.

"Grayson…" River said softly, hovering next to the bed. "What did you do?"

Grayson lifted his head, his eyes a little glassy as if he'd been holding back tears. He looked up at River and then me, letting a choked sigh leave his lips. "I-I...I'm sorry."

"We understand that. What exactly are you sorry for?" I pressed, crossing my arms and leaning against his dresser.

"Is Riley okay?" Grayson asked, his voice shaking.

"That's not something we can really answer right now." River ran a hand through his hair, small pieces sticking up and not going back into formation.

"She's alive. That should make you happy, right?" I narrowed my eyes.

Grayson widened his eyes at me. "Of course it does, I never hurt her! I brought her back home and made sure she was safe."

"Safe?! Bringing her back home covered in blood is your definition of fucking safe!?" I pushed away from his dresser. "The way she says your name doesn't really put you at the top of the list of people who would never hurt her."

"Why do you even care?" he asked, his dark eyes piercing into mine. This whole conversation wasn't about me or whatever feelings I did or didn't have.

"This is about you and the fact that you are going to open your fucking mouth and explain what the hell happened after Riley's necklace was destroyed."

Grayson pressed his hands to the side of his head and closed his eyes. "I'm sorry! I didn't know she was involved!"

I knocked his desk chair over, letting it slam against the ground. "Involved in what? You being fucking sorry doesn't mean anything to us or to her unless you explain what you did."

River got in front of me, pressing his hands into my chest. "Calm down and shut up. Yelling at him is not going to get us anywhere."

I remained in my brother's face, never losing eye contact. "Do *not* fucking coddle him."

"I'm not," River hissed. "I'm trying to get the whole story, and that won't happen if you don't stop yelling at him. He'll just retreat into himself."

I lifted my hands up, scoffing. "He's your friend. You know him better than I do."

"I-I didn't know anything about her necklace or about what she could do. Once it all started, I was t-told to take her. I didn't w-want to, I swear, b-but you don't understand…"

River turned around and sat on the bed. "You were *told* to take her?" He turned his head to look at me, but I nodded towards his friend. He didn't want me to open my mouth and scream at him, so I kept my thoughts to myself at the moment.

Grayson fidgeted a little as if he was afraid to say his next words. "Yeah." He grabbed River's arm, pulling at the fabric of his shirt. "You have to b-believe me. I-I didn't know she was involved. I didn't know she was who he was looking for."

River ripped Grayson's hand from his shirt, keeping his hand over his when he sat on the bed. "Who told you to take her?"

Grayson bit his lower lip, a few tears that had welled up in his bottom lids finally dropping down his cheek. "Your dad."

"Excuse me?" I asked, getting closer to the bed.

"I thought since nothing we'd done had worked then they would just leave me alone. Our deal was done."

River moved his hand away from Grayson's. "Your deal? You've been working with my dad to somehow get to Riley for whatever reason you aren't fucking telling us?"

Grayson shook his head. "No, well, we did have a deal, but I didn't know about Riley. River please! I wouldn't have done any of this if I had known that she was the one he was looking for."

"What did our dad want with Riley?" I inquired, inclining my body towards him so I wouldn't miss a thing.

Grayson wiped his hands over his cheeks. He tried to reach for River's hand again, but my brother kept his hand away. Grayson tried to keep the look of hurt from his face and continued, "He needed her for Chancellor Fowler."

"Chancellor Fowler?" I asked, remembering how Riley had mentioned him before.

Grayson smacked his lips together, gathering his words. "He's the one who killed Mr. Monroe."

"Wait, what?" River scrubbed his hand down his face.

"And he's her real dad."

I nearly choked. "What the fuck, Grayson?!"

"I didn't know! I went to figure out shit with my scholarship and Chancellor Fowler and your dad were there waiting for me. They gave me an ultimatum; I either do what they asked or I lose my scholarship and my entire life, everything I've fucking worked for would be completely fucked."

I pinched the bridge of my nose; surprised steam wasn't erupting from my ears with how fucking pissed off I was. I let out a humorless laugh. "You shadow wielding little shit. The disappearing witches... that was you."

"Yes, but I brought them back!"

River pushed off the bed with a harsh groan. "That doesn't fucking matter! You didn't see what she did in her comatose state! You didn't see the look in her eyes when she even mentioned your name!" I came up behind him, reaching for his shoulder. River shrugged me off. "Whose blood was it?"

Grayson's eyes looked down towards his comforter, picking at the material. "Chancellor Fowler did it, not me."

"I didn't ask who did what. I asked you whose it was." River's voice was less and less comforting and more stoic. The charm he'd mastered so well was fading away.

Grayson moved his mouth around, looking as if he was chewing on the inside of his cheek. "I didn't know she was going to be a part of this. I didn't know it would end like that. I never hurt Riley, he did!"

I quickly moved past my brother and lunged onto the bed, pulling Grayson up by his shirt. I could hear the fabric strain under my hold. "It's too late for regret. Blame it on Chancellor Fowler all you want, but in the end, she still sees you as a villain in her story and hiding out in your room isn't going to change that. I don't care what you didn't know; I'm only interested in what you *do* know. Whose. Blood. Was. It?"

Grayson opened and closed his mouth, peeking over my shoulder at River. "Marianne's."

I heard a sharp intake of breath behind me.

"Marianne?" River asked, his voice shaking. "Marianne!" The next time he said it, the anger that was threaded in his words was obvious.

"Who is Marianne?" I asked, letting Grayson go and shoving him back on his bed.

"She's one of Riley's best friends," River said, crossing the room to the other side of the bed. "That's why she didn't want to talk about it..."

A knock came at the door that made us all jump.

"Grayson, sweetheart. You should really eat something." Grayson's mother's voice entered the room with its light-hearted energy, but even that wasn't enough to break the tension.

"We can't continue this conversation here," I said in a low voice.

"I'm fine, Mom, really," Grayson said reassuringly.

"Where do you want to go then? We don't have a random secret warehouse to keep him in like in the movies." River whispered, rolling his eyes.

"Our place. We have that spare room. I think your little friend is far too upset with himself to try anything." I turned to look at Grayson, my eyebrows turning down. "Go tell your mom you're leaving with us."

Grayson hustled off the bed, stopping at his bedside table and opening up a drawer. He pulled something out and tossed it over to me. I opened my hands to catch it, looking down at what it was. A cellphone.

"It's Riley's. Your dad told me to grab it before I let her loose at

Chancellor Fowler's house." Grayson didn't wait for us to say anything. He ran a hand through his hair, opening up his door and stepping out to speak to his mother.

I waved her phone at my brother. "You sure know how to pick your fucking friends."

River narrowed his eyes at me, deciding to pull his phone from his back pocket instead of argue with me. I cut her phone on realizing it had a little bit of battery left. Twenty missed calls and ten missed texts from Corrin. There were a few missed phone calls from her mom that were only about thirty minutes ago.

"Hey Mrs. Monroe, slow down. What's wrong?" River's voice caught my attention. He had his phone to his ear. "Wait, she just left? I haven't heard from her, no."

I turned my eyes back towards her phone. As much as I knew my brother would want to go on the hunt for Riley, we needed to deal with Grayson. I clicked on one of Corrin's missed calls.

She answered in one ring. "Riley! Holy fuck! You can't do that shit to me!"

"It's not Riley."

She was quiet for a moment. "Uh, this voice sounds eerily like my professor."

I sighed. "That's because it is, Corrin."

"Oh shit, why do you have Riley's phone?"

River looked over at me, telling Riley's mom to give him a minute. He pulled his eyebrows in as he waited to hear how my phone call was going.

"Apparently she left her house, and her mom doesn't know where she is."

I heard rustling around on the line. "Does this have to do with what happened at the meeting?"

I groaned. "Listen, I don't have time for this. Can you just go get her?"

"I'm sure the attitude is just from stress so I'll let that shit go for

Riley's sake, but fun fact, I can't find her if I don't know where she is."

River kept his eye on me but was starting to talk to Riley's mom again. It sounded like he was reassuring her. I let out a breath and dipped into my powers. My brother was already stressed out enough, but if this didn't work, I would *make* him use his powers again. I tried to be optimistic and thought that she could be at another friend's house, taking what I could only assume would be a well-needed nap.

I'd been in her dreams before and even if she was just casually daydreaming, I could find my way in. My mind rattled and pulsed when I found her. She was half asleep from what I could tell, but it was like she was trying to stay mildly alert for some reason. I had to get in there and I had to make it quick. I'd taken to dream walking easily and Riley would be no exception.

I found my dream self in front of her, while she sat on a bench of some kind, staring at nothing. I reached down and shook her gently. She jumped, shifting away from me.

"Asher?" Her voice was so small. It was so hot and muggy in her mind, it felt like flames were licking at my skin every so often. I ignored it, hoping to be out of here shortly.

"Where the hell are you, Riley?"

"Leave me alone and get out of my fucking head," she barked back.

"Tell me where you are and I will."

"I'm literally fine. I have Beau."

I wiped the sweat from the back of my neck. "Ah, yes. The dog will save you from any harm."

She scoffed at me and despite my irritation, I still couldn't deny that she was beautiful even in her obvious sadness. "I would much rather have his company than yours."

"I'm such a monster. The guy that's trying to make sure you're alright."

She ignored me, not even looking in my direction.

"Your mom is worried about you. And so is River."

She sniffed, running a finger under her eye as if she could quickly hide the tears that were attempting to overflow. "San Jose Caltrain station. It's like forty minutes from my house."

No wonder she needed to stay at least partially awake. She was at a fucking public train station. "Stay put."

"Yes, sir." The way she said it was almost sarcastic.

I pulled myself out, speaking into the phone. "She's at the Caltrain Station near her house in San Jose. I'll send you the location." I hung up before Corrin could say anything back.

River nodded at me and then returned to his call with Mrs. Monroe. Grayson stepped into the room with his head down but kept his door wide open.

"We know where she is, Mrs. Monroe. It's going to be okay. We..." River fiddled with the studs in his earlobe, "we know where she is. Yes, she's safe." He said a few more things and then finally hung up.

I settled my attention on Grayson. "Where's your ring?"

He looked down at his naked forefinger where he usually wore his dampener ring. "It's on the bedside table."

River turned around and searched, finally finding it and placing it in his pocket.

"Is she okay?" Grayson asked in a tentative voice.

I scowled at him. "What do you think?" I tilted my chin up, silently telling him we were leaving.

Grayson's parents gave us cordial goodbyes. Grayson tried to act like everything was fine, keeping a somewhat believable smile on his face. He gave his mom a quick hug, pulling away too swiftly for her liking.

"*Psssst*. Get back here." The sound she made had Grayson turning around without another thought. She held her arms out and kissed him on the cheek. "*Ingat ka anak*. Call to check in and eat something."

I didn't know what he'd said to them, but they seemed to trust their son, especially when River was involved. His mom gave my brother the biggest hug and he gave her a small side-smile, walking out behind us.

"He can ride with me on my bike—" he offered, getting his keys out.

"Fuck no." I took Grayson by the arm and nearly dragged him to my car. "He rides with me."

5
RILEY

I was thankful that it wasn't overly humid tonight and that the breeze was coming through every now and then. I was extra thankful that the station wasn't as busy as I remembered it being. No one paid me any mind, but despite Beau staring down every person that passed, I still felt vulnerable. I made myself comfortable on the bench I'd claimed and played with the ends of my braids. I wanted to scream, but I was far too tired to even consider it. My mom still tried to reach me, comfort me, even though I'd hurt her.

She had lied to me about my lineage for my entire life, but that didn't constitute violence. That didn't make what I'd done okay. I would understand if she never wanted to see me again, but I knew that would never be what she wanted. Seeing her face in my mind now hurt my heart, but it also made it rage from all the half-truths and full-on lies. I was sorry for what I did, but that didn't make me any less fucking angry.

I pulled at the ends of my hair, looking left and right. I no longer felt like sleeping since Asher had jump scared me. I didn't think he'd be the one to seek me out, but I clearly had been wrong about so many things before. Beau hopped onto the bench, nearly falling off, but settled against me.

Can we go home now? Beau asked in my head.

I sighed. *Not yet. I don't like what I did.*

You didn't mean it.

That doesn't matter, buddy. I stroked the top of his head, running my fingers along the back of his ear and massaging. He started making grunting noises and one of his legs started kicking.

I heard arguing to my left, but it was too dark to make out what was going on. Even the lights in this place were too dim to help me out. Beau lifted his head up, jumping off the bench and staring right into the darkness. His tail stood up, on high alert.

"*Ay Dios!* Do you two ever stop fighting?" A familiar voice sounded, a laugh rumbling out of them.

"If he just stopped complaining, then we would be fine. I'm twenty, not twelve, you overprotective idiot." My ears perked up and Beau's tail dropped lower and started wagging incessantly.

"I'm not about to have my sister go off to a train station at fucking eleven o'clock at night. You are out of your mind." I got up from the bench, sidling up next to Beau who looked up at me with his silly little smile.

His front paws tapped the ground as if he was anxiously excited. His bark flew through the open air and I waited but he only barked once as if it was some kind of signal. I heard the sound of someone running and then a shriek.

"Oh my god! Riley!" I noticed her neon pink headband before I realized Corrin was sprinting over to me, our bodies colliding when she embraced me in the fiercest hug. I held her tight, pressing my face into her neck. She pulled back, scanning my face.

Mateo and Ike were behind her, keeping what I assumed was a watchful eye on the perimeter, like two unnecessary guard dogs.

"What are you doing here?" I asked, watching as Beau circled around her legs.

"Asher called me. He somehow has your phone, but that part isn't important." She squeezed my arms. "The important thing is that you're okay."

"Uh, yeah," I mumbled.

"Or...not." She rubbed her hands up and down my arms, pulling me into her again. "You can tell me or not tell me, but we'll take you back to my house."

"You couldn't have picked like I don't know, a twenty-four-hour diner or something?" Ike complained, looking around.

I shrugged, not really knowing how to answer.

"*No se.* It's eerie and quiet here. It's kind of a vibe." Mateo winked over at me, causing Ike to narrow and roll his eyes.

Ike pointed from his sister to her partner. "You two are made for each other with your never-ending optimism."

Corrin widened her eyes at me shaking her head. "You should try it sometime, maybe you wouldn't be so grumpy." She bent down and scratched Beau behind his ear. "Aren't you the cutest! You want to meet my cat?" Beau's tail thumped as he panted in her face, fogging up her glasses.

"I think the only person Jax likes is you, *mi amor.*" Mateo bent down next to her and reached out to pet Beau as well.

I moved to head back to the bench I'd been sitting on. "I don't think that's a good idea."

"From the looks of it, you don't want to go home, so where else are you going to go Riley?" Ike questioned, walking over and sitting down next to me.

"It's not that, well it's not that completely. Things are different..."

Corrin came to sit on the other side of me. "You mean when you blasted one of your boyfriends across the room?"

I clamped my mouth shut, whipping my head around to face her. She wrinkled her nose.

"That look on your face is insulting. I have two eyes, Riley. Also, that whole ordeal has been all the school gossip mill has been talking about the last few hours. While I am very fucking interested in how my roommate was a witch and I didn't know it, I am more concerned with getting you to a safe place." She placed her hand on my leg, patting it reassuringly. "And from the look on Beau's face, so is he."

I looked over at Beau, who was happily getting chest scratches from Mateo.

"How can you tell? Can he talk to you too?" I wasn't really all that sure how magic, being a witch or having a familiar even worked.

Corrin giggled a little. "No, he can only talk to you. But he can understand anyone." She called Beau's name and he cocked his head to look at her. "Do you want to head to my house, so Riley's comfortable?" Her voice had an excited tone that made his ears perk up.

He let out a few short barks and ran up to me, jumping up so that he could place his paws on my legs. His weight was heavy, but I didn't mind. I grabbed his face and smushed his cheeks in. "Fine. I'll go."

"Oh, thank fuck." Ike slapped the bench and started walking back the way they came.

"You and I both know Jade is going to want the dog to sit up front," Mateo said, lightly punching Ike when they sidled up next to him. Corrin held onto me while we walked behind them, her tight curls tickling my face as she leaned her head towards me.

"Jade is here too?" I asked, confused.

"Well, we were already all together when Asher called and my sibling was not about to miss out on a search mission. It's that *lobo* instinct, always on the hunt." Mateo turned around, giving me a big smile.

"There was no hunting. Asher sent us the address. Stop making yourself sound cooler than you actually are, *mi amor*," Corrin pointed out, softly sighing when Mateo blew her a kiss before turning back around.

Loud music blasted from the van while Jade sat in the driver's seat singing along to the lyrics with the windows down.

"It's the middle of the fucking night. Common courtesy," Ike scolded, reaching into the drivers' side and turning the volume down.

Jade took her dark loose curls and tied them into a bun on her head. "You're no fun." She gasped and clapped her hands. "Ah! *Un perro!* He sits up front."

Mateo looked over at us, snickering. "Told you."

Mateo had given Corrin nearly a million kisses before they left with Jade, who told Corrin to put her number in my phone when I got it back. I sat on the floor of Corrin's bedroom watching Beau and Jax have a face off on either side of the room. Jax initially was highly uninterested in Beau, but my overly friendly boy wanted into the cat's personal space more than anything. After being swatted nearly three times in the face, he'd retreated to the other side of the room, pouting.

I picked at the dog hair on my leggings, trying to get my thoughts together. Corrin healed the wounds on my arms, but the phantom pain of the heat that had been pressed into them by Chancellor Fowler still gave me trouble. Corrin's door opened slowly, revealing my roommate and her mom. Corrin had this strained smile on her face as if she'd just gotten scolded, but it wasn't as bad as it could have been.

"Do you need anything, Riley?" Her mom asked, her voice soft and polite.

I shook my head. "Everyone keeps asking me if I'm alright, if I'm fine or if I need anything and honestly...I can't answer that right now."

Her mom ran a finger over her eyebrow piercing and sighed. "I understand, but I would like to call your mother and tell her you're staying the night."

"Right. Yeah. That's probably a good idea." I didn't look at her, but I continued to stare at Corrin's dresser in front of me. My back was settled against the foot of her bed and I was comfortable exactly where I was.

"Okay, good. Uh…Riley…" Corrin's mom started, the sound of her walking over to me causing me to blink and turn my head towards her. She knelt down, giving me a perfect view of her flawless face. Her dark skin didn't have a blemish in sight, and she had given some of that physical perfection to her daughter. "Corrin only told me a little bit about what happened."

I flicked my eyes over her shoulder at her daughter. Corrin gave me a small smile, fiddling with her headband.

Her mom grabbed my chin and forced me to look at her. "Don't be mad at her. She fought hard to fumble around the truth, but I can be quite scary when I want."

"Ain't that the truth," Corrin mumbled.

Her mom pulled her hand from my chin. "It must be scary to come into your witch powers so suddenly. I knew that necklace meant something strongly for you, but I just couldn't put my finger on what it was. I also don't know if it would have been my place to tell you." She gave me an apologetic expression.

I sucked in a deep breath. "It's okay. Thank you for letting me stay here. I just…it's been a day." That sounded like a less than impressive way to explain what my life had become.

"You're a fellow witch. Our door is always open." She patted my knee, giving it a squeeze. "We can talk more in the morning, but for now get some rest. In the morning we'll see where you're at and discuss some things then, alright?"

I gave her a forced smile and then proceeded to give her my mom's phone number. I heard flapping wings and then running. Ike busted into the room, almost knocking over his sister. Ted, his bird familiar, perched himself right on the top of Corrin's dresser. Beau wagged his tail, jumping up and clawing at the air to get to him. Jax successfully jumped onto the piece of furniture prepared to swat the bird down.

"Ike! Get Ted out of here!" Corrin stomped her foot, pushing her brother forward.

"Ted, let's go!" Ike patted his shoulder, staring the bird down.

Ted squawked at him and then flew over, perching perfectly on Ike's shoulder.

"Next time, I should let Jax just eat him," Corrin threatened, giving her brother a stiff smile.

"Next time I should let him shit on your bed," Ike spat back as he walked out of the room.

"Enough. Go to bed, both of you." Their mom rubbed one of her temples. "You too." She nodded at me before kissing Corrin on the forehead and leaving.

Corrin let out a loud sigh before collapsing next to me. "Are we sitting in silence? Because I can do that. I know that sounds impossible coming from me, but I promise I can zip my lips with the best of them."

I peeked over at her, looking at the sincere way she was looking back at me. "It's my legacy, or so he says."

"What is? Who said?"

"Celica."

Her eyes nearly came out of their sockets. "Wait, *my* Celica coven?"

"Mmhmm."

"How are you even remotely intertwined with the founders of Celica? I mean your mom is human right?" She pulled at one of her curls and then snorted. "I mean obviously that would have to mean that your dad was a magic wielder..."

My breath caught causing her to clamp her mouth shut.

"That's not right though...because your dad was a human who helped students at Mystic Riegan. He was the best person to come to when you had a problem, no matter where you came from." She sounded so sure of herself.

I brought my knees up to my chest and whispered, "He wasn't my dad. Not my biological one at least."

"What?"

"Please don't tell your mom any of this."

"Sure, whatever you want." She placed her hand gently on my forearm.

I told her everything I could about Chancellor Fowler and River's dad. I tried to sum up Chancellor Fowler's history with my mom and tried not to get too choked up by telling her about my dad. Her eyebrows raised when I stuttered out Grayson's name. She listened carefully, never trying to interrupt me. Once I was finished, she waited a moment to see if I had anything left to say.

Corrin bit her thumbnail, thinking. "He ordered Grayson to get those girls from the coven so he could get a memory pulling witch to search through their minds." Her words came out like they were fact.

"Seriously?"

"It makes sense. Telekinesis is a pretty dominant power, so he likely knew you'd inherited it, but he couldn't figure out if you were well...*you*. Best way to do that, since your mom gave you that necklace, is to search in your mind, find visuals of your mother, your life, anything to identify you. When they didn't pan out, he sent them back. Quite literally mind fucked."

"I'm sorry, Corrin," I said, placing my head in my hands.

"For what?"

"Unknowingly putting you in danger. Getting you involved in any of this."

She wrapped her arm around me. "The guy is the supreme leader of my coven from what you've told me, so I've always been involved. Even if you didn't transfer, he was still siphoning magic from his own coven witches like the greedy pig he is to keep just being powerful. Classic villain. That goes for Mr. St. James as well, although that guy always gave me weird vibes anyway." She pulled me into her side tighter. "I am sorry about Grayson though. As much as I want to beat his face in for what he did, it does sound like he had no idea."

"I'm sure he didn't. I just can't— I don't really even want to look at him right now." Every time I thought about Grayson, I saw him bringing in Marianne. I saw the stunned look in his eyes and heard his pleas of forgiveness. All the happy things I tried to remember about us were now doused in this shadow of darkness, coated with the blood of my best friend. All because he didn't know how all of this would pan out. All because he thought he was saving his future, and well, I guess he did at the expense of my trust. But...he didn't know.

My hands were shaking and my heart started beating intensely in my chest. The drawers in Corrin's dresser rattled and a few items on her desk were shifting around as if there was an earthquake. Jax jumped off the dresser, leaping onto Corrin's bed for safety. Beau stalked over to me, laying down on top of my feet.

"Riley, hey look at me." Corrin shook my shoulders a little. She didn't beg me to stop like others might have.

I blinked over at her, hearing the soft rattling of objects around me.

"I don't know if there is more to your time with Chancellor Fowler and I won't push. Just know I'm here, okay?"

I could feel myself wanting to explode, wanting to tear this whole room apart with my anger and sadness. Heat raged in my veins and knew I could set this room on fire if I was given the opportunity, but I found myself looking at Corrin and suddenly all I wanted to do was cry.

"He hurt someone I cared about. He really hurt them. I–I just–" My voice cracked.

She stopped me. "You don't have to say anything else."

I let the tears fill my eyes and spill over. I dropped my head into the crook of her neck and sobbed. It wasn't loud and obnoxious, the kind of crying that strained your throat. It was the kind that was soft and nearly silent because you still didn't want people to know the kind of pain you were in, the kind that hurt your chest because you weren't sure if the tears would ever stop falling. My cries were muffled into her shirt, soaking the fabric, but she didn't care. She smoothed her hand down my arm and rocked her body into mine.

I don't know how long we were like that, but somehow, I fell asleep.

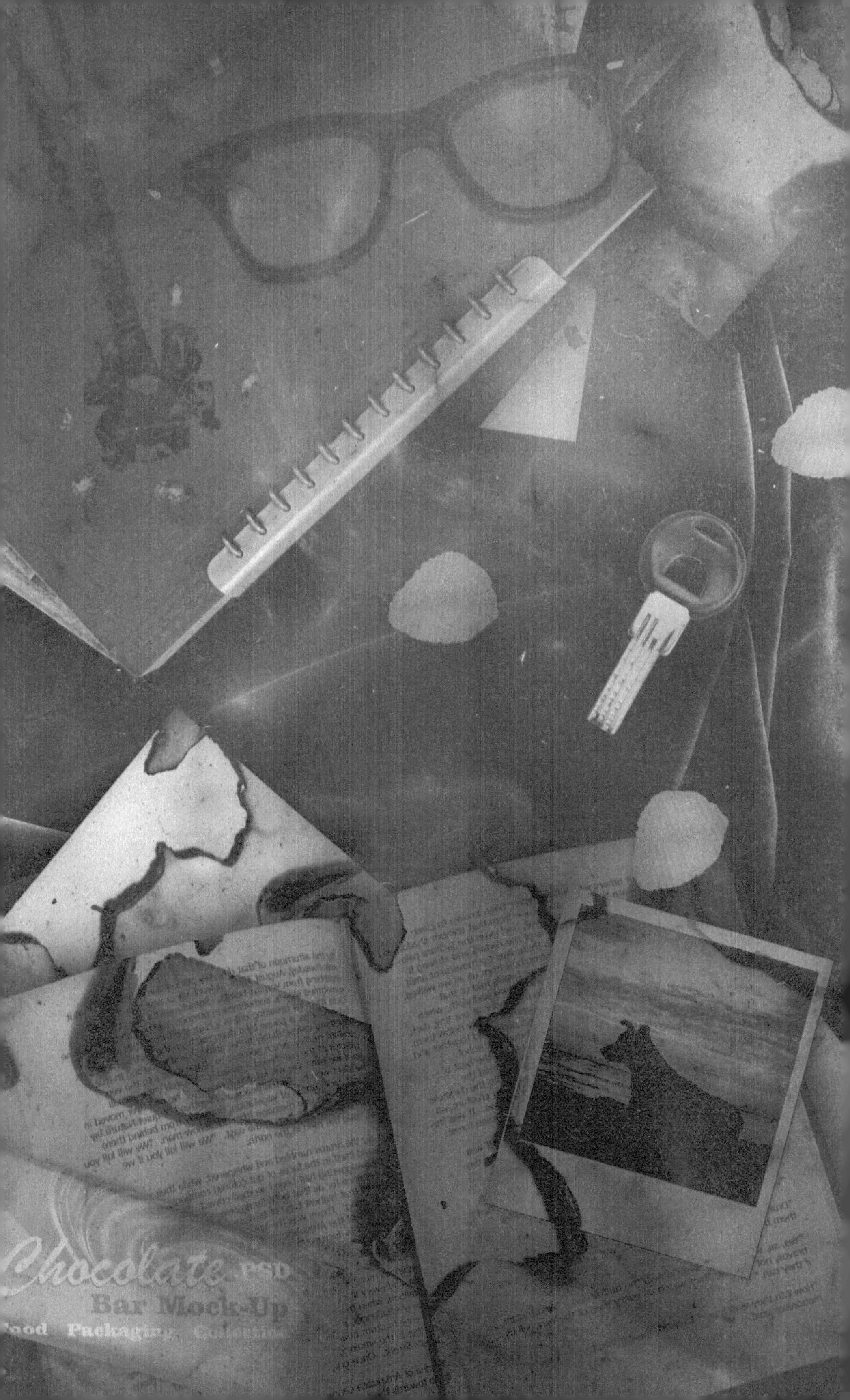
Chocolate .PSD
Bar Mock-Up
Packaging

6
RIVER

I watched Asher speed out of our driveway and down the street before heading into the kitchen. He had mumbled something about still being a teacher and needing to do some stuff at school. I couldn't imagine heading back to school right now. Even though it was only closed for two days, Mystic Riegan would do what it always did: it would rally. We would be a little awkward going back to the normal everyday college student things, but somehow everyone would eventually end up acting like it was old news.

The university did the same thing with Riley's dad. It kind of made sense now that Chancellor Fowler had been revealed to be her *actual* dad. He had more pull than most and never had to really show his face. If I was being honest, I didn't even know our school even had a fucking chancellor until my junior year. I scrubbed a hand down my face, shuffling over to the coffee maker. I leaned against the granite counter while I listened to the machine rumble and pulled out my phone.

I'd woken up to a text from Riley's mom, thanking me for finding her daughter and letting me know she was at Corrin's. I planned on heading over to Corrin's house today and giving her back her phone, then taking her back home—or maybe bringing her back here. She had run away from her house, so maybe going back to her mom wasn't something she wanted. What the fuck happened between us leaving that night and her ending up sleeping at her roommate's house? We would unpack that later.

I grabbed a mug, ironically it happened to be one with the school's name on it, from the top cabinet and poured my coffee into it. I sighed looking towards the open entryway to the kitchen, knowing that around the stairs near the laundry room was the spare bedroom. I knew my best friend was in there and I hadn't talked to him since Asher threw him in there and threatened to beat the shit out of him if he tried to shadow himself out of here. All Grayson had done was nod and make his way to the air mattress we had since neither of us had made time to actually turn that room into a proper guest room.

I groaned, tapping my fingers on the counter before I started making another coffee, thinking about the first time he met Riley and how even then I knew there was something between us— all of us.

"Is your friend always this late?" Riley asked, kicking her legs as she checked her phone.

Grayson was running a little behind, but I would give him shit for it later. It was July in San Francisco, and the fog was more than apparent which told me that he was probably driving five miles an hour. I didn't know why I was so nervous about him meeting her. She had been a big hit with all my other friends, but none of them were my best friends. He had heard me talk about her for the last two months, I'd shown him pictures and he'd promptly stated that she was out of my league.

I'd picked Rheya's Kitchen, which was a small but well-known restaurant. Grayson and I had eaten here a few times and I'd brought Riley once about a month ago—where she admitted she enjoyed this place much more than where I took us on our first date, so I knew it was somewhere we all liked and would have no trouble finding something on the menu.

I placed my hand on her shoulder. "He'll be here, okay? Stop fidgeting."

"I'm not fidgeting." She played with her ruby necklace that her mom had given her years ago, chewing on her bottom lip. "You just talk about Grayson a lot and I don't know, if he hates me then how am I supposed to come back from your best friend hating me?"

I laughed. "He isn't going to hate you, gorgeous. No one in the history of the world could ever hate you."

She stuck her tongue out at me. "You underestimate the world."

"Perhaps, but don't worry, if you're a good girl tonight, then I'll show you how much I don't hate you later." I leaned in and gripped her chin, tilting her head up so I could kiss her.

She molded her mouth to mine and moaned a little. It was the most enticing sound I'd ever heard and it took every piece of restraint I had to not get down on the floor and bury my face between her legs. We'd been taking things as slowly as she liked and although we hadn't slept together yet, she had let me taste her and I was more than satisfied with just that. We'd celebrated her nineteenth birthday a week ago and I'd made sure she and her body were taken care of.

Riley pushed against my chest, giggling. "Okay, okay. I'm calmer, thanks to your distracting mouth." She pecked my lips and looked around. "I'm going to find the bathroom."

She got up, giving me a perfect view of the dress she had on. I knew she had little shorts on underneath so the wind that picked up this time of year didn't completely expose her if it decided to whip her dress around. It was burgundy with a sweetheart neckline, a lace bodice and short sleeves. The hem was mid-thigh and moved when she walked. She must have felt my *eyes on her because she turned around before she turned the corner and wrinkled her cute nose at me, her nose ring sparkling in the overhead light.*

I sat back, readjusting her oversized jean jacket that she had thrown on the back of her chair

"Did she get tired of you and leave?" Grayson joked, pulling a chair out across from me and sitting down.

I chuckled. "Unfortunately for you, no. She's in the bathroom."

"Unfortunately for me?" My best friend raised one of his eyebrows.

I nodded, leaning forward and brushing a piece of his hair from his face. "Yeah, you can't have me all to yourself." I winked at him, before I settled back in my chair again.

Grayson gave the waitress his drink order when she came back over which I followed with an order for an appetizer.

"She's really not going to Mystic Riegan for college?" Grayson asked, removing his jacket and placing it on the seat next to him.

I shrugged. "Nope. She's pretty set on community college. I'm not going to push a school on her that I didn't even want to go to at first. Seems a little hypocritical don't you think?"

"Ah, well fair enough. Look at you being all mature. Big brother must be so proud."

I rolled my eyes at the mention of Asher. "Oh yes, very proud. He's thoroughly impressed that my GPA is still sitting at a 3.8. He hasn't said much to Riley though, which you know, isn't surprising from Professor St. James."

Grayson laughed, nodding in agreement. "And she's a person you immediately mentally locked onto at the bar?"

I ran my fingers over the tattoos on my arms. "Her thoughts were the first thing I noticed about her. They were so frantic and chaotic but like in a cute way. It didn't hurt that once I got over there, she happened to also be gorgeous. I liked her for her rambling thoughts first and foremost."

He started laughing again but stopped when he looked over my shoulder. He sat up a little straighter, interlocking his fingers together and placing them on top of the table. I looked to my left, seeing Riley pull her chair out and slowly sit down.

"Grayson, right?" she asked, smiling that casual smile she gave anyone she didn't know very well.

"Uh, yeah. Yeah, that's right. It's nice to meet the girl that River never stops talking about." Grayson said, nodding his head towards me.

The waitress came back with his drink and our starter. "Are you guys ready to order or do you need a minute?" She started to reach for her notepad.

"Can you give us a minute?" Riley asked, tapping her fingers on the menu.

The waitress gave us a small nod and sauntered off to another table.

"Well, River never stops talking about you either by the way. Should I be jealous?" Riley snickered, nudging my shoulder with her own.

I let out a cough, flicking my eyes to Grayson, who was grabbing a breadstick and hadn't taken his eyes off of her.

My best friend bit off a piece of bread. "Oh no, he loves you. Believe me."

Riley had started chewing a piece of her own bread, but his words caused her to end up in a coughing fit. I narrowed my eyes at him because as much as his words rang true, I hadn't exactly said 'I love you' yet. It was early and I didn't want to scare her off, but I may have admitted that to him at two in the morning, at a bar where I spent hours unloading how much I enjoyed her very existence.

Grayson pressed his lips together, flinching. "Heh, I'm just kidding. He doesn't love you at all. I'll shut up."

"Yes, shutting up would be a good thing right about now," I scolded.

Riley placed a hand on her chest. "It's okay." She slapped my arm. "Are you saying that it's not true?"

I opened my mouth and then closed it, running my index finger over my forehead. "When did this entire night become about me? I will not be ganged up on, thank you." I looked at my girlfriend, giving her a small smile and kicking her foot under the table.

Grayson cleared his throat. "Fine, we'll talk about something more interesting. Someone just had a birthday, hmm?"

Riley lifted her menu up, so it hid part of her face. "Yes, but that was last week. We are done celebrating me."

I ducked behind her menu and kissed her cheek. "You should always be celebrated, gorgeous."

I scoffed when I heard Grayson mutter the word 'obsessed' into his hand. Riley's giggle brought music to my ears. They both started talking at the same time, laughing and finally got to the topic of books, which sent them into even more frantic rambling. She got distracted by something on her phone, giving me some relief from trying to keep up with their conversation, when I heard a familiar voice tapping against my mind.

Out of your league. *Grayson thought to me.*

I side-eyed him but he was engrossed in his menu.

I mentally answered him back. You think I don't know that. She is practically dry heaving over here because you can actually have a conversation about the books she likes.

I watched the corner of his mouth lift up before he placed a hand over his lips.

She's gorgeous. *He thought back.*

I had to stop myself from letting out a barking laugh. Ooh...does Grayson have a crush?

He looked up at me and I watched him swallow slowly. Of course not.

I peered over at Riley, down at the table and then back at my best friend. I let my thoughts travel like silk. I won't be mad if you do. You are very good at fixing your face, but I can tell when you want to practically devour someone. I've seen it before, remember?

He reached for his water glass, downing half of it, but somehow maintaining eye contact with me.

"Are you guys having a mental conversation about me?" Riley inquired, giving each of us a skeptical look.

"What would you say if I said yes?" I asked, wiggling my eyebrows at her.

She pushed her bottom lip out. "I would say it's rude, since I'm sitting right here." She pressed her hand against my cheek and playfully shoved my face away.

"We were talking about how pretty you look tonight," Grayson offered. "The pictures River showed me really don't do you justice." As if on instinct, I watched his eyes do a quick look over her entire body and then return back to her face if it never happened.

Her eyes widened and she placed her hands against her cheeks as if she could feel them heating up. "Thanks." Her voice was small and a little shy, it was like she enjoyed the attention but didn't know what to do with it if it didn't come from me. I wasn't going to think too much about it at the moment, but I could see a tiny smile growing on her face, almost as if she enjoyed the compliment now that she thought about it.

Interesting. It was early in our relationship, but I was more than excited to learn everything I could about this girl.

The waitress came over to get each of our food orders and while Riley was explaining the certain substitutions she wanted, I heard Grayson in my head again.

Fine, it might be a little crush. She's all yours though.

I sighed, picking off a piece of bread and throwing it at him. That got me an eye roll from my girlfriend as she checked her phone. I clucked my tongue before answering him and getting a heated stare back.

Ah, but your flirting may or may not turn me on. Besides, we both know I don't mind sharing.

I OPENED THE DOOR SLOWLY, CAREFUL NOT TO SPILL THE TWO COFFEE MUGS I carried. I leaned against the wall, looking out the one window that let light filter into the room. It was getting closer to the end of August, so the days of random fog were becoming less and less. The sun wasn't as bright as it could have been due to some various clouds, but the natural light still flooded in, covering the room.

He looked over his shoulder when he heard me come in, immediately looking down at his feet. I kicked the door closed behind me, hearing it click before I made my way across the room. He had made the sheets I'd given him to use with the air mattress look nice, almost as if he'd never used them to sleep.

I held the mug out to him, the steam rising between us. He looked from the coffee to my face, hesitating.

"It's just coffee," I said, inching the mug closer.

He nodded, reaching out and taking it. "Thanks."

I peeked over at his hand, trying to get a better look at his forefinger. He noticed my staring and lifted up his hand.

"I have it on, don't worry. It's not like I need it though. If I wanted to leave I could, but I know your brother would make you find me and then beat my face in." He shook his head, taking a sip of the coffee.

"Asher doesn't make me do anything."

"Alright, fine. But he isn't my biggest fan, so—"

"Can you blame him?"

Grayson swallowed, looking down into his mug. He started to worry his bottom lip. "No, I can't."

I turned around, walking towards the other side of the room. I took a long drink of my coffee—nearly draining it— wishing I had added something of the alcoholic variety to it. "I'm not going to pretend like I don't understand why you made your decisions. I know school means a lot to you and doing right by your parents, but fuck, you were working with my dad? Do you understand how fucked that is? You know how I feel about him and so much shit I don't like talking about."

He placed his mug on the ground, taking a deep breath. "I know, okay? It's no excuse and I knew you would hate me for it. It's not like I enjoyed it. Your dad can be a scary son of a bitch, especially when Chancellor Fowler is right next to him."

I faced him, running a hand through my hair in frustration. "Did you even consider telling me? Even once?"

He took a step towards me. "Your dad told me if I did, I would regret it. He told me the best way to make sure no one got hurt would be to keep my mouth shut and just do what I was told. I didn't know if he meant my parents would be hurt, I didn't know if he meant you... so I just followed their rules."

My dad could have a short fuse and I would be lying to myself if I didn't believe that he would use threats to get what he wanted. He could have used any shadow wielder to do his bidding, but he picked Grayson. It fucking hurt me to think about, but it hurt even more that the end result ended up being Riley in any sort of pain, especially pain I couldn't fix quickly.

I sucked in a deep breath, I let it out shakily, rolling my shoulders. "And all of that resulted in kidnapping witches and hurting Riley."

He ran a shaky hand over the back of his neck. "I tried to get them to tell me why, but they wouldn't. I already told you I made sure those girls weren't hurt. I would never have knowingly put Riley in danger if I knew this had anything to do with her. River...I would never..."

I ran up to him, throwing my mug past his head and hearing it shatter against the wall. I got right up to his face, feeling his breath on my skin. "But you did! I know you didn't know, but it happened! I can put myself and my hurt aside but whether you meant to or not, you fucking—" I grabbed the sides of his face, forcing him to focus solely on me. My words came out through my teeth. My frustration elevating immensely and I knew my hold on him had to hurt, "you fucking hurt her! You hurt our girl, Grayson!"

"I fucking know! I want to tell her that I made a bad choice, that I didn't know what else to do! The threat of all my hard work, everything my parents wanted for me being torn apart scared me and I panicked!" He didn't try to remove himself from my hold. He didn't try to push me back. He just stood there, accepting what I had to say, letting it sink in. His lip quivered before he spoke again, He sucked in a breath, looking up at the ceiling. "I saw the look on her face when Marianne died, River. Believe me, I know I fucking hurt her. I didn't make those pieces of glass hit Marianne's body but to Riley I might as well have."

If the moment was any different, I would have kissed him with how close we were. I could tell he was sad and defeated; I wanted to make it better and kiss away his pain. I knew he would have done the same for me. As much as Asher wanted me to feel disdain for him, I just couldn't. He had no tension in his body and if I let him go, he probably would have collapsed against me. His mind was quiet and tired when I went into his head to listen to his thoughts. I hated that this whole thing with Riley involved him in this way.

Grayson meant a lot to me. I could admit that I loved him, but Riley and her feelings were my priority. Until she could look him in the eyes and forgive him, I had to keep him at a small distance.

We just looked at each other for a minute, time not meaning a fucking thing.

"River..." he whispered, looking down at my mouth and back up into my eyes. His dark brown irises looked the most innocent I'd ever seen them.

I pressed my lips together, feeling my heart palpitating. I closed my eyes. "Does my dad still talk to you? Mentally?"

I opened my eyes, noticing that he had placed his hands on my biceps. "No. I promise you, I would have told you if he was. I know Asher won't believe me, but my concern is for Riley. Chancellor Fowler might have given her up but that doesn't mean he has loosened his grip. He is letting her be free because he *can*, he told her as much with closing the school. She can't just decide to run away or not show back up. Whatever the chancellor and your dad want, I won't do it, but he knows who she is now and that's dangerous."

I moved my hands from his face to his shoulders, letting my thumbs skate against his collarbones. I chewed on the inside of my cheek in thought. "I won't let him, or my dad, hurt her. She's at Corrin's so I know she's safe, but I'm going to go get her...."

The door opened and my brother leaned against the threshold, his eyebrows furrowed behind his glasses. He let out an annoyed sigh, giving Grayson the most lethal death glare I'd ever seen. "River, we need to talk. Now."

Chocolate .esd
Bar Mock-Up
Food Packaging Collection

7

ASHER

I'd spent most of the time in my office attempting to do work and prepare myself for when school reopened, but the minute I opened my computer, I found myself just staring at the screen. The past day replayed in my head and every little noise outside my office door sent my shoulders sky high and my pulsing anxiety elevated. Campus was quiet for the most part except for the students who had chosen to stay in their dorms, but overall, the majority of people went home.

I wish I wasn't as connected to this fucked up situation as I was. I was only in this mess because my brother had decided to be in love with a girl who just happened to be the focal point of an insane person. An insane person I technically...worked for?

I could have been on the outside of this. I could be monitoring my brother and offering my aid from a healthy distance, but oh no, of course I had to be involved because River was my fucking brother and I had given into a carnal need not too long ago with Riley. I didn't even know if I liked her enough to even care this much, but somehow, here I was…. caring.

Thirty minutes of me trying to let myself believe that it was just sex and her pussy was probably pure magic, so that's why I cared, turned into me rushing out of my office and heading to my car.

I pulled up to my parent's house, clutching my keys in my hand so tightly I thought the metal would stab through my palm. I used my key to let myself in, slamming the door behind me.

"Dad!" I yelled, looking around the pristine entryway. "Dad!"

"Asher, stop yelling, please," My mom scolded, rushing out from where the kitchen was to the right. "Your father is in a meeting."

"A meeting? Where is he?" I asked, looking towards the staircase.

She grabbed my arm, holding onto me with more strength than I knew she had. My mom was human and ultimately obsessed with my dad. He had given her everything she'd ever wanted when they'd met, made sure she was well taken care of and with his powers, he knew what she wanted before she even opened her mouth. I didn't think she was ever privy to what this man had put us through or why. She had always gone on some spa trip or something else my father had to do to get her out of the house, knowing she was happy and elated to have a doting husband.

I took after my mom so much that looking at her face was like looking into a mirror. Her features were more delicate, but she was still so beautiful and I remember telling her that often when I was younger. I reached for her hand, removing it from my arm and squeezing.

She smiled at me. "I miss you. You and your brother. You never visit anymore. I know your father can be a little hard to be around, but I miss my boys."

"Mom, you have to listen to me…"

"I'm right here, Asher. Don't bother your mother. If you wish to speak, come to my office," my dad bellowed from the top of the stairs. He looked so relaxed and unbothered.

I groaned, moving around my mom, but not before planting a kiss on the top of her head. I took the stairs two at a time and turned to head to my dad's office door. The room was cold when I walked in, like just being in here with him sucked any warmth from the room. He was casually sitting in his chair, leaning back and staring at me.

My jaw tightened with the way I was grinding my teeth together. I closed the door, trying to keep my voice leveled. "You need to fucking explain to me what—"

My mouth clamped shut when I noticed that we weren't alone. The other person filled my insides with just as much if not more rage than my own dad did.

"It is very impolite to not greet guests, Asher. I know your father taught you better than that." Chancellor Fowler leaned up against the wall, his arms crossed over his chest. His voice was like honey, charming and smooth. His words came out with such easiness and playful energy, almost like he hadn't just turned Riley's life upside down in a matter of a few hours.

"I don't make it a habit to listen to my father, especially if you're the company he keeps," I snapped.

"Oh, you raised a feisty one, Thomas. He reminds me a little of myself when I was growing up." The chancellor laughed, clucking his tongue and wagging his finger at me. "Students must love your wit."

"What the fuck are you doing here?" I demanded. The two of them here couldn't be good and I didn't think they would be forthcoming with anything at all, but I couldn't leave here without something new to mull over.

My dad waved his hand back and forth as if dismissing my question. "Just assessing our options."

"Nothing major," Chancellor Fowler added, shrugging nonchalantly.

I turned to my dad. "You picked Grayson to fuck with River, didn't you?"

He sighed. "You both always think the worst of me. I don't pay much attention to students' powers; there are faculty members for that. He was the first shadow wielder that came to mind. Lucky for us, he had a lot to lose if cooperation was going to be difficult for him." He picked at something on his sleeve. "I won't pretend like I don't know about your brother's affection for him. I did not do it maliciously, but if it, I don't know, was a way to somehow get it into River's ungrateful little head that he should learn to respect me then well, so be it."

I didn't want to defend Grayson by any means, but this was wrong.

"If it makes you feel any better, poor Grayson put up a fight, but ultimately, his family and his education were a priority, and I commend him. I didn't know he had such a connection with my daughter. The look on his face, the devastation was..." I had to blink before I realized that Chancellor Fowler was almost smiling at the memory of Grayson becoming a victim of circumstance and unintentionally throwing Riley under the bus.

My long legs got me over to him in seconds and I got in his face. "Leave her alone. Leave all of us alone. You traumatized her, what in your delusional mind makes you believe that she will ever want you in her life, you sick fuck?"

Chancellor Fowler raised his eyebrows in surprise. "My daughter sure has put a spell on you boys. Her mother was just as enticing. I really should visit her, let her know that despite her deceit, she raised a beautiful young woman." He sighed giving me a curious look. "What do you plan to do, hmm? Fight for her honor? She is perfectly fine, Asher. I've already told Riley that I don't want to hurt her. Let's not pump our chest out and play hero." He slapped my cheek twice before walking around me. The feeling of heat from his hand caused me to hiss.

I scoffed, whirling around, my dad blocking me from following after him.

"Asher, you are the smarter one between you and your brother. You can help us if you want. That girl has lived her entire life not really knowing who she is, and all Erik wants to do is give his child all the things she should have had."

My eyes nearly bugged out of my head. "You almost sound like you know what it's like to be a good parent, like you can somehow understand. I won't help you. Helping you only hurts her."

"And you would never do that because you.... care for her?" Chancellor Fowler questioned, tilting his head to the side as he looked at me. "You didn't seem to think about her much when you were willfully letting Oliver in on her whereabouts, or is that how the kids show their affection nowadays?"

I ignored him, trying not to let the sting of what I did weigh on me so much. I did what I had to do for River's sake. I didn't know that something I'd done could escalate into a much bigger issue. I hated the fact that I was starting to understand Grayson right now. "It isn't right! I am not going to reward everything you've done. You killed her dad. You can't come back from that so stop being pathetic and thinking your daughter will give a shit about you." I looked him up and down, disgusted by his very existence.

He let out an exhausted sigh, like a restless child. "I used a little magic so that he went out a window. Can we please move on? Your father is the one who waited for him to stop breathing instead of calling the police right away, do not give me all the credit."

My dad didn't even flinch at his words. He kept looking at me, catching my eyes and never breaking contact.

"Y-you did what?" I didn't want my voice to stutter. I wanted to appear strong and like I had my shit together, but this caught me off guard.

He rolled his eyes. "We were the only two left in the office besides Thomas. Erik told me what he'd done and my reaction was to help. Thomas wasn't going to make it anyway, alright? I had to sit there and wait for the poor bastard to die."

"Fuck! Dad, what the fuck?"

"It was a lot of work for us, Asher. Make it look like he'd been drinking. Pouring alcohol down his throat, shattering a bottle near his body..." Chancellor Fowler prattled on, but I was walking backwards away from both of them.

"You told River a security guard found him. You talked about how much the school would miss him and how distraught you were. You stood there and watched him die. For what?" My back pressed against the wall. I took off my glasses, rubbing at my eyes, trying to press my fingers into them hard enough so that I didn't have to see either of these horrible people anymore, but it was no use.

"Power," Chancellor Fowler explained. "Family and power are one of the two most fought for things, well, I guess love but that can be achieved from either of these things eventually. You think everyone you know isn't seeking more power, more strength for their family? You clearly do not know the people you surround yourself with, trust me." He said it with a smirk like he knew something I didn't. "I know how to get your father more power and I can do the same for you and your brother. I'm not selfish, I can siphon powers from my coven for those who are loyal." He nodded towards my dad and I curled my lip upward.

I shoved my glasses back on my face, running my hand over my mouth and down my short beard. "I don't want that. I don't *need* power. I need you to fuck off and leave her and the coven alone." I turned my head to look at my dad. "Leave River out of this."

My dad's eyes gleamed with this look like his mind was working overtime. I felt a tug inside my head, but nothing happened. I knew what he was trying to do. He snickered, smirking at me. "Oh, my son, you're strong enough to push me back. You've grown those mental powers, that mental block and it makes me proud to know you're a worthy opponent."

"You can't make me do anything. I. Won't."

Chancellor Fowler let out a low laugh, it was condescending and made my skin crawl.

"Ah, but your brother...." My dad continued, "he hasn't been so disciplined."

I watched my dad tap his chin as if he was in deep thought. "The fuck does that mean?"

"River is smart. I didn't raise children who weren't intelligent—"

"You didn't raise us at all," I spat at him. I felt my lips clamp together; something was holding them closed. I tried to open my mouth but couldn't. I eyed Chancellor Fowler who had his index and thumb almost touching, telling me he was using his powers to keep me quiet.

"So rude to interrupt," he scolded, inclining his head towards my dad to keep going.

My dad wrinkled his nose. "I may not be able to get to you, but your brother is an entirely different story. I don't like forcing his hand, but we do what we must to achieve the things we deserve."

I narrowed my eyes at him, a small smile tugging at the corner of his mouth. "You get that girl to go back to school, push past her reservations. We both know your brother will comfort her while your little shadow friend wallows in his shame." He perched on the edge of his desk, clasping his hands together and placing them on his knee. "You use that wondrous power of yours to make her mind a place she can't stand, that fighting against herself is wrong, that the only way to relieve her pain is to seek her father's help."

The chancellor let me go and I rubbed my lips together. I let out a humorless laugh, catching my breath. "That is the most ridiculous thing I've ever heard. She knows my power anyway, she would know it's me. And that's if I was even considering this, which I'm not."

Chancellor Fowler took my dad's place in his office chair. "Ah, but along with your brother's comfort will come yours. You can't tell me you got that masters degree and don't know how to make a dream infiltration look natural, almost like she conjured it up herself." He tapped his fingers along the arm of the chair.

My jaw ticked and he nodded as if my silence was answer enough.

I grabbed him by his suit jacket, pulling him towards me. "I don't answer to you. I got my brother out of this house the minute I had the chance and I'm not going to let you manipulate me into doing your fucked up dirty work because you like being this psycho's bitch." I nodded towards Chancellor Fowler. I pushed my dad away from me causing him to hit the desk hard.

I turned to leave when he called my name. "Asher, it is simple. I want more, and despite you and your brother's disrespect, I know with help from Erik we could be stronger and better. You don't do this and I'll be forced to use your brother. His mind is not quite the steel trap that yours is. I can make it hurt and I can make *him* hurt. He will fight and hate every minute of it, but he will do what I say. It will make what happened to Grayson look like child's play."

"Fuck you," I grumbled.

"You want to protect your brother then do what we ask. Or do you want to protect her and leave your brother open to persuasion?"

Grayson had the excuse of not knowing Riley was involved. I would know the entire time and I would have to live with that and know that River would never understand or forgive me.

PRESENT

I noticed the way River dropped his hands and stepped away from Grayson as if it pained him to do it. Grayson looked at me, letting out a loud sigh and turning towards the window. My brother stalked past me, not saying a word. He moved to the entry table by the front door, grabbing my car keys.

I tugged on his wrist, causing him to drop them. He huffed, facing me head on.

"What do you want to talk about?" His words came out annoyed.

"Are you seriously letting him off the hook that easily?" I asked, nodding towards the room Grayson was in.

River pinched his eyebrows together. "What? No! Give me a

fucking break. I'm still pissed, but I also still have feelings for him, okay? It's complicated. Riley needs to be face to face with him and decide how she wants to proceed before I do anything."

I nodded, looking off to the side. "Smart move."

He gave me a fake smile. Sarcasm laced every single word that came out of his mouth. "Thanks. Your validation means so much."

"Is that where you're going? To go get Riley?"

River crossed his arms over his chest, his tattoos on full display. "Yeah. I would rather she be comfortable in your car than on my motorcycle."

"I really should argue with you about just deciding to take my car without asking, but I'm inclined to agree that it would be better than your bike."

Before he could reach for them again, I was faster and snatched them up. He gave me a frustrated expression. "You are way more involved in this than you should be. What happened between all of us was an experience, sure, but it's not like it hasn't happened between us—" he motioned between the two of us. "—before."

"What are you getting at?" I pressed, keeping my keys firmly within my grip.

"You found her at the station using your powers. You are ready to fight Grayson without another thought because he caused her pain, which I understand completely—and your first instinct was to run to her at the meeting when it all went down. You are so fucking transparent; you might as well be a fucking window."

I licked my lips, breathing through my nose. "River, none of that fucking matters at the moment."

He placed his hand on his chest. "I'm not upset by it. But if you want to be in this, then be in it. She doesn't need whatever pros and cons list you're drawing up in your head. I don't need to read your mind to know how you feel, big brother."

My eyes turned to slits. "You couldn't right now if you tried."

River cocked his head to the side. "Excuse me?"

I grabbed his arm, pulling him into the kitchen. I threw my keys on the counter, gripping the edge. "I am able to block you out when I want to because I've worked years learning about mental magic and improving my skills. I told you forever ago that you needed to do the same, especially with people just like you. You make yourself vulnerable to anyone with ill-intentions."

"What the fuck are you talking about?" River leaned his hip against the counter.

"I'm talking about our father. Why didn't you tell me that he could so easily get into your head, manipulate your thoughts and moves?"

I watched my brother's face flush as if he'd just been caught doing something he wasn't supposed to. He opened his mouth, but nothing came out.

I shook my head. "Actually that doesn't matter because before I came here, I went home. I saw dad and Chancellor Fowler." I explained everything to River and the more I said, the more nervous he looked. I didn't know if it was the potential of Riley being in harm's way or if he was freaked out by the thought of our dad meddling around in his head again.

"Dad really is a piece of shit. I don't understand; he had to know you would come and tell me all this." River rubbed the back of his head, eyeing the keys on the table.

"That doesn't matter. Learning to block out others takes time and focus. You are too worried about Riley and still very much in love with your deceiving little shadow wielder to master it any time soon." He opened his mouth to argue but I held my hand up. "Don't even try to tell me I'm wrong. The main thing right now is getting her to school; we have to act like we are playing into his hand."

River snagged my keys and gave me a small nod, then a skeptical look graced his features. "You haven't considered going through with it right?"

I raised one of my eyebrows.

"Getting into her dreams in the hopes of saving me from dad."

I dropped my head, sighing. "I've saved you from dad's wrath more times than you know." I looked up seeing a confused look on his face. I didn't want to get into that right now, so I shooed him away. "Go get your girlfriend and we'll reconvene."

He jogged towards the door but stopped just before turning the knob and pulling it open. I sent a thought to him.

Please watch yourself and watch your mind, especially where dad is concerned.

River looked at me, one corner of his mouth tugging upwards before he left.

8
RILEY

Beau rested his head on my lap while I stretched my legs out on the floor, leaning my back against the front of Corrin's couch. An awkward silence had settled over everyone when we'd all sat down to eat this morning, but I didn't know what to say to ease anyone's mind, so I just kept quiet.

Jax purred on Corrin's lap while she sat cross-legged in her dad's recliner. His eyes were trained on Beau just in case my familiar decided to do anything spontaneous. I looked over at Corrin, who was watching me with a tiny smile on her face.

Beau rolled over, showing me his belly. *Can we go home to River?* Beau had taken to River quickly and it was nice that he thought River was a sense of comfortability.

Before I could think up an answer, the front door opened revealing Mateo and Jade. Corrin squealed, jumping out of her chair. Jax screeched and scurried across the floor, jumping all the way to the back of the chair and holding on for dear life.

"Venaqui, mi hermosos bebe." Jade bent down and stretched out

her arms for Beau to run into. She smushed his face and rubbed along his body, making his tail wag. Her thick, spiraled curls were tied up in a loose bun and she wore a strapless top that showed off the large shoulder to shoulder tattoo that decorated her light brown skin. A moon sat on one shoulder blade and stars cascaded towards the other. A wolf was delicately drawn, its nose turned up so that one of the stars was perched on its snout.

Jax hissed over at us. Mateo kissed Corrin on the cheek and nodded to her cat. "*Hola*, Jax. I see you are still as pleasant as ever." Their hair was combed back, away from their face, but tiny curls peeked out and around the sides.

I stood there watching them and the easy way they all interacted. If my life hadn't imploded, I would easily be full of energy and a glowing personality. Currently, I really didn't know how to do much of anything except overthink and attempt to reevaluate something I didn't even understand in the first place.

Ike came from outside, the sound of the back door slamming startling me out of my own head, bringing me back into the present.

"Hey, *estámos aquí para apoyarte*, but I'm personally here to play with the cutest *perro* ever." Jade squeezed my arm, patting the side of her thigh so that Beau would trot along after her.

"Support me how? There isn't much you can do. I'm pretty fucked." I didn't mean to sound like a downer, but it wasn't like the words were a lie.

"Well for one, we are here, so that's something, right?" Ike pointed out, taking Corrin's spot in the recliner.

Corrin walked over, smacking the side of his head. "Can you please stop being such a grouch?"

"How was that grouchy? That was an honest answer! Don't forget I told mom and dad that anger management should be a very real possibility for you." Ike rolled his eyes, poking his sister in her side.

Mateo started to step between them. "Time out, okay? As much as we all enjoy your bickering, that's not the priority. Can you please settle down, *por un minuto?*"

"I think that is an excellent idea." Corrin's mom walked in with a tray of snacks. Everything from basic potato chips to candy to corn on the cob that was smothered in what looked like mayo and cheese with bits of chile.

Jade gasped, nearly crawling over to the coffee table to grab the messy corn treat. She started taking full bites without another thought. Her hands were instantly messy and so was the surrounding area around her mouth.

"What is that?" I asked, grabbing the snack by one of the skewers and examining it. It smelled delicious, but I placed it back on the tray knowing my stomach could only handle something as simple as chips.

She giggled. "It's Mexican street corn. Our Mamá used to make it for us all the time when we lived at home. Nothing rivals hers, but this is a very, *very* close second." Jade praised.

Corrin's mom sat on the arm of the couch, letting out a laugh, but then the room settled into that familiar quiet. We each got some food, but once the small amount I'd consumed was gone, all I could do was fidget.

"Like I said last night, you don't have to say every single thing that happened, but..." Corrin's mom started, easing herself onto the couch near me.

I looked over at her daughter, who was now seated on the floor between Mateo's spread legs. She gave a little shrug and a nod of encouragement.

"I can only tell you what I know." I continued to fidget, twisting my fingers together over and over. This would have been the time I reached for my necklace but instead I found Beau's head pushing against my hands.

"That's all I ask, sweetheart." Corrin's mom leaned back against the couch, prepared to listen intently.

I told them what I had told Corrin last night, watching as her mom's eyes widened and the way she placed her hand over her chest at certain parts. I stuttered a bit when Grayson came up, so I moved past that as quickly as I could. I tried to force Marianne's name out of my mouth, but it wouldn't budge. That part wasn't important to them, but she was important to *me*, so why was that part so fucking hard to open up about?

"That's what was happening with your coven, *mi amor*?" Mateo asked Corrin, taking her chin in their grasp and forcing her to look at them.

"Yeah, but I promise I didn't know all the insider details until last night." She turned to her mom, pointing her finger. "And don't start. If I had known her evil bio dad was in charge, I wouldn't have been insistent on staying in."

"Damn, a Celica legacy...." Ike trailed off, blowing out a breath. "That man takes 'I'll do anything for my family' way too far."

Corrin's mom shook her head, her twists hitting her cheeks. "I knew something was off with that whole thing. I can report him, and seek the witch's council's help. You'll be under the council's protection seeing as you are one of us now."

I pulled at the ends of my braids, the tension at my scalp giving me something else to focus on. "No, doing anything like that would likely anger him and I don't want to d-do t-that..." I shut my mouth the minute I found myself stuttering. I wouldn't talk to the man that night after the meeting and he'd murdered someone right in front of me because of it. "I'm sure he's skated his way by the council for years now. He isn't stupid so doing something like that would be too obvious."

"He still siphoned powers. He's probably still doing it, despite finding you," Jade pointed out, wiping her hands on a napkin. "Your boyfriend's dad is also a piece of shit, by the way, just in case we weren't clear on that. You trust that boyfriend of yours? Where exactly is the shadow wielder that was helping them?"

Mateo threw her a look. "Yes, we are all aware of how awful these men are so slow your questions. You are just as bad as Mr. Metal Magic over there." Ike threw them a middle finger.

"Yeah, I trust River completely. And no...I don't know where Grayson is." A part of me wanted to know, but I couldn't let myself go there, not yet at least.

Mateo gave me a sympathetic expression. "If not the witches council, then what? I, myself, and a few other wolves can watch you from a distance."

"I don't need bodyguards," I grumbled, placing my face in my hands.

"You wouldn't even know we're there. Stealth is like wolf 101." Mateo nodded to their sibling, who nodded as well in her agreement.

I scoffed. "You say things like I'm going to just go back to school. I can't do that."

Ike placed two of his fingers against his temple. "Do you plan to just stay here? Be a hermit? Chancellor Fowler expects you to submit, so you'll just go against him by doing...nothing."

Corrin grabbed a bunch of chips and chucked them at her brother. "Can you give her a fucking break?"

Ike grabbed a chip from his lap and popped it into his mouth. "Am I wrong?! The man wants you to take over his legacy—he isn't about to, like you said, let the council get in the way of that—but with everything that happened you just think that he's going to let you sit and rot away with your thoughts and *not* lash out on anyone who is associated with you?"

I flinched at the last thing he said. I knew Chancellor Fowler would do just that, which was why this entire thing had no right answer.

"Ike! Just shut the fuck up!" Corrin screamed, the sheer volume of her voice sending Jax into a panic. He jumped up at Ike, clawing at him, which caused her brother to leap from the recliner. He swatted at the orange cat, yelling at Corrin to discipline her fucking animal.

A deep rumble erupted into the room. It sounded like a growl, but not the kind that Beau let out when he sees a squirrel, The kind of annoyed, frustrated kind of growl. Jax hissed, but pranced away from Ike as if nothing happened and Beau picked his head up, staring right at Mateo.

"Way to set the tone, alpha." Jade stuck her tongue out at her sibling.

Mateo vigorously shook their head. "Do not put that on me. Alpha tendencies, yes. Actually alpha, I am not." They rolled their eyes, getting up from the floor and pulling Corrin along with them. They held their hand out for Jade to accept.

Ike rubbed the back of his head, a few claw marks showed on his forearm, tiny blood droplets falling along his dark skin. I swallowed hard when I looked at it, feeling a little dizzy. Just the smallest droplet had me seeing more, suddenly the droplets were a pool of thick, red, liquid.

"Riley, I'm sorry if I came off harsh, I just—" I could hear Ike's voice, but it was becoming background noise to the loud static that went off in my brain. I clutched the couch, trying to breath, but it was like air had no way to enter my fucking lungs.

"Riley, please calm down, it's okay. It's okay, sweetie." I heard my roommate's mom, her voice soothing, while her arms rested on my biceps. Beau's large head rested against my legs, whimpering.

I loosened my grip on the couch, blinking over to Mrs. Hayes. "I —I don't...."

Corrin looked down at my side. "Well, Dad wanted a new couch anyway." I followed her gaze, noticing that I'd created two large burn marks into their couch.

"Fuck, I'm so sorry. I don't know how to...I can't..."

"I have a feeling that that is also a reason why you would not like to be in society right now?" Ike inquired, running his fingers along his chin.

Jade got up and grabbed his arms, pulling him away from us. "You really don't know how to read a room, do you?"

Mrs. Hayes grabbed my hands, enveloping them with her own.

"Your magic is undisciplined. You need a dampener. Especially if you intend to go back to school the day after tomorrow."

I let out a little laugh with no happiness in it. I really didn't know what to say.

"Let me talk to Ike and Samia." Samia was one of the main witches in the bay area that helped produce dampeners. She did basic jewelry with simple metals, or she could make custom pieces that were fancy. The kind that you saw on celebrities or high-profile people. Her wife was a metal magic user and if you wanted the piece made in-house, then it tended to cost more. Most people I knew, based on what River had told me, had jewelry made somewhere else and only went to Samia to turn the piece into your dampener.

"You don't have to. I'm fine." I heard a bark which startled me. Beau was looking at me, his big dopey eyes narrowed.

You are not. He sounded concerned and just a little pushy.

I kissed his head. "If you feel inclined to talk to Samia, then fine. I'll give you whatever money you need to pay for the dampener."

Corrin's mom waved me off, her voice going soft. "Have you spoken to your mother?"

My breath caught in my throat as I digested her question. My brain didn't have time to short circuit the way it wanted to because a car door slammed from outside. We all shifted our attention to the front door.

Mateo went to the window. "Ah, your knight in dashing good looks and artful tattoos is here."

Corrin shuffled to the front door, throwing it open and letting River walk in. I shot up from the couch, walking around it and taking a few steps toward him. My boyfriend looked around the room, throwing a few casual nods towards the people around me.

"Maybe you should just stay here. You seem to have a whole army of people." He chuckled softly.

I shrugged. "I was considering it."

He cleared his throat. "Actually..." He stepped closer, bringing his hand up to caress my cheek. "I came here to pick you up, if that's what you want. We don't have to go to your house, but I was thinking you could stay with me. Your mom knows you're safe and I know she'll want some kind of proof of life from you, but I just…"

"River —" I started, but I felt Beau shove his face into the back of my calves so that I would step closer to him.

"No matter where you go, the wolves will look out for you," Mateo offered, giving me a reassuring look.

"And since your boyfriend texted me for my address, I now have his number just in case you go radio silent again." Corrin let her phone swing back and forth from her fingertips.

River pulled my phone from his back pocket. "Here. You might want this back."

I had wondered where it went, but that didn't matter at the moment. I sighed, letting my body do what it wanted to do the minute he walked through the door. I fell against him, feeling his large arms wrap around me. He pressed his face into my hair, kissing the top of my head. "I'm happy they were able to keep you safe."

"Yeah, but…" I pulled back, looking up into his green eyes. "I do want to sleep in your bed tonight."

"Whatever you want, gorgeous."

Corrin reached out for my hand and squeezed. "Call me and let me know you're all squared away, okay?"

I nodded, heading up the stairs to Corrin's room to double-check that I didn't leave anything behind. I did a once over and sighed, closing her door to head back to the main room. Mrs. Hayes was waiting in the hall. She had a melancholy look on her face.

"I'm sorry if this sounds like overstepping, perhaps my daughter gets it from me, but I do hope that you give your mother a chance."

I moved a few of my braids over my shoulder. "It's not that. I just did something, and I can't really face her right now. What she kept from me was a lot, but I don't know how to deal with my emotions and these powers simultaneously."

"What you did can't be that bad?"

I raised my eyes to the ceiling, not wanting to cry.

Corrin's mom ran a shaky finger over her eyebrow piercing. "Oh honey, I'm sorry. I didn't mean to upset you. Just, as a mother, I know there is nothing my children could do to make me never want to see or hear from them again."

I sniffed. "I know you're right."

"Then maybe think about what I'm saying. Just think about it."

I let out a small cough and gave her a helpless smile. "I guess, I just don't know what to say when I do see her."

Mrs. Hayes grabbed my shoulder and slid her hand down my arm and over my hand. "I think seeing you is the most important thing to her. Whatever you say after that is secondary."

9
RILEY

We pulled up to the house, the entire drive a mix of music and River's attempts at charming small talk. I gave a few answers here and there, but at some point, I realized he understood that I would much rather be in my own head. He had rolled the back windows down so that Beau could stick his head out, his tongue slapping against his face.

River walked around the car, opening my door and holding his hand out for me to take. I narrowed my eyes. "I'm not a princess, River."

He kept his hand out. "And I'm not a prince, but I've been doing gentleman type things since we started dating and it's not about to end now."

I begrudgingly took his hand, letting him pull me from the car. I got on my tip toes and kissed his cheek, turning away so I could let Beau out. River headed towards the house, pulling out his keys, but before he could start to unlock it, the door opened quickly.

"Took you long enough." I heard Asher's voice before I saw him. Beau ran ahead of me, pushing past River and sliding between Asher's legs. He ran around the house, starting to explore every room he could.

"What the hell?" Asher said, pointing at Beau's fast-moving body.

River opened his mouth, stepping through the threshold, but I cut him off. "He's a dog." I shouldered my way between both of them, getting inside the house and calling for my familiar.

Beau skidded to a stop, trotting over and sitting down nicely next to me.

Asher let out an aggravated groan. "Of course, your dog. Why is it here?"

"Ash, let it go," River pleaded, throwing the keys on the entryway table.

"He's here because I want him to be." I placed my hands on my hips, tilting my head to the side. I peeked down at Beau, realizing he was tilting his head as well.

Asher pinched the bridge of his nose, pushing his glasses further up his face. "I wouldn't let my own brother get a dog, what makes you think I'll let yours just gallivant around my house?" He stepped up to me while River sighed heavily behind him. Asher raised both his eyebrows, his green eyes shining a little brighter this close.

"Hmph," I grumbled, standing my ground. My hands balled into fists as I let them fall at my sides. "Your dad is one of the reasons my life is a fucking mess, so you might owe it to me—" I leaned in a bit. "—just a little."

His chest rose and fell as he studied my face. "Neither of us had any part in that. I detest what my dad did." His words came out harsh, like his father was in the room with us and he was throwing the words at him and not me.

I shook my head, watching the ends of my braids swing back and forth. "I know, okay? It's a fucking dog, Asher. He won't be a problem for you. Besides, he'll keep me occupied so you won't have to deal with me that much while I figure my fucking life out."

Asher ran a hand through his hair. "Riley... you make yourself sound like a burden and that's hardly the case."

I hummed, noticing the way his beard was slowly starting to grow out again and needed to be trimmed. I had to snuff out the need to run my fingers along the unruly hair. "I'm surprised you could say that with a straight face."

Asher groaned and it was meant to come out annoyed, but the sound sent a weird sensation to my core of all places. I was too far in my own head that I was finding the things Asher St. James did over-whelmingly appealing, and it needed to stop. I didn't like feeling immensely sad, but this was not a feeling I wanted to exchange it with. I felt eyes on me and noticed Beau was staring, the look of judgment that I knew only pitbulls could pull off was in his eyes.

River stood between us, putting his hands up. "Simmer down, both of you. Like she said it's a fucking dog, Asher. And he's her familiar. You really want to see what happens if you try to separate him from her?"

We all looked down at Beau. He fixed his gaze on Asher and bared his teeth. A deep growl came out, but he didn't make a move to cause any damage. It was more that the idea of his removal didn't sit well with him. It made my stomach turn thinking about it.

Asher gave Beau an annoyed look, rolling his eyes. "My concern is what happens to him when she goes back to school."

I reared my head back. "School?"

"Yes, school," Asher repeated.

"I haven't decided what I'm doing. Besides, everything about me is very unstable and I don't know if heading back to Mystic Riegan is what I want. Chancellor Fowler gave me two days so don't assume that's what I'm doing."

River and Asher exchanged a look that had my eyebrows furrow-ing. River took my face in one of his hands. "Riley, when you get settled, we need to talk to you about.... something."

"What aren't you telling me? Are you really going to lecture me about school?" I started to argue, but Beau's incessant sniffing and high-pitched bark nearly had my brain short circuiting, so I gave him my attention.

He was over near where the guest room was, far too interested in whatever was behind the door.

Asher snapped his fingers, trying to get Beau's attention. "Away from there!"

"He's not going to listen to you," I said, making my way over to my dog. "What's going on buddy?" I felt River grab my arm, pulling me back.

"Why don't we just go upstairs, gorgeous? We can talk about everything when you're settled. You and Beau."

I stole my arm back, looking over my shoulder. "What's behind the door, River?"

Asher's exasperated laugh filled the air. It wasn't that he found something funny, but more so that whatever needed to be said was so wildly insane that laughing was the only way to deal.

I looked up expectedly at my boyfriend, who pressed his lips together. He placed his hand at the back of his head and looked up at the ceiling. He was avoiding my question and I wanted to combust. "I swear if you don't tell me I will rip that door off its hinges." I made it so we were so close in proximity that he could feel my breath. "We both know I can do that."

He huffed in defeat. His green eyes already had a look of pleading, and I didn't even know what was going on. "Grayson."

One name. One word. A small breath escaped my lips and I had to cross my arms over my chest, tucking my hands into my armpits to keep them from shaking. "He's here?"

River slowly nodded, reaching for me. I stepped back, shaking my head. "Why?"

Asher raised one of his hands. "That was my idea. After what happened, it was the best case scenario."

"Your idea?" I reiterated, looking back at the door and then at him. He put his hands in his pocket, turning and heading up the stairs. I rested my gaze on River. "You agreed to this?"

River shifted from one foot to the other. "It seemed like a good idea to keep him close, after everything. He told us what happened, and I know he hurt you. What happened with Mari—"

"Shut up! Stop talking." I felt my palms getting hot and I knew it was more than just anxiety. I took a deep breath and shoved past him, hearing him let out a groan. Beau's familiar footsteps followed after me, almost right on my heels.

I stomped up the stairs, seeing Asher coming out of the bathroom near River's room. "Are you expecting me to go in there and talk to him right now? Hear him out?" I shoved him lightly and he peeked over my shoulder. I heard River creeping up the stairs but not interrupting us.

"Who, Grayson? No, I don't. You can talk to him whenever you think you'll be okay to do so. I don't actually care what you do."

I snorted. "Right? Says the guy who just told me I couldn't have my dog and claimed I was going back to school."

"Fuck's sake, keep the dog. You want to fight me like a child to keep your companion, fine. River is right, he's your familiar so as long as you pick up his shit and he stays out of my room then we're all good. School is non-negotiable though."

"Non-negotiable?" My mouth dropped open. "You can't just make all these fucking decisions. We aren't in a classroom, *sir*. You can't just tell me what to do and expect me to just nod my head and submit. I just had one insane fucking man try to tell me what I am and who I'm going to be, so fuck you, if you think you'll be another one."

"Hey, Riley, it's okay. Let's just go to my room and talk," River coaxed, tentatively touching my shoulder.

Asher scanned my face, taking in my heavy breaths and likely over-stimulated demeanor. His eyes dropped to my mouth, moving them back to meet my eyes so quickly it was almost as if it never happened.

The tension in my body started to fall away and I sighed, letting out a breath that came out like a light cough. "I really don't know if you do all this because you like control or because you actually give a shit."

I swiftly turned around, my body knocking against River's, heading towards his room.

I SAT ON RIVER'S BED, HAVING CHANGED INTO ONE OF HIS SHIRTS AND PLAYED with the hem while he was out in the hall with his brother. I jumped in surprise when I heard Asher's door slam. I stopped fidgeting, listening as the door opened. River closed it with his back, leaning against it with his head bowed.

"If you guys were arguing out there, you are both surprisingly quiet about it."

He laughed softly. "Asher is very good at whispering harshly. He did say he was sorry."

I gave him a leveled look. "No, he didn't."

"He did not," River admitted, walking over to his bed and sitting on the edge. He gave me a bit of space and something was holding me back from telling him that he could get as close as he wanted. He took in my change of clothes. "It's the middle of the day. You look like you're dressed for bed."

I drew circles on my exposed knees, since I had on his shirt and nothing else. "I didn't sleep well at Corrin's despite crying until I was practically dehydrated." He opened his mouth but I continued before he could interject, "Please don't ask about it. I spent most of the night in and out of sleep, tossing and turning and being here...." I splayed my hand out on his comforter.

River placed his hand over mine, the feeling of it warm and loving. "Being here, what?"

"I think I could sleep soundly. I just keeping seeing b-blood and I—"

River ran his hand up my arm and over my shoulder, so he could cradle my neck. The thick lines of tattooed black vines that decorated his bicep in my eyesight. "Grayson told us about Marianne and Riley..."

I shrugged him off and vehemently shook my head. "No. Don't talk to me about that." I shuffled off the bed, walking away from him and towards one of his dressers. "I *don't* want to talk about that." A pit was developing in my stomach and I wanted to vomit from the feeling. "I don't want to bring up what happened in that room. I'm already trying not to think about the fact that you have Grayson in this house and all that does it make my fucking heart hurt."

Beau watched me from where he'd curled himself up in River's closet. The door was open and he had made a makeshift bed out of some of the clothes that had fallen off of their hangers. I gave him a small smile, letting him know I was fine. His eyes drooped closed again, letting himself drift off to sleep.

"Grayson is—"

"I need to talk to my mom." I interrupted.

"Okay, I can take you there if you want to get dressed." His words had a cautious tone to them.

"Tomorrow. I want to go by myself."

The air stilled and River sucked in a breath. He was hesitating.

I turned on my heels and faced him. "Are you going to tell me no?"

He groaned. "Not exactly, but I don't think it's a good idea. Not without one of us with you."

"You sound like your brother. She's my mom, River. I don't need to be babysat or watched like some sort of ticking time bomb."

He got up from the bed, his mouth pressed into a hard line. "You didn't want to go home hours ago, but now you do. I'm happy for it, truly I am, but your powers are still new, they are still pretty unstable and—"

"I know that!" I yelled, nearly all the furniture in his room rose off the ground and then dropped. A loud banging sound echoed in the otherwise quiet room.

River didn't let it phase him. His gaze went distant for a moment and then came back.

"Let me guess, you were alerting Asher that everything is fine?"

"Would you like him to rush in here and give you a lecture?" he volleyed back.

I bit my bottom lip, flinching a little when I accidentally bit too hard. "I go and you stay in the car, will that suffice?"

He let out a sigh in defeat. "Yes, gorgeous. That is good enough for me." He stepped closer to me, leaning down to kiss my forehead. "We need to talk about school."

"I already told Asher that's not his decision to make."

A painful look passed over his eyes. "You going to school isn't Asher being a hardass. It has to happen, for your safety, your future.... for all of us."

"Says who?"

River took my hands and pulled me back to his bed, waiting for me to sit down next to him. "Our dad and Chancellor Fowler."

"You talked to them?" I gasped.

"Asher did. If you want to take a nap or something before I get into it, then I understand, but I don't want to keep you in the dark about this."

My phone buzzed and I looked over at the end table, grabbing it and seeing a text from Corrin.

CORRIN

Please show signs of life.

Ike had said something along the lines of Chancellor Fowler not letting me just sit idly by. It was laughable that I even considered that I had a chance of getting even a moment of solace about this. Of course, he would involve people I cared for, I had said it myself. He was an adult, but he acted like a petulant child, lashing out and causing havoc if he didn't get his way. He wanted me under his thumb, living my life as a college student and embracing my powers, yet he wanted me unfiltered and undisciplined so he could fix it. He was my connection to these powers I had; he was the closest thing I had to that part of myself, that part of my mysterious family. Did he just expect my mom to come running back to him now that he'd removed my dad from the equation? Now that he had me?

That admission sent a shiver down my spine.

My phone beeped, alerting me that it was getting too hot, my hands feeling like fire. I willed my hands to stop shaking so I could be able to type. I took methodical deep breaths before I wrote my reply.

> I'm good. Beau and I are both settled.

CORRIN

> Thank god. I'll let you know what my mom says about the dampener and all that. We've got you.

I sent her a heart emoji and then set my phone back down. My head was a little woozy from lack of sleep and any information that River tried to give me would just not sit right without my undivided attention. His pillows looked so comfortable and even though my face wasn't buried in his sheets, I could smell his scent wafting off of them.

"Just let me, I guess, recharge, and wake me up in a few hours. Don't just let me sleep till whenever, okay?"

He placed his hand on my knee, sliding it up so that his fingers hid beneath the bottom of the shirt. "I got you." He ran his fingernails along my chin as he curled his fingers into his palm, pulling his hand away. The amount of restraint in his expression was palpable.

He tilted my chin towards him and kissed me. The kiss was chaste and sweet, probably what I needed right now. He walked over to his dresser, pulling out my silk pillowcase and tossing it at me, so I could replace the one behind my head with it. The door closed behind him and I settled into his cool sheets. In a matter of two minutes, I had ultimately been told in one way or another that I wasn't alone. Whether it was through text or through spoken word, it came out with conviction. I should probably start believing them.

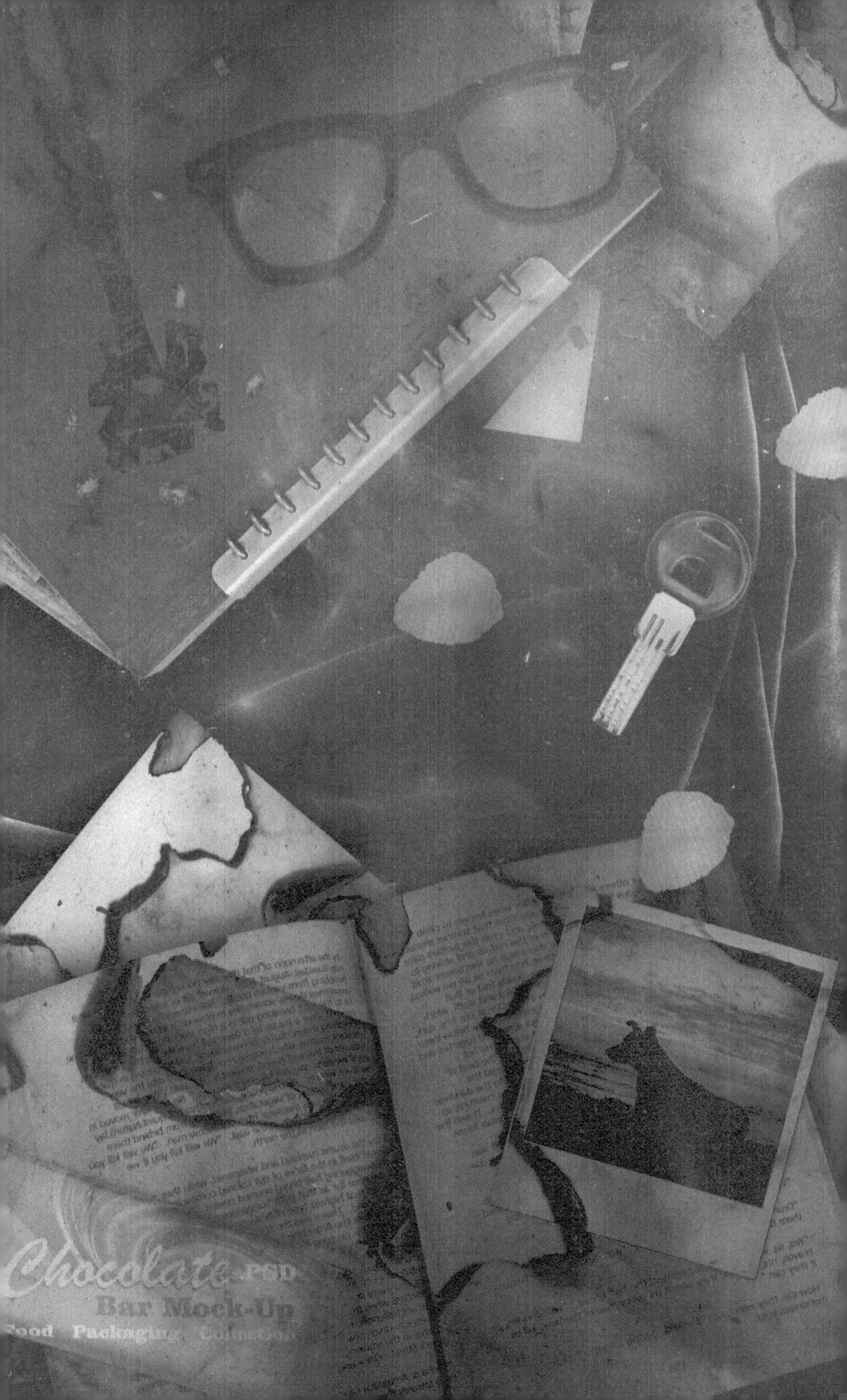
Chocolate PSD
Bar Mock-Up
Food Packaging

10
RILEY

’d woken up earlier than I wanted to, but trying to get back to sleep was harder than I imagined, so I stopped trying. I sat up in River’s bed and reached for my phone. I tried to read a few pages of one of my ebooks but I couldn’t focus. I don’t know why I did it, but I went to my photo app. I swiped through until I found ones of me and Marianne. I should have closed my phone and stopped, but I didn’t. I clicked through more pictures, each and every single photo filling me with a kind of sad rage that I’d never felt before.

I had no idea what the chancellor had done with her after I blacked out. I hated that she was scared when she died. I hated that she had been a part of my life and this is what happened. I shut my eyes, letting my phone fall from my hands. The last picture I’d seen was the one from when we’d driven all the way to Los Angeles because she had done so much research and was determined before she went off to college to get a real celebrity sighting. And by ‘real’, she meant a celebrity she deemed as A-list and would make all the others at Virginia Tech jealous.

It never actually happened, but we spent an entire weekend in the city and way too much money, but that time was something I'd always remember, and it made my heart hurt. I opened my eyes and tears spilled down my cheeks. I quickly wiped them away when the door cracked open.

River poked his head in and his eyebrows raised when he noticed I was up. "I was coming to wake you."

I tossed my phone on the end table and put my hands in my lap. I looked around the room. "Where's Beau?"

River nodded beyond the door. "He's napping on the couch. I took him for a walk, fed him a sandwich and then I put on some cartoons for him to watch in the living room."

I laughed softly. "You fed him a sandwich?"

"Well, we don't have dog food here, so I made him a sandwich. Don't worry, all dog-friendly items. It was like peanut butter and ham. He thought it was delicious. That's at least what he thought to himself."

I made a disgusted face. "That sounds gross."

River shrugged, walking further into the room and closing the door. "He liked it. That's all that matters." He didn't make a move to sit on the bed, but instead just stood near it as if he was contemplating his next words. "Can we finally talk?"

I lifted my head towards the ceiling and sighed, "Did you talk to Grayson while I was asleep?"

"I did. He asked how you were for the tenth time. I let him in on what's going on and despite what you might think, he isn't loyal to my dad or Chancellor Fowler. He wants to help and..."

I widened my eyes as if to tell him to keep going.

"And he called his parents and told them he was going to head back to the dorms early before school opens back up, but he's actually just going to stay here, in the guest room. He doesn't want to bother you until you're ready, but he is on your side, Riley." He almost started to flinch like I was about to argue with him.

"He can do whatever he wants. We can cross paths for all I care; I'm not ready to look at him and say much of anything. He isn't the problem, but he's a constant reminder." I mumbled the last words under my breath, pulling myself together. "Now inform me on why school is so fucking important."

River had a relationship with Grayson, one that went beyond ours and I knew he was hurting in a different way then I was. I couldn't just forget what happened for the sake of my boyfriend. I loved River, but he didn't live in my head and see the continuous fucking pain that liked to replay.

He started pacing as he spoke. "Asher went to see our dad and well, your dad was there too."

I fisted the sheets, tampering down my anger. "That man *isn't* my dad."

River slowed his steps and looked at me, nodding. "Right, sorry." He started up again, clearing his throat. I let him tell the entire story and he tried to gauge my reaction when he'd mentioned his dad being a part of how mine died. I swallowed hard, knowing something had always been off with Oliver St. James. I didn't want to pat myself on the back about it because I didn't like being right, not about this.

When he was done, he finally sat down in the middle of the bed, facing me. "Does it all make sense now?"

All the information suddenly made my braids feel far too tight and I rubbed my scalp. "What?"

"Asher's insistence."

I pulled my braids up off my neck and pulled them over one of my shoulders. "Yeah, I guess. He doesn't have to be so pushy about it. It's not really helpful..."

"I think it's his odd way of caring about me...and about you."

"River, I don't think—"

He shook his head. "That is for you and him to discuss. I only know about my own relationship with my brother, and I've always known Asher had a weird way of showing he cares."

"As long as Asher doesn't turn to the dark side, then fine, I'll go to fucking school. I'll listen to you guys, but he needs to cool it. He can keep his abrasive tendencies for the classroom and not bestow it upon me, that's all I ask. I don't want Chancellor Fowler to ruin anyone else's life, so if I have to go and show my face, be seen as some type of pariah, then fine."

"You won't be a pariah, Riley. That school has much bigger problems than you and your secret magic." River reached out and squeezed my leg over the sheets. "Besides, if you have any problems, I'm a phone call away."

"You won't read my mind and just know?" I challenged, cocking my head to the side.

"I wouldn't do that."

"River, let's not pretend like you didn't try when Grayson brought me back into my room, unconscious. I may not be able to prove it, but I do know that you would want to help me no matter what and even fight against how much you conditioned yourself not to." I slipped out from underneath the covers, shuffling over to him.

His mouth was slightly open as if he wanted to retort and go against what I was saying, but his defense would be futile. "Riley, I didn't want to and it's not like your mind would let me, but you were scaring me and I really didn't like seeing you like that. Marianne, your dad, I hate it for you. I hate that I can't fix it."

"I know and I'm not mad. I can't blame you." He looked a little relieved and I stuck my tongue in my cheek. "You really care about me, don't you?" I asked, poking his arm.

"What gave it away?" he joked, smiling at me. It was that charming smile that I'd fallen in love with.

I reached out and traced my finger along his defined jaw, watching the way his Adam's apple moved as he swallowed. There were so many things out of my control lately that it wasn't fair. I didn't ask for this fucked up family history. I didn't ask for my dad to get thrown out a window and left for dead. I didn't ask to have power, but then again, they felt like they have always been a part of me and I never wanted them to leave. I'd hurt my own mother because of them...and I needed something that was tangible. Something I knew was a constant for me.

I leaned in, pressing my mouth to his. He let an immediate moan slip out and I took that as my cue to open my mouth and take more. I wrapped my hands around the back of his head, moving my lips over his and he gripped my sides. The shirt rode up my thighs and I felt heat up my spine. Never breaking our connection, I maneuvered myself so I was straddling him.

I brought my hands down and tucked them under his shirt, wanting it off.

He broke our kiss, dodging my attempts to capture his mouth again. "Riley." His voice was a whisper in the small distance between our faces.

"What?" I asked, more bite to my words than I anticipated.

He ran his hands up my sides and then back down. "I think maybe we should talk some more or I don't know...."

"No, you don't know. You are trying to tell me what I need and that's not how this works." I cocked my head to the side, my frustration building.

He gripped my face in his hands, keeping me steady. "That's not what I'm trying to do, gorgeous. I would never. I just don't know if right now is the best time."

I scoffed. "I have no fucking sense of direction at the moment, but I do have this," I wiggled a little on his lap, causing him to stifle a groan. "I am coherent enough to know when I would like to stop talking for a minute and just have sex with my boyfriend. If you don't want to have sex or you don't want me, then just say that. Don't turn this into something about my well-being."

He removed his hands from my face and placed them on my thighs. His fingertips touched the exposed skin and it tickled. He let his thumbs lightly run against the soft skin of my inner thigh. I was about to get up and move back to my place on the bed, but he held my thighs tighter, keeping me on top of him.

River let out a deep breath, gazing up at me. His eyes were thoughtful yet determined. "I will *always* be concerned about your well-being. And I will *always* want to have sex with you. Those are non-starters, gorgeous. I will never tell you how to feel, but you have to fucking understand that I will make sure that you want me inside of you because it will make you happy or clear your head, not because you think it will solve your problems or because you think you'll come and your life will go back to normal." He reached up and held my chin, brushing his thumb over my lips. It was a feather-like touch that had me squirming on his lap. "So look at me and honestly tell me that fucking me would make you happy, right here in this moment."

I bit my lower lip, letting my hands run through his hair and bringing his face closer to me. Our foreheads touched and he placed his hands back on my thighs, inching them a little higher, but keeping his fingers away from the place I wanted him. His tattoos were such a beautiful contrast to my inkless brown skin, that it was hard to look away, but I focused on him.

He was waiting. He was being patient, like he always was.

My nose grazed along his and his breathing was steady, as if he was a master of self-control. "It would make me happy."

I tried to kiss him, but he pulled back, giving me a tiny smile. "That's not what I asked. Tell me those words *specifically*."

I moved on his lap again, but he held my thighs. I nuzzled into his neck, kissing the side of his throat before pulling my head up and pinning my eyes to his. "You fucking me right now would make me happy." I brushed my lips along his, whispering against his mouth. "Please."

His mouth connected with mine with the kind of fierceness that only someone who had a singular goal could achieve. River had this way of making me feel like the only girl in the entire world, even in a crowd full of people. We were alone right now though and every kiss, every movement of his hands felt meticulous and comforting. I moaned against his mouth, our tongues dueling together and I scooted closer to him, grinding my lower body down on his lap.

He was hard between my legs and the friction was incredible. He grabbed underneath my thighs and moved me so I was laying on my back. My braids splayed out around my head and I tilted my head up, missing the feeling of his body underneath me. He ran his hands down my thighs, kissing the inside of each one, back and forth.

"Do you need me to make you feel good?" he asked, running a single finger over my panties. He lifted up the shirt I wore and kissed right below my belly button. "Does my girl need to be taken care of?" He pressed his finger against my panties, sending more wetness between my legs.

"Y-yes," I stuttered, moving my hips so I could press against his finger.

"Tell me what you need, gorgeous. I like when you tell me what I can do for you." He ran his nose along my panties, teasing me. His tongue darted out and he licked the fabric, soaking the material even more.

I fisted my hands into his sheets, my breathing becoming a little unsteady. "I want you to take care of me and make me feel g-good." His tongue licked me again and I wanted him to just devour me, but I knew what he was doing, and it made me very fucking needy.

"That's a good girl." He slipped his fingers into the sides of my panties, moving them down and slipping them off. He peeked up at me, that look of focused need in his eyes before he wrapped his lips around my clit. My hand went immediately into his hair and a sharp moan fell from my lips.

He sucked hard, letting go and circling his tongue around my clit before diving back in to give it more attention. He lapped up my arousal, sticking his tongue inside of me, trailing his hands up my body and grazing the pads of his fingers along my nipples.

"Fuck, that's so good, Don't stop," I begged, pulling his face against my pussy harder.

He groaned against me, keeping his mouth firmly latched onto my clit, but used his other hand to circle my entrance. Sliding two fingers inside of me at an agonizingly slow pace, my vision started distorting. There was this vibration beginning in my body that had nothing to do with the pleasure from his mouth. It was my power and it was brimming.

It was a different kind of intensity, not the kind that had me wanting to throw objects around the room or cause pain. I let go of River's head and focused my power on keeping him in place, steadying his body and head right where I wanted him. I couldn't let this moment get away from me, so the simmering fire was sent through my body, warming me.

River flicked his eyes up at me like he could tell something was different but if it was a drastic change, it didn't bother him. He simply let me continue to keep him between my legs; it wasn't like he planned to be anywhere else anyway. His fingers moved faster and curled, his tongue moving over my clit in a rapid motion.

"River, just like that, please," I whined, my thighs muscles tightening.

"Let that pretty pussy come around my fingers, gorgeous," he coaxed, curling his fingers again and again. I closed my eyes, my back arching and a long moan erupted from my throat. The searing heat I had thrumming through my body pulsed, sending a shock wave of warmth through me.

I opened my eyes to see a shadow looming over me and I watched my boyfriend place his fingers in his mouth, sucking them. He reached behind him, grabbing the collar of his shirt and pulling it off. His fingers quickly undid the button of his pants and he removed them, his cock hard and thick between us. The silver balls of his piercing shined, and I ran my fingers over them gently. He hissed at my touch, picking me up in one swift movement and placing my body on top of his while he positioned himself on his back.

The head of his cock rubbed against my clit and I whimpered. I wanted more, I wanted to feel that closeness we had, that overwhelming comfort that brought me so much happiness.

River took hold of himself and placed it right at my entrance. He slowly slid his hand up and down his shaft. Watching him stroke himself so casually, my thighs trembled and I could have come just like that. I walked my fingers over his chest and down his arm, tracing the colorful tattoos he had. He used his free hand to run his knuckles over my cheek and I turned my head, kissing his hand.

"Be happy and get yourself off." It came out like one of his normal dominant commands, but there was a softness to it that had tears sitting in my lower lids. I looked down, firmly pressing my knees into the mattress and sunk down on him. I let the feeling of his piercing force a moan from my lips and the fullness that I always felt with him had me sighing in relief. He let out a long breath, rubbing my thighs and his jaw ticked. "Ride me like a good girl, gorgeous."

I rolled my hips, finding what felt good. I lifted myself up a little, then felt the thickness of his cock all over again. I pressed both my hands to his chest, steadying myself while I rode him. He watched me, keeping his eyes fixated on my face. I moved on his cock slowly, leaning forward a bit so my clit could rub against him. The position let his piercing move inside of me in the right way that had me moaning repeatedly.

River ran his hands up my shirt and played with my nipples, sending a jolt through my body that had me moving quicker. He let out his own low groans every time I bounced up and down, his hands palming my breasts.

I let my power and mind drift to what I wanted, what would make me happy. His face contorted a little as if he was trying to figure out what was happening, but he let my telekinesis move his hand out from under the shirt and up towards my throat. He quickly understood what I was doing and let his fingers be wrapped around my neck. He willingly gave me a gentle squeeze.

"You are so fucking beautiful," he complimented, moving his other hand to my clit and rubbing.

My heart pounded in my chest with the way he looked at me. That was how he always looked at me, but right now, that look meant more than any time he'd ever done it.

"Fuck, River…" I leaned further down so I could be near his face. He instantly kissed me and I eagerly kissed him back. "River, I need you to fuck me." My words came out breathy and wanting. Sweat collected at the back of my neck and the overwhelming heat I was producing, percolated throughout my body more and more.

There was no hesitation when he lifted himself up, keeping hold of me and turning us over so he hovered over me. He remained inside of me and I caught my breath the moment I felt the shift in power between us. It wasn't unwelcome and I wanted the feeling of him taking over to consume me.

He took my arms and moved them above my head, holding my wrists together with one of his hands. River buried his face in my neck, finally moving inside of me. His thrusts were deep and meticulous. Tiny pleas to not stop and please keep going came out of my mouth and he didn't let up. His pelvis slapped against mine, letting every inch of him fill me over and over again.

"You're so fucking perfect, Riley," he groaned into my neck. "You take my cock so well, baby." He licked at my skin, moving his mouth to my ear. "You're going to come so beautifully."

His chest was sweaty and I didn't know if it was just the exertion or if I was somehow sending some of the heat from my powers onto him, but I didn't care. My orgasm was building and every thrust was pushing me closer and closer. He moved his face back into my view and pressed his forehead to mine, moving inside of me quicker than before. His bed was starting to shake and I let out a long, unbridled moan when I came.

His movements started to become a bit erratic until he moved his hips a few more times and I felt him release. Our mutual breathing mingled, and we kissed; it was messy and lazy, but a smile formed on my face as our mouths danced.

I wiggled my lower body and he let out a strangled groan. He pulled out of me, taking me with him when he settled us into his bed. He lifted his arm so I could cuddle into his chest.

"I feel happy. Happier than I have in the last day or so," I admitted, knowing that he needed to confirm that I indeed got emotional satisfaction from this.

"I love making you happy, Riley. Unfortunately, my dick can't fix everything." He sighed like he wished that what he was saying wasn't true.

I traced lazy lines along his abs. "I know. Sometimes I just need you, okay?"

He pressed his face into my braids, kissing my head. "I'm yours, always." I snuggled further into his body. "I find something very interesting though." River ran his fingers over my shoulder.

"Hmm?"

"You aren't as undisciplined as you think, gorgeous."

I peeked up at him through my lashes.

He smiled down at me. "We don't have to talk about it, but I could tell you were using your powers in a way that felt right for you. You could have destroyed my room and that would have been okay, as long as you came." I noticed his smirk and my face started to heat from my blush. "The fact that you held back at all tells me that you are a lot stronger than Chancellor Fowler gives you credit for."

I let myself consider that, then sighed. "Can we not bring up Chancellor Fowler, especially not when I'm in a post sex high?"

His chest moved when he laughed. "Sure, sure. It is very hot to say my girlfriend is a sexy little witch though. You can force my face between your pretty thighs any time you like." His hand roamed around to my side and tickled me.

I knew that all the things that needed to be figured out, all the bad things would find their way back to me. River was right, he couldn't fix everything, he couldn't change what's happened, but he *could* give me a sense of peace. Right now, I wanted to remain in my happy bubble for just a little longer.

11
GRAYSON

River left the room and I tried to get myself to believe that every conversation we had got a little bit better, but that was a stretch. The fact that he was talking to me at all was good enough and I knew that he didn't think I was a bad person. I *knew* I wasn't a bad person. I made a choice and I thought that choice only involved me and people I didn't know.

That was an odd way to think about it. The fact that I would have made different decisions based on the fact that I cared about the people involved. I should have stood up and fought back the minute the idea of kidnapping witches even came up, regardless of my familiarity with them. Did that make me a coward? I didn't know how to answer that. Chancellor Fowler wasn't a particularly scary man, but what he could do, how he spoke... that was what sent a chill down my spine.

I couldn't comprehend how Riley could be related to him. She was this little ray of light that I liked being around and associating myself with Chancellor Fowler had shattered that light into a million pieces and ultimately, I *had* helped him. That's all she saw when she looked or thought about me. I was determined to change that and help her. I wanted to help all of them.

My *lolo* used to say: *hindi mahalaga kung ano man ang tagumpay na iyong narating kung hindi mo naman kayang ipagmalaki kung paano mo ito nakuha*

The achievement doesn't matter if you aren't proud of how you acquired it.

I ran my fingers along the dampener I wore and it made me think about my powers. It was times like this that I wished I had just inherited my father's shifting ability. Shadows had gotten me in trouble and the fact that I had worked so hard to understand and perfect them made the situation even worse.

I sighed, looking around the room. Their guest room had a half bath and a window that let in natural light. I wasn't complaining and I had been doing fine until I heard her voice. I kept quiet because if I'd bombarded into their conversation, it would have escalated to a level I didn't want. All I wanted to do was let my shadows out and move towards her. Comfort her with them like I used to and make her feel good. I could wait...I was patient enough. I had been patient and waited for her to be okay with accepting both me and River into her bed, so I could wait for this.

River had eaten lunch with me, made small talk and left. It was just me in this room now. I heard a throat clear and the door nudge open. Asher pushed it open some more and leaned against the threshold.

He looked annoyed, but honestly, that's just how Asher always presented himself. "My brother has informed me that you'll be staying here for the time being, even though your dorm room is perfectly adequate."

I pinched my eyebrows together. "I would think you would want me under your thumb for the long haul."

Asher sighed. "One would think, but now that she's here, I'm worried this will cause more problems then solve them."

I walked over to him, placing my hands in my pockets. "I'll tell you what I told River. I want to help, and more importantly, I want to help *her*. If she wants to talk to me then I'll be ecstatic about it. If she wants to pretend that I'm not here then okay, I'll deal."

Asher looked me up and down and chuckled. He removed his glasses, cleaning them with the bottom of his shirt, then placing them back on his nose. "You really think you can be around here and not just assert yourself into her space?"

I smirked, crossing my arms over my chest. "It can't be that hard. You do it."

"What's that supposed to mean?"

I rolled my eyes. "I can admit that I fucked up. I can admit my relationship with her might not ever be the same. I can even admit that I am a little bit in love with her, but you can't even admit that you have to work to restrain yourself and try not to be in her personal space."

"Stop making something into a bigger issue and also deflecting. I'm her teacher, so I think I know how to act professionally."

I scoffed. "Oh right, I'm sure it's very professional for teachers to fuck their students on a bathroom sink or you know, shove their dick down their throat until they gag. You ask me if I can deal with being in this space with her, when I wonder the same thing about you."

Asher sucked his teeth, staring me down. He was the kind of person that could have a full-on hour-long debate, but he had to know that I could also spend an hour on the defense, throwing things right back in his face. I was trying to get back into Riley's good graces, not his. Eventually, he clucked his tongue. "You aren't really making me lean your way in the whole staying in my house decision. You should work on your negotiation skills."

"Well, that's okay, because despite how amazing the St. James brothers are, you guys probably need me. I'd like to use my powers for something good this time and shadows can be quite versatile."

He turned away from me, leaving the door open. I took that as my cue to follow him.

"I've never been a fan of group projects, hence why I never fucking assign them," he muttered under his breath.

I ignored him, asking my own question. "Where did River go?"

He looked over his shoulder, stepping into the kitchen. "He took out Riley's dog. I have a feeling a trip to the pet store for dog food will be in River's future."

I drummed my fingers on the counter, considering how I wanted to proceed. "She's officially going to go back to school?"

Asher paused before opening the fridge. "She has to, Grayson."

I looked up towards where River's room was and every fiber of my being wanted to rush upstairs and talk to her. I blinked, removing my eyes from the second floor and focused back on Asher, who was staring at me.

"Don't even think about it. I'm pretty sure she's sleeping." He threw a stern look in my direction, but instead of intimidating me like I knew he wanted it to, all it did was make me way more curious about his intention with her.

"I wasn't planning on it. Like I said, I'll respect her wishes."

"Good. Maybe this won't be such an awful idea after all." He poured himself a drink and then went to a cabinet, pulling out a bottle of Jack Daniels.

I narrowed my eyes. "It's like four in the afternoon."

He stared at his glass, letting out a sigh, but continued to make his drink. "In a short period of time, a lot of alarming shit has happened, so excuse me for wanting one drink. And don't ask me for one because the answer will be fuck no." He took a sip, swallowed and ran a hand along the back of his neck.

I walked around the counter, closing our distance. "Do you have an actual plan for when school starts, Asher? Or are you just hoping that a plan will arise, but making all of us believe that you have it together?"

He licked his lips and turned to look at me, his hip leaning against the counter. "The school wants to act like everything is fine, so we will too. At some point she *will* have to want to get close to Chancellor Fowler. But as long as it doesn't look like we are hiding her or she's running then it will feel like compliance. When the time comes, are you willing to use that incredibly versatile power of yours to trap someone, snap a neck, seep into any orifice and infiltrate enough to kill from the inside? I mean you kidnapped people, but could you take it a step further?"

"I—" I opened my mouth, but nothing came out.

"Chancellor Fowler is more than willing to do those things, our own father is more than willing to ruin lives to achieve what he wants, so hesitation isn't acceptable."

I gave him a confused look. "You think I don't know that?"

"Your lack of an answer is very telling."

I stepped back and turned around, needing to stare into the empty front entrance, I blew out a breath, thinking back to that moment in that disastrous meeting. The moment I heard their dad's voice in my head.

It's her. She's the one. Take her now.

I'd looked at Riley and I'd...hesitated. Of course I hesitated. I still had no idea what I was doing any of this for. I didn't want her to be like the other girls. I'd seen their faces when I'd pick them back up to leave them somewhere to be found. I'd refused him in my head, but he'd just gotten louder.

Do it! Take her to him now. You understand what's at stake.

I reasoned and rationalized with myself in a matter of seconds that she would be fine. This would all stop once I took her and then I could take her back. I would stay and apologize for bringing her into that situation and we could work through it. If she was the one, then Chancellor Fowler wouldn't need the witch he used before to go into her mind. They could have a civil conversation or something. Everything should have been fine.

Oliver St. James's voice reverberated through my head constantly.

It's her. She's the one. Take her now.

Their own father was more than willing to ruin lives…I was well aware. I'm sure the chancellor would have found her at some point, but I'd sped up the timeline.

My voice was a whisper when I spoke, "I hear him in my head sometimes."

I heard his glass slam down on the counter. "Our dad is still talking to you?!"

"No, not anything new, just from before."

The house was quiet around us and I felt like I was back in that room with her. The moment right after Chancellor Fowler had thrown those glass pieces at Marianne and the world shifted. The moment I knew my association with everything that happened would make her hate me.

I slowly turned around. "It was clear. His voice telling me to take her. His voice telling me she was the one. I knew what it meant in the sense that Chancellor Fowler had found what he'd been looking for, but I didn't know what the bigger picture was. Your dad screamed at me to take her and I fucking rationalized about it, Asher. I thought everything would end up fine."

He pressed his lips together, bringing his drink to his lips and downing the rest of the liquid. Asher placed his glass in the sink, pulling up the sleeves of his shirt, exposing his forearms. He walked up to me, his expression unreadable. "I'm not like River, Grayson. I don't give a lot of thought about mental invasions when it comes to keeping people safe and protecting others. So, I've been in your head when you sleep. I've witnessed your sadness. Intentions be damned, you hurt my brother and you hurt that girl upstairs so that made me want to create the worst type of nightmares for you. And then I would bring them out of your dreams and make them haunt you in your real life." His eyes flared with this hostile kind of darkness, but his face remained neutral. Then his voice got softer. "I stopped myself though, because despite what I think about what you did and your part in it, my brother believes in you and still actually loves you.

I can't speak for Riley, but for me, somehow when you say that you're sorry, that you didn't mean to hurt her, I believe you."

"Asher..." I started, reaching across my body and running a hand down my arm.

"You fight back in your dreams, Grayson. I could make you fight back in reality if I truly wanted to, but that wouldn't do you any good. As a teacher, reasoning is good, it makes for solid structure and clear thoughts. In situations like this, you don't have time to reason, because the minute you do, people like my father, people like Chancellor Fowler take that as vulnerability and they will use you just the same as they did before. If you would have just come to us ahead of time, you wouldn't have had to reason with yourself, but that's in the past." I cleared my throat to speak, but he continued, "I'll ask you again, are you willing to use those shadows—"

"Yes," I snapped, pinning him with an intense stare. If it meant protecting the people I care about, I would do whatever it took. I didn't know if I had the stomach to actually take a life, but I couldn't think about that when the people I was up against had such a disregard for life itself it seemed.

He raised his eyebrows and huffed a breath of satisfaction. He turned away, stepping back further into the kitchen.

I swallowed, clearing my throat. "Thanks for not mentally debilitating me."

Asher let out a deep chuckle. "I can be very nice when I want to. It doesn't mean I like you. It just means I still think you're most likely a decent person and even decent people deserve second chances."

"Hmm." I didn't know what to say. He was being nice to me, but in a way that only Asher could. "I'm sorry about your dad. River has only told me so much about your family life. I never liked pushing."

Asher shrugged. "Your family deserves a fucking medal for dealing with him so much."

"I would say he's like a brother to me, but that seems kind of gross since we've... you know..." I trailed off, tilting my head down so I could smile thinking about the awkward conversation I'd had with my parents after the twentieth time River had stayed over and they'd blatantly asked me if River was my boyfriend and then proceeded to express how much they liked him. The answer was no, neither of us really wanted that, but the affection we had for one another was palpable to the point of suffocation.

Asher cleared his throat, a slight cough coming out. "Mhm, super aware of that. And that fact is why you need to be all in."

"I am, Asher. Don't worry," I said in my most reassuring voice. "Do you plan for me to keep my dampener on while I'm here?"

He eyed me skeptically, pulling another glass from the shelf. I watched him do everything he did before, pouring the whiskey and replacing the cap. "If your shadows need to stretch then, take off the damn ring." He picked up the glass and walked over, handing it to me.

I looked down at it and then back up at him. My hand was steady when I reached out to take it, but he pulled his hand back a little. I stopped, eyeing him suspiciously. "If she finds it's too much, if she wants you out of this house, then you leave. You don't argue."

I tilted my head to the side, a smirk playing at my lips. "No wonder you make her call you sir. You are good at that."

He pulled the drink back even further. "And you're a brat, so no wonder my brother is so enamored by you. Just do what I say."

I pressed my tongue into my cheek, thinking about Riley. At some point, she had to hear me out. Then again, that was more wishful thinking. She didn't *have* to do anything. I would gratefully accept her yelling and screaming at me. I've seen her in tears and it gutted me. I would crawl on my knees for her.

I grabbed his wrist to keep him steady. I took the drink from him with my other hand. "You got it, *sir*." I looked at him from over the glass as I took a sip.

He gave me an unamused look. His voice was stern and monotone when he said, "Don't call me that."

I took another sip. "You mentioned how you protect the people you care about, keeping them safe. That doesn't just stop at River, does it?"

"Just go back to the guest room, Grayson."

I downed the rest of the drink and placed it on the counter, lifting my hands up in surrender. I reached up and slipped my ring off. It was like my body relaxed and could breathe. My shadows came out and picked up the glass, easily placing it in the sink. Asher watched my movements with a keen eye.

I started walking backwards, but caught his attention when I said, "I remember your face in that bathroom, Asher. You were done the minute you kissed her. You're already obsessed. I know the feeling."

12
ASHER

I headed towards the stairs, after taking the time to clean up and spend some time alone, running into my brother as he was coming out of the bathroom. He looked happier than he'd been when he'd left to take Beau for a walk. I gave him a curious expression when he followed me down the stairs.

"What?" he asked, taking the steps two at a time. When he reached the bottom, he went to the entryway table and grabbed my keys.

"Where are you going this time?" I inquired, eyeing my car keys.

"You were the one who said and I quote 'I'm not paying for that dogs food so you better make sure it has what it needs if it's going to live here.'" He raised his eyebrows, ending his impression of me.

"I don't sound like that."

He wrinkled his nose, shrugging. "I'll be back. I promise if I get him a toy, it won't have a squeaker." He turned the doorknob, heading out but I called him back.

"How is she?"

River moved his mouth to the side as if he was attempting to bite the inside of his cheek. "Based on everything that's happened, she's doing better than I thought. She is really trying here, Asher. If she is going to deal with these things and eventually rid herself of Chancellor Fowler, then she needs to trust us. All of us."

I tilted my head to the side, crossing my arms over my chest. "Why do you say that like I'm the problem? I'm trying to keep all of you in fucking line and make sure nothing goes sideways."

River looked up at the ceiling, groaning. "I'm not calling out *you* specifically. She needs to handle the Grayson thing and she knows that, but in the meantime..." He leaned forward, poking me in the chest with his index finger. The king chess piece he had tattooed there in my view. "Be nicer to her. You know you want to."

"I'm realistic, River. If that doesn't make me her favorite person, then so be it. At least we will all be alive when it's over."

He furrowed his eyebrows. "You are very dramatic. Dad pisses me off, but the man doesn't scare me." He let out a *hmph*, before adding, "She must have you wrapped around her finger if you are this wound up about something."

"It's called being concerned."

"That's one word for it." He winked at me and turned to leave.

I ran a hand roughly through my hair, flexing my hands from all the tension I was trying to release. I had spent my time doing everything I needed to do for when school started again and I wasn't the least bit hungry. I looked over to the couch, seeing Beau lazily staring at the TV screen. A colorful cartoon was on and his eyes drooped a little, telling me he was starting to fall asleep.

He was kind of cute, I admitted to myself. That couch would be covered in dog hair and I would most likely be the one to clean it because that's what always happened. Beau let out a loud sigh and I mimicked him. I went into the kitchen to get a glass of water and headed back up the stairs when I'd chugged it in one sitting. River's door opened as I passed it.

Riley jumped when she saw me staring at her. I scanned her face and then my eyes traveled down to my brother's shirt and her bare legs.

"This feels a bit like déjà vu, doesn't it?" I joked. "Are you also going to ask me if I spied on you guys having sex too?"

Her mouth dropped open. "You just have really weird timing, that's all."

"Perhaps," I said nonchalantly, finding myself working very hard to not stare at the legs, her brown skin looked so smooth and I was aching to touch her. I tried *very* fucking hard to not remember what was between those legs and how it felt to have her contract around me and come. She opened her mouth to speak, but I ignored her, turning to my room and nearly ripping the door off its hinges to get inside.

I heard her footsteps following closely behind me. "I was figuring out a way to come and tell you that I maybe overreacted a bit to you claiming that I was going back to school, that I was sorry that your dad is just as insanely diabolical as the chancellor."

"There is no need actually. I've been over your outburst for a while now."

"I'm trying to be civil here, Asher."

I gave her a forced smile. "Again, not necessary. I'm not the one you need to be deciding to have civil conversations with."

She reared her head back, a look of shock on her face. "What the fuck is that supposed to mean?"

I pinched the bridge of my nose, feeling the need to step back when she walked further into my room. The instant memory of what happened here was always vivid anytime even a fragment of it entered my mind. The way her eyes looked up at me when she took me in her mouth, so willing to let me fuck her throat. I felt the overbearing need to throw her on my bed and do it all over again.

"Grayson is going to be helping us, so maybe find a way to make all of this less of a hassle for the people you seem to trust."

Her brown eyes widened. "Oh, I'm sorry if my apprehension is a hindrance to you. I am working my ass off to understand everything and find my footing. Do I need to show my work, Professor? Do I need to get your approval before I can be graded on how well I'm moving on and improving?" She pointed over at me and a canvas that was hooked on my wall flew off and hit the floor.

I looked behind me, thinking that anyone else in this situation would have been nervous or trying to calm her down. I found her eyes again and noticed how all this was tied up in her emotions. Anger was something that held a lot of weight, especially in magic. Most definitely for magic that had never been nurtured.

"So, we're back to overreactions again, hmm?" I placed my hands at my hips and waited for her response. I wasn't riling her up on purpose, but I wasn't going to run and coddle her either. She had River for that.

"I am going to step on that campus and know that he is probably around, watching me. I have to fucking pretend like that man didn't just infiltrate my entire life in the blink of an eye. He smiled about it, he fucking *smiled* about it and kill—" Her voice caught, almost as if she wanted to cry. She wet her lips with her tongue and pushed her braids out of her face, steeling herself. Little sparks of fire danced along her fingertips, and she focused her gaze on them, curling her hand into a fist so she wasn't forced to look at what she'd created.

River and I knew about Marianne already, but even I wasn't that much of an asshole to touch that subject. That memory would haunt her forever; it was something she would never be able to change. There were things that graced my mind, things I would rather leave in the past and didn't like bringing it up because I didn't want to relive it. I had the luxury of doing just that because no one really knew about them.

We were all aware of her situation. She had nowhere to hide when it came to that loss she dealt with, so the best place to go was to retreat within herself, keep it buried down so that no one would inspect or poke at it. I heard her sniff and I focused my attention on her again.

"There are more lives than just ours when you really think about it and you want to stand in front of me, without an ounce of empathy and tell me in a less pretentious way that I should just deal with it better?"

"Don't put words in my mouth, Riley. That is not at all what I said." I let myself step closer to her this time. "You are allotted your time and space to grieve and feel fucking upset, but I won't have you deciding at any random moment that we are changing the plan, that you don't want to do this or that you are going to go it alone, whether that be due to Grayson or whatever reason that pretty brain of yours can conjure up."

I wasn't sure if the heat I felt from her body was due to the fact that she could turn into a human inferno at any point or if it was entirely natural. Up close, I got to notice more things, like the way her eyes were dilated and the nonchalant way I could tell she was pressing her thighs together. Her shoulders were slightly tensed, and a light pink hue appeared on her cheeks from her frustration. Her hoop nose ring glinted even in my dim bedroom light.

I could have kissed her. I *wanted* to kiss her. She could be so infuriatingly upset with me. Fuck, she could hate me, and I still wanted to kiss her and then let her leave because I wouldn't let myself have anything more than that.

She huffed, her eyes narrowing to an almost lethal degree. "If I know you at all, you would have been fucking pissed at Grayson. You would be fighting against him, yet here you are defending him in some weird way."

"Let me remind you again, don't put words in my mouth. I am not defending your little shadow wielder. Rage and upset were my first reactions to what he did, but I realized something that I hope you are slowly figuring out. You are all in your twenties and every thing that comes your way, every single inconvenience, causes you to think that there is no way out. There are a few who are the exception, but he is not. He's a smart kid and you can't just look me in the eyes, little liar, and tell me that isn't true."

She sucked in a sharp breath and I sighed harshly. "We've all fucked up, Riley. We've all made shitty decisions and some of those decisions deserve punishment. The individuals also deserve to be heard and it may fucking hurt to listen, but you need to do it. And then you speak on your demands, what you want and how you see things moving forward." My voice was stern and precise.

She pressed her lips into a hard line. I could tell she was taking in what I was saying and maybe I should have waited to throw all this glowing wisdom at her later on, but she had me impatient with how she continuously fought against me.

"Please, stop telling me what I need, for fucks sake," she said the words through her teeth. "You speak like you seemingly have my best interest at heart, like you have everyone's. Your dad tasked *you* with getting into my head and making me hurt." She pushed her finger into my chest, pressing into the fabric of my shirt. I didn't feel any pain, but maybe that wasn't the point. "The ultimatum between your brother and me. That seems like an easy choice, Asher. Hey, River might not ever look at you the same if you fuck me over, but at least your dad will leave him alone. I'm not dumb!"

I pushed against her finger at my chest. "I told him no. I've already told River I would never. This whole argument is ridiculous, even for you."

A pulsating shove hit my chest. I was thrown backwards onto my bed, planting my hands on the comforter. I sat up, adjusting myself so that I was on the edge when she came up to me, placing herself between my open legs. She leaned towards me, placing her hand on my shoulder. I felt a force holding me down. It was like my bones, my body mass, everything was bolted into place and there was no way of getting out.

She was still undisciplined, but she wasn't so feeble. Her emotions would always get in her way and at some point, she would use her powers to really hurt someone that didn't deserve it. Fuck, maybe she already had. Being a Celica legacy gave her magic a lot of strength and I was afraid she had no idea what to do with it when it all started to come out in waves. That kind of magic could consume her in an unhealthy manner.

"Just because I go along with you and listen to your plans does not mean I trust you. For now, River is the *only* one I trust. Your brother seems to believe what you say, but anyone with half a brain knows that it's because he's your family, Asher." Her breath washed over my face and my hands nearly tore at my bedspread, wanting to slide up her legs and under her shirt. "I'm just a girl you fucked because your resistance got weak."

I cut my eyes to her mouth and then quickly looked back into her eyes. "Don't insult me. And it's beneath you to insult yourself." Her power quickly lessened and the minute I felt my own strength return, I popped up from the bed and started walking forward. I towered over her causing her to walk backwards towards the wall next to my door. I placed both my hands on either side of her head against the wall, caging her in. "You asked me if I simply liked control or if I actually gave a shit. My control allows me the luxury of giving a shit. That control is being tampered with by my fucking father and now you're undermining it by thinking I'm not on your side. If you want to believe that, then fine, I can only continue to do what I'm doing."

My fingers slowly curled into my palm against the wall. I berated myself internally over and over again not to touch her. If I touched her, that resistance she mentioned would deplete yet again. "You want to harp on me about resistance, so be it. I went easy on you in my bathroom anyway, but oh, little liar, let's not forget that you were less than amicable to me until you realized my thoughts. Your resistance weakened, same as mine."

I could have sworn I heard our hearts beating rapidly, the sound thrumming in my ears. I watched her throat move as she swallowed and that pink hue at her cheeks got deeper. "You didn't even think about it a little when your dad told you what he wanted you to do?"

I let out an exasperated breath. "No, Riley. I can resist my father. I have learned to withstand his threats."

She reached up and lightly touched my hand, tracing her fingers against the skin. "Lucky you. I have to figure out how to withstand mine." Her touch was searing, and I wanted more of it. "Asher, do you think our resistance fumbled because—"

I cleared my throat, pulling away from her. "I need to do some things that don't involve you being in my room, especially without pants on."

She looked as if I'd just slapped her in the face. Her eyes darted from the open doorway, then back to me. "Okay, if you want me to leave all you have to do..."

"Leave." The word was harsh and I surprisingly regretted it. "*Please*. I just need to concentrate, and I can't do that with you here." I definitely couldn't since instead of focusing, I would be bending her over my work desk, pressing her face into the wood and making her thank me for letting her come.

She could get that kind of distraction, that kind of care, from my brother. I shook my head and watched her start to leave. I closed my eyes, tapping my fingers on the outside of my thigh. "Wait."

She had grabbed the doorknob and was about to close it when she stopped. "What?" she snapped.

I opened my hand and she watched as a translucent gray outline formed in my palm. It pulsed and soon, it burst into something that made her place her fingers over her mouth.

"Is that..." She tentatively pointed at my palm. "Is that my necklace?"

Her previously shattered necklace sat in my palm, the delicate piece of jewelry shined as if it was brand new. The ruby color was vibrant and sparkled.

"What? H-how?" she stuttered, picking it up as if it might disappear.

I ran a hand through my hair, giving a slight shrug. "I think it's common knowledge that oneiromancy can involve pulling things from dreams and into reality. It's easy when it's your own dream, but it takes practice and lots of headaches to be able to do it with someone else's."

"Hmph." She unclasped the chain and placed it around her neck.

"It is just a normal necklace. It isn't enchanted like the other one." I walked over to the door and held it open for her. "Once I've been in your dreams, I can go back and remember what I've seen. You have it on constantly, so it wasn't hard to find."

She stopped at the threshold and gave me a confused look. "Thank you, but Asher, why did you do this?"

I lightly grabbed her shoulder and kept her moving so that she was outside of my room. The threshold was between us now. "Accept the gift, Riley." Her mouth opened slightly as if she was going to say something else, but I gave her a stiff smile and closed my door.

13
RILEY

I remembered being next to Beau on the couch, but then I must have fallen asleep. I felt familiar arms carrying me upstairs. The light from River's window had me shutting my eyes again the moment I opened them, hoping to adjust quickly. The sound of feet padding around the room had me opening my eyes again and I saw Beau on the floor, curled up in his little dog cocoon. I dropped my arm and scratched the top of his head. His tail thumped, but he didn't make a move to wake up.

"Ah, you're awake." I turned over and saw River fumbling around with what looked like shopping bags.

"I didn't even know I fell asleep."

"You were pretty out of it." He tapped his lips as if he was thinking. "You moved around some of the stuff in my room. You didn't break anything, but I will say I watched you most of the night, so I'm exhausted as fuck."

"I did what?" I looked around, confused.

"I think you were having a nightmare. Not strong enough to

cause a big reaction, but enough to get your powers to surface even when you're unconscious." He gave me a sympathetic smile. "The only person I know personally that can do that is Asher."

"You didn't try to get into my head and I don't know, ask questions?" I started to get up, throwing the covers off my body.

River sighed, walking over to the bed. I shuffled over to where he was, getting on my knees so I could press my hands to his chest. "Just because I tried to get into your head under dire circumstances doesn't mean I'm just willing to do it all the time now." He kissed my forehead. "Beau was watching you as well. You would toss and turn a little, things would rattle and then you would stop."

I groaned. "Listen, I understand that this entire relationship started because you couldn't keep your powers to yourself and I'm grateful for your little invasion because now I have you, but please don't hesitate to force your way in because you think I'll hate you for it. You've been very good about honoring my wishes, but I'm telling you that it's okay. Okay?"

He opened his mouth, but I quickly added, "Don't argue with me."

"I wasn't going to. And I would never anyway because you should get ready." He leaned down to kiss me and then turned away.

"What is all that?" I jumped off the bed, walking over to his dressers. On top of the furniture were about three tops, two bottoms and some underwear. I pursed my lips, inspecting the items and then throwing him a perplexed look.

He grinned sheepishly, staring at the clothes as he spoke, "I went to the pet store to get Beau's food and I might have stopped by the mall before it closed to get you some stuff. I know you are going to your mom's today to talk to her and I assume you are getting clothes and anything else to stay here." He peeked over at me. "I just didn't think you'd want to wear the same thing today and well, I assumed you also needed options. You may not think I pay attention to your clothes or sizing, but I can be quite observant when I want to be. Oh and the bag over there has some books because I stopped at one of those small bookstores you like and that other bag has snacks. Tiny pretzels, those gummy bears you like—"

He was rambling and it was very cute. It almost took my mind off of what he'd said about talking to my mom today. That was enough to make me get up on my toes and kiss him. "I love you. Thank you."

"Anything for you, gorgeous. I love you as well and I would ask if you want a shower buddy, but I'll respect your space until you give me the okay." He ran his fingers under my chin and winked at me. His green eyes found the necklace that dangled between us and his eyebrow inched upward. One corner of his lips threatened to lift, but he stopped it, kissing my forehead again and leaving the room.

I lightly touched the ruby gem and it caused me to go right back to my conversation with Asher. Well, not really a conversation. Asher and I never had *conversations*. He was usually just an ass who had to always have control of the room, but something about what he said got me thinking. He put on a good front, but I knew his dad had upset him and threw him off with what he was asking him to do. I knew he was an advocate for his brother, even though they didn't always see eye to eye.

Asher making any sort of sense during what that was last night just pissed me off even more. He was so fucking irritating. I knew I needed to talk to Grayson; there was a part of me that wanted to forgive him for what he'd done, but my stomach would do backflips every time I thought about it. Maybe I was afraid of what he'd say and that I would crumble right in front of him. Or maybe I wouldn't think it was enough, and we could never attempt to rebuild.

I steadied my breathing, not wanting to fall too far into my own thoughts. I was an adult. I had decided to stay here, knowing full well that he was going to be around. Grayson was the type that would authentically try to give me my distance as best he could, probably shadow himself away when he saw me coming. I could have laughed at how ridiculous that sounded. It was even more ridiculous that I wanted everything to go back to normal, but that goal was nonexistent and only the idea of a new normal was within my reach.

He could be a part of it, if I let him.

He wasn't Chancellor Fowler, so I didn't hate him, I didn't loathe him with every fiber of my being. What I did hate was that when I pictured Grayson it was followed by this awful thing that happened, but somewhere in the very back of my mind, I could also still see the guy that would stand in lines at bookstore signings with me and not complain once, especially since he always had a few books of his own to get signed.

The sound of footsteps and voices caused me to flinch and I shook my head, needing to face one problem at a time. My phone buzzed and I went to grab it, noticing a few unread text messages.

The top one was from my mom.

MOM

Honey, whatever happened, just know it's okay. I hope you're safe. I love you always and always

I hovered my fingers over the keyboard. I couldn't think of a response worthy of what I did. 'I'm sorry' just seemed stupid. I'd been out of control, just like Chancellor Fowler wanted me to be, like he'd known I'd be at some point. That probably wasn't even the tipping point of what I could do.

I love you too. Always and always

I switched to the next unread message.

CORRIN

Checking in. Mom is headed to Samia's shop today. She wouldn't let me go with her because I've involved myself enough.

She has a point. Maybe you should take a step back

She sent me a shocked face emoji. Along with the one that was rolling its eyes.

CORRIN

I will disregard this bullshit you are spewing because you are going through things. But I'm not going anywhere, Riley.

I blinked down at my phone, remembering how all of them had rallied for me at Corrin's house. I thought about how Marianne should have been one of them. No, that wouldn't have even needed to happen if Chancellor Fowler just left me the fuck alone. I dropped to the ground, landing hard on the wood floor. I curled my knees against my chest, holding the sides of my head.

My skin was too hot and I pushed down every ounce of my telekinesis as I could. I didn't need River coming in here and trying to make it better. I didn't want him seeing me like this. My whole body felt like it was shaking, and I wanted to throw something, destroy something. I wanted to take all that power I had and blow a hole through the wall. All I could do was feel the pain beat against my chest, constricting my heart.

I removed my hands from my head and looked at them, sparks of flames were licking at my palms. They dissipated and started up again, over and over. The fire felt good along my skin and the smell was intoxicating. It was like something I'd been waiting for, something I'd been missing for a long time.

I had to stop. I had to fucking stop. I pressed my lips together, closing my hands and digging my nails into my palms, feeling the sting of pain. I returned my hands back to the sides of my head, silently willing it to just stop for a moment.

Beau was at my side instantly and nuzzled his face between my face and knees. He was trying to push his way through, whimpering slightly. I felt tears streaming down my face as I rocked myself through the pain. I focused on the weight of Beau's body leaning against my sternum the minute he forced his way in. I sucked in a deep breath, my exhale coming off choppy and choked.

Mom, it's okay. You're okay. You always like to scratch my head. It makes you feel better.

He pushed his head up and even through my tear-stained vision, I locked eyes with my protective familiar. *I don't want to hurt you.*

He leaned his body as much as he could towards my hand and licked it. *You won't hurt me.* He licked my hand again. *You're a good person, Mom. Grandma knows it and so does everyone else.*

I nodded, sniffing, placing my palm against the top of his head. I bent my fingers and started scratching, feeling his short fur along my fingertips. There was no heat there, my chest still hurt but my breathing was beginning to become easier. I leaned down to press my face against the place between his eyes. "I'm sorry I can't get my shit together," I said out loud, my voice muffled against him.

Beau tilted his face up and licked my nose. *It takes time. You're the strongest witch I know, even if you can't see it yet. I found you when you needed me and I'll always be here.* He pushed against my body, sending me backwards so he could climb on top of me, laying down. His weight was a lot of pressure, but for some reason, it made me feel better. He had his face between his paws, staring at me. *You'll stop the bad guys. I know you can do it. So does Marianne and so does your dad.*

Fresh tears fell down my face and all I could do was wrap my dog in my arms, letting him crawl closer to me, so that his face was in my neck. I sobbed against his thick body, making sure to not alert anyone outside of this room. My magic was quiet as we laid on the floor, but the thumping of his strong heart, a heart that loved me unconditionally, had me wanting to smile.

I felt much better after changing clothes and taking a shower, using the dark purple shower cap River got me so that I didn't have to worry about my braids. Beau waited patiently by the bathroom door, springing up the minute I walked out as if he had fallen asleep. I'd made sure my face wasn't splotchy anymore from crying and gave myself the most lackluster pep talk, but it would have to do for now.

Beau was right on my heels when I descended the stairs, trying to be somewhat inconspicuous. Asher had a coffee in his hand and looked up at me the moment my feet hit the last step. His phone was in his hand and the grip he had on it was lethal.

He had on a simple black t-shirt that was tight around his arms and gave me a prime view of his biceps. The tattoo of stars was in full view on his forearm, and I couldn't help but stare at it. I had to keep my eyes from going anywhere else because as much of an aggravating dick Asher could be, he was still insanely good looking.

He snapped his fingers in front of my face and I shot my eyes up to his. "Are you good?" he asked, lowering his hand.

"Yeah, I just— what has you so tense?" I pointed to his hand that still held his phone in a death grip.

He opened his mouth but then closed it, readjusting his glasses and shook his head. "It's nothing, just school stuff, that's all."

"Shouldn't I be made aware of school stuff?"

He tucked his phone into his pocket. "I don't know. Did you get a teaching degree since the last time I saw you?"

I fiddled with my necklace, fighting down my urge to just punch him in the face. I watched him follow my movements. His green eyes that once held indifference, softened. It happened in slow motion, and I would have fucking recorded it if I'd had the chance.

He sighed as if I'd worn him down when I hadn't said anything at all. "It was an email from the school to faculty, specifically from the chancellor."

"Of course it was," I muttered.

"He quite literally mentioned how the witches and everything that troubled the students and school before has been rectified. The culprit has been identified, and the authorities are doing their job." I could hear the disdain in his tone. It made his voice deeper than it was and it sent an odd shiver through my body. I focused back on him when he continued. "You should be getting one too. All the students will get one tomorrow about coming back. Probably with a lot of flowery language that puts people at ease or well, I should say it is *meant* to put people at ease."

"Students who don't know a fucking thing." I looked down, focusing on my shoes.

"We knew they were going to treat things like business as usual. Students will fall for it. And so will parents because they all believe this school has so much history and integrity. There isn't much we can do about the masses. Worrying about everyone else makes you lose focus and—"

"We need to have control of the situation. I know Asher." I placed my hands on my hips and my cropped shirt rode up just a little, revealing a sliver of my skin. His eyes darted to the exposed area and he cleared his throat when we heard the sound of a door closing.

He cast a glance over my shoulder, and I followed his eyes. River walked up to us, rubbing his hands together. "I'm going to feed Beau and Gray—," he stopped himself mid-sentence.

I cocked my head to the side. "You can say his name in a normal conversation, River."

He nodded toward the guest room and then looked at his brother. "Grayson needs to go to the dorms to get stuff, so are you good with taking him?"

Asher looked at his brother, dumbfounded. He sat his coffee down with more force than necessary. "No, especially since this is the first time I'm being told I'm playing chauffeur."

I looked between them. "Why can't he just shadow in there and grab things, then shadow back out? The school doesn't prevent the use of magic on campus, it just prohibits it when it comes to students, give or take some exceptions so..."

"Riley, it's just not—" Asher started but I turned my head sharply to look at him.

"What? Trust, right?" I made sure my words hit him directly and he rolled his eyes, so they were looking at the ceiling. "If Grayson really means to be on our side, then let him off your proverbial leash." He watched my mouth when I spoke, his eyes narrowed as he leaned against the kitchen counter.

He ran his index finger over his bottom lip. "Maybe someone actually listened to me last night." He pushed away from the counter, grabbing his coffee and walking past us to the living room. "Fine, he can go, but I'm clocking him the minute he shadows out of here. I'm not bailing him out if he gets caught by university police for using magic."

River's top teeth bit into his lower lip like he wanted to laugh but he held it back. I followed him further into the kitchen, silently watching him get Beau's dog bowl prepared. "Are you all ready to go?"

"Go?" I asked, pushing my braids over my shoulder, watching Beau scurry over to his food bowl when River sat it down.

"Your mom's."

I instinctively grabbed my necklace, knowing that even though it didn't hold my magic hostage anymore, it still brought me some kind of comfort like it used to. "Oh, right. Yeah, let's go. You stay in the car, remember?"

River nodded dutifully. "Of course, whatever makes you happy." He ruffled his hair before coming over to me and lightly held the jewel of my necklace between his fingers. He was giving it the same look that he'd had upstairs. "Didn't this get destroyed?"

"Um, it did."

He let it fall back against my chest. "O-kay, so how is it here now?" He raised his eyebrows playfully, letting me know that this wasn't an interrogation.

I hadn't really thought this through, and I wasn't the absolute best at thinking on my feet. Footsteps came from behind me and Asher ran into my shoulder as he passed by, placing his coffee mug in the sink. He was literally just washing the fucking mug and I could tell he was watching me. I flicked my gaze back to River who was also looking at his brother.

He had an amused smile on his face. River was so unassuming that it amazed me how observant he was.

"You know what, gorgeous? I don't need to know. Between you and me, we can assume the giver of such a caring gift can remain..." He threw his voice so Asher would definitely hear him, "anonymous."

The dishwasher rattled when Asher slammed it shut. "Shouldn't you two be going now?"

River rolled his eyes, leaning down to kiss my cheek and went to grab the car keys. "Watch the dog, Asher. We'll be back."

Asher waved him off, giving Beau a disinterested look as my familiar munched on his food. Beau said goodbye to me in my head, much too interested in breakfast. I followed River out the front door, realizing I'd forgotten my phone inside.

"I'll be right back," I informed him, pointing over my shoulder to the house.

I pulled open the front door, not paying attention when I ran into a chest and heard a sharp breath. My eyes widened when I stepped back and saw Grayson in front of me. My mouth was suddenly dry and I felt a pit in my stomach. I had assumed I would feel disgust or anger when I saw him. All I felt was hurt. It was like everything I had thought I would feel was consumed by *hurt*.

Disgusting hurt.

Angry hurt.

Distrusting fucking hurt.

"Riley..." His voice was soft and calm. I could tell there was a nervous tone to it that he was trying to cover up.

I shook my head quickly. "I have t-to..."

"Riley." I heard Asher, who was a few feet behind him. The look he gave me was similar to the one from before. It was caring and sympathetic.

I placed my hand over my face, trying to wipe away the shock. "I have to go see my mom, umm...okay..." I heard a growl and looked around seeing Beau with his eyes locked on Grayson's back, his food not quite as important anymore. Grayson looked over his shoulder, hearing Beau's continuous growls.

It's alright, buddy. Go back and eat your food. I thought, gracing him with a lackluster smile. He sneezed, then turned to head back to his bowl.

Grayson turned back to me and nodded, not trying to say anything. I looked down at his hands, noticing how his fingers twitched like he was itching to touch me.

"I have to go." I didn't make eye contact when I went right back out the door. I had tunnel vision when I made my way over to the passenger's side of Asher's car. Him saying my name felt like old times, it sounded like the Grayson I trusted.

That happiness was distorted when I remembered what he sounded like when he'd shadowed me to Chancellor Fowler, when I remembered what he said and what it meant.

Riley, I'm sorry.

14
RILEY

I kept readjusting my posture on the drive to my house. Nothing worked when it came to my overwhelming anxiety, but then River let go of the steering wheel and put his hand on my knee. He stroked his thumb along my skin, keeping his eyes on the road. I focused on the tattoos on his fingers, following up his arm to the other colorful pieces of artwork. I let my eyes get lost in their designs and before I knew it, we were pulling up to the driveway.

He put the car in park and I looked out my window, biting the inside of my cheek.

"I don't know what exactly happened with you and your mom, but I'm sure she'll be happy to see you." River patted my knee, giving it an encouraging squeeze.

"Mmhmm." I nodded, opening the car door and starting to get out. I quickly turned around and pulled his face to mine. Our lips met in a rushed manner, and he laughed a little, pulling away just enough to find my eyes. "Thank you." I got out of the car, holding the door open.

"I'll be here when you're ready to go. My phone will be on."

I furrowed my eyebrows. "Oh, my phone is still at your house. I forgot it."

He waved me off, opening his mouth to respond when I heard my name. My mom's voice was something I'd know anywhere and this time when I heard it, it gave off hopeful sadness. I closed the car door and turned around, seeing her standing outside the front door. She had her hands clasped together and she made no move to rush over to me, but just stood there, waiting.

Once I was a few feet in front of her, I noticed her neck had a few markings on them. They looked like bruises and it had me wanting to vomit. I'd done that and I couldn't take it back. My lips suddenly felt dry and so did my throat. I didn't know what to say and I didn't want to just go inside without any sort of invitation.

She reached up, lightly touching her throat, and I sucked in a breath. I really couldn't do this. Fuck.

I made a move to turn and leave. Maybe I could do this another day. A hand reached out and grabbed my forearm. She yanked me back and I practically flew into her arms. She held me close to her with a tightness that was nearly suffocating. I remembered holding her just like this when she'd told me my dad died. I buried my face into her neck, smelling her familiar scent and letting my shoulders relax.

"I'm sorry, Mom," I mumbled into her neck, keeping her as close to me as possible. It didn't even feel like she had any plans to let go anyway.

"I know, honey."

"River doesn't want to come inside?" she asked, heading to the kitchen with me tucked into her arm.

"I told him to stay outside. I need to do things on my own, but he likes to hover."

She chuckled, kissing the side of my head. She had to peel me off of her so that she could comfortably move around the kitchen. "That's a good man. I'm grateful that he's been taking good care of you. I was worried sick."

"You really didn't need to worry. What I did..."

She paused before opening the cabinet she was reaching for. Her face scrunched up into one of frustration. "I worry about you constantly, Riley. My worrying started the moment I found out I was pregnant with you and it's not stopping anytime soon. I don't care about what you did. I care about *you*."

"But, Mom..."

She pulled open the cabinet, taking out a box of tiny pretzels. The ones I liked the most to be exact. "No buts. You can't tell me all about how Erik showed up and frightened you and then just run off into the night. I forgave you before you even did what you are so scared of. That power is a part of you, baby, I'm sorry I ever made you think I wouldn't accept it. You may be a witch, but you are first and foremost, my daughter." She passed me a pack of pretzels, clasping her hand over mine when I went to grab it. "That means nothing you do could make me love you any less, especially when the things you do are because you are hurt or scared. All I ever want to do is help you."

"I hate that I hurt you. He told me I would be out of control. I think he thinks I'll need him," I explained, my voice low as I intertwined my fingers with hers.

"He always thought he knew better. He masked it with charm back then and maybe he's still doing that now. His father was actually the chancellor back then and Erik surprisingly didn't want anything to do with the school in that way. His father was fine with that, he was a nice man, but his mother...."

"You told me that you guys didn't get along."

She opened up the other pack of pretzels she brought out, picking one out and popping it into her mouth. "Right. She didn't like that I distracted him, I guess. She was Celica's leader and she wanted him to have the same drive, the same mindset as her. I could always tell when he'd spoken to her because he'd come back with such a temper. She always pushed the fact that he had both his parents inherit powers, so he was stronger. He could rival even his own father if he truly wanted to, but he didn't." She grabbed my shoulders and walked us to the couch. She kept me close to her when we sat down. "His father died a month or so before I found out I was having you and it devastated him. He actually thought his mother had something to do with it and I wouldn't have been surprised if she had."

"If he disliked her so much, why take her name? Why go by Erik Fowler instead of Erik Lowe? And so, what? His father's death, his mother's annoyance and your pregnancy announcement sparked his insanity?"

She watched me put a pretzel in my mouth and placed her arm on the back of the couch. "I suppose. I think he thought that with the pregnancy, he would have a better family. A few days after I told him, we told his mother and boy, did that not end well. He started going on and on about how his mother wouldn't control him or his family. He spouted off about how he would find a way to rid us of her and the coven would be a safe place for our baby. That you could have a legacy you would be proud to be a part of. I guess he became everything his mother wanted, just not in the way she wanted it."

A shiver went down my spine and I placed my bag of pretzels on the coffee table.

"He scared me, Riley, and I already loved you so much that...I didn't know what he was going to do, but I didn't care about a legacy, I didn't care about having a powerful family. I just wanted you to be safe."

I hummed, leaning against her body. "The way he spoke to me, Mom, it was like he wanted me to have all the luxury in the world, like I should be thrilled to know I was associated with the school and coven in that way. His mother didn't think he deserved anything, so maybe he just took what he wanted when you left. Maybe not having me and you just kind of sent him over the edge." It sounded just as wild out loud as it did in my head.

Her eyes turned sad, her voice filled with an odd kind of regret. "Maybe I'm to blame for the way he truly turned out. If I would have stayed with him, I don't know how your life would have been, but maybe leaving wasn't the lesser of two evils." She kissed my forehead. "I don't regret protecting you. Or at least trying to. I really thought he had let me go when all that time passed or he had just moved on and disappeared like people said, but he was right under our noses."

I sighed. "The crazy thing is that he *had* moved on. And then he talked to dad." I fiddled with the chain of my necklace. "Under any other circumstance I would respect his determination towards his family, but I hate him, Mom. I've never hated anyone before, but I hate him."

She pulled back, holding the side of my face and stroking my cheek. "I know. I also know your voice and the different tones and inflections you use when you are trying to convey your emotions. What aren't you telling me?"

I avoided her eyes, twisting the necklace chain around my finger. Her eyes shot to my movements and her eyebrows rose. "You fixed it?"

I let go of the chain and ran my hands down the tops of my thighs. "No, it's not magical. Um, it was a gift from Asher."

I could see that she was trying to figure out where she knew that name. "River's brother?"

I slowly nodded, hoping she would stop asking questions about it. "Yeah, he's a professor at the university."

She casually looked off to the side, almost as if she was trying to understand something. Her phone went off, saving me from this very, *very* awkward conversation we could have had. She patted my leg before going to retrieve her phone from the other room, leaving her opened pretzel bag on the couch. She sounded friendly when she answered almost like she was speaking to an old friend and then her voice got nervous and frantic. She sucked in a sharp breath causing me to swivel my body so I could look at her over the back of the couch.

My mom had her hand over her chest. "Oh my god. Sarah, how? What happened? Do you need me to do anything?" My heart stopped for only a moment because I knew that name. There were probably a million Sarahs in the world, but only one that my mom would be this devastated for.

Sarah was Marianne's mom.

"Okay, okay. Please let me know if they find out anything. Sarah, I don't know what to say. My god." Her hand flew to her forehead as she pressed her fingers into her skin. She said a few more words and then hung up.

She wiped under her eyes and then looked over at me. I swallowed, waiting for her to speak. She took a deep breath and started walking back over to me. "Riley, honey, that was Marianne's mom."

I kept my mouth shut, deciding to just nod.

Her voice was shaky. "You know they usually speak frequently, but it's college, so she thought Marianne wasn't communicating because she was just busy. She called around and no one had seen her, so she called the police." She pressed her lips together, frantically wiping the tears that were falling from her eyes. I held my breath since that was the only thing keeping mine back as well. "They found her body near a wooded area close to one of the local bars to the school. They are looking more into it but I'm so sorry, Riley. She's gone." Her tears were coming full force now and watching my mom cry unleashed my own.

I choked out my words because it hurt my chest far too much to hold it in. "I know."

She grabbed my hands. "You know?"

I slowly released myself from her hold, running my fingers quickly under my eyes, removing the tears. They felt thick and heavy; when I looked down at my hands the wetness was a deep blood red. I slapped my hands against my thighs, shaking my head. "I already know."

My mom watched as her coffee table shifted against the floor and how the items on the mantle teetered back and forth. I was trying, I was trying so fucking hard. I bit my tongue to stop myself.

"Riley, how could you possibly..."

"That's why I hate him."

Even though her face was stained with tears and her mind was muddled with the idea that Marianne was found dead, alone in the woods, I could tell the moment I had her undivided attention. He had her moved, he cleaned all traces of him, he covered his tracks... because he had the power to do it. He treated her like she was nothing.

I looked down at my hands, they burned from a fire only I could produce. "He killed her right in front of me and there wasn't anything I could do about it." I closed my hands; more tears trickled onto my knuckles. I watched as my mom let out a small breath, her mouth slightly opened. "He killed her because of me. That's why I hate him."

15
GRAYSON

I fumbled around my dorm room, trying not to let Riley flood my mind. The look on her face, the way her lip quivered when she tried to speak, the way her eyes didn't have that flirtatious look to them, and I had noticed all of it in a matter of a minute. It took everything in me not to pull her into my body and start pleading for her to let me back in, let me back into her circle of trust and into her heart.

There was a small moment, like her instinct was to let me hold her, but she'd refrained. When she was gone, I'd let out the breath I'd lodged in my throat and listened while Asher went on about how I could get my stuff from my dorm room. He just so happened to let it slide that Riley may or may not have been the one to tell him that I shouldn't need a babysitter. If I knew Riley at all, that didn't mean she was on my side one hundred percent, but it did mean that we could be getting somewhere.

I grabbed the duffle bag from the top shelf of my closet and started transferring my clothes into it. I'd already placed all the school items I needed into my backpack, so I had one last look around to do before I headed back. My phone rang in my pocket and I plucked it out, reading my mom's name on the screen. I let out a deep sigh, feeling a twinge of guilt in my chest.

"Hi Mom," I answered, trying to sound more upbeat than I felt.

I heard what sounded like something being sprayed on the other end and my best guess was that she was cleaning the house. "I'm just checking on you. The last time we spoke you sounded a bit distant."

The last time I had her on the phone I'd told her that I was going back to the dorms early. I *thought* I'd sounded pretty normal. My parents always pushed when it came to school, especially because I equally pushed myself. If I had decided community college and an associate's degree were where I saw myself, they would have been right there and cheered me on. My personal life, on the other hand, was something they let me have free of judgement or critique. They both grew up with strict parents themselves and didn't want me to feel that kind of pressure.

I cleared my throat, putting my phone into the crook of my neck and using my shoulder to keep it to my ear as I zipped up my duffle. "*Huwag ka nang mag alala.* You being stressed causes me to be stressed and that's not good when classes are about to start back."

She hummed. "Right. *Di ko gusto kapag na-iistress ka.* Besides, you have River and I know he'll keep you on track."

I rolled my eyes. "I knew you liked him more than me."

She laughed and that pulled at my heart to hear the happy noise. "*Huy! Tigilan mo yan!*" Although, I do like him for you and I think you two would make a very nice couple. "*Bagay kayo!*"

"I told you then and I'll tell you now, we are not a couple."

I heard some shuffling on the other side of the phone. "I know. He is just much better than that one awful girl you dated your freshman year of high school and then that one boy the summer of sophomore year..."

I smacked the top of my bag. "Yes, I get it. River is the best." I felt the smile creep on my face the moment the words left my lips. I was only speaking the truth.

I heard my dad's voice next. "You can't blame us for assuming since you two were intimate."

I nearly tripped over my own feet when I let myself fully take in what he said. I wish I could have turned back time and unheard it. "*Anong sinabi mo?*"

My dad cackled on the other end. "*Sinasabi ko sayo.* Invite River and that girlfriend of his over for food. We like her too."

I rubbed my fingers into my eyes. The mention of Riley mildly dulled the feeling of my parents even remotely being aware that I had a sex life.

"We are not so old that we think you don't do adult things." She tsked me over the phone in only the way my mom could.

I groaned. "I am now very embarrassed, so if that was your mission, good job."

My mom yelled something at my dad about getting some things out of the fridge for lunch before she gave me her attention again. "I am a parent, embarrassing you is what gives me joy." She giggled, but then her tone turned serious. "I do mean it though, Grayson, you did sound off on the phone. *Anong nangyari?*"

I readjusted my phone, relaxing my shoulder. I went to grab my backpack, catching myself looking out the window that overlooked the courtyard. "I promise I'm okay, Mom. That meeting kind of shook me, but everything is fine now. Graduation is coming up sooner rather than later and I just want things to go off without a hitch. *Pasensya na at pinag alala pa kita*"

It was almost like I could tell she was nodding on her end even though I couldn't see her. "You will do great, *syempre anak kita*, you always find a way to do good work. Sunday dinner next week?"

I gripped my desk chair, tightening my hold around it until I felt a strain in my hand. I fucking hated this. "I'll see what I can do. I might have to do some major library time. Who knows what teachers will give us, even if it's just us being gone for two days."

"*Syempre*. I have to go before your dad ruins my kitchen, love you."

"Love you," I said back, taking the phone away from my ear and looking down at it. My parents were good people, they didn't deserve this.

I wanted to pick up my desk chair and chuck it across the room. I groaned loudly, looking down at the floor when wisps of black smoke and a small noise caught my attention. I looked at my window, seeing a tall figure staring back at me.

"Ah, why so frustrated Mr. Ypulong?" His voice sent my spine ramrod straight. He didn't make a move for me, so I spun around coming face to face with Chancellor Fowler.

"What the fuck are you doing here?" I looked around trying to find the source of his intrusion.

He looked around along with me as if amused by my skepticism. "Honestly, I could have just walked in here and used my master key to get into your room, but I thought we should be evenly matched, so I got here the same way you did."

I felt the wisps of my shadows playing along my neck as if to soothe me, but nothing was going to help right now. "I thought we were done. That's what you told me when you had me take her back."

Chancellor Fowler placed his hands in his pockets, sauntering over to my bed and sitting down. "We are. Grayson, I'm not here to get you to do my bidding. I promised you that you were off the hook, and I keep my promises."

I scoffed, grabbing my backpack and trying to pretend like he wasn't even there. "Then why are you here? You've caused enough problems."

He crossed his legs and leaned forward so that his elbow could be propped up by his knee. He placed his fingers under his chin, sizing me up. "I kept my promise when it came to that adorable family of yours. They really are quite sweet, much better than the family I grew up in, and I admire you for holding them so close. You don't have to try to prove yourself for their love even when you weren't the perfect little shifter they thought you'd be."

My eyebrows furrowed. "How do you know that?"

He clucked his tongue, smiling at me. "You wound me with how little you think I know."

"Whatever, okay. Stalk me all you want, I don't care—"

He uncrossed his legs, getting up and sliding his hands down the front of his cream-colored button-down shirt. "How is my daughter?"

I pulled my backpack over my shoulders. "Oh, you don't know the answer to that? I'm surprised."

"Your attitude delights me. I can see why she liked that witty nature of yours. Obviously, *liked* being the operative word here, of course. Past tense as in before you eventually betrayed her." He blinked, looking at me with curiosity.

I opened my mouth to push back, but he tutted me and moved his hands around so that my backpack was removed from my shoulders. He motioned his hand towards my desk chair and slid it over to me, letting it hit the back of my knees and forced me to sit down. I whipped my head around and grinded my teeth.

"The technicalities don't really matter, do they? You can explain yourself and run around in a circle of rationalization, finding a way to justify when none of that really matters. What's done is done and all we can do now is deal with the consequences." He leaned his face down, getting to my level.

I met his gaze with a harsh glare. "You think you are above consequences though. You somehow think that despite everything that you've done, Riley will ever want to be in the same room with you, sit down and have a father daughter heart to heart? You are delusional if you think she'll ever want to look at you again without throwing you across a room."

He laughed, the sunlight coming through my window shined a light on each of his curls. Up close, the resemblances he shared with Riley were so much more apparent. "Ah, that is something we share,

I guess. Riley's disdain. How are you dealing with the idea that my daughter can't fathom looking at you without knowing the hand you had in everything?"

I pressed my lips together but said nothing.

"If she is as stubborn as her mother, well then, you and I have much work to do. You have your good looks and your charm, Grayson, but that doesn't mean much when she can't even trust you, hmm. I, on the other hand, am her father. I have her best interest and whether she likes it or not, she will be exactly where she belongs. Maybe as soon as that imposter of a father was dead, Hecate was able to refuel me with the energy to search for her again."

I got up and kicked the chair back. "I'm not even a witch and I know Hecate would never bestow anything to you for something so cruel. You stole pieces of magic, pieces of other witches' essence for the sake of being fucking greedy. You deserved to be miserable if this was always your intent. Any *real* father would want a happy and willing daughter, not someone they have to control."

He crooked his finger and I was thrown over to him. He had me by my shirt, not too tight, but tight enough so that my muscles tensed up. "I have left my daughter alone for two full days. I told her as much and now she will come back to my territory and play by my rules. She will want this because at the end of the fucking day, I understand her. She will think she has it under control and you may even be able to worm your way back into her good graces, but when all is said and done, she is mine. If my own mother taught me anything, it's that you can't run away from who you are, we all eventually end up exactly where we are meant to be. The more you run, the worse off you will be and that person you're running from will eat you alive."

"You don't know her at all if you think she will ever willingly come to you. You can't scare her into submission." I shook my head, feeling my shadows start to wind around my arms.

He let me go, shoving me back. "Why not? It worked with you." He smirked at me, rolling his shoulders. "I would never intentionally cause her physical harm, but Riley's emotions will be her downfall. I think you are all forgetting that she isn't a simple witch, she can't just read a few books on magic meditation and understand how things work."

"And you think getting Asher to mentally scare her straight is part of the solution?" I asked, keeping my voice leveled. "I'm sure you have a secondary plan in place because he won't do it."

He scanned my face, the corners of his eyes crinkling every now and then. "I mean I don't think getting you to restrain her again with your shadows will work this time, so a new strategy is in place. I have many ways this could go and it will be fun to watch it all unravel. As you know I do have other shadow wielders so if all else fails, I will do whatever is necessary. My power isn't just from what I've siphoned but it is also from the control I have over others simply because I know the right people, have the right connections and I've spent a good part of my life learning how to lure people into thinking that helping me is what is good for them. Riley, Asher, even her little telepathic boyfriend are no different."

"I'll kill you if you hurt any of them." My shadows swirled around my wrists, pushing off my hands and racing towards him, but they were stopped, bending and contorting into any direction that wasn't aimed at him. That force he was using went further down, all the way down to where my shadows grew and settled. I felt it in my chest and I couldn't breathe. My shadows were being yanked and thrown around; I wanted to pull them back, but he wasn't letting me.

"You'll kill me, Grayson? Really? You could have done it a long time ago, but you didn't. If you were wanting to do it because you felt the overwhelming need to murder me then so be it, but you are doing it for her, for them, and it is slightly pathetic. You think it will get you back in with them, but all you'll be is a murderer. Your parents will see you that way, the school certainly will because I have made a few people aware that I came to your dorm to see you. You will never get to live out that happily ever after with my daughter because yet again, you fell into my trap." He let go of my shadows and I choked out a breath. My shadows weren't so constricted and I rubbed my hands down both my arms, shaking them out.

Chancellor Fowler cleared his throat. "Finish out your senior year, Grayson. Make your parents proud. You did work hard to keep them alive this year and I commend you on your commitment to your family. Try to make amends with my daughter, if you can. Truly, I am keeping my fingers crossed for both of you." He reached out and brushed his palms against my shoulders as if he was making me look presentable.

His fingers tightened around my shoulders and I swallowed the lump in my throat. His voice got low and his eyes turned dead and soulless. "You come at me with your shadow again, you try to get the upper hand against me and I will make Professor St. James' decision easier. I'll have Oliver forgo the plan and mentally debilitate Riley's precious telepath and then I'll crack his head against the pavement over and over again. You and I both know you care about him just as much as my daughter and I'll make sure Riley is aware that you could have prevented this if you just listened. You all seem to want to help her, but in the end all she'll end up being is hurt and if I'm who she wants to cry to well then I'll shoulder that burden." He smiled at me, almost like a glowing politician. "I hope we have an understanding."

My voice shook when I spoke. "You really are a monster."

He cracked his neck as he turned to head to my door. "No Grayson, I'm just a father who loves his daughter."

Chocolate .psd
Bar Mock-Up
ood Packaging Collection

Chocolate.psd
Bar Mock-Up
ood Packaging collection

16
RILEY

"You were gone way too fucking long!" Asher's voice thundered when River and I walked through the front door. My boyfriend insisted on carrying both suitcases of clothes and also didn't make a move to interrupt me when I spewed my entire conversation with my mom at him.

She had been stunned at what I told her, but it was like my words weren't hard to believe when she gave me an empathetic smile. I was far too upset to start sobbing, but I did let her hold me and rub my back. She kept repeating that she was so sorry, but she didn't try to figure out what to do next because.... there was no helping Marianne, there was no *fixing* that.

Chancellor Fowler had cleaned up his mess. Well, one big mess of many.

I turned my head to look at River, really hoping Asher wasn't talking to me because I was not in the mood for his fucking attitude. River quietly closed the door behind us, rolling my suitcases towards the living room. I walked towards the kitchen where Asher's voice grew louder and then a familiar voice, Grayson's voice, responded.

"For fuck's sake, were you timing me!? Give me a break."

Asher let out a booming laugh. "A break! I told you I thought you were truly sorry for what you did, but I've also made it clear that everyone's trust will take time and doing fuck knows what in your dorm room isn't helping!"

They hadn't noticed me yet, so I stood over by the threshold. I felt River's body heat at my back. He placed one of his hands at my waist but was silent.

Grayson groaned, dramatically sliding both his hands down his face. "Oh my god! I was getting my stuff! I got a call from my parents and then I was going to come right back here and he—" He choked on his words, placing his hands on the counter and dropping his head between his arms.

Asher let out a breath, tilting his head to the side. "He who?"

"Chancellor Fowler," Grayson admitted, looking up and those deep brown eyes looked both sad and scared. My heart stopped for just a moment when he said his name. River's hand at my waist tightened as a way to tell me he was still here.

"I thought you weren't in contact with him or my father. Grayson, what the hell?!" Asher sounded flustered. His body was angled away from me so all I could see were Grayson's eyes widening.

"I'M NOT! I want nothing to do with that man!" He slammed his fist against the counter. "I wasn't lying when I said I wasn't talking to them anymore. They haven't been in my head and there hasn't been any communication between us; then he decided to just show up. I didn't want to talk to him, Asher. Please just believe me."

Asher removed his glasses, placing them on the counter. "What did he say?"

Grayson swallowed. "It was threats and warnings basically. It's like he wants Riley to come of her own free will, but then again not really, because we are meant to be that driving force to get her to pick him. Everyone is used as his scapegoat even though he actually has no issues proving that he's the bad guy."

"The man is insane, Grayson. He will say whatever he needs to get what he wants."

Grayson stepped closer to him. "That may be true, but I fucking believe him. Behind all the sick, twisted nature, he loves Riley. He loves her so much he is willing to break her heart to get her. He wants to be needed and maybe this is some fucked up projection of his past," He turned around, placing his hands on the back of his head before swiftly turning on his heels to look at Asher again. "You claim it's so easy, but River is your brother. You can't look at me and actually tell me that your decision was so obvious; that there wasn't a miniscule moment when your brother was much higher than her on your priorities. A few dream infiltrations are nothing when the end result is saving him."

I didn't have to look too hard to know that Asher was seething. "You don't know anything. I will not be pushed into a corner by my dad, let alone Chancellor Fowler. I care about River, but that doesn't mean that I don't..." He stopped himself, letting out a sigh.

Grayson shot back his response, his voice shaking. "He fucked with my shadows from like the inside of my body, Asher. We try to fight back, we get in the way of his fucked-up relationship he thinks he has with her, then he will make it hurt. He threatened to forcibly smash your brother's head in! Insane doesn't cover it!"

I gasped louder than I would have liked and both their heads turned to face me. The color drained from Grayson's face and Asher picked up his glasses and gave me a stoic expression. I felt the moment River's hand left my body as I started walking forward. My eyes were trained on Grayson, but I stopped about halfway to maintain some distance.

"Did he tell you what he did with Marianne?" My tone was harsh and nearly accusatory.

Grayson opened his mouth but then closed it. He ran his fingers over his lips, the space between his eyebrows crinkling. "No, he—"

He flicked his eyes behind me and out of my periphery I noticed River coming to stand next to me. Grayson gave me a look of confusion.

"Marianne's mom called mine. That man moved her body, was nice enough to bring her home and I guess made it look like some kind of unsolved murder. I had to explain to my mom how I watched her bleed out, how there was nothing I could do but fucking *watch*." I licked my lips and narrowed my eyes at him. "Don't worry though, I left out the details about you. My mom knows how close we are—*were*—and I didn't want to upset her anymore then she already was." I noticed the hurt look on his face and I wanted to care, but I just didn't have the strength.

River touched my arm, but this time I brushed him off. "Did he ask you to do anything else for them? Did he ask you to keep a close eye on me just in case you need to shadow me away somewhere?"

"No, Riley, this was a scare tactic and a really fucking good one, that's all." He raised his hands up as if meaning no harm and then let them fall back at his sides.

"And his comment about River?"

Grayson glanced over at his best friend, snaking a hand behind his neck and rubbing. "It looked like he was dead serious about it. I tried to attack him and he rambled on with more threats. That being one of them."

"Ruin everyone I care about until there is no one," I muttered under my breath, shaking my head. I gave one solid nod and pressed my fingers to the center of my forehead. I set my eyes on Asher who was watching me silently. I heard whining from upstairs, focusing my eyes behind me on the staircase.

"Beau is in River's room," Asher explained, crossing his arms over his chest. His eyes roamed over me like he was inspecting every inch.

"That's where I'll be then." I swiftly turned around and started to head out of the room when a hand caught my arm.

"Grayson, I don't think—" Asher started, but the act of me harshly removing my arm from Grayson's hold cut him off.

He stood before me, much closer than before and my heart constricted. His being this close had me wanting to feel his warmth and let those shadows that once caressed me do it all over again. I wanted the guy who literally hung onto my every word whenever we were alone because he thought what I had to say was important. The guy who wanted to make me happy with his books, his family, his words.... his mouth. I closed my eyes tightly. His closeness made it hard for me to think and as much as I missed him, I couldn't let his sad eyes and relentless pleas get to me. "You don't get to be this close." I pressed my hand against his chest causing him to take a few steps back.

"Riley, please." The begging tone in his voice sent a shock through my chest and it sounded so sincere.

I shook my head, keeping my hand out to maintain our separation. "You can stay here and help. You can hate Chancellor Fowler just like the rest of us, and you should. You can be around me and look at me and think up all the ways you can win back my trust, but you don't get to be that close. Not right now." My throat had developed a lump that I tried to swallow down and it hurt.

I started to turn around again, but his voice echoed through me. "Riley, I'm sorry. I'm so *fucking* sorry that—"

"I KNOW!" I whirled around, nearly inducing my own vertigo from how fast I'd spun. "I know you're sorry!"

River covered his mouth but didn't make a move to follow me when I stormed off, running upstairs and into his bedroom. I didn't make it to the bed, but just slid down the side until my ass hit the floor. Beau came up next to me, circling a few times before laying down near my legs.

Do you want me to bite him? he thought, laying his head on my thigh.

I furrowed my brows. "Thanks, but that's a little drastic."

Beau sighed. *It's not drastic to me. If it will make you feel better, I'll do it.*

I stifled a laugh, hearing my phone buzz on the bedside table. I reached around and grabbed it, seeing Corrin's face blown up on my screen. I swiped to answer her call.

"Hey, what's up?" I answered in a steady voice.

The line was silent on her end and I pulled my phone away from my ear thinking I had accidentally hung up. "Hello?" I asked again.

"What's wrong?" she inquired, sounding a little far away, but I could still hear her clearly.

"What do you mean? All I said was hey."

Corrin hummed. "Mhmm, and the way you said it was all weird and not like an everyday 'hey'. So I shall ask again, what's wrong?"

I rolled my eyes to the ceiling, playing out all my options. Then Mateo's voice came through the line. "Riley, she'll just keep going if you don't give her a reason to stop, so say something."

I pulled my phone away from my ear for the second time. "Mateo? Where's Corrin?"

"I'm still here, you're just on speaker," Corrin responded. "Mateo absconded my car and made me a passenger princess for the day."

I let out a little laugh. "Sounds nice and like something you shouldn't complain about."

"I happen to like driving, thank you very much. We all can't be transit gurus like you," Corrin grumbled. "Don't change the subject. I will not ask a fourth time, what's wrong?"

I groaned, rubbing my fingers into my eyes. "I saw my mom today."

"Really? How did that go?" Corrin asked, intrigue peaking in her voice.

I told her what I could, yet again leaving out the parts about Marianne. The guys already knew, so speaking about her in a way that started to bring it all back was okay because I didn't have to explain so much. They knew what she meant to me in so many words. Corrin knew my dad, so speaking about how his death made me feel was easier because I didn't have to tell this long, drawn out story. I didn't care about background listeners, none of the people I'd surrounded myself with would judge me, but my head wouldn't connect with my heart to form the words.

I simply told her something else that was just as important. I let her know about how my powers had taken over and I'd hurt my mom. I told her how regretful I felt and how her mom was right when it came to my own mother's forgiveness.

"Riley, you're a novice witch and they make mistakes. They fuck up, believe me. You can ask Ike and he'll eagerly tell you all the ways I've made a fool of myself. Of course, he's never made a mistake in his whole fucking life, but I digress, your powers are understandably unstable which is something I'm sure you're aware of."

"Yes, yes, I've been told that before." I rolled my eyes.

"I was actually calling to tell you that my mom talked to Samia and I have your dampener ring. You'll need to put it on for the first time so it can sync to your magic, so I'll bring it tomorrow before school. We can meet in the parking lot, just text me when you leave the sausage fest that you live in." I heard Mateo bark out a laugh on the other end.

"Don't call it that. Even though my mom and I are fine, I just think being here is my best option right now."

"Whatever you say, but Mateo needs your mom's address so they can have one of their wolf people on patrol."

"That's not necessary."

I heard Mateo scoff. "I didn't ask if it was necessary. I just asked for the address. We won't bother her, but if something happens then you'll be upset, which will make *mi amor* upset, which doesn't make for a very happy Mateo. Does that make sense?"

I let out an obnoxious sigh but begrudgingly told them I would text Corrin the address. "And you trust these wolves?" I don't know why but I was starting to get constantly skeptical of everyone.

"With my life. They are eager to help," Mateo reassured.

Corrin's voice came through the phone again. "Do you feel overly protected with the St. James brothers at your disposal?"

I clucked my tongue. "I guess. Grayson is here too."

Corrin let out loud, obnoxious gasp, which caused Mateo to let out a loud fuck and I heard the skidding of tires.

"Fuck! *Estás loco!?* You can't do shit like that. Made me almost have a fucking heart attack," Mateo scolded, breathing hard.

"Gasping is a normal sound. And information like that deserves a solid, loud, chest-grabbing gasp. I'm sorry that I almost made you swerve into traffic, honey," she apologized, getting a grumbling huff from her partner. "So, how is that going?"

It took me a minute to realize she was talking to me again. "It's going. He wants to help and that's a good thing. He's sorry and I might believe him, but I don't know..."

"Listen what the guy did was fucked up. Trust has been broken and it's valid that you need time or whatever it is you need for you to come to terms and accept him back into your life. That is if you even want to. I say make him crawl and beg for your love, I'm sure he's very cute on his knees, but I have a very active imagination."

I pressed my lips together, setting up that entire scene in my head. There was something about it that intrigued me and it had me pressing my thighs together in a way I didn't think was possible with something like that in my mind. I looked down at Beau who was casting his judgement face upon me. I scrambled off the floor, keeping the phone to my ear.

"You are quite the menace, but thanks for the idea. I just need to make it past this first day. Grayson is a mildly avoidable problem. Invisibility would have been a great power to inherit right about now."

I heard an engine turning off and keys rattling. Muffled voices mixed with a car door slamming filled my ears.

"You're busy, I should let you go."

"Blegh, they can wait. Mateo has brought me to a shifter brewery like an hour away. An hour which felt like a million hours because they obey stupid traffic laws. I like the Marth Moon beer and that's about it. I am far too picky to try anything new." She made a disgusted sound. "Anywho, I'll be right there by your side tomorrow and I hate to say it, but I have a feeling you'll get an invite."

"Invite?"

"To Celica. Probably in your student mailbox for the dorm. Or maybe Chancellor Fowler will find some over the top creepy way to do it. I know he is basically the devil, but that coven despite its upbringing has a connection to you and well, I hate getting all sappy but if you join then that would make us like hot witchy sisters."

I smiled to myself, but then that smile faltered. "Joining would be another way for him to control me."

"Maybe, but infiltrate from the inside, right?"

We had already decided that going along with everything in small doses was the best way, so ideally joining the coven would be the most organic way to add to my supposed compliance. They wouldn't like it, but I didn't need to ask their permission. I rapped my knuckles on the wood of the bedside table. "You do make a point. I'll think about it."

"I'll be just a minute, leave me alone!" Corrin shouted, letting out a harsh groan. "Mateo is getting irritated, which is very, very cute. Before I let you go, my mom got to talking with Samia about your necklace. Even if she wasn't the one who created it, then maybe she might know who."

"And?"

"Mom described it to her and she remembered your mom and dad coming in all those years ago. Dampeners are different, they subdue until you remove them. What your necklace did was hold your magic in a ruby encrusted prison, taking away any magical signature you could leave in your wake. Samia doesn't do that kind of thing, so she outsourced it to someone named Evie Malcolm, she was a Celica coven witch but obviously before my time."

"I'll have to jog my mom's memory, I suppose. Your mom didn't have to do that, you know."

"Hmph, well if my mom encapsulated my magic for years, I would want to know all the people involved just for my own knowledge. I think she thought you deserved to know all the facts, even when you didn't ask."

The door creaked open and River stepped inside. He raised his eyebrows and I pointed to my phone. "That actually means a lot. Keep me posted if anything else happens."

"You got it."

"And Corrin?"

"Yeah?"

My chest warmed with how much I wanted to say it. "I'd be happy to call you my witchy sister."

She squealed and I knew Marianne would be so proud of me for not pushing her away. My dad used to think I wouldn't open myself up to anyone like I had with Marianne, so maybe they would both be proud of me.

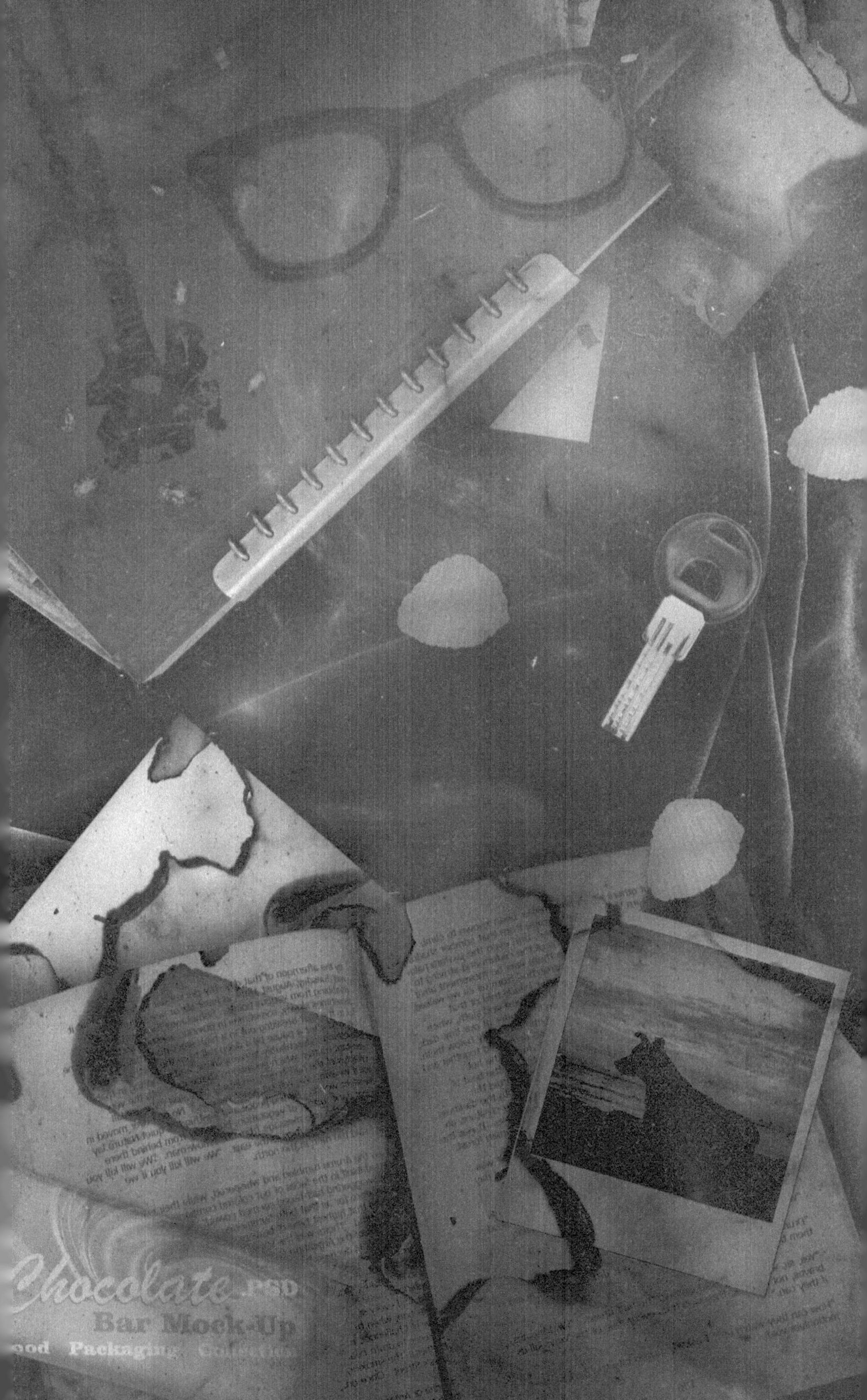
Chocolate.PSD
Bar Mock-Up
ood Packaging Collec

17
RILEY

I thrashed my arms out, not knowing where I was or what was happening. I saw Chancellor Fowler's face and the easy way he conducted himself. How he simply took Marianne's life without a second thought. A simple flick of his wrist and my best friend was dead. I kept seeing my dad's face as he was propelled through that window and how even in the past, I wanted to do something and I failed.

My hands reached out and caught onto nothing; I felt like all the air was being taken from my lungs and the walls in this space were closing in on me. I was asleep but it was like I was falling into a much deeper darkness than sleep would provide. My eyes wouldn't open and an overwhelming heat surrounded me. I wanted it all to stop. I needed it to just fucking stop.

The darkness and drowning started to let up, the heat that threatened to swallow me whole was now warm and soothing on my skin. The dim and dank space I had placed myself in opened up and expanded. My airways didn't feel so constricted and the moment I inhaled easily, I smelled the relaxing scent of lavender. Underneath my body wasn't the hard ground I'd felt before, but it was a plush blanket. One that I could see myself snuggling in with a book, falling asleep to all the adventures and romances I'd read about.

This was so much different than my nightmare, this was a dream I could have stayed in for the rest of time. This was....

A gentle shake at my shoulder had the dream slowly drifting away as my eyes opened without difficulty. I was sweaty and the sheets around me were in disarray. I noticed Beau at the end of the bed curled up into a ball. I pushed my braids out of my face, feeling another body next to me. I assumed it was River, glancing over and shifting my eyes up to his face.

It wasn't River at all. It was Asher.

The room was still shrouded in darkness, the tiny nightlight in the corner the only source of light. It wasn't hard to make out that his lips were pressed into a hard line and his hair was unruly, like he had spent a lot of time running his hands through it.

It took me a few swallows to finally speak. "What are you doing here? Where's River?" My voice was small and almost a whisper. I don't remember screaming in my nightmare, but with the way my throat hurt, I wouldn't have been surprised if he told me I'd been screeching in my sleep.

Asher didn't move, nor did he give any signs that he planned to answer me.

"If you are going to just appear in someone's bed—uninvited, I might add— then telling them why you're here is not that much of an ask." I sat up, pulling the damp sheets around me. My tank top felt sticky to my skin and I really wanted to change my clothes.

"River went out for a night ride, despite the fact that I told him to just stay here, but he's stubborn. He does it when he's stressed but doesn't want to talk about being stressed." He shrugged a little as if it was no big deal, but I could tell it bothered him. "And as for me being here.... he wanted me to make sure that I checked on you."

I flicked my eyes up and down his body. "How long have you been here?"

He scrunched his mouth to one side. "Hmm, a few minutes. I've been awake for a while now though."

I slowly nodded, clucking my tongue.

He sighed heavily, removing his glasses and rubbing his temples. "Your dog was hanging out downstairs and I couldn't sleep so we were having quiet time on the couch when he took off upstairs. I followed him and you were fine, but then you started tossing and turning like you were being attacked in your sleep, Riley. Would you like me to have just left you alone to deal with whatever the fuck was going on in your head?"

I bit my bottom lip, trying to find my words. "And you invaded my dreams...again?"

Asher let out a frustrated huff. "Are you going to detail everything that happened because that would be really annoying. I wasn't trying to be nosey or malicious. I was trying to..."

"Help me?"

He raised an eyebrow at me, putting his glasses back on. "Sure."

My heart beat a little faster at the look he gave me. Something passed over his green eyes that almost looked like genuine care. Maybe because it was. His eyes flicked down to my mouth, only for a moment, then he looked away.

"Thank you," I muttered, running my hand across my sternum and feeling the sweat that sat there.

"Yeah, don't mention it," he answered quickly.

"There was a moment I thought it was *you* doing those things. It was fleeting, but I thought you were creating that mess in my head," I admitted.

"I figured as much, but that was all you. You are your own menace this time and all those feelings are going to eat you up inside, you know. Your skin was scorching to the touch; it was like you were trying to consume the fire you can create within yourself. You kept your telekinesis in check, so there is at least that."

My shoulders stiffened. "I'm allowed to feel things after what I saw."

He nodded. "Don't put words in my mouth. I *said* that the feelings will eat you up. I can see your nightmares, Riley, but I can also feel them. I've never felt something so viscerally debilitating. Is it like this every night?"

"Shouldn't you be able to answer that, Mr. Dream Magic?"

He pressed his tongue into his cheek. "You'll be saddened to know that me getting into your dreams is not a nightly occurrence. I simply came up here to do what my brother asked and I found you practically being held hostage by your own mind. I thought it was a good idea to ease you out of it, create a better visual, rather than just shake you awake."

"You sound worried about me." I shoved his shoulder, trying to bring the moment out of the trenches he was letting it fall into.

He ran a hand over his mouth, his fingers trailing along his trimmed beard. "Would that be so bad?" He wasn't looking at me when the question came from his lips. It came off like he was asking himself and all I could do was stare at the sheets.

"It's probably due to everything that comes with going back to Mystic Riegan and the fact that I can't just pretend like my life choices aren't being watched. My mind just got a little overstimulated; my imagination can run a little wild, okay? I'll work on it. I can only promise you that."

He softly chuckled to himself. "You don't have to promise me anything. I'd prefer you didn't."

Asher started to get off the bed, but I caught his hand. I could have sworn a small spark expelled from my fingertips. The way he looked down at our hands, I thought maybe he noticed it as well. If that tiny spark had hurt him, he didn't let it show. "Don't tell River about this. He's witnessed a small instance of me having an odd dream and this felt like so much more than that. I don't want to worry him or burden him or anything like that. I told him that it was okay to get in my head if it was completely necessary and if it happens then so be it, but he doesn't need to know about *this*. I'm okay and that's all that matters, right?" I sounded like I was trying to convince myself and the look on his face told me that he felt the same way.

"Riley..."

"I haven't asked you to do anything like this for me, Asher. *Please*. Everything with your dad and Chancellor Fowler and just fucking everything, I don't want him to put all his energy in worrying about me."

"River is always going to worry about you. It's his thing, Riley." He took a long look at my hand on top of his, raking his eyes up my arm and to my face. "Fine, but only because my brother has seemingly become a person of interest to the people trying to ruin our lives. I would rather him be aware of his mind and his surroundings. I do also know that your shadow wielding friend hurt him like he hurt you, so he's dealing with that in his own way. I won't put this on him either."

I nearly flinched thinking about Grayson. My mind started to wander towards how he was doing downstairs. Asher had his reservations about him, but he thought he was genuinely sorry based on their yelling match I'd walked in on. And I knew River would follow in whatever direction I decided to go in when it came to Grayson. I didn't know what I needed from Grayson to bring me any resemblance of solace, but I wanted to figure it out because the minute I did— he would do it in a heartbeat. "You're a good brother." The compliment rolled off my tongue easily.

He smirked at me before ripping his hand away from mine. He pushed up the sleeves of his henley, running a hand through his hair. "Don't sound so surprised. I do know that I'm not perfect though. I've made mistakes with him and with.... other things." He looked like he almost wanted to say something that went along with that statement, but refrained. He rounded the bed and headed for the door.

My skin began to cool when he wasn't in close proximity to me. I didn't know whether I liked the fact that I might have wanted him to continue lounging on the bed next to me. He was almost at the door when I spoke next. "Are you going to continue to check up on me?"

Asher froze, rolling his shoulders and staring at the door. "River will be home soon, so I don't have to."

I reached up and fiddled with the necklace he'd given me. "You could, if you felt so inclined. I like the beach, or like one of those bean bag chairs that I see people comfortably reading in. Also, if you could add in Beau that would be nice." I reached down and ran my hand along my familiars back. His ears flickered but then they settled back down.

I looked up to see Asher staring at me like I had five heads, clearly confused. I rolled my eyes, explaining. "If you want to send me into good dream land, that's what I'd like."

"I don't take requests. I'm not a dream DJ." Asher shook his head, narrowing his eyes at me.

I cleared my throat. "I just thought..."

"I'll see what I can do." he grumbled, cutting me off and rubbing the back of his neck. He looked like his kindness o-meter was at full capacity and he was about to explode.

I bit the inside of my cheek to stop myself from grinning at my tiny victory. I swiftly moved the sheet from my body, feeling the cool air against my sweaty skin and padded over to where he stood. "Don't hate what I'm about to do."

"I don't follow..."

I leaned up and kissed him. His lips were stiff at first, his body like a statue. Little by little, that icy exterior melted away and his arms coiled around my body. His hands touched my skin, creating a different kind of heat. He leaned down, causing me to arch my back and wrap my arms around his neck.

I'd meant for it to be a simple peck. A 'thank you' kiss that we could both shrug off as nothing. He pushed my body into his, moving his lips over mine. I whimpered into his mouth and he groaned, turning us and shuffling our bodies so that my back was pressed against the door.

He ran his hand down my leg, gripping my thigh and hoisting it up and over his hip. I felt how hard he was and he wasn't shy about grinding it against my core. I raked my hand through his dark hair and pushed my body into his. He bit down on my bottom lip, a growl ripping from his throat and into my mouth.

His lips found their way to my neck as he pinned me against the door. His teeth grazed my throat and his fingers dug into my thigh. I rubbed my body feverishly against his and the friction was deliciously welcoming. He kissed up my neck and found my mouth again, whispering, "You need to go back to bed, Riley."

His words said one thing, but his other hand gripped my ass, pulling me into him, while he kept a hold of my thigh. I let out a small desperate sound against his lips, moving my lower body against him.

"I'm not tired."

"After what you just went through and what's to come, you should be, little liar." He nipped at my lips, pulling me back in to kiss him. He pressed me harder against the door, his cock hitting my clit with each movement of his hips. Even with clothing between us, the sensation was no less exhilarating. I moved my hips forward, rubbing against him harder, needing more friction and probably wanting more than I should have.

"You can't control my sleep schedule, *sir*." The last word came out in a moan when he released my ass from his grip and started roughly rubbing his fingers between my legs.

I closed my eyes when his fingertips hit my clit again and again. His mouth was at my ear when he said, "Maybe not, but you would like me to control you in other ways, wouldn't you?"

I knew I was soaking wet and he could feel it through my boyshort panties. It was that same heat, that same need and all because I'd wanted to kiss him for simply choosing to be a decent person. I reached down and ran my palm along his cock. It was pressed up against his pants, straining to be released.

He quickly gripped my wrist and put it above my head. He did the same with the other one, staring at me as if he was trying to collect himself.

I felt uneasy on my feet when I placed my leg back on the ground and Asher eventually stepped away from me. I could have choked from the heavy breathing I was trying to get under control. Asher placed his hands against his face and gripped his glasses, taking them off and cleaning them with the bottom of his shirt. His chest rose and fell rapidly like mine, but his demeanor was one of a stoic nature now. Gone was the man who could have very easily picked me up into his arms and fucked me against the door.

"What's wrong?" I asked, the words came out a little rushed and very fucking confused. I could see the outline of his erection even from the small light throughout the room.

He huffed, nodding towards the bed. "Go to bed, Riley. I need to get some sleep. We both do." He moved closer to me, but just so he could get to the doorknob.

I let him turn the knob as if he could escape this without another word from me. I stepped away from the door, hugging my body. "You could have said you didn't want to kiss me. You could have stopped me, but you didn't. I assume we are chalking this up to your weak resistance," I said the words sharply, so that he would feel them through that ice wall exterior that he had reconstructed.

His shoulders dropped a little when he was halfway out the door. He turned his head a tiny bit, giving me a sliver of his attention. His green eyes scanned down my body and I heard a small whine come from the doorknob. He had to be holding it with all his strength so that it would leave an imprint in his palm. A surprisingly shaky breath escaped him. "Yes."

The door shut with a soft click. The arousal and tension I felt wasn't so palpable anymore. I could breathe easily, but I was quickly trying to figure out why I didn't enjoy that so much. My eyes found

Beau, who was no longer peacefully snoozing, but he was looking at me. His head was tilted as if he was sizing me up.

I'm really not interested in what you think. I thought to him. I wasn't embarrassed in the slightest that he was right there. He'd witness some pretty heavy make out sessions between me and River, so he should be used to these things by now.

He huffed, his mouth opening so his tongue could stick out. *I like him.*

I rolled my eyes, speaking out loud. "You are aware that's Asher and not River, right?"

Beau yawned and tilted his head again. *I have two eyes, Mom.*

"You just seem a little confused, buddy."

He got up and circled the end of the bed a few times, before he laid back down in the same spot. *He likes my Mom. He wants to protect you. He's just a little grumpy, like Jax.*

I opened my mouth and then closed it. I padded over to the end of the bed, petting the top of my familiar's head. His eyes drooped a little, like he was falling back asleep. I leaned down to kiss his snout. "He doesn't like me. He tolerates me and might be a little attracted, but that's something I'll explain when you're older." I let out a small laugh and he sighed.

He wants to protect you. Beau mentally repeated. *They all do.*

I absentmindedly started to stroke his body, feeling his soft hair under my fingers. Beau started snoring as I remained awake.

They all do.

And by all, I knew he was including Grayson. One minute Beau could be bearing his teeth and growling at you and the next he was claiming you as one of his owner's protectors. I kissed his snout again, pressing my nose to his damp one.

I truly hoped I was worth protecting.

18
RILEY

I bent down to scratch Beau under his chin, his tail swaying against the floor while he sat down near the front door. He tilted his big head to the side, panting when I hit just the right spot.

I'll be back before you know it. I mentally said to him. I would have been happy just snuggled up with him in bed, but that wasn't an option anymore.

Auntie Jade will take care of me. He did a small hop and licked my face.

Right on cue, a knock came at the door. River moved past me and opened it, letting Jade inside. She practically knocked me over to get to Beau. "Before you say anything, no, you are not burdening me or Mateo with anything that is happening. They are happy to play big bad wolf and keep an eye on you, while I am more than happy to play dog sitter." She smushed Beau's face and his tongue slipped out the side of his mouth. She started to speak in a baby tone. "Isn't that right? *Sabes que eres la cosa más linda del mundo?*"

"I'm sure you could be working at the bar or something. Asher would have an aneurysm if someone wasn't around to keep an eye on him." I rolled my eyes, knowing full well that Beau was probably the best trained dog ever. River didn't think an argument with his brother was necessary for something like this, so I'd texted Corrin to ask Jade if she was free to watch him for us. The wolf shifter was more than eager to offer up her services.

Ten minutes ago, Asher had jogged down the stairs, muttering something about prepping for his classes so we needed to hurry up, and didn't bother even looking at me before he rushed out the door to wait for us in his car. River had mumbled something about not taking it personally, which I didn't—well, I didn't think I did. The guy gave me a replica of my necklace, pulled me out of a nightmare and kissed me like he was the world's most desperate man, yet he pushed me away constantly and pretended like none of the previous things had any merit.

River had mentioned that Grayson's car was still in the student parking lot, so we wouldn't be forced to ride with Asher all the time. If things didn't get better with Grayson, then I actually didn't mind being in that close proximity with his brother.

"No problem at all. Mateo has one of our best at your mom's. She has already offered him water, lemonade and tiny pretzels because apparently, she has so many." Jade straightened up, picking dog hair from her shirt. Her dark ringlets were styled into two low ponytails that fell down her back.

"Yeah, they're my favorite. My dad actually used to add like four more boxes of them to the shopping cart just because he always knew that one wouldn't be enough," I rambled, clearing my throat when I realized I had drifted a bit.

Jade gave me a small smile, placing her hand on my shoulder.

"I really don't know why I just told you that."

She shrugged. "Neither do I, but I'm happy you did. If talking about your dad keeps him close to you in some way, then please keep talking. Also, I enjoy snacking on walnuts and cashews. I blame it on the bar." Her laugh was soft and it eased the tension in my shoulders.

"Ready to go?" River's hand rubbed my lower back and I nodded. I heard the guest bedroom door open and I swallowed down a lump in my throat when I locked eyes with Grayson. He adjusted his backpack on his shoulder and licked his lips, not so subtly shifting his eyes from me to anywhere else in the room.

Jade tapped the sides of her legs. "I'm just going to go feed this big guy and get myself away from this umm... awkward situation." She gave us all a tight smile and quickly walked into the kitchen. Beau trotted behind her, clearly eager to remove himself as well.

The car ride was full of mutual breathing and the sound of various cars going by. River kept his hand on my leg, tapping his index finger occasionally against my jeans. I saw my phone light up, so I picked it out of the side pocket of my backpack.

"Hey Mom," I answered, not wanting to be too loud, but there was really nowhere to hide.

"Please be careful," she blurted out.

I sighed. "Mom..."

"I'm serious, Riley. That man is proving all the reasons why I ran away all those years ago and I'm just scared all over again. That school is just... I know you are an adult and you are going to make your own decisions despite what I say, but just please say, 'yes Mom, of course I'll be careful'." Chancellor Fowler instantly saw my dad as a threat once he realized my mom had moved on and was happy. He wouldn't lay a finger on me, but everyone else was inconsequential in his need for my loyalty and love, therefore they were disposable. I could understand and respect her apprehension.

I ran my hand over River's, laying my fingers over his. "Yes Mom, of course I'll be careful."

"Good. I'm going to be going over to Sarah's house to check on her cats and get her mail for the next few days. She is flying to Virginia this morning to settle some things over there before she prepares for the funeral. She asked about you when I spoke to her again last night. I think it was a nice distraction."

"I wish things were different. Let me know the details about that...the uh, funeral." My voice lowered and I had no idea if any of them were listening, but I made myself believe they were all blocking me out. "I have to go, Mom. Can I talk to you later?"

"Sure. I love you. Always and always."

"I love you too. Always and always." I hung up the phone, tucking it away.

"Riley..." Asher started from the driver's seat, but then he stopped himself, looking into the rearview mirror at his brother.

I looked over at River who was staring intently back at him. I knew they were silently communicating through their minds and I really didn't have the energy to consider what they must be saying. Asher let out a rough sigh and flicked his eyes to me in the rearview mirror and I challenged his stare.

He quickly looked away, remembering that he was driving.

Asher pulled into the student lot a few minutes later and texted Corrin.

I'm here

CORRIN

Do you see me waving? Ike is waving too.

I pushed open the car door, grabbing my backpack and looking around. I found Corrin instantly with the way she was flailing her arms around. Ike was doing a much less enthusiastic imitation of her movements. River and Grayson got out, slamming their doors behind them. Asher opened his door, folding his arms on the hood of the car.

Corrin made her way over to me, holding out her arms to pull me into a tight hug. "I missed you so much. Jax feels the same way."

I pulled back, rolling my eyes, and watched her pull her backpack in front of her and unzip the smallest compartment. She pulled out a tiny box and handed it to me. I looked over my shoulder seeing that the guys were just watching me, prepared to stand there for however long. I opened the box, revealing a ring that was a dark ruby color. It felt like the normal metal that River's was made out of, but there was something unique about it.

"That makes me wish I had gotten mine decked out," River said, suddenly standing next to me and inspecting my ring.

"I would have been fine with something plain." I eyed Corrin who just shrugged.

"Mom thought you would like it. We can always go to Samia's and have her change the color or..."

I shook my head, holding the ring between my fingertips. "No. I love it." I smiled at her, but that lasted only a few moments when I finally considered the people watching us. I moved my head around to see the groups of students whispering in their circles, their eyes scanning me and likely making their assumptions.

"Are you going to put it on?" Ike interrupted my thoughts, lifting his backpack higher on his shoulder.

"Uh, yeah." I slipped the ring onto my finger and it felt just like it did when Chancellor Fowler had done it, when he'd made me wear the ring he had for me. All my powers fell silent, like they were put in a trance-like sleep.

River tapped his fingers against my hand. "How do you feel, gorgeous?"

I wiggled my fingers and rolled my shoulders. "Fine, the same I guess. Um—" The people around us continued to whisper and even though I couldn't read their minds, it wasn't hard to figure out what they were saying. None of them could help themselves. The fact that I showed up on this campus again was the most shocking thing overall.

River groaned, rubbing his temples. He grabbed the back of my neck, making me look at him. "I can hear them and they're all a bunch of fucking idiots. Don't let it bother you. Any issues and you text me, okay?"

He kissed me and it went on longer than I'd assumed it would. A throat clearing had us breaking away from each other. Asher gave us a disinterested expression before rapping his knuckles on top of his car. "Some of us actually work here and need to get to their office to get ready for their class. So, am I dropping you two off at the lot where Grayson's car is parked or are you walking?"

He was talking to River and Grayson, but out of the corner of his eye, he was looking at me. River swiveled his head from Asher to me, dropping his head, a small laugh escaping him. He wagged his finger at his brother. "You say I need to work on things up here," he tapped the side of his head, "well, so do you."

Asher groaned, pushing away from his car. "Fine, okay. You want to be funny so you can walk." He gave his brother a lackluster smile, then dropped back into his car, slamming the door behind him.

River chuckled next to me and pulled me closer.

"That was dramatic. Although, I really shouldn't be all that surprised anymore," Ike pointed out, lifting his wrist to his face and looking at his watch. "I'm already going to be late for my meeting about my teaching assistant position, so I have to go." He started to leave our little group but then stopped, looking at me. "I made sure the metal was pristine with no jagged edges. First ring I've ever made and the design is flawless. " He looked pleased with himself.

My shoulders shook with my laugh. "I appreciate it."

Ike gave me one small nod, the sunlight shining down on his dark skin and close-cut dark curls. River cleared his throat, gaining all our attention. "Do you want to get some food? I know your class doesn't start for another hour or so and I thought we could..." he stopped talking, realizing where he'd made a mistake.

My eyes immediately shot over to Grayson who already had his attention on me. *We.* I wasn't quite ready for sit down meals where we were a *we* again. I wanted it, I missed it, but dealing with all these strangers judging me and knowing that somewhere Chancellor Fowler was watching me, was all I could attempt to handle. People walked by us and looked from me to Grayson, likely remembering everything that had transpired. They probably felt bad for River, having to deal with all this bullshit. I wrapped my arms around myself, rubbing my arms. "I'm not really hungry and I need to go to my dorm anyway."

River peeked over at Grayson, preparing to open his mouth to speak when Corrin cut in. "You guys do whatever you need to do. Did I hear something about Grayson's car? Go take a leisurely walk and I'll head back to our dorm with Riley. Okay? Okay!" She hooked her arm through mine and swiftly turned us towards the school gates.

"WELL AT LEAST IF IT EVER GETS STUFFY ON MAN ISLAND THEN YOU CAN always come here," Corrin offered, sitting on her bed.

"Man island?"

She rolled her eyes. "My jokes are not always the best. I am a healing master with an affinity for potions, not a comedian."

I opened my desk drawer, fumbling around inside.

"What are you looking for?" She craned her neck to try to see from her side of the room.

I pulled out the pack of tiny circular pills. I waved them in her direction.

She pushed off her bed and grabbed them from me, raising her eyebrows. "Birth control pills?"

I took them back from her, popping one of them out and swallowing it. I tugged my backpack off my shoulders, unzipping it and threw the rest of the pills inside. "Life altering revelations, traumatic deaths and betrayals tend to get in the way of remembering to take these."

Corrin's mouth formed an 'o' and I tugged my braids to one of my shoulders. "Ah and I assume you and one of your boyfriends have—"

"Yes." I chose not to mention how I had been more than willing to have sex with Asher the other night. Nothing happened and maybe it had been for the best.

Corrin smirked, rocking on her heels. "Well, I suppose that means you'll be using good old fashioned condoms for the next week. Or I can mix you up an elixir. I know they're nasty, *but* at least you won't have to worry about remembering to take a pill for like three months." She gave me a soft smile, tugging on the straps of her backpack. "Also, if you're nervous about...*anything*...I can cook you up a different kind of elixir that's the magical version of a Plan B."

"I will actually take you up on that. Both of those things, better safe than sorry. I got out my phone, looking at the time. "I have to go meet with the Dean of Students in a few minutes."

I walked towards the door to our room, Corrin at my heels. "Dean of Students? Why?"

I tried not to make eye contact with the students that passed us in the hallway while we walked towards the elevators. "The school was bound to pull me aside at some point."

Once we were safely tucked away in the elevator, she spoke again. "Are you going to expose Chancellor Fowler? I mean, Dean Wales was pretty nice to us after the whole thing in your dad's office, so I mean she could be a good ally."

"What is she going to do, Corrin? She works under him. She answers to him. As much as I want to put faith in this faculty, I just can't. This campus is a giant fucking chess board, and he is just looming over, waiting until I'm out of moves so he can yell checkmate."

Corrin slid her hand down my arm and folded her fingers in with mine. "Just make it through today and then you can say you did that. And hey, despite knowing that you and River— I will assume the one you had sex with was River —would have very cute babies, you remembered your pills so that you can prevent unwanted pregnancy. I call that a win and you know, a solid start to the day." She gave me a large, shining smile and all I could do was laugh.

I knocked on Dean Wales's door, hearing her soft voice telling me to come in. She gave me a warm smile and motioned towards the seat across from her. I sat down, crossing my ankles and fidgeting.

The dean pulled out some papers and her eyes glanced over the top page, then she looked up at me. "You aren't in trouble, Riley. If that's what you think, then rest assured, you are not."

"That's a relief."

She let out a small, casual laugh. "The Admissions Department would like to understand why you didn't mark 'witch' on your application. You are well aware this university is integrated; your transfer application would have been treated just the same as any other student."

I interlocked my index fingers, pulling them against each other until it hurt. "I didn't....I didn't know."

"Didn't know what?"

My voice grew smaller. "That I had magic. That I was a witch. My —" I reached up and fiddled with my necklace, deciding to not finish my sentence. The silence between us was thick and all I could do was stare at a blank spot on her desk.

She blinked a few times, scanning over her papers again as if the answer to everything would be somewhere within them. "That explains the outburst at the meeting." She sighed, placing her hands gently on top of her desk. "It isn't my job to question anything beyond this university's walls, so I won't ask details about your personal life. The school is required to move your status from human to magic wielder, and if you plan to change your major toward a magical focus, then..."

I cut my eyes to her. "I don't. I want to keep an English major. I can keep that right?"

She got up and walked around her desk. "Of course you can. You will have to get a dampener, that is rule number one. This is pretty odd territory for the school, but we are prepared to help you. Are you fully aware of what your magic is?"

I stopped fidgeting and settled my hands on the arms of the chair. "Telekinesis and fire."

"An interesting combination. If you'd like to take any classes related to those things we can help fix your schedule. I'm not the liaison for human-magic relations, so anything regarding stress or just trying to get yourself back on track with all this newfound information you have at your disposal, I can't help you with, but I can help you set up a meeting with her."

I scrunched my face up in confusion. "My schedule is fine. I don't want a change." I licked my lips, letting her words wash over me. "Wait, you replaced my dad?"

She perched on top of her desk. "Your father will be missed, but his position was vital on campus, and it was important that we fill it with a worthy candidate. You will love her, I promise."

Sentences were formulating in my head, but nothing was coming out of my mouth. He gave so much to this school and they chewed him up and spit him out. It wasn't fair. My mental rambling got overthrown by the sound of the dean's voice.

"Everything that happened with the witches left such a horrible stain on the school and we want to make sure that all of you are watched over and that things are never just glossed over anymore. You caught some attention that night, but rest assured, not all of it was bad. Our students' well-being and making sure they get an education that suits them is our top priority." A knock came at the door and she gave me an encouraging smile. "Come in!"

Caught some attention? If she meant the agonizingly skeptical looks I'd gotten all morning then yeah, she would be right. I don't really know why that would be her concern or how she would even know that.

Unless...

"Ah, Chancellor Fowler please sit."

His steps were calculated but smooth as she walked around my chair and sat comfortably in Dean Wales's seat. She stood next to him, far too eager as if she thought him being here was good for me, like I should be thrilled to have one on one time with this school's handler.

Chancellor Fowler sat back in the chair, his elbows on the arms with his fingers crossed. He was examining me and then the corners of his lips pulled into a smile that made my stomach turn. "It is so nice to finally meet you, Riley. You've caused some trouble, haven't you?"

19
RILEY

I opened and closed my mouth a few times before deciding that whatever I was trying to say wouldn't help me out of this. I looked from the chancellor back to Dean Wales, hoping that my eyes would give her some indication that the man next to her was a fucking monster. She just leaned against her desk, comfortable in what she thought was a normal situation.

Chancellor Fowler chuckled. "I'm only joking. I'm sure Dean Wales informed you that you are not in any sort of trouble. The university hopes that you will let us help you and stand by you through this sudden change." He sounded like he actually cared, like his sole mission was to make me feel welcomed. He was so good at playing the charismatic villain that I feared I might have to pinch myself if I ever started to believe him.

"I already let her know about Lena and how she's more than happy to be a helping hand in all this," Dean Wales offered.

"Lena?" I asked, focusing my attention on her.

"The human-magic wielder liaison. Her name is Lena. She's

worked at a few other hybrid universities before, albeit smaller ones, but she cares so much for the students." Dean Wales explained, wiping her hands down her skirt.

"I don't usually show my face around the university much, but after what happened, after what I witnessed, I thought you should be aware that you won't get lost in the shuffle. I've taken a look at your transcript and you are quite impressive; it does sadden me that along with your exemplary test scores you couldn't amplify your magic as well." He rocked back in the desk chair and gave me a smile that was meant to be sympathetic.

"I'm sure my magic being hidden away was for a good reason," I responded, crossing my arms over my chest and leaning back.

Chancellor Fowler cleared his throat and scowled. "There is no good reason to dim a witch's magical abilities, well, unless whoever did it was ashamed." I narrowed my eyes, but he continued, "You shouldn't be ashamed of your powers, they're a gift."

"A gift indeed, sir. Both telekinesis and fire," Dean Wales added, looking pleased.

The chancellor's eyes widened in faux surprise. "Well then, that is impressive. Lucky girl to be born with something like that. I'm sure your *father* would have been so proud of you." His jaw ticked when he said that word, like he hated having to mention my dad at all. There was a small glint in his eye though, that led me to believe that he at least enjoyed speaking about him in the past tense. I could feel my whole body wanting to vibrate from anger, but any power I would have displayed was dormant at the moment and right now wasn't the time to go nuclear.

"I'm sure," I answered through my teeth.

Dean Wales pointed to the papers on her desk. "I spoke to her about the next steps. Dampener, of course, speaking with Lena, and—"

"I already have a ring," I announced, holding up my hand.

Chancellor Fowler lifted up one corner of his mouth in a smirk. "You are on top of things, aren't you?" It was a rhetorical question, so

I kept my mouth shut. He fixed his gaze on Dean Wales. "May we have the room for a moment?"

She nodded. "Of course, I'll be down the hall." She walked past me, squeezing my shoulder as she went. Once the door was closed behind her, the tension that was already heavy in the air became so thick I could have choked on it.

Chancellor Fowler let out a laugh that had me raising an eyebrow in his direction. He shook his head, placing a finger at his temple and tilting his head. "It's nice to know my daughter gets things done in a timely fashion. Magic is an addictive thing. And even dampeners can't help that. You can't look me in the eye and tell me that using it hasn't given you a sort of...high."

I looked down at the ground, ignoring him.

He sighed. "You don't have to tell me. I already know. When my powers manifested, I ended up accidentally burning part of my house because I got a little too angry at what was probably the smallest thing. I'm not saying that you'll start fires, but let's not pretend since the last time I've seen you that you haven't let your magic gain more power over you than you have over it."

I kept my head down, refusing to acknowledge him when I felt a jolt at my chin forcing my head up.

"This isn't a one-sided discussion, Riley."

I tried to pull away, but it was no use. "You don't know me. You don't know anything about me."

He let out a frustrated groan. "Can't you see I'm trying?"

"All you've done is murder and threaten people. Why would I ever want to know anything about a person who does that? I would never want to call someone who does those things my dad!"

He slammed his hand against the top of the desk, letting my face go. "You watch your mouth!" He ran a hand through his hair, taking a deep breath. He slid his hands down the front of his crisp button-down shirt. His voice was calmer and leveled. "I was defiant, just like you, and my mother tried to force me into my role. If she had just let me prosper, then maybe things would have been different. I don't want that with you, which is why you'll simply come to me because you need me. Not because I'd confined you to a room and forced you. I could do those things, but that's not the kind of father I want to be."

I scoffed. "I know you threatened River's life. You tormented Grayson." I shot up from my chair. "You wanted me at this school and now I'm here. You can't force anything else; I know what you want Asher to do, but he won't, so what now?"

Chancellor Fowler sucked his teeth and slowly walked around the desk, trailing two of his fingers along the edge. "What makes you think he won't?"

"Because he..."

"Because he told you so," he finished for me. He wiped his hand over his mouth and stood in front of me. "That's what you wanted to hear though, right? That he wouldn't do that to you; he would never harm you in that way."

I looked at him confused, wondering where he was going with this. "Even if he did, I would know. I could push back; it wouldn't be some big mystery."

Chancellor Fowler gave me an encouraging nod as if he knew what I was saying was true, yet he always had more to add. "Hmm, that is true. Asher is well aware of the consequences, and we all know how much that telepath means to both of you. You and I both are fully aware that the minute the decision was between you or River, you automatically became wary of your place with those boys."

"You don't know what the fuck you're talking about."

He lightly grabbed one of my braids, sliding his fingers down until he could curl the end around his finger. "You could be told a million times that they will protect you, they will choose you and somehow in the back of your mind...you never really know, do you?" He let go of my braid and reached up to touch my cheek. I felt his magic keeping me in place, forcing me to withstand his touch. "What makes you think I don't have another well-disciplined mental magic user with oneiromancy that is more than willing to do what I say? Asher could be oh so innocent, but you would be quick to judge because his brother, his family, is his priority. And like I said, distrust. Can. Ruin. Everything.

So much anxiety, so much agitation can lead to dire consequences. Life would be so much easier if you stopped thinking those boys can save you or that you can save yourself. Your mother thought the same thing and look where that got her." He leaned down to be right in front of my face. Eyes that looked so much like mine stared at me. "Right back where she left off. She tried to run from me, but in the end here you are."

"You *don't* get to talk about her." I reared my head back feeling his magic slip away, so the resistance was gone making me stumble back. I caught the chair, getting my balance back before looking at him again. "You want me begging for your help, pleading for you to show me the way? Is that what you want?"

"You make it sound so bad." He wanted me broken and so far down that he was my only option. He couldn't control all my decisions, but he could control what came from them.

"Fuck you. Fuck you and your entire twisted idea of a family."

He walked around me, rolling his shoulders. "How about I do this, since you think I'm such a monster. I'll back off, just a tiny bit and you join Celica, like you were always meant to."

"Celica?"

"I'm sure the interim leader has already sent you an invite of some kind. Form bonds with your fellow witches. It would bring me joy to see you in great spirits with the others."

I curled my fingers into fists at my sides. "I don't want it. I don't want a legacy. I can find other witches, make connections without having to step foot in that coven."

Chancellor Fowler gave me a cheeky grin. "You were erratic and all over the place at that meeting, do you really think many witches will want anything to do with such a spectacle? The coven will give you support and shoulders to lean on. Plus, you'll have your friend in there, right?"

"And it's a way to keep me close, *right?*" I mocked, rolling my eyes.

"Closer. I mean, you are already on a campus that our family built."

I nearly shivered at that thought. I wanted to wretch at the term *our family*. "Fine. I'll join. And you'll back off."

He held his hands up as if he was the most innocent man in the world. "You have my word. Although, I have no jurisdiction on how Oliver wants to handle his family. I can keep him on a leash when it comes to you, but I have no say when it comes to his sons. The man is power hungry, and once you've gotten a dose of power from someone else, it's a feeling you start to crave."

"The magic you siphon, you plan to give it to him?"

He shook his head. "No, not all of it. Men like him need just enough to feel better than the rest. The St. James family needs to keep up that prestige somehow." He grabbed my backpack from the floor and handed it to me. "You will meet with Lena. Monday morning, after your class."

"I don't need to meet with Lena. I have nothing to say. I'm fine. I won't talk to someone you replaced my dad with. I'm not going to sit in that office and pretend like months ago you didn't shove him out a window," I spat, yanking my backpack out of his hands and shoving his shoulder.

He looked over at his shoulder and shook his head as if he was disappointed. "I'm just trying to do what's best as your father."

"I said I would join Celica, so that's all I'm doing. Everything you've done negates any talk of you being a good dad. We are never going to eat dinner across from each other or sit on a couch and talk about our day. I'm never going to cry on your shoulder because I'm sad or ask you to make me feel better when I don't feel good. I already had someone who did all those things!"

His jaw ticked. "You have a class you should be getting to in thirty minutes." He nodded his head towards the clock on the wall.

"How do you..."

"Never mind wondering how I know things, Riley. I do find it rather interesting that Professor St. James, who happens to be your boyfriend's brother, is someone who feels so strongly about you. I can understand being apprehensive because you are dating his brother, but the way he looked...hmm, there was so much more there. That is something that I feel the school should be made aware of, if it ever becomes a true problem. I've heard he's a firm yet fair teacher, and it would be unfortunate if his effort went to waste."

My feelings were constantly mixed when it came to Asher, but I knew he liked teaching even when it frustrated him. I also was more than aware that anything that happened between us would be tricky and very delicate territory. Tears threatened to escape my eyes, but I held them back. "I thought you didn't want to control me?"

"Oh, honey I'm not. I'm presenting a choice. Just like I always do. I gave your mother a choice. I could take over the coven, learn to siphon powers to keep getting stronger so I could protect our child because those witches owed me. All the things I'd endured from my family to get where I was, they owed me. Or I could still siphon powers, but we could end up leaving, go somewhere and start over. She chose neither and left me; she took you. Now I leave no room for error. No room for detours. I will look after my family this time."

My lip quivered and it took everything in me to force it to stop.

He walked over to the door and started to open it, but froze, turning to me with a sad smile on his face. "Asher and I have that in common. Looking after our family. He was never going to let his brother get into trouble. That's why he told Oliver about where you were that night in Thomas' office. Or oh, wait...did he not tell you that?" He bared his teeth as if he'd just accidentally let something slip.

My breath got caught in my throat and I remembered back to my phone call with Corrin. Asher had heard bits and pieces, but I didn't think he'd gone and ratted me out to his dad. My feet felt like lead weights as I walked. Chancellor Fowler opened the door for me, and I stopped next to him, trying to maintain my composure. "You should really be more selective about who you surround yourself with."

The open hallway was bustling with faculty engaged in conversation or headed to their offices while on their cellphones. They didn't really notice me and how I got a bomb dropped on me just now.

He raised one of his eyebrows, leaned towards me and whispered, "Are you still so sure that you aren't better off with me?"

Chocolate.PSD
Bar Mock-Up
ood Packaging Collection

20
RILEY

My entire body felt like it was vibrating while I sat in my class, hardly listening to anything my professor had to say. All I could hear was Chancellor Fowler's voice over and over again. The upside was that I hardly noticed the eyes that seemed to land on me every so often. I would occasionally look in their direction whenever I tried to refocus and they would look away quickly.

I tapped my phone screen to life and found my text thread with River.

> Does Asher have office hours today?

The three dots appeared letting me know he was typing.

RIVER
> I think so, why?

> Any clue when they are?

RIVER

What's this about, Riley?

Nothing. I just need to talk to him.

RIVER

Nothing is your way of saying it's something. I may have a pretty face, but I do pay attention, gorgeous. Did he do something to piss you off already today?

More than usual, I mean.

I wanted to laugh because River had a way of turning a dark moment into something worth smiling at.

I would love to let you in on every detail, but I need to talk to him first.

RIVER

Does this little talk have anything to do with why his mind was a dirty mess this morning? You might have broken my brother and I am highly impressed.

It wasn't my intention I assure you.

RIVER

Haha, well here's his number. Talk away, gorgeous. We'll take you back home later today.

The next message I got was Asher's phone number which I quickly saved into my contacts. Students started getting out of their chairs and barreling out of the room, so I waited patiently in my seat.

Are you busy right now?

ASHER

who is this?

your favorite student.

My screen changed from the text thread to an incoming phone call. He was fucking calling me. I started to leave the room when I answered.

"Hello?"

"What do you need, Riley?" There were some echoes and background noise on his end.

"Are you headed to your office?"

"Why are you asking?"

"Why don't you answer?"

He groaned, clearly annoyed. "How did you get my number?"

"River is very helpful. Now are you headed to your office?"

"Yes, are you planning to stalk me?"

"Wouldn't dream of it."

I hung up before he could think of some snarky way to respond and headed to the Department of Mental Magic.

My determined footsteps slowed when I realized I was now on the same floor as Asher *and* his dad. The elevator doors closed behind me and I stared at Oliver St. James' door, wondering if he was in his cushy office, so proud of himself and what he'd done. I wanted to rip off my ring and burn that entire half of the building down, hear him beg for me to save him from the flames while I just watched. I would treat him just like he treated my dad.

I knocked on Asher's door, hearing a small laugh and then, "Come in." His deep voice came through clearly and I turned the doorknob, surprised when I realized he wasn't alone. A girl with fair skin and short dark hair sat across from him, a notebook in her lap.

"Can I help you with something, Miss Monroe?" Asher leaned forward in his chair, running two of his fingers over his lips.

"I—I didn't know that you were meeting with someone."

"Well, these are my office hours, so it's always a possibility. You can email me if you want to make an appointment outside of them." His voice was so professional and precise. I would have never guessed this was the same man who dry humped me against a door.

The girl tucked a piece of her hair behind her ear and batted her eyelashes. "It's totally okay. We were just chatting now; we got done a few minutes ago." She tucked her notebook away in her bag, getting up. "Thank you, Professor St. James. You're always so helpful." I had to catch myself from letting a laugh escape when she legitimately bit her bottom lip. She left the room and took all the humor from that moment with her.

"How about I repeat my question. Can I help you with something?" Asher took a stack of papers from his right and grabbed a red pen.

I rushed over to his desk, curling my fingers around the edge. "I think you can. Help me understand why you decided it was a good fucking idea to open your big mouth to your dad."

He stopped scribbling words down with his pen, placing it down next to his papers and looking up at me. "Excuse me?"

"You told your dad where I was that night. You ruined my entire plan."

He pushed his chair back, standing up and meeting my stare. "How do you know that?"

"I had a nice chat with Chancellor Fowler today. One of what I assume to be his many random check-ins he'll do." I knew my face showed nothing but disgust. "That part isn't important right now, what's important is the fact that you didn't tell me yourself."

"Are you hoping that you'll get an apology out of me?"

I scoffed. "I'm hoping for some kind of explanation."

He licked his lips, keeping his eye contact with me. "You came in already upset, so what difference would it make?"

"I deserve to know. That's why." I leaned further in, bringing us a little closer.

He knocked his knuckles against his desk and walked around it. He pressed his fingers to his forehead and turned to stare at the wall.

"You were hiding *a lot,* Riley. River is a fucking handful and yes, but I still don't want him getting involved in avoidable things. He would do damn near anything for you, so I was safe to assume he was going with you."

"Safe to assume? No, Asher, assuming anything is the dumbest thing you could have done. You told your dad! Grayson working with your dad hurt him, so this is literally no different!"

He whirled around, furrowing his brow. "I know, okay! I am well aware of the choices I made. You've been face to face with our dad *one* time, Riley! He doesn't have to use his powers to aggravate your mind; he's gotten very good with just his words. He likes to speak so highly about how he wants the best for us and all this bullshit that I was just tired of it, so I let it slip. He wanted to be a good dad, so he should go check on his son." He let out a sigh and shook his head. "I can admit it wasn't the best laid plan, alright?"

"Your dad got me put in the hospital. I got lectured by my mom and was made to look like I was fucking insane. He told lies about me being erratic and hostile. If you had just kept your mouth shut, none of that would have happened." I pointed my finger at him, trying to breathe through my anger. "You had the fucking audacity to fuck me and then throw me under the bus. Who does that?! You looked me in my eyes and gave me a lecture on trusting people. It's laughable."

I turned to go, so tired of being in this room. I caught the look of sincerity in his eyes before he wasn't in my view anymore.

"Riley."

"Fuck you. I'll be sure to take this into account when you fuck me over to appease your father, yet again."

A sharp tug on my backpack sent me spinning around to face him. Asher was just a few inches in front of me. "I didn't know he was going to hurt you. I won't apologize for always considering my brother, but I will apologize for putting you in harm's way. I will *never* be okay with that." His voice had this air of protectiveness that I hadn't heard before until right now. He ran a hand down his short beard, actually avoiding eye contact with me this time. "You're right though."

My body went still from him actually admitting something like that. "What?"

"I shouldn't have had sex with you and then made that choice. I'm sorry about that. I should have never let it go as far as it did." He peered over at me and my heart beat a little faster with each second that passed. His green eyes fell to my mouth and I wanted to step back, leave the room and try my best to avoid both him and Grayson for a while, but then again, I wanted to step closer.

"We're both adults, Asher. We both made a decision." I found myself looking at his mouth as well and the room felt too hot, the air too stuffy.

He inclined his head towards me. "You may not believe me, but I would never want to see you in any sort of real pain." He took a tiny step towards me. "That's the last thing I want."

"Tell me what you did was dumb. Tell me it was stupid. Tell me it was one of the worst decisions you've ever made," I challenged, my breathing becoming heavier with each word. "I'll forgive you."

He took a deep breath and continued his walk over to me causing me to back up against the door. I dropped my backpack on the ground, placing my hands along the wood behind me. "You think I want your forgiveness that badly?" He planted one of his hands next to my head, leaning his body into mine.

"I think that's up to you. It makes no difference to me." I partially closed our distance so that my lips were a breath away from his. "Resistance is a tricky thing, isn't it, *sir*?" I let the word linger and my tongue peeked out, touching his bottom lip.

He tilted his head to the side and brushed my lips with his own. His breath washed over me and if he listened hard enough, I'm sure he would have heard my heart thrumming away in my chest. "It was dumb." His free hand ghosted over my side and down to my hip. "It was stupid." He used his knee to part my legs. "It was the worst decision I've ever made."

I let out the smallest whimper and his mouth was on mine, capturing that sound and claiming it. He removed his hand from the door and grabbed my face, opening his mouth to fully welcome our kiss. I grabbed his waist, tugging him into me and kissing him deeper, our tongues dueling. He pushed me harder against the door and I shoved him away from me. He staggered back, a confused look on his face. I let out a few breaths, tenderly touching my lips.

"She likes you, you know," I pointed out, giving him a knowing look.

He narrowed his eyes, taking off his glasses. "Who?"

"That girl that was here earlier."

His eyes raked down my body and instead of putting his glasses back on, he tossed them onto his desk. "I hadn't noticed."

I gave a small shrug. "Of course not. You would never go that far with a student, right?"

"Of course not," he repeated, taking a few steps towards me until he was close enough to tug on my shirt, yanking me up against his chest. He bent his knees, trailing his hands behind my thighs and lifting me up so that I could wrap my legs around his waist. I hooked my ankles together against his lower back as he walked us to his desk. He placed me on top of it, so I was facing his desk chair, and he stood in front of me.

He nuzzled into my neck, kissing my throat, bringing his lips to my ear. "Unless the student in question has a pussy I can't stop thinking about." He started to unbutton my pants with a speed I didn't know he possessed. "A pussy I've been wanting to bury my face in and pound my cock into." I bit my lip so hard it hurt.

"Asher…"

"Lift your hips." It was a demand and all I wanted to do was follow.

I did as he said, watching him rip my pants from my legs. He took the front of my throat in his hand and tilted my head up. "You forgive me, Riley?"

His other hand cupped my covered pussy and I gasped, feeling his fingers rub against me. "Y-yes." I actually did. There was a haze of lust and desire, but despite all that the past wasn't something I could change and all we could do was make a plan for the future. Maybe that was something I needed to consider for others as well.

He rubbed harder, biting at my earlobe. "Yes, what?"

"Fuck, yes sir."

"Good girl. You don't get to show off to the others right now. You don't get to make all those dirty noises that I like for anyone else but me." He moved my panties over, sliding one of his fingers inside of me and I let out a sharp moan. He licked my earlobe continuing, "It's just me, you and your pretty wet cunt that I'm going to make very happy and you're going to come on my desk like the needy little slut that you are, aren't you, little liar?"

He fucked me hard with his fingers and I grabbed his arm, digging my nails into his shirt, likely bruising his skin. "Y-yes, sir."

He tore his fingers away from me and got down on his knees, grabbing my hips and bringing me to the edge. He licked up my thigh and my mouth dropped open when he gripped my panties with his teeth, pulling them down my legs. Asher gripped the back of my thighs, pushing my legs back so that he had the most intimate view of my core.

"Fuck it's so pretty," he praised, not letting a moment pass before burying his face between my legs. I held onto his desk, losing feeling in my fingers from how intensely I was holding on. He moaned against my pussy, flicking his tongue over my clit repeatedly and sucking it into his mouth.

Asher lapped at me as he held my thighs apart, the muscles in my legs burning. He never looked up at me, he never focused on anything else but the task at hand. He devoured me, stuck his tongue inside and explored. His fingers joined in and he started to focus all his attention on my clit, while two of his fingers curved, finding that spot that caused me to nearly see stars. His skilled tongue circled my clit. With the way his mouth moved and his fingers, I was going to come soon.

My mind went into almost a lustful daze the closer and closer I got. I realized my mind was still in the moment, but the euphoria was getting higher. This feeling felt like a fucking dream and I didn't want it to end. Was he doing this? Was he intensifying my brimming orgasm like a lucid dream? Fuck, I didn't care. My legs started to shake from the way he was sucking on my clit and I pressed my hand over my mouth,

He kept pumping his fingers into me but lifted himself off the ground as my orgasm continued. Asher removed my hand from my mouth and gripped the back of my neck. "Taste yourself." He kissed me as I moaned against his lips, his beard scratching against my face. The orgasm felt like it would never end.

Eventually the feeling subsided and I came back to reality. Asher released my mouth, slipping his fingers from my pussy. I yelped when he swatted it, smirking at me when I widened my eyes. "Did you use your powers on me?"

He didn't say anything, putting his previously occupied fingers in his mouth and sucking them. He casually bent down to pick up my panties and jeans, handing them to me. I couldn't help but stare at his erection, which seemed like it was screaming to be released, as I put my clothes back on.

Asher grabbed my arms and turned me around to face him. He brought his thumb to my lips, pulling my bottom lip down. It was a gentle move and I didn't really know what to think about it. "I don't care about other students."

Six words said so much. "So does that mean you care about me?"

He dropped his hand, backing away and plopping down into his desk chair. He glanced at the clock on his wall, then pointed towards his office door. "You should go. I have an appointment in ten minutes. I'll see you at home."

I rolled my eyes, not at all surprised by him. My legs were still shaky, but I kind of liked this lingering feeling of knowing what happened. "What about your—" I nodded to his obviously hard cock.

"It'll go down."

I didn't know what else to say so I started to walk to the door, picking up my discarded backpack. His voice caught me by surprise before I left.

"I don't get to have your mouth on my cock because I made a dumb, stupid decision. You deserved to come because of it. Simple." He had his glasses back on his face, marking up papers with his red pen, when I turned around to see him. My eyebrows rose. "Don't forget to close the door behind you."

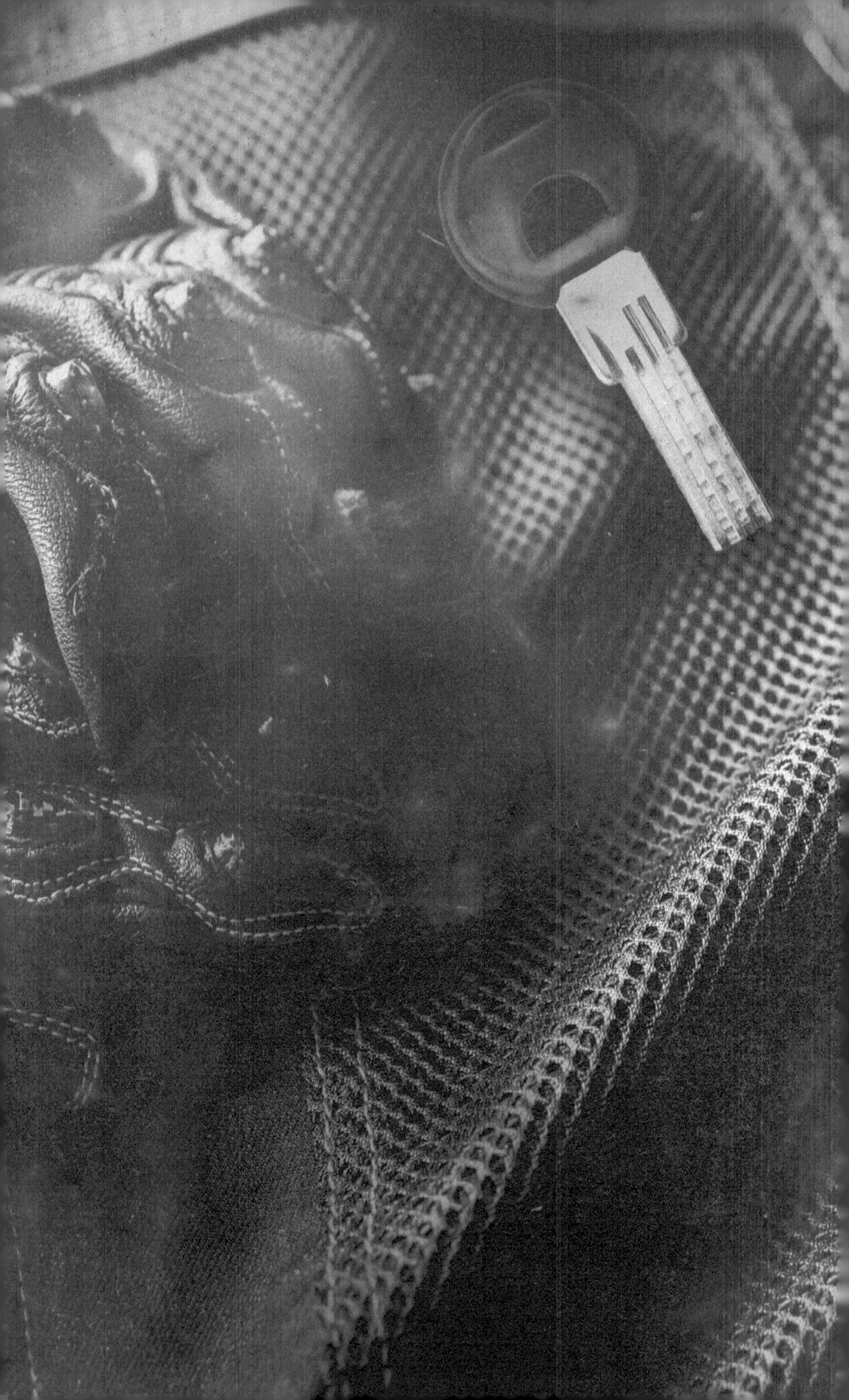

21
RIVER

I crumpled my napkin up, throwing it on my empty plate. I watched Grayson from across the table, sucking some of the salt from his fries off his fingers. I moved my plate to the side, sighing. This was way harder than I'd imagined. We could have conversations, we could even have lunch like we were doing now, but there was this shift that I didn't like. I knew exactly what it was, but the fact that I couldn't do much about it was what tore my heart apart.

Riley needed to take her time, however long that would be and I'd patiently wait. I'd waited far too long for someone like her to come into my life, so respecting her need to figure out how she felt and what she wanted was something I was more than willing to do.

"Earth to River." Grayson waved his hand in front of my face.

"I'm listening," I lied, straightening up on my side of the booth. Leif's was busy and it had taken close to an hour to get our food, but it was always worth it.

"Your eyes do that thing where they glaze over like you're in your own world, so I know you aren't."

I laughed, throwing a sugar packet at him. "Fine, you caught me. What were you saying?"

"What were you thinking about?"

I shrugged. "A lot of things. If you haven't noticed there is a self-righteous wacko running this entire school who is obsessed with our girl." I pressed my lips together, acknowledging my words.

Grayson's eyes fell down to the table. He started tearing up his straw wrapper. "Y-yeah, that makes sense."

I reached across the table and placed my hand on his wrist. "Hey, I'm trying to figure out how to navigate this."

He placed his other hand over mine. "I know. I just want to do whatever she wants. You have to have some kind of idea what that is. She actually talks to you." His tone had him sounding a little jealous.

"Believe me, if I had any idea, I would tell you. Anything I say to her now is just all the things I've told her before. She knows where I stand and that I've forgiven you, but Riley is her own person." I squeezed his wrist. "She'll come around, and I'll keep you company until she does."

"Aren't you sweet," Grayson chuckled, sticking his tongue out at me. His eyebrows furrowed for a moment.

"What is it?"

He looked up at me with his deep brown eyes that were filled with sadness. "It was really easy to be just friends and pretend like I didn't know what you sounded like when you came because you were so genuinely happy with her. When she wanted to add me to that happiness, when I got to have both the people that seemed to, I don't know, complete me in some way, it was something I couldn't describe. And yes, that happiness includes your brother, as much as he doesn't want to admit his feelings for her." I laughed, until he moved his hand away from me, placing them both in his lap. "Now it's starting from square one, just being your friend and trying to pretend that I don't know what you sound like when you come. I guess it's a little worse since I also know what she sounds like too."

He let out a laugh that had little to no humor in it. I let out a sigh, running a hand down my face and throwing him a soft smile. "You also happen to love her and I think she knows that. She doesn't hate you, Grayson. I think that fact alone is why this is so hard for her. I mean the song does say 'Love is a Battlefield.'"

Grayson snorted, a full genuine smile appearing on his face. The waitress came by and placed down our checks. I grabbed both of them before he could even reach his and walked over to the register. I tugged my wallet out from my back pocket, smiling over at the girl in front of me. I handed her the checks, noticing how she let her fingers linger on my own before pulling away.

I always had a good laugh when the women and men seemed to do this to me, but right now I just really wasn't in the mood. She read me my total and I handed her my credit card. When she handed it back, she tilted her head to the side. "It must be exhausting."

"I don't know what you mean."

She giggled. "That girl who went crazy at that meeting. That's your girlfriend, right? It must be exhausting having to deal with all that."

"She didn't go crazy, she—" I started but she handed me my receipt, cutting me off.

"I've never been with a telepath. I'm just saying, if you want something easier, I get off at seven." She looked me up and down and I commended her on her confidence, but she was barking up the wrong tree.

"That's really not as appealing as you make it sound," I stated, snatching my receipt from her hand. "And for the record, I'm not a fan of um," I snapped my fingers, "desperate pussy."

Her mouth dropped open at my blunt response.

"I prefer the taste of my girlfriend's. I'll make sure to let her know how exhausting she is after she wears me out later tonight." I winked at her, turning around and locking eyes with Grayson. I nodded towards the door and he looked from me to the cashier before slipping out of the booth.

He followed behind me as we rounded the corner, falling into step beside me. "What the hell happened just now?"

"A day in the life of being very good looking but tremendously faithful." I slapped him on the back.

He shook his head, running a hand through his hair. "It's a good thing you can't use your powers on campus because I can only imagine what you'd be hearing right about now."

"Their looks say enough. Riley can handle herself though."

Grayson nudged my shoulder. "We both know you would gladly handle things for her."

"That makes two of us, hmm?" I challenged, nudging him back. He knocked his shoulder against mine and the contact felt fun and flirty. While we walked, I had to flex my fingers out, willing them not to hold his hand. It didn't hurt, holding back, but just like Grayson had said...it just made me sad. "Riley is likely in the library since her second class is—"

I heard nothing but static. I stopped walking and shook my head, the sound never ceasing.

"River?" I heard Grayson say, but the static got louder and it was piercing. I grabbed the sides of my head, stumbling back and pressing my back against the side of one of the buildings we passed. "River, hey what's wrong?"

I pressed my palms against my temples, needing it to stop. I vigorously shook my head, grinding my teeth together with how the sound grated on my mind. I closed my eyes and heard a voice, it was so faint. I couldn't truly make it out, but it didn't sound like anyone I knew, but I couldn't think straight.

I felt myself being shaken, but it wasn't doing me any good. I slapped the side of my head over and over again. I didn't know why, but I was doing it. My head was throbbing from the hits, but I continued, it was like I needed to obey.

"For fucks sake..." Grayson's voice sounded so far away and

when I pulled my hand back for another hit, I felt something slither into my ears. When I tried to open my eyes, they were clouded by a black film. A sudden bitter taste developed on my tongue. The static, the voice, everything was blocked and constrained.

My whole body shook and I backed away from my best friend, running my hands down my arms and stomach. I stuck my finger in my ear, still feeling the sensation like something was in there. My eyesight was clearer, and I ran my hand over my tongue to try to remove the bitter taste. Shadows wafted in front of me, looking as if they came off of my tongue. I watched as Grayson put his dampener ring back on.

I opened my mouth, but he beat me to it. "What the fuck just happened, River?"

"I-I don't know. That's never happened before. I didn't..." I sucked in a breath, rubbing the side of my head. "I didn't want to."

"Was it your dad?" Grayson asked, stepping closer to me and placing his hand on my cheek. I looked around and it seemed like he had moved us in between buildings.

I rested my hand on top of his, leaning into his touch. "I don't think it was. I know my dad's invasions. I've felt them before...more times than I'd like to admit."

"Okay..." Grayson moved his thumb along my cheek. "What now?"

I let out a heavy sigh. "I have to tell my brother."

"And Riley?"

"I'll tell her. Just let me talk to my brother." I didn't want to hide anything from Riley, but Asher would be a pain in my ass if I didn't tell him immediately.

I licked my lips, the foul taste still lingering. I tenderly touched my ears. "Did you...ear fuck me with your shadows?"

Grayson pressed his lips together trying not to laugh, dropping his hand, but I caught it. "That's one way to put it, sure. It's the only way I could get to you from the inside. The downside is that it ends up everywhere, your mind, eyes, nose and mouth, hence the bad tasting aftereffects."

I brought his hand to my mouth and kissed his knuckles. He blinked, using his other hand to rub the back of his neck. I moved to text Riley that we would be a little late getting her, but all I could think about was how easy it had been to let myself be taken off guard. I knew how to shield my mind, but I'd never kept up the practice.

Maybe Asher was right to worry about me.

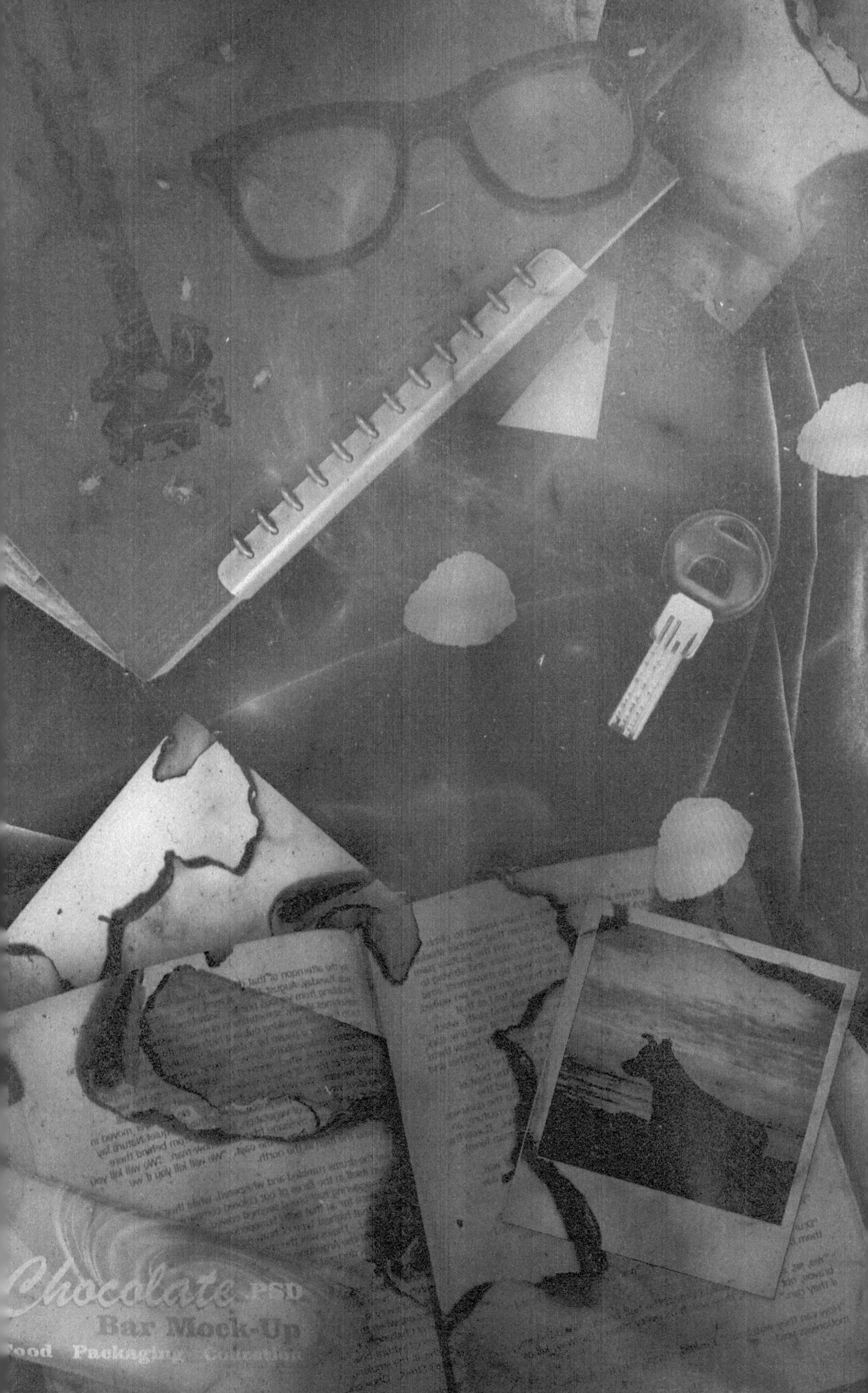
Chocolate PSD
Bar Mock-Up
Food Packaging Collection

22
RILEY

I sat on the floor in between two bookshelves flipping through one of my textbooks. I scribbled down notes, hoping that secluding myself to the third floor of the library would give me some sense of privacy. I sighed, looking past my textbook to see students at the various desks on this floor trying not to stare at me, but they were doing a terrible job at being discreet. I pretended like I didn't care as I tilted my head back, banging it against the wall.

I tapped my pencil against my book, realizing that I was retaining none of what I'd read for the past thirty minutes and closed it. I searched inside my backpack for the novel I'd been slowly working my way through. It was a monster romance that involved a different planet and I really needed something I could lose myself in. I had only read about two pages when two bodies were hovering over me.

"There you are!" Corrin yelped, getting harsh stares from a few students. She turned around, throwing them her middle finger before rushing to sit down next to me. Ike grunted as he sat down in front of me, trying to get comfortable spreading his long legs out.

"I will just say, I'm missing an entrepreneurs club meeting for this," Ike pointed out, getting his phone out and tapping away.

I narrowed my eyes at both of them. "How did you know I was here?"

Corrin waved her hand dismissively. "I tried texting you, but I guess you didn't hear it. I texted River. He told me you were probably here."

I took my phone from the side pocket of my backpack, realizing I had two missed texts. One from Corrin and one from River. "So, you just happened to pick the right floor?"

Ike snorted. "No, we looked like idiots ducking down each aisle on the first two floors."

Corrin shushed him, taking a book out from her bag. "I get bored very easily, so I decided to do a little digging on the coven, especially Evie Malcolm, the lady that created your necklace."

I sat up a little straighter, putting my book down and placing it next to me. "And?"

"Ike is really good at researching and doing archive stuff, so I asked him if he could find anything relevant to that time. And as annoying as my twin is, he never disappoints."

"I am right here you know." He kicked her foot with his own. "Compliment aside, there were some articles about Mystic Riegan's chancellor dying suddenly and that took over a lot of the headlines. That guy really had the school thriving during his time. I collected a few old pictures of the coven, but the craziest thing I found was something I guess the school tried to bury but clearly not good enough."

I raised my eyebrows telling him to continue.

His dark eyes danced with excitement as he explained. "Evie Malcolm was apparently having an affair with the chancellor."

I pursed my lips, feeling Corrin grabbed my arm. "When he told me I was like, oh my god, that was something the coven always talked about as like a world class rumor. No one could really verify if it was true or give that much detail, especially about the chancellor's wife. Celica and Mystic Riegan being an intertwined legacy means that that kind of scandal would have to be covered up, especially after the chancellor's death."

"Not well enough, it seems," Ike said, smugly. "Evie Malcolm and the affair is as close as you get to any details on that time besides the fact that the guy died."

I moved my braids to my back, sitting cross-legged. "Chancellor Fowler's dad was the Chancellor back then. My mom told me all about how when his father died, things changed for him. She told me he always accused his own mother of doing it. His mother was the coven leader, so she would have had to know Evie."

Corrin opened her mouth, letting a small breath escape before frantically flipping through her book. "In all the searching, we found this." She finally found the page she wanted and stopped, bringing the book between us so I could see. She pointed to a slightly grainy picture of a collection of men and women together.

"What am I looking at?"

"This is the coven during that time and that," Corrin pointed to a girl with wispy dark hair, "is Evie Malcolm." She moved her finger over to a woman with dark brown curls down to her waist. She looked older than all of them, but she was beautiful, the picture of pure regal grace. "That's the coven leader, Teresa Lowe. Riley, I recognized her because she was the coven leader up until your dad died."

"Wait, the one you said just up and left?"

Corrin nodded, her bright pink crop top sliding down one of her shoulders. "Yeah. Teresa and Erik never really show up in pictures together or anything. It's like they damn near avoided each other. She never even talked about her son when we interacted. Maybe the change to his mother's maiden name was some kind of fresh start when he took over, since Erik Lowe stopped showing up in any kind of research we've done about a year after his father's death. It's like he disappeared for a while." Corrin eyeballed the picture some more like she was searching for something. "Then all of sudden, after a number of different chancellor's all related to that family, he pops back up with a different last name. I couldn't find any other details on it though."

She tapped her finger against someone else in the picture. "That's Chancellor Fowler, well, the bottom says Erik Lowe." I peered at the photo, seeing him as a younger version of himself. He didn't look happy or sad; he just looked content. I wondered if this was after my mom had left or before. He was handsome in a way that had me understanding why my mom fell for him, but I knew what he was, what he would become and I had to look away from the photo.

I closed the book, placing it back in Corrin's lap. "Yeah, my mom said that she was told he just went off the grid when she came back to California. She thought it was over. What does this all mean?"

Ike cleared his throat. "If you were going to do that type of magic, the kind that involves housing whole magical abilities into an object for supposed infinite dormancy, you would consult your coven leader or your coven leader would be the one bringing you the project in the first place. That's big magic and not something you just go off and decide on your own."

"So...that would mean Teresa had to know what Evie was doing. She would have been aware that the necklace was for my mom... for me," I spoke my words towards the ground, trying to make it all make sense. "She knew my mom was back the entire time, but she never told Chancellor Fowler."

Corrin hummed. "I mean, you said they didn't get along, maybe that was her way of keeping your mom at bay. Or maybe she wanted to help your mom. The past could be in the past, you know?" She nibbled on her bottom lip, her eyebrows furrowed.

"Corrin, what are you thinking?" Ike asked, his voice full of knowing skepticism.

"Nothing terrible, just maybe if I can find out if Teresa Lowe is alive, then perhaps she can help us with getting her son to chill the fuck out. Get rid of him. Remove him from the situation." She flinched when she was done, waiting for her brother to explode on her.

Ike groaned, running both his hands down his face. "Are you trying to give mom and dad a heart attack? The witch kidnappings, the chancellor being way too connected with a coven you happened to still be in and now this?!" His voice raised a little and a few students shushed him.

"Okay, calm down, both of you. I can take this to the guys and we can figure it out, without you. I should have never involved you. Ike is right; your parents have been great to me and I don't want to be any more of an issue for them." I took her knee in my hand and squeezed.

She pouted, grabbing my hand and pushing it off her knee. "That's very kind, but I'm in. I've been in this the minute you told me about your dad, and I'm not leaving now. A cheating husband, another mysterious murder plot, a cover up and your still unfinished love connections? I mean come on, how could I *not* stay involved?" She tapped my nose, doing a little shimmy with her shoulders.

Ike let out an exhaustive sigh. "I sometimes wonder how we share the same DNA."

Corrin pointed at him. "You have to help find Teresa. We sleuth better together and you know it. Besides, mom and dad would hate for you to let me venture out all by myself."

"You are the fucking worst," her brother whispered, opening his mouth again to say more, but I stopped him.

"She won't be in the coven by herself," I said, hoping to end their bickering.

They both looked at me, their eyes widening.

"You decided to join?" Corrin asked, tucking her legs under her thighs and settling back on her heels. "Did they send you an invite like I told you they might?"

I tapped my fingers on my knees. "Uh, no. I had a fun conversation with Chancellor Fowler and that was my best option when it came to keeping him satisfied."

"You met with him? Oh my god, Riley, why didn't you tell me?" Corrin shuffled closer to me, placing her hands on my arm.

"It was a surprise attack and I don't really want to talk about it. I told him I'd join Celica, so that's that." I patted her hand. "Witchy sisters, just like we talked about."

Marianne had prattled on and on about how she planned to rush a sorority when she got to Virgina. She'd promised that none of those girls would ever be more like a sister to her than me, but they could try. She had gotten into the sorority of her choice, but she still made time for me. She always chose our video chats over mixers with fraternities. Marianne was like my sister and I couldn't protect her because I didn't even know what was coming. I wouldn't make that mistake again.

"Your mom can blame both of us if anything happens," I said to Ike, who just huffed out a breath and rolled his eyes.

He got up from the floor, slinging his backpack over his shoulders. He gave each of us a pointed look before helping his sister off the floor. "If—and that's a big *if*—we find out she's still alive, do you plan to just casually knock on her door and say excuse me, I'm Corrin, a witch in the coven you used to lead and this is your granddaughter and I know you didn't really like her mom all those years ago and you probably don't even like her now, but can you please come back and tell your son to stop doing illegal things and seek therapy?"

Corrin tapped her chin. "Well, obviously not, that's a terrible introduction."

I almost snorted, but then I heard a familiar voice, followed by a familiar face peeking around Ike's body.

"Riley?" Grayson loomed over me, while I sat on the floor, unmoved.

I swallowed, grabbing my stuff that was around me and shoving it into my backpack. "What are you doing here?"

He pointed to where we could see part of the help desk on the other side of the room. "For my work study, you know I'm a library assistant."

"Yeah, I remember. Is that the truth?"

"What?" He gave me a puzzled expression.

"Just making sure that you aren't going to go off to make more unwise decisions that could hurt the people you care about."

Ike pressed his lips together, putting his head down to avoid looking at either of us. Corrin fiddled with a piece of her hair, letting the tight curl spring back when she pulled on it.

Grayson sucked in a deep breath and then let it out, his shoulders sagging. "No, I'm done with that. You *know* that. I just..." He stepped closer and I stood up, shaking my head slightly. I had told him that he couldn't get too close, that he couldn't be that close to me until I was ready to embrace him with everything I had. When or if I did that, that would be it. If he fucked up again, there wouldn't be a second chance.

He left some space between us, holding onto the straps of his backpack. "You weren't answering your texts so I'm just letting you know that River is at Asher's office waiting for you. I have my car, so I'll be home when my work is done."

"Okay," I mumbled more to myself.

"I can probably make the tail end of my meeting. Let's go Corrin," Ike nodded his head towards the elevators. There was no denying how incredibly tense and awkward this situation was.

Corrin threw the book into her backpack and jerked me to her in a tight hug. She pulled away, digging into the side of her bag and pulled out two tiny bottles. "Take the purple one first. Then take the teal one and you'll be set for three months." I realized they were the elixirs she had promised me and snatched them from her, clutching them in my palm. She faced Grayson, giving him a full closed-mouth smile. "I forgive you for kidnapping my fellow witches. Be grateful for that, because Mateo was very ready to bite your dick off." She patted his shoulder as she left, earning a grumble from her twin.

He let out a soft chuckle before focusing on me again. I tucked a braid behind my ear, shifting from one foot to the other. He stepped to the side, so I could get out of the aisle. I walked past him, that familiar pull that I'd always felt with him snaking its way along my skin.

I exhaled through my nose, turning back around slightly. "When you get done, um, just get back home safely."

Grayson nodded. "Yes ma'am."

I found myself wanting to keep looking at him, but I needed to leave. Being in a library with him made me think about what had happened the last time we were alone together in one and that wasn't happening with him right now. I couldn't help but feel like I was missing something without him, but how I wanted to go about letting him back in took priority.

I got off the elevator, heading for the doors towards the main campus. I reached for my phone, checking the time when I saw I had another message from Corrin.

CORRIN

on his knees, Riley. It's actually more liberating than you think.

That same feeling of desirable intrigue warmed my veins, like it did the last time I thought about this. I didn't know if I liked it because I coveted the way it made me feel knowing I could ask that of someone, or the fact that I knew he would do it in a heartbeat.

Chocolate PSD
Bar Mock-Up
Food Packaging Collection

23

RILEY

Beau had been at my side while I sat on River's bed ever since I'd gotten home. He'd moped a little after Jade left but she'd promised that she hadn't overfed him treats while we were gone. I didn't believe her, but the moment we found them asleep on the couch together instantly made up for it.

The car ride back home was more awkward than it had been getting to school. River had sat in front and the tension between them was palpable, but I didn't ask questions. The minute I walked into Asher's office, their shoulders were tense, and the immediate silence when I walked into the room already told me something was off. I wondered if Asher had told River about how he'd gone down on me on that very desk they stood in front of, but knowing River, this wouldn't have been the attitude he ended up in.

They wouldn't be ecstatic with me joining Celica, nor would they be delighted that Corrin had added 'search for Chancellor Fowler's mom as another means to defeat the big bad' to my to do list. From the outside, in a small way, I was offering him a little bit of what he wanted, but it was a means to an end; just like him using Grayson and killing my dad was for him. I hated comparing us, but it was staring me right in the face.

I considered what would happen if the worst came and I was faced with killing him, if his life was dangling by a thread and I held the sharp blade that could cut that thread. Would I do it? Maybe I had humanity left if my answer wasn't an immediate yes. Was I that hurt by everything if I didn't just want to tear him to pieces? I hated him; I knew and felt that with every fiber of my being, but murder... thinking about it boiled my blood but it also made me queasy.

The bitter taste of both of the elixirs still sat on my tongue, but I kept telling myself it was a necessary evil. Beau snuggled closer to me and I looked over his head at the end table. My dampener ring sat on the wood, looking innocent and not like a piece of jewelry that held me back. I shouldn't say that. It didn't necessarily hold me back, it just.... made sure I stayed calm and collected, right?

I let out a loud, obnoxious sigh. Thank God it was Friday, because even after one day I needed a fucking nap and then I heard shouting. I grumbled, throwing my legs over the side of the bed and rushing to the door. The arguing was coming from Asher's room and I was prepared to tell both of them to shut the fuck up, when the words they said stopped me.

"You don't have to keep yelling at me!" River shouted. "I know this is bad, okay? I didn't try to hide it from you, so that should count for something."

Asher scoffed. "Ah, yes, thank you for not keeping the fact that dad ravaged your mind. I appreciate your honesty and the fact that you came in and told me what happened as if we were discussing the weather."

"How would you have liked me to explain it? Either way you were going to be pissed off." River explained. "Besides, I told you that it wasn't dad."

That's why the drive home was so awkward. That explained the tension when I'd come to the office. I gently leaned against the door.

"You keep saying that, but it doesn't make any sense how it couldn't be."

"I know dad, okay? I know what his magic feels like. It stings and I—" River cleared his throat. "I would know if it was dad. You also didn't need to go barging into his office either. I told you to keep you in the loop, not have you come to my fucking defense like I'm a little kid."

Asher barked out a sharp laugh. "I can tolerate dad speaking to you and being the normal self-righteous prick that he is, but the minute he pushes too far, the minute he threatens you, that's my cue to step in. It's always been my cue, whether you appreciate it or not. So, yes, when our dad decides he is going to mess with you in the middle of the fucking school day for no reason whatsoever, then I will come to your fucking defense whenever I damn well feel like it."

The one thing I always understood about Asher was his infinite love for his brother, even though he didn't put it on display for the world to see. His actions as fucked up as they were sometimes always shifted River out of harms way by any means necessary.

"It wasn't dad! I don't know who it was and I clearly don't know why!" River sounded exhausted and all I could do was slump against the door and keep listening. "It felt more like an aggravated warning than anything else."

"Even if it wasn't dad's magic directly, he was still involved. He always is."

"You can try to protect me all you want, Asher, and as much as you grate on my last nerve, I would do the same for you, but this all boils down to Riley. I know I'm just one of many pawns to get her to submit to Chancellor Fowler. Dad wants us to be this super family with mom as our doting human who is so fucking blind to what's in front of her. He's willing to see us so unhappy, just so we can pretend to be the luckiest family with all the money and power to gloat about. He will never be satisfied, so if for one second you think that choosing me over Riley will appease him, I would think again. I'll work on my shit, but I would rather him destroy every little piece of my mind than give her up."

I meant to place my head against the door lightly but the sound that reverberated from my skull meeting the wood was louder than I intended. My body froze and I stepped back from the door, praying to whoever that I could walk back to River's room unscathed.

I heard the doorknob turn and came face to face with my boyfriend.

"How long have you been there?" River asked, his voice soft.

"Not long, I was just about to knock—"

"How about the truth, little liar." Asher came up behind his brother with his arms crossed.

I rolled my eyes at him and focused on River. "A few minutes."

River looked over his shoulder at Asher, who raised his eyebrows and shook his head as if to say, 'your call.'

I didn't let either of them speak. "Someone tried to mind control you today?"

River rolled his lips together and sighed. "Well, not exactly, but they just..."

"Yes or no, River? Did someone get into your head and try to hurt you?"

"Riley, it's not that simple. I don't know if they planned to hurt me, it just felt..."

I cut him off again. "Yes, I heard what you said. An aggravated warning. It's still a threat of some kind and you didn't think to tell me the minute you saw me?"

He opened his mouth to argue but then closed it. His eyebrows turned down and he looked to Asher, as if his brother had the answer.

Asher ran a hand over his beard. "Oh, don't look at me to save you now."

River stepped out of the room, moving closer to me. "I was going to tell you. This was about our dad and anything associated with him...telling Asher just seemed like the most logical first step."

I hummed. "Fine, makes sense, so why didn't you say anything when we got back here? You let me go into your room and still nothing. Does that come with more logical reasoning?"

I heard Asher let out a small chuckle.

"Okay, I know it looks bad, but—"

I smacked the side of his head, and he gave me a shocked look, blinking a few times.

"Ow! I'm sorry! I should have told you."

"Hmph, you think." I turned on my heels to take the stairs two at a time. I heard footsteps following behind me.

The minute I hit the kitchen, River grabbed my arm, spinning me around to face him. "Riley, I am sorry I didn't tell you, but I don't particularly love adding to your plate that is already toppling over every fucking minute. My dad is an issue, but this wasn't my dad at all, not directly. I don't know if that makes it better or worse; I don't know anything. All I *do* know is that even if this situation has to do with me, I will always wonder how it affects you." His words came out breathy like it was taking a lot for him to make sure he was saying things the way he wanted. He looked over my shoulder and I noticed Asher was behind me, leaning against the kitchen counter.

"Did you confront your dad?"

"We tried." Asher offered. "He wasn't in his office. Surprise, surprise. If he got that one student to rip off your necklace at the meeting, then what's to say he didn't enlist someone to do this as well?"

I tilted my head to the side in thought. "Compulsion isn't taught anymore. There are a lot of mental magic classes and workshops at the university, plenty of different majors, but that isn't one of them, so unless our dad has been secretly preparing a student for this very moment, he has to be using an outside source."

"Those mystery books really enhance your deductive reasoning skills," Asher joked, smirking at me when I frowned at him.

I touched River's arm, feeling this warm skin on my fingertips. I dragged my hand up to his shoulder and over this neck, cradling it. "I need to know everything from now on."

"Riley, I was going to—"

"Everything." I pressed my fingers into his neck for just a tiny hint of emphasis. I considered bringing up Celica and my choice to join them, but I pushed that thought away. River's dad seemed to be the one who couldn't play by the rules of a game they created, it was only the first day and he was getting a head start that no one had offered.

He wrinkled his nose, clutching my hand and removing it, but he didn't let it go. "Yes, Riley. Everything. Since we are saying everything, then you should know Grayson helped me out. I won't get into the details cause they're honestly a little weird, but he was there. I didn't go through what I did alone."

My eyes never left his face, staring directly into his green irises. Grayson made sure he was alright. "He used his magic," he cut his eyes to Asher, "yes on campus, so don't pull your university rules shit on me."

"I wasn't going to. I'll thank the shadow wielder when he gets home. I can be nice," Asher said, the tone in his voice full of sarcasm.

I remembered his shadows feeling unfamiliar and cold when they'd wrapped around me when he was operating under Chancellor Fowler's influence. I imagined them doing something good, something good for a person I loved. He hadn't done it to seek my affection, but he'd done it because he cared about River. Maybe I needed to create new memories with the Grayson that wanted a second chance.

On his knees, Riley. It's actually more liberating than you think.

"Hey, you okay?" River had slightly bent his knees to meet me at eye level. "You kind of zoned out for a minute."

I lifted his hand to mine and kissed it. "Yeah, no, it was nothing. I was just thinking that maybe it's time we had a talk. Grayson and I."

"I'm sure Grayson will talk about whatever you want if you decide on that plan," Asher pointed out, catching my attention.

"Excuse me?" I asked, watching him narrow his eyes at me when I turned around.

"Zoning out is just another form of daydreaming in my humble opinion, so believe me it was hard to keep a straight face when the visual of him on his knees manifested. I could have told you very quickly that Grayson submitting to you was more than possible. His yearning is palpable."

My mouth formed into a hard line. "You just adore being able to use your powers on me, don't you?"

He clucked his tongue. His next words were said in a deeper voice, lower. "You didn't seem to mind earlier today?"

My lips curved into a smile. "I seem to recall that earlier you didn't mind getting on your knees."

His eyes darkened and neither of us looked away from each other when River stepped up behind me. "Is that why your mind became a steel trap when she came into your office today and why it smelt faintly like sex in there?"

Asher reared his head back. "We didn't have sex."

River wrapped his arms around my waist, leaning down to place his chin on the top of my head. "Mmkay, well, if you didn't have sex, what *did* you do exactly? What would constitute you being on your knees?" His voice was playful while he pulled me further into him.

Asher groaned loudly, running his index finger along his eyebrow. "I'm not even going to consider entertaining that with a response." He snuck a glance at me before attempting to leave the room.

"Did you get on your knees so you could taste her pretty cunt?" River moved my braids to the side so he could nuzzle into my neck.

Asher hadn't even made it two feet away from us before he turned around and scanned his eyes over both of us. River left kisses along my neck, each one followed by a tiny bite. Asher stood there, his eyes focused solely on me and my reactions.

River moved his hands to the hem of my shirt, gracing his short nails along my stomach. "Did you spread her out on your desk, so you could make sure that needy clit was taken care of?" He moved his fingers to unbutton my jeans and slid down the zipper. My eyes fluttered closed when he dipped his hand inside and started playing with me.

I let out small moans while he lazily drew circles around my clit, nibbling on my earlobe. I let my eyes fall open to see Asher lick his lips as he watched his brother's hand. He suddenly flicked his eyes to me and they were filled with this kind of fiery lust that I'd only ever seen that night in his bathroom.

River's seductive voice lingered in my ear. "Is that what he did, gorgeous? Did he spread those sexy thighs and lick your pussy?"

I stared right at Asher as I nodded. River brought his other hand to the front of throat and tilted my head back. "Say it. Did he lick your pussy?"

"Y-yes."

River smiled against my cheek, releasing my throat. He stuck a finger inside of me, causing my ass to move back and graze against his hard cock. I gripped his arm, feeling his bicep muscle flex with the way he moved his hand.

"Tell me Asher, did you make her come?"

Asher shifted his eyes from me to his brother. Slowly, as if in slow motion, he walked over to me. River never let up, so I was forced to control my breathing with every movement of his fingers, every light touch that sent my clit into overdrive.

Asher cupped my chin, getting close to my face so that our breath mingled. "I don't know. Did I make you come, little liar?"

I gasped when River stuck another finger inside. "You d-did."

Asher granted me a smug look which faltered the moment I reached out and grabbed his erection through his pants. I rubbed it causing his mouth to drop open slightly and his breathing to become a bit unsteady. I reached behind me, finding River's cock and mirroring my actions. My boyfriend's deep chuckle against my skin, sent a shiver down my spine.

River took my face and turned it, so that I could look at him from over my shoulder. He kissed me, his soft lips moving over mine like an art form. I pulled away saying my next words against his delicious mouth. "I want more."

His eyes sparkled with that mischief I adored. River looked at his brother, his eyes unmoving and I knew he was telling him something mentally. I hadn't ceased my efforts on Asher's cock, but when I turned to look at him, he bent his head down to capture my mouth. The kiss was desperate and hungry, the sounds I made from River's invasive fingers were absorbed by this kiss.

Asher liberated himself from my hold and I almost whined. River slipped his fingers out of me, putting them in my mouth for me to taste. He dragged his wet fingers from my lips and down my chin, then leaned in to pull my bottom lip between his teeth.

Asher inclined his head towards my ear. "You want more, Riley? You need us to take care of your greedy cunt and make sure our pretty slut is satisfied?" He ran his hand up my stomach and over my breasts, palming them.

"Yes, s-sir."

His eyes closed in a satisfying way as if he had just heard the most beautiful music. Asher started to undo his belt and River's breath washed over my ear. "Get on your knees, gorgeous."

24
ASHER

She was beautiful with that desperate, desirable expression on her face. Her lips trembled with this whimpering need that made my dick twitch. I wanted that mouth on me, I wanted to watch her swallow my cock until her brown eyes watered. My heart thundered in my chest, but I kept my composure and stepped back, messing with my belt, undoing it.

"Get on your knees, gorgeous," my brother said, while I watched her throat move from the way she swallowed.

I had started to get my zipper down when, with agonizing slowness, she knelt on the ground. She looked up, her braids moving around as she took in both of us before her. She used her top teeth to pull her bottom lip in, reaching to slide her palm over my erection. I noticed how River watched her every movement, his mind solely set on her. His eyes scanned down her body in this way that told me he was committing everything about her to memory.

Riley tucked her fingers into the top of my pants and started to yank them down. I stepped out of them, my cock directly in front of her face. I could feel the heat of her breath at the tip and I fought the urge to grab myself and trace her lips with it. She peeked up at me through her lashes, forcing me to give her my attention. Looking away from her wasn't an option I would even consider taking.

I stifled a groan when she grabbed my cock at the base, tilting it up and licking a long strip until she got to the tip. Her tongue flicked across the head and her eyes never left mine. She repeated herself, but this time she swirled her tongue around the tip. Her hand started to stroke me up and down, her grip tight but not suffocating. Riley moved her mouth further down my shaft, starting to bob her head back and forth. Her tongue massaged the underside of my cock, while her hand maintained its movements over the parts she couldn't get to.

She moaned around me, her mouth full, and I pressed my hand to the back of her head. She slid down further and I hissed at the feeling of her teeth slightly grazing against my cock. Small gagging sounds came from her throat as I moved my hips forward to get more of me into her mouth. I pulled back, tilting her chin up and seeing how glassy her eyes were.

"I think you can do so much better than that. I want to feel the back of your throat and hear you choke on it." I ran my thumb over her lips, watching her tongue peek out and catch the side of my fingertip.

River stepped up behind her, stroking the top of her head, twisting some of her braids around his finger. "She knows how to use that mouth, don't you, gorgeous?"

Her eyes looked so innocent when she peered over at River, nodding her head. She pawed at his pants and a short laugh escaped him. He turned her head, so that her lips brushed the head of my cock. "Then show him."

River started to unbutton his pants, keeping his eyes trained on her. Riley ran her hand along my cock, flicking her tongue at the tip and swallowing the pre cum that leaked from it. Her eyes were pools of brazen need when she looked up at me. "Make me choke on it, *sir*."

Her tongue came out and licked at me again. I nearly growled at the way she teased me, the way she was playing with me.

"Fuck, you're a brat. Open your mouth," I demanded, gripping my cock and pressing it against her lips. She opened her mouth and I held the back of her head so I could keep her in place. I fucked her mouth, hearing the moans and small breaths of air she tried to take when I wasn't hitting the back of her throat.

River smirked over at me and picked up her hand that was closest to him. He had gotten his pants down, helping her wrap her fingers around his dick. "Show us how well you multitask."

She started moving her hand up and down his length, her fingers skating over that ridiculous piercing I still couldn't believe he'd gotten. I looked down and saw her looking up at me again, tears decorated the corners of her eyes and a shiver went down my spine. She didn't ask me to hold back or slow down, letting me use her mouth.

I didn't want to come just yet. I wanted to be inside of her when I gave her everything. I found my way into River's mind.

Give her mouth something to do.

He had his eyes closed, but he popped them open to focus on me. *Don't mind if I do. That pretty mouth was about to make you come, wasn't it?*

I ignored his words, watching as he took her head in his hand and turned her face toward his waiting cock. "Fuck, good girl," River mumbled, clenching his jaw when she took him in her mouth. He moved her braids out of her face so he could get a better view, watching her sucked him down and gag.

I squatted down and reached for her jeans. It was easy for me to maneuver her lower half and drag them down her legs, along with her panties. She didn't let my contortion of her body stop her from continuing to work her mouth over River's shaft. I got her back on her knees, facing my brother completely. I got down behind her and she ceased her movements, looking over her shoulder and realizing I had lowered my head so my mouth was at her ear.

"Don't stop, little liar. I just want to play with your wet pussy and hear you moan with a cock in your mouth."

River brought her face back over to him, shoving himself back in her mouth and I trailed my hand down her stomach. I cupped her pussy, her arousal coating my fingers. She was soaked and slippery and so fucking perfect. I rubbed two fingers against her clit, wrapping my other hand around her waist when she jolted from the sensation.

My brother held her still and I kept toying with her. I circled my fingers around her entrance, pressing two of them inside. She whimpered, moving her hips as if she was trying to fuck my hand and I held her tighter. I plunged my fingers into her, rougher this time, curling them. My breath caressed her ear. "Fingers aren't good enough for you? Your slutty little pussy needs to be filled and taken care of?"

I pulled her off of River's cock and brought her head back so she could look at me. River grabbed the back of his shirt, taking it off. "Is that what you want? Answer me," I commanded, swatting my hand against her clit.

She moaned and let out a breath. "Yes, s-sir. Yes, that's what I want."

River grabbed her face. "Tell us exactly what you want. Words, gorgeous."

I pinched her clit, rubbing it at a quick speed. She kept trying to take in breath after breath. "I, *fuck,* I want you both to fuck me. I w-want you to take care of me and f-fill my pussy."

My brother kissed her, hard. "That's my girl. Fuck, you're so sexy when you know what you want."

He snuck a look at me over her shoulder, mentally letting me know how he wanted to move her. I shuffled backwards, letting River take her waist and turn her around. I unbuttoned my shirt, removing it and throwing it to the side. I laid down on the kitchen floor, pushing up on my elbows. I slowly started to stroke my cock while River bent her over so her face was parallel to my shaft.

He pressed a hand to the small of her back, bringing her ass up to meet his pelvis. He backed up a bit, so that he could bring his face down. From between her legs I could see his tongue come out and lap at her pussy. She let out a deep moan, her tongue appearing and licking at my cock.

River straightened up again, smacking her ass. "You taste so fucking good, especially when your pussy is such a dripping mess." He smacked her ass again, her shoulders tensing and then relaxing.

She mumbled a sharp *fuck* when River pushed inside of her. He took hold of her hips, bringing her back to meet his slow thrusts. She opened her mouth, taking in as much of me as she could. I moved her braids out of her face, wanting her to have as little distractions as possible. Her body swayed back and forth with each snap of River's hips. He went harder, the sound of his pelvis slapping against her skin echoed around us.

"I could spend hours fucking this pussy."

She used one of her hands to move along my cock and placed her other one at my chest to steady herself. River pounded into her causing my cock to hit the back of her throat and she choked. If she kept this up, I wouldn't make it much longer.

Make her come. I told my brother. He was looking down, focused on watching his dick disappear inside of her when he flicked his eyes up to me.

What do you think I'm trying to do?

I groaned internally. I also literally groaned, since her mouth was pure magic. *Do it faster.*

You can be honest and just say you want to fuck her. We can just switch.

I want her to come first.

He reached underneath her and started playing with her clit. She got her mouth off my cock and let out a sharp moan.

Aren't you generous? You want her to come so you can fuck her and feel her come on your dick. Admit it.

She dragged her nails down my chest as River kept up his movements.

Yes. Okay? Fuck, you are so fucking aggravating.

River let out a deep, throaty chuckle, his fingers working overtime on her clit. Her body shook when she came.

"Oh god, fuck fuck fuck." Her voice cracked as her orgasm barreled through. She started to slump against my body, but I shifted out from under her.

"Come on, gorgeous." River gently picked her up and placed her on her feet. She turned to face him and I got behind her, putting my hand between her shoulder blade and bending her over.

I kicked her legs apart and let her get adjusted to this new position, holding onto River's hips. I slid my cock over her slit, feeling her thighs twitch with every swipe at her clit.

"How bad do you want it, little liar?"

River cradled her face in his hand, nodding his head as if to tell her to answer me.

"Please *sir*," she begged, her voice shaky as she tried to move her ass back against me. "Please fuck me."

I kept teasing her and she whined. "Do you want me to fuck you slowly, be gentle? Or do you want me to fuck you hard, fuck you like the needy slut that you are?" I squeezed her ass cheeks.

"Slow or hard, gorgeous. Decision is yours," River coaxed, moving his cock against her lips.

She pressed her lips together, her whimpers growing thicker. "Hard. I want you to fuck me hard. I w-want," she stuttered, swallowing before she finished her sentence, "I want you deep, please, *sir*."

My knees nearly buckled with the desperate way her voice sounded. I would give her anything she wanted if she kept talking to me like that. I would likely give her anything she wanted regardless. That was something I needed to figure out later when I didn't have a beautiful girl to thoroughly exhaust.

I fed my cock into her pussy, letting out a satisfied sigh when I was fully seated inside of her. It hadn't been that long since I'd last been inside of her, but it felt like the first time all over again. I didn't remember her being this tight and the way her pussy clenched around me would be my undoing. I moved meticulously, groaning with every small motion, needing to savor the way she felt right now.

I heard her muffled noises, watching her head bob as he fucked her mouth. He collected her braids into one large ponytail above her head, gaining better control of her movements.

I started with sharp, shallow thrusts and then gradually found a solid rhythm. I kept up my pace, leaning over her back so I could trail my hands under her shirt. I palmed her breasts, running my fingers over her nipples until they were tight peaks at my fingertips. She moaned against River's cock as I fucked her deeper. I wanted to make her squirm and writhe until she couldn't take it anymore.

I moved my hands away from her chest and reached for the top of her arms, pulling them back towards me so I could firmly take each of her forearms in my hands.

River controlled her mouth, using the fact that she was hands free to fuck her throat harder. "Fuck, swallow that cock baby."

I used my hold on her forearms to keep her steady. Her ass bounced back against my pelvis over and over again. I fucked her hard and fast, her garbled, throaty sounds were mixed with the heavy breathing coming from all of us.

I felt her pussy start to contract around me and her body shudder from her orgasm. She held me tight inside of her and I had to bite my own tongue not to release everything I had right now. River let out a deep moan, his hips moving erratically and then he pumped his hips a few more times before letting out a sigh of contentment.

My brother stepped away from her, holding a hand to her mouth. "Swallow it, gorgeous." He ran his thumb over the side of her lip. "All of it."

She started to straighten but I grabbed her waist, causing her to yelp. I brought her over to the kitchen wall, meeting her face to face before I quickly bent down and grabbed her behind her thighs, hoisting her up. My biceps flexed as I used my forearms to hold her up and keep her legs apart. I angled her just right and slid myself inside of her.

Riley leaned her head back, exposing the column of her throat. I peered down between us, watching her take my cock. I pounded into her harder with every sound she made, every time her tiny cries got louder.

"Does that feel good, little liar?"

She leaned her head on my shoulder, becoming literal putty in my hands. "Oh fuck."

"Does my cock feel good? Answer the fucking question, Riley."

"Yes, sir. Your cock feels good."

I pressed her harder against the wall, her body moving up and down with my thrusts. "That tight cunt is going to make me come and you're going to thank me for making you scream. You are going to feel me for days. You are going to sit in my class and squirm, wishing I could be buried deep in that needy pussy like the pretty little slut that you are."

"Fuck, Asher, I'm going to—" her words were cut off as my thrusts got rougher and I grabbed onto her ass, keeping her in place so I could pound into her with more speed.

I could tell she was going into that euphoric dream-like state, so I helped her along with my powers. I made every sensation in her mental state better and much more delicious. She gripped my shoulders and I felt heat creep along my arms, it didn't burn but it brought a warm pleasure to my body.

Was she using her fire power on me? I didn't hate it, surprisingly. "Come for me."

She let out a whimpering scream before I kissed her. She welcomed my mouth, moaning against me and riding out the rest of her orgasm with her lips on mine. I bucked up into her until I felt my own release spill inside. I broke our kiss, blinking at her as my chest felt tight from my harsh breathing. A few of her braids fell into her face as she looked at me, her eyes a little hazy.

River stepped up next to us, rubbing his hands together. He had put his pants back on, leaning against the wall a few inches from Riley's head. "You two put on a very good show. Quite entertaining." He winked at me and held arms out, mentally telling me I could give her to him. I slowly slid out of her, moving my arms so I ended up cradling her. I transferred her to River, who burrowed his face against hers and whispered, "You did so good, baby. Such a good fucking girl."

Her eyes were half closed, but she presented us with a little smile. She turned her face to me, the smile never leaving. "Did I do good?"

Before I could stop myself, I leaned down and kissed her forehead. "You did very good." My words were muffled against her skin, but I knew she heard them. I stepped back quickly so River could take care of her upstairs.

You can perform some aftercare for our girl too, if you want. River offered, not turning back to me when he got to the first step on the staircase.

No, you got this. I insisted, picking up my clothes from the floor.

Our girl. I didn't really know why...but fuck, I liked the way that sounded.

25
RILEY

I tiptoed out of River's bedroom, not having had a minute to myself since what I was now calling 'the kitchen incident'. River doted on me, running a shower for me and setting out my clothes to change into. He kissed me in a way that almost made me want to beg him to get into the shower with me but fuck, I was sore. Deliciously sore.

Beau followed me down the stairs and into the kitchen. I couldn't help but stare at the space where I'd been touched and caressed by two brothers. I ran a hand down my face, sneaking a look at Beau who ran his big head into the back of legs. I'd mentally told him I was coming down here to get some water and he'd replied with *hydration is very important after exhausting activities.*

I quietly turned on the sink, filling up a glass and downing it within seconds. As much as I wanted some alone time, I found myself not really knowing how to fixate my mind on one thing. I eyed the clock on the stove: two o'clock in the morning. I looked down at my finger, bringing it up to my face and examining my dampener ring. I'd put it back on before we went to bed; I assumed that with the stress of seeing Chancellor Fowler, Grayson, River and everything that was brought to my attention by Corrin and Ike...I would just take a precaution.

I trusted myself. At least, well, I thought I did. I could breathe easy with my mom, since early on the ride back to the house, Mateo had informed me everything was fine. They said they would continue to monitor my mom and Jade would be around the house here whenever I needed. Even through a text, Mateo sounded very much like I presumed an alpha wolf would sound, even though they profusely denied being one.

I leaned against the counter, setting the glass in the sink. Scare tactics were just that: scary. Even though Chancellor Fowler had threatened River's life, Oliver wouldn't kill his own son. Emotionally scar him, maybe physically hurt him, but end his life? I just couldn't wrap my mind around a parent doing that to their child. Maybe I couldn't think like that. Maybe I had to assume everyone had the most heinous intentions and that was the only way I would get out of this.

I reached up and fiddled with my necklace. I walked out of the kitchen and over to the living room. Beau curled up onto the floor and I sat down on the couch, my necklace still in my grasp. This kind of thought provoking logic was the kind of thing I'd talk about with my dad.

"WHO DO YOU KEEP TEXTING OVER THERE?" MY DAD ASKED, TRYING TO PEEK over my shoulder.

I cut my phone off, twirling around and lightly shoving him back. "No one."

"That smile on your face says otherwise."

It was a nice, sunny day while we walked around the San Diego Zoo.

He liked to spend his last few days before school started with me at one of our favorite places. He liked watching the koalas and while they were cute and all, my favorite was the clouded leopards. I wasn't much of a cat person, but something about them intrigued me enough to stare into their enclosure for hours.

"I wasn't smiling."

He laughed, grabbing my shoulder and keeping us moving. "I wasn't born yesterday, honey."

"Ah yes, we can tell." I ran my fingers across some of the gray in his beard.

He swatted my hand away. "Okay, smartass. Is it that boy you've been seeing?"

I rubbed my lips together, trying to decide how much to say. I'd only told them so much about River and I wanted to keep him as close to my chest as I could. We were just dating for now; he wasn't my boyfriend...at least not yet. I'd met all his friends, including his best friend Grayson, and we'd gotten more than handsy with each other over time, but I hadn't really brought up the idea of putting a label on things. "Maybe."

"I'll take that as a yes. You've been on quite a few dates with the guy, Riley."

"So?"

He turned to follow down a pathway and a group of loud children ran by us. "So... you don't have to be so secretive about him. You'll be in college this fall and I want you to always be open with us. I'll be busy at the university, your mom has her job and you'll be running around being the smartest woman I know. I just don't want you to think we're too busy for you to talk to."

I chuckled. "That's very sweet, but I know I can talk to you guys. I just don't want to say a lot right now, okay? I like him and he is the first guy I've ever liked this much." I felt my cheeks heat and it wasn't from the sun. "It's just dates for now. When things get really serious then I'll let you know. We can all have dinner and you guys can thoroughly embarrass me."

He pulled me to his side and kissed my cheek. "Alright, your wish is my command. He isn't going to use those mental powers on us, right?"

I shook my head. "No, well, I'll tell him not to. He doesn't with me."

My dad's eyebrows raised. "That's honorable."

Pride swelled in my chest hearing that. River was the best from what I knew about him so far. He was sweet and an enormous flirt. He liked who I was as a person and treated my looks as secondary. His powers were intriguing, but I wanted him to learn about me without all the magic. He was always more than willing to make me happy.

"I like to think so." I pulled out my phone and dragged my dad over to one of the exhibits. I stood next to him and put my phone out in front of us. "Smile!"

We laughed as we looked at the picture and I sighed. "You're really not upset that I'm not going to Mystic Riegan?"

He narrowed his eyes. "Of course not. It's your education, Riley. If college wasn't something you wanted to do, I would still be okay as long as you had a plan. Your mother would be a different story, but I can persuade her easily." My dad waggled his eyebrows.

"Okay, gross. Have you thought about transferring to a closer school? Maybe even one that doesn't keep you so late. I've heard the University of San Francisco is pretty great, even though it's a human's only school." The topic had been lingering on my mind for a while.

He hummed, pulling us in the direction of my favorite clouded leopards. "Perhaps. I like the dynamic of Mystic Riegan. I like being able to help all kinds of people. I may be just a human, but the fact that I can help a magic wielder through the scary times of doing something new is incredible. Those people confide in you and value your thoughts and opinions. Eventually you stop thinking about powers or no powers and who is stronger than the other. You just start seeing them as people, especially when they're just kids."

"Well now you made me feel shitty for even asking." I faux pouted, letting him fake drag me to the leopard enclosure.

We stopped when the big cats came into view. They looked majestic and beautiful.

My dad squeezed my hand. "You look at River and you don't see powers, you just see a man who is probably already ridiculously in love with you. You talk to him without considering anything else because none of it matters." I opened my mouth to retort his one comment but he tsked me. "Having powers doesn't define a person, baby girl."

I leaned against my dad and watched the leopards stalk around their enclosure. A few people crowded around to see but I just leaned my head on my dad's shoulder. My phone buzzed in my hand, and I looked at the screen.

RIVER

I miss you. Tell your dad I said hi. Also tell
him I'm your boyfriend, please and
thank you.

I almost snorted. I felt my dad's shoulders move from laughter. I turned my head to him, seeing that he was eyeing my screen.

"Ridiculously in love, indeed."

I WAS DROWNING. I COUGHED AND TOOK IN MORE OF WHATEVER WAS MAKING it hard for me to breathe. The air smelt smokey and things were collapsing around me. It felt like my life. It felt like everything I'd worked for, everything I thought was fine was falling apart, piece by piece. I tried to use my powers to stop them from crumbling, but it was no use. I couldn't focus on my powers when I couldn't fucking breathe.

I was drowning and thick liquid coated my throat. It tasted like copper. I was choking on blood and I had no idea if it was mine. It had to be, right? I looked down at my hands and they were stained with dark red, the floor around me the same. There was no one around to save me, no one to help me, because maybe I caused this.

A hand reached out to touch my shoulder from behind. It felt cold and not at all welcoming, like a façade of comfort. My whole body shook as my world imploded around me and I slowly turned around to face who had come to my rescue...

I was being shaken awake and the force of it was enough to make my head spin. As if someone had let me go, let me escape from my own thoughts, I shot up from the couch, nearly falling off of it. Asher sat next to me, his eyes wide behind his glasses. I pressed my fingertips under my eyes and realized I had been crying. He got up and turned on one of the lamps in the room.

He tentatively reached my arm and I shuffled away from him. "Did you..."

"Did I what?"

"D-did you do whatever it is that you do? What I saw, did you—"

"No!" He looked over his shoulder up the stairs, then lowered his voice. "No. Why the fuck would you think that?"

I shook my head, retreating further into the side of the couch. "I d-don't...I don't know." My hands were shaking so I pressed them underneath my thighs.

Asher sighed. "You don't trust me enough to believe I wouldn't hurt you like that." He said it as if it was fact and as much as it stung to admit it to myself...it was the truth. It was an odd thought, since I trusted him with my body but not with my well-being. I was a fucking mess.

Soft snoring sounded from the floor. Beau was fast asleep still curled up, his tail twitching. My mouth moved but no words came out. Asher glanced over at my familiar. "I came downstairs and you were passed out on the couch. I wasn't going to bother you and then you started to have a fit. I knew Beau would get loud and wake the entire house, so I sent a little dream sedative to his system. I'm sure he's chasing all the squirrels he can in his head right now."

I furrowed my brow at him, maintaining my distance.

He nodded, clearing his throat. "It's the truth, Riley."

"Why didn't you just ease my dream. Use your sandman magic on me like you did before?"

He placed his hands on his thighs, squeezing his eyes shut. "I tried." He wiped under his nose with the back of his hand. Small drops of blood decorated his skin and more trickles came from his nose. I blinked and without thinking, scooted over to him and used my fingers to wipe away the blood that was finding its way to his upper lip.

"What the hell, Asher?" The thick liquid stained my fingertips.

Asher tugged on my wrist, moving my hand away from his face. "It's nothing."

"Don't do that. Don't treat me like I'm dumb."

His expression softened just a little. "It happens when I push too hard. It's a common side effect for any heavy use of magic. When I said I tried, I meant it. I could get into your head and help you out last time but whatever just happened wasn't *you*. It was someone else who has magic just like me, but it seems like they are much stronger. I couldn't—"

I watched as he wiped the rest of the blood from his nose and lost his words.

"You couldn't what?"

He ran both his hands through his hair, saying under his breath, "I couldn't help you."

I reached out and touched his knee. "You really didn't cause any of this, did you?"

He grazed his hand down my forearm and placed it on top of mine. "No, Riley, I really fucking didn't."

Asher wasn't the kind of person who threw out his affection so openly like River and Grayson. You had to look through his steel-coated exterior to get to even a fraction of something soft and warm. He showed his cards sparingly and you were lucky if he bestowed you with a smile that wasn't condescending. Despite knowing all those things, right now, I liked being with him. I could even admit that I liked him a little mean. He was a delicious contrast that challenged me, but I was honored to be one of those people that got his softness on occasion.

"Riley, we should—"

I inclined my head towards him and found his mouth. Unlike the last time we were alone and kissed, his body didn't stiffen. He embraced what was happening and kissed me back. He brought his hand to my face and cupped my cheek. He pulled me in a little closer, deepening the kiss, then a vibration from within the couch cushions stunned us both.

He wiped his mouth, sticking his hand in between the cushions, pulling out my phone. "A little late to be getting text messages."

I took my phone from him and looked at the screen. It was from Corrin.

CORRIN

I tried to sleep but I couldn't. Ike may be annoying as fuck but he's the best little researcher. We found her.

I took in a breath and peeked over at Asher, who was watching me intently.

And?

CORRIN

Well, she's alive. She never left California. She's living it up in Napa Valley.

That's not far.

CORRIN

Weekend road trip?

I stuck my tongue in my cheek, considering this. It was only about an hour or two depending on traffic, but bombarding a woman out of nowhere wasn't something I'd ever considered doing. She up and left once my dad was killed, so seeing her and getting to question someone about the past and then praying they could shed some light on the future had me wanting to type out an immediate yes.

My fingers hovered over the keys.

> I'll give you an answer when the sun is out. Go to bed.

CORRIN

> Bossy, but I like it. Fine, I will await your thoughts. It can be a girl's trip! Well, including Beau but he's one of us. I'll look up dog friendly hotels!

> I haven't said yes, Corrin

CORRIN

> yes, but you will. You are playing hard to get and it's cute. Sleep tight!

"All good?" Asher asked, concern etching his tone.

I placed my phone face down on the coffee table and nodded. "Yeah, just fine."

"Right. What was it you said earlier? Oh, right. 'Don't treat me like I'm dumb'." He raised an eyebrow at me.

I let out a soft laugh, but chose to talk about something else. "We should let everyone in on what's going on...with me?"

"Your erratic nightmares?"

I bit my lower lip. "Yes. I told River that we all need to be more open and it's only fair. Whoever got into his head is probably associated with the same person who did this to me. They are probably people we don't even know who either got manipulated just like Grayson or are just inherently bad people, I don't know, but everyone being so in the dark isn't helping."

Asher ran a hand over his mouth. "All? So, you were actually serious when you spoke about having a talk with Grayson?"

"I guess so."

Asher let out a *hmph* and then rubbed his hands on the front of his thighs. "You are aware that means no more throwing accusations at any of us? None of us are out to get you."

"Baby steps, Asher. Your brother was just mentally harmed, so you can't blame me for assuming you made a choice."

He pinched the bridge of his nose, removing his glasses. "How many times do I need to tell you…"

"I'm sorry, okay?"

He left his glasses resting on his thigh and grabbed my chin, forcing me to look at him. He was so close to me, his words whispered against my mouth. "I invade your dreams to mess with you, help you or bring you pleasure, but that is all. I can protect my brother and I can also protect you, got it?"

I moved my eyes over his face seeing the need for me to understand in his eyes. "Yes, *sir*."

He removed his hand from my chin and put his glasses back on. I watched as he rose from the couch, rolling his shoulders. He headed for the stairs and he didn't look back.

I turned my phone over, settling back on the couch and scrolling to my email. I found one from yesterday evening.

Miss Riley Monroe,

We look forward to your attendance at the Celica coven meeting this coming Monday at 7 o'clock pm, If this interferes with any classes, please respond to this email. If not, then we look forward to welcoming you into the family.

Attached below you will find the meeting site posted for your convenience. Please be prompt.

I tilted my phone so that it touched my forehead and I sighed. This was all moving very fast and I just wanted it to slow down.

But it seemed like even that was asking too much.

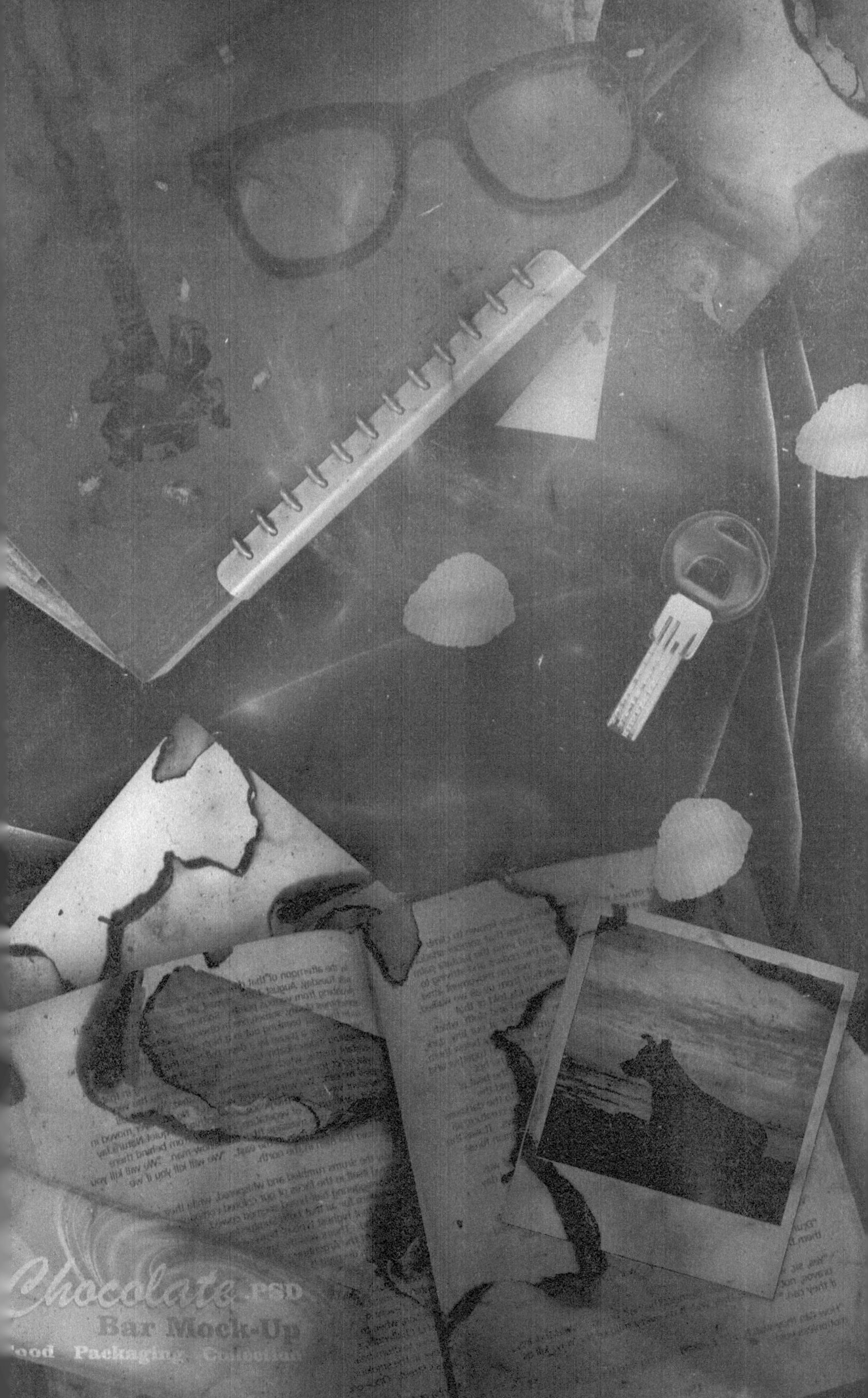

26
GRAYSON

"O*o, okay lang yung unang araw.* I told you yesterday it was fine." I kept my voice on a reassuring level with my mom. We'd spoken for three hours on the phone last night and the conversation had gone like every time we'd ever spoken while I was at school.

"Don't get snippy with me. You sound stressed."

I sighed, hearing footsteps on the stairs. I turned around, keeping the phone to my ear. Riley was at the bottom step, focusing her gaze on me. She had some of her braids tied together in a bun on top of her head, while the rest fell down her back. The casual pink dress she wore had tiny purple lilies and it hit right at mid-thigh, leaving her legs and the miles of brown skin exposed and glorious.

"Grayson. *Nakikinig ka pa ba sakin?*"

I cleared my throat, focusing on my mom again. "Yes, I'm listening. I have to go, but I'll call you later, love you." I tucked my phone in my pocket and watched as she walked into the kitchen, breezing past me.

Asher sat coffee cups down in front of both me and River. He placed one down in front of Riley, then River went to the fridge, getting a bottle of vanilla creamer and pouring a hefty amount into her cup. She gave him a genuine smile which he responded to by giving her a quick kiss. I was fucking jealous of my best friend.

Riley took a sip of her coffee, drumming her fingers on the mug. Asher removed his glasses, keeping his eyes on her as he cleaned them.

"I'm joining Celica. Don't fight me on it. It's happening." She took another sip of her coffee.

River's eyes widened. "I'm sorry, what?"

She peeked over at him and casually shrugged. Riley smacked her lips together and continued, "I'll have Corrin, so it's not a big deal."

"Ah yes, let's just let your witchy friend protect you," Asher said, shaking his head.

"You didn't mind her helping out when she picked me up from the station," Riley spat back, raising one of her eyebrows.

Asher narrowed his eyes. "Touché."

"Is that what you were talking about when I found you, Corrin and Ike in the library?" I asked, keeping my eyes on her.

She moved her eyes over to me. "Yeah, basically."

"Baby, why would you even want to do that?" River ran a hand through his hair, far more agitated than I'd ever seen him.

"I'm trying to be as smart as possible when it comes to Chancellor Fowler and being a part of Celica will make him happy enough to get him off my back for now. He said so. I might not be able to do fuck all with whatever your dad is up to, but I can do this."

"So, you plan on stalling?" I pushed, tilting my head to the side.

She threw me a disgruntled expression. "No, well…I don't know. Isn't that all we *can* do right now?"

River waved his hands in front of his face. "Wait. He said so? Like during your time with him after—" he snuck a look in my direction. "Um, after the whole meeting catastrophe?"

Riley shook her head slowly. "No, yesterday morning."

"YESTERDAY—"

Asher put his hand up to stop his brother. "That part isn't important. The one thing Grayson said a while back rings true. The chances of Chancellor Fowler hurting you are slim, at least physically anyway. He'll use everything around you before laying a finger on you."

Riley used her top teeth to tug at her bottom lip. "I also had an odd nightmare when you went out riding one night."

River's eyes widened for the second time.

"And last night as well."

My best friend's eyes nearly exploded out of their sockets. "What the actual fuck is going on?!" He looked from me to Asher, zeroing in on his brother. "Did you know about this?"

Asher sighed. "Yes, I helped her through it each time." His tone was leveled and clear.

"I appreciate that, but fuck, is today give River a fucking heart attack day?" River placed his elbows on the counter, dropping his head into his hands.

"You waited to tell me about your mind fuckery while you were with Grayson, so let's just call it even." Riley rubbed his back while she stared at me. "Everything keeps piling up, so I wanted nothing to be a surprise. I already called Corrin this morning. She's going to try to make something to help shield my mind. *Try* being the operative word."

"Everything that happens to you is far more important than anything happening to us. We will never be even, gorgeous." River grabbed her arm, moving it so he could hold her hand.

Asher drained the last of his coffee. "Well, since we are offering things up..." he looked at his brother. "I told dad where Riley was the night she got caught in her dad's office."

River choked on his coffee, groaning. "What the actual–"

Riley sighed. "It's in the past. I forgave him and we can move on." She batted her eyelashes at him and my best friend seemed to settle down, giving his brother a mild glare.

"Anyone else want to offer up anything worth mentioning?" Asher blinked over to Riley. "Unless you have more to say."

She threw him a fake smile, rolling her eyes.

I reached behind me, rubbing the back of my neck, clearing my throat. "Theo Ellis."

They all turned their heads to look at me. Asher furrowed his brows. "Who?"

"He's a junior and also has a work study at the library. I went to talk to him yesterday after you left—" I nodded towards Riley. "—and he's been in contact with Oliver and Chancellor Fowler."

"And he just told you that?" Riley questioned, her voice almost full of disbelief.

"It didn't take much, but I know how to get information when I want it. Especially when I know it's for your wellbeing." I raised both my eyebrows and I heard her breath hitch.

"You didn't hurt him, right?" She walked around River, getting closer to me.

I sighed, knowing that question was coming. "No, of course not. He may have pissed his pants, sure, but he left unharmed and probably relieved he told someone."

"Told someone what?" River pressed, the color of his tattoos sharper under the kitchen light.

I chewed on the inside of my cheek, leaning forward on the counter. "He's the one who went and got Marianne."

I watched Riley's throat move as she swallowed. Her eyes glazed over a bit, like she was returning to that moment that broke her. She blinked a few times before responding. "Was she the only one?"

"Chancellor Fowler had him keep an eye on the coven as their shadow. He told him that 'he's using his powers so think of it like extra credit.' Theo is also on a scholarship, Riley. He was literally shaking the entire time he spoke to me. Chancellor Fowler told him Marianne was someone who was threatening the coven, so if Theo wanted to be a hero, then he'll do what he asked." I clucked my tongue. "He asked me if she was okay, if everything ended up alright.

I really didn't have the heart to tell him so I just changed the subject. He told me he hadn't heard from the chancellor since taking Marianne and he was better off for it. He kept apologizing to me and asked if I was going to tell his parents." I rubbed my forehead with two of my fingers.

"He fucked with a lot of people." Riley was speaking more to herself than to any of us. Her words were muffled under her breath as she stared right through me.

"Is the kid okay?" Asher asked, running his hand along his beard.

"Yeah, I guess so. I don't know how Chancellor Fowler is picking his helpers, but at least we know he isn't afraid to go for the most vulnerable and not just the strongest."

"So basically anyone who isn't in our immediate circle is a threat?" River asked, pursing his lips.

"It's a little harsh, but yeah, for now that's how it has to be." Asher explained, crossing his arms over his chest.

River came up behind Riley. "Which brings us back to you joining Celica. We don't know who is on his side. They may not know he was siphoning power but someone in Celica could be dangerous to you."

Riley looked over her shoulder. "I can't just sit around. Complying doesn't mean giving up. It's just giving us more time. I can fake smiles with the best of them."

"Our little detective strikes again," Asher joked, licking his lips.

Riley let out a small chuckle, taking in a short breath when I delicately clutched her wrist. She looked down at my much larger hand. One of her braids swung near the side of her face and I wanted to take it between my fingers and casually play with it...like I used to.

"I can go with you to the Celica meeting. I can do what Theo did." My heart was beating hard against my chest, but every word came out without an issue. No stutter, no mumbling. I meant everything I said. "I can be your shadow, *aking sinta*."

She hadn't stopped staring at my hand placement, but the minute the endearment came out of my mouth she ripped her hand away. She took a few steps back, colliding with River who held her steady.

I closed my eyes, taking in air through my nose and opening my mouth to let it out. I understood but I still fucking hated this. I pushed away from the counter, watching Asher run one of his fingertips over his eyebrow, looking as if he didn't really know what to say.

"I'm sorry, Riley. Just let me know what you want, I'll do anything. I'm at your disposal. I always have been despite what you think."

River gripped her arm, but she brushed him off, taking a small step towards me. She knitted her eyebrows together as if she was thinking. She opened her mouth to speak but then closed it. Her shoulders slumped like the words she had wanted to say were gone now.

I gave one solid nod and turned around, walking towards the guest room.

"Grayson." I heard her say my name the minute I closed the door behind me. I leaned against it, tilting my head back.

If she didn't want me to go to the meeting with her then I would go without her knowledge. I just wanted to make sure she was safe. A small part of myself wanted to prove something to her, but I also just instinctively wanted to prove to myself that I was a good person. Even if I'd broken our relationship permanently or I never got to touch her skin or kiss her lips again, that wouldn't stop me from always watching her and making sure she never got hurt ever again.

"I'm fine, it's okay." I heard her say from outside the door and then footsteps came closer. I moved away and the doorknob turned. I backed up to the other side of the room, focusing my attention on Riley and River.

She stepped into the room; her fists balled at her sides. River stayed at the threshold, watching her like his life depended on it. I was mentally preparing myself for all things she could say to me, all the venom she could rightfully spew in my direction. Her eyes scanned my entire body and she pressed her lips into a hard line.

"You'll do anything?" she asked, her expression neutral.

"What?" The way she looked at me made my shoulders stiff.

"You told me you would do anything."

I nodded, not knowing where this was going, but for her, I honestly didn't care.

27
RILEY

I stared at Grayson from across the room, my hands shaking at my sides. I had so many feelings: love, anger, regret, lust.... they were all too much and I had to work to swallow down every bit of need I felt to let all of them out at once. Every time he said those stupid fucking words, 'I'm sorry', I wanted to take them and shove them back into his mouth. They were just words and once they left his lips, once they were out in the world and floating around, they didn't mean much anymore. I couldn't do anything with those words.

They were just *fucking* words.

My mouth dropped open a bit, taking in a small breath. Grayson remained silent, flicking his eyes from River to me. I glanced over his features, at every inch of him and he looked defeated and upset. His deep brown eyes seemed to always have this look of pleading whenever I granted him my attention and something inside my chest sparked.

Just let me know what you want, I'll do anything.

My lips pressed into a hard line and I peeked over my shoulder at my boyfriend. "We'll be fine. You can go."

I caught River's skeptical expression and then he nodded, giving Grayson one last look and then stepped out of the room. The door clicked and I brought my hands up into my braids, lifting them off my neck and then letting them fall. My gaze fell to the floor, staring at my feet.

"Just tell me what you want, Riley." His tone matched his eyes. Pleading, again.

I blinked and before I knew it, I was walking over to him. I slipped off my dampener ring this morning, leaving it in River's room. My hand was still shaking, but now it was just tiny twitches of my fingers as I skated them over his arm, across his chest and towards his throat.

"What do I *want*?" It was a simple question that held so much weight. "I want my life back, I want my best friend back, I want that 'ignorance is bliss' feeling back." He lifted his hand up to try to comfort me, but I swatted it away. My fingers traced his Adam's apple. He watched me closely; his eyes trained on my every movement. I examined the way he swallowed under my hand. "You want to know what I want from *you*, Grayson?"

"Yes, Riley, just tell—" His last words came out choked when I wrapped my hand around the front of his neck. I used my powers to put pressure around his throat, pressing and pressing. I started to move forward, forcing him back with more of my power so that he stumbled backwards. I made it quick so that his back hit the wall and I kept him in place.

I wasn't choking him enough so that he would suffocate, but it was enough to get his attention. He wasn't clawing at his neck the way my mom had. What happened with her was uncontrolled, but this...this was different. My powers didn't feel overwhelming in this moment, like they had with her. I felt like I was back in River's bedroom with just him and I, his face between my legs with that sensationally content feeling.

I stood up on my tip toes and trailed my nose along his jaw. "You worked for Chancellor Fowler and Oliver St. James; you gave them your loyalty. You were scared, you thought you had no other options, so you did what you thought was best, hmm?" I pulled back, slowly nodding my head. "Say yes or no, Grayson."

"Y-yes." His answer came out strangled, but it was clear enough. I was giving him enough air, feeling his pulse point along my fingers.

I let my nose rub against his, our lips barely touching. I pressed my body more into his chest, feeling his heart thump. "You made me feel safe. And now you want to know how we get back to that place, how you earn me and get back in my good graces?"

His breath was against my lips. "Yes. Y-yes."

He wasn't pulling away from me and he wasn't scared of me. It felt like he was pushing towards me, like he was leaning into the force I had against his throat. I shoved my powers against his chest, jolting him back against the wall. He let out a groan, closing his eyes.

"Everything you gave Chancellor Fowler, every ounce of effort you put into all the fucked up things they asked of you, you give that to *me*. You don't answer to them anymore; you don't owe *them* anything." I brought my face back to his, letting my tongue come out and flick against his bottom lip. "I want your loyalty, Grayson. That's how you get me."

His eyes opened and they were filled with this kind of unbridled desire that I couldn't look away from. I liked where I had him, the power I had over him and from the looks of it, so did he. I never let my eyes leave him when I placed my free hand at his stomach, sliding it down until I could cup my hand around his erection. He hissed the minute I made contact and the sound sent a shiver down my spine.

"I want your shadows to never be used against me again. You get my heart and those shadows will protect it because part of it will be yours," I started to rub him through his pants, my teeth sinking into my bottom lip. He remained against the wall, taking in small breaths against the strain on his neck, but his eyes pierced into my soul. His eyebrows furrowed when I rubbed harder, "and you'll be mine. You'll be my good boy again."

I nearly thought I heard him whimper. I fumbled with the buttons on his jeans, unzipping them and plunging my hand inside. He was so hard and I added a tiny bit more pressure to his throat. "Can you do that?"

He was panting now and his lips pressed together each time I stroked his cock. "Fuck, yes, Riley. You have my loyalty. You'll always have it. I'm yours, I'm your good boy."

I let out a satisfied *hmph* and ripped my hand out of his pants. I used my powers to shove him away from me. He sucked in a breath when his throat was released and watched me. I turned around, but I didn't plan on leaving the room. No, I was getting what I wanted. I sauntered over to the mattress, settling down on top of it. I bent my knees so that the hem of my dress inched up and slid a little up my thighs.

Grayson noticed every single thing, running a hand through his hair. One of my braids fell into my face and I left it there, sticking my tongue out to lick at my lips and watch him. He started to come over, but I lifted my hand letting the force from my magic stop him. He gave me a confused expression but didn't make a move to challenge me.

My eyes slowly moved to the floor and then back up at him. I tilted my head to the side, giving him a small smile. "Crawl."

He reared his head back, taken aback by my demand.

"I want your loyalty and I want you to crawl to me. Crawl to what you want the most."

His chest rose and fell as he regarded me for a moment. It was like he had to readjust to understand what he was seeing, what was happening right in front of him. On the outside I said my demands and I didn't hold back, but on the inside, I was a bundle of nerves. I had never been *this* forward. It was different when I was being playful and giving them both the go ahead to have their way with me, but this was me knowing that I somehow held a lot of power over Grayson and using it.

I wasn't trying to be malicious and I didn't want to hurt him. I wanted to be the reason why he stopped and thought about his decisions from now on. He wanted me and I couldn't help but want him too, but I'd been through far too much to make things easy.

He looked at the floor and as if it was in slow motion, he descended to the ground. His knees hitting first and then he bent over, placing his hands flat in front of him with his head down

"Hmm." I hummed, looking over to the door. "Make sure he knows what's happening."

Grayson brought his head up, following my eyes. "River?"

I smirked at him. "Yes, River."

"Whatever you want." He looked away from the door and back at me, staring straight into my eyes. My breathing started to increase as I watched him start to crawl over to me. One hand in front of the other, he moved with this sexy elegance that I didn't think was possible. It was almost like he wanted to impress me with how well he could obey. The sudden urge to rub my thighs together for friction surprised me and I could feel myself getting more and more turned on.

He got closer and closer until he was right in front of me. I spread my legs a bit, so he could get between them. Grayson sat back on his heels, his fingers flexing as if he was itching to touch me, but he kept them on top of his thighs. I leaned over, taking his face in my hands. I tilted his chin up and ran my lips over his. His body shuddered and I sighed with a kind of satisfaction I didn't know I could feel. "You are very obedient."

"For you, always," Grayson declared, adoration in his tone.

I dragged my hand into his hair, letting his silky dark locks fall between my fingers. His face scrunched in a bit of pain when I tugged on his hair, keeping his face up. "All your loyalty, all your effort, is mine."

"Yes," he answered, trying his best to nod under my hold.

"Say it."

"All my loyalty, all my effort is yours."

I used my other hand to cup his cheek, my thumb running over his lips. "I give you my heart back and you take care of it. You come to me if you are in trouble, you let me—us—help you." I tried not to let my voice crack, feeling a strain in my chest from the effort I put in. I didn't want to see him or any of them end up like Marianne or my dad.

"I promise. I'm with you. You. Have. Me," he enunciated every word, throwing each one at me and hoping they would hit.

He looked like he was ready to kiss me. And I knew that kiss was going to make me feel so many things I'd been missing. I wanted one more thing.

"What does it mean?"

He tenderly touched where I had grabbed his hair the moment I let him go. "What does what mean?"

I placed my hands on the bed, picking at the material. "What you used to call me."

He closed his eyes, letting out a breath. He brought his hands up to my knees, hovering before they touched my skin. His eyes looked at me in question, asking for permission. I nodded, feeling a familiar heat between my legs when his fingers caressed my skin.

"It means," he started, inching his hands up my legs, tucking his fingers beneath my dress, "my love or my darling, whichever you'd prefer honestly."

I caught him off guard when I gripped his shoulders and held him in place with my powers, kissing him. It took him a matter of five seconds to kiss me back, moaning into my mouth. It was overwhelming and needy, the way our tongues danced together was sensual and I missed him so fucking much.

I pulled back, seeing the dazed look in his eyes. "Say it. Call me it again."

He got closer, rubbing his nose against mine, whispering at my lips. "*Aking sinta.*"

The place between my legs grew wetter and squirmed. I slid back a little on the bed, opening my legs a little more. "If I'm your love, if I'm your darling, then be a good boy and make me come."

We both heard a sharp *fuck* from beyond the door and I knew River was clearly getting a play by play of everything.

"Do it quickly," I added, letting out a soft moan when he slid his index finger up my inner thigh.

Grayson settled himself between my legs comfortably. "Yes, ma'am."

In a matter of seconds, my panties were yanked down my legs and his face was buried in my pussy. He licked me like he was starving and his need for air was nonexistent. I arched my back, feeling his tongue circle my clit. He held onto the outside of my thighs, digging his fingers into my skin as he stuck his tongue inside of me. I reached down and threaded my fingers through his hair, pulling him closer to me. He hummed against my pussy, sending a shockwave of pleasure through my body.

"Fuck, you taste so good," he complimented, flicking his tongue along my sensitive clit. One of his fingers slipped inside and my eyes rolled back. His shadows stroked my inner thighs, tickling me and making me whimper.

"Keep going," I urged, moving my hips up and into his face.

"I've missed this pretty little cunt." He pressed another finger inside, fucking me with them while keeping a rhythm at my clit with his tongue.

I was panting and my pussy clenched around his fingers with each stroke. I ran my hand over my breasts and into my hair. I could feel the sensation of my orgasm rising with the way he sucked on my clit and I couldn't take it anymore.

My thigh muscles tightened, and I tugged on the fabric of the mattress as I came. He kept licking me through it, never letting up, even when I was shaking. His lips touched my inner thighs, planting kisses and causing me to twitch even more.

He looked up at me with a twinkle in his eye. "How did I do?"

I let out a breath. "Very good. You did very good."

He continued to kiss up my body, over my dress and between my breasts. He moved his fingers over my nipples. "Was I a good boy, *aking sinta?*"

I hummed, his kisses finding my collarbone and then my throat. "Yes, you were such a good boy for me." He started to descend his mouth on my lips, but I pushed up, grabbing his arms and shifting away from him. I managed to get him to turn over, kicking my leg over his body and straddling his lap. I tucked my fingers into his waistband and shimmied his jeans down towards his knees, letting his cock spring free.

I readjusted myself along his lap, letting my pussy rub against his hard cock. He groaned, planting his hands firmly at my waist. His eyes were transfixed on where I was grinding myself against him. My arousal coated his cock, while I slid back and forth, the head of his dick hitting my clit.

His breathing was sharp and I ran my hands up his shirt, raking my nails down his chest. "Does that feel good?"

He audibly gulped. "Fuck, yes."

I stuck my tongue between my teeth and did something I had only done one other time. I opened up my mind and let it travel to River.

I need you.

It took all of two seconds for him to come through the door. Grayson and I both swiveled our heads to look in his direction and River stopped dead in his tracks. I hadn't stopped moving my hips and Grayson hadn't let go of my waist. My boyfriend's mouth dropped open and he slowly looked over his shoulder at the open door.

He focused back on me. *I can call Asher and...*

No, not this time. I just want you.

River was silent when he closed the door and walked over to the side of the mattress. His green eyes glazed over with desire as he tried to take in the scene in front of him. He cut his gaze to me.

You haven't talked to me in my head since you gave me your phone number.

You really want to go down memory lane right now?

He chuckled. *The fact that you are choosing this moment is sexy as fuck. My naughty little witch.*

Heat creeped up my cheeks as I watched the dimples in his own cheeks appear with his smile. He crouched down near the mattress, swiping my braids over my back. He looked down at Grayson's cock that was coated in my arousal.

"Fuck, you're so wet. You two put on such a good show." He pressed a knee into the mattress and shuffled over so he was behind me. River looked over my shoulder at Grayson, placing his hands over his best friends and helping me move. "Is he back on your good side?"

I bit my bottom lip, nodding, leaning back against his chest.

"Did he eat your pussy the way you like?"

I moaned as I rubbed myself harder against Grayson, whose hips flexed with each movement. His groans were making me wetter and River's voice in my ear was almost too much. "Mmhmm." It was all I could muster.

River reached down, so that his fingers grazed my clit. He rubbed it, his fingers getting wet from me. I sucked in a breath, feeling another orgasm begin to build. River took his fingers and extended them towards Grayson's mouth. My shadow wielder eagerly took his best friend's fingers between his lips and sucked off my taste.

"That's a good boy," River praised, kissing my shoulder. "Is he good enough to be inside of you?"

I lifted my body up, taking his cock in my hand and rubbing the tip along my soaking pussy. Grayson's hooded eyes watched as I sunk down onto his cock, his mouth falling open in a silent sigh. His shadows came out slowly, slithering over my skin and caressing me.

"Oh my god, oh god," I moaned, rocking back and forth feeling him inside of me. River cupped my breasts in his hands, nipping at my earlobe.

"Fuck, you feel good. That tight pussy is fucking choking my cock." Grayson's biceps flexed and tensed as I moved. He held my waist tighter and I knew what he wanted.

"You want to fuck me, Grayson?" I asked, rising and falling back down on his length.

"I'm sure he is dying to pound that wet cunt." River pinched my nipples through my dress. "You come first and then he'll get his turn, right?" His question was intended for Grayson.

"Yes. She comes first." Grayson lazily nodded, as he trailed his hand up my body and found River's hand. He pulled on the center of my dress, exposing one of my breasts. River released the other one and they both played with me while I rode Grayson's cock. I started to bounce up and down, rotating my hips and bringing myself closer and closer to a climax. Grayson let his shadows circle my hips and travel to my clit, fluttering over it and causing stars to shine behind my eyes when I came. I felt my body heat up, the fire within me simmering, but I made sure it didn't get to be too much. I could control myself...I knew how to be with them and I felt safe.

River held onto me while Grayson sat up, pulling my face forward and kissing me. I felt high but this just felt right. My face was pulled away from Grayson and turned so I could kiss River. He tugged on my lower lip. "Such a good girl."

I kissed him deeper and this time I nipped at his top lip. "Make him come."

Chocolate .PSD
Bar Mock-Up
ood Packaging Collection

28
RIVER

Riley eased herself off of Grayson's lap, collapsing next to him. She turned over so that she could face him and kissed his shoulder. His cock was still so hard and glistening from being inside her perfect pussy. My girl wanted me to make him come so I would do exactly as she asked. I leaned down, taking Grayson's face in my hands and kissed him.

It hadn't been that long since the last time our lips touched, but right now, this moment was everything to me. His tongue came out and tangled with mine, while my hand snuck down his body and gripped his dick. I stroked it, licking at his lips as he kissed me back deeper and with more aggression. I pressed my forehead to his, glancing over at my girlfriend who had this look of utter adoration, her tongue poking out and licking at her bottom lip.

I inclined my head towards her and pecked her lips, granting me a giggle.

Grayson huffed out a breath from the way I continued to jerk his cock. Precum coated my hand along with Riley's arousal. I removed my hand, bringing it to my face and licked my palm. I sucked each of my fingers into my mouth, making sure I didn't miss anything. They both looked at me with desire in their eyes and all I did was smirk and shuffle back so that I could be eye level with my best friend's cock.

I gave no warning before I licked the underside, still tasting her on the smooth skin of his shaft. I held his dick towards his stomach, flatting my tongue to lick stripe after stripe over his length.

"Oh fuck," Grayson moaned, pressing his head back against the mattress.

My tongue swirled around the head of his cock before I sucked him into my mouth. I relaxed my throat, taking him further down. The choking sound I made had his thighs tensing, a guttural sound expelling from his lips.

I flicked my eyes up and noticed his eyes were closed, his stomach hollowing out each time I bobbed up and down. Riley placed her hand at his cheek, making his eyes flutter open.

"Don't close your eyes. Watch him."

He nodded as if he was in a daze and focused his deep brown eyes on me. I stroked his cock with my mouth and one of my hands, while I worked to unbutton my pants with the other. I freed my cock, immediately beginning to jerk myself off.

"The way you two look at each other is so hot," Riley admitted, running her hand along Grayson's stomach and licking his earlobe.

I continued to gag on his dick, letting it nearly hit the back of my throat and I let my mind wander to his. *You can have both of us now that you've learned your lesson.*

One of his eyebrows twitched. *I missed you. I missed this.* He moved his eyes over to Riley, who kissed him deeply before maneuvering his head to continue looking at me.

I've missed this too.

He sighed, instantly groaning when I popped off his cock, needing to slow my own hand down so I wouldn't come yet. I licked every inch of his shaft, playing with his balls and then diving back down to take him in my mouth again.

Your cock tastes amazing, especially when it's covered in her. You plan to fill my mouth up like a good boy? I thought, causing his hips to jerk upward. He slowly started to fuck my face and I let him. The metal of my piercing ran across my fingers as I stroked myself, feeling a pleasurable sensation creep up my spine.

Only if you plan to swallow all of it. He thought back, reaching down and gripping my hair.

Believe me, I don't plan to waste anything. Do what she wants and come for her.

Riley was lightly scratching his skin and breathing against his neck, but when Grayson connected his eyes with mine again, I knew he was done for. He thrusted into my mouth roughly, releasing down my throat. Riley lifted herself up to watch me swallow. I let go of his cock a minute before I came, coating my hand, parts of the mattress and Grayson's pants that were still hanging at his knees.

Riley walked on her knees over to me, swiping her thumb over the corner of my mouth. She popped that thumb between her lips. "Missed some." She leaned in and kissed my chest, surprising me by bending over and taking my cock in her mouth.

I was way too sensitive right now for that, but fuck her mouth felt good. Her tongue ran over my piercing, and I hissed. She let out a soft laugh before straightening up. She fell back on the mattress and Grayson kicked off his cum stained pants. I settled down next to her, moving my body towards her so she was squeezed between me and my best friend.

"I could go for a nap," I announced, placing my arm behind my head.

Riley laughed, pushing up and away from us so she could get on her feet. "Well, I have to go to the bathroom but get comfortable." She stepped over Grayson and padded towards the bathroom.

She made it to the side of the mattress before the door opened. We all stared wide eyed at Asher, who looked unamused as he took in everything he was seeing. He started to rub his temples. "So, I'm going to assume there will be no more silent treatment or awkward cold shoulders anymore?"

Riley nodded. "You assumed correct." She walked over to him, resting her hand on his chest. His shoulders stiffened, but he didn't back away. "Do you want to join in on the snuggling?"

I couldn't see her face, but I knew she was batting her eyelashes.

Asher peeked over her shoulder at me and Grayson. "I'll pass, but by all means, take a nap at noon."

"We exhausted a lot of energy, Ash," I answered, smiling at him.

He rolled his eyes, reaching for his back pocket. He plucked out Riley's phone, handing it to her. "Corrin has called eight times since you've been in here." Asher pointed at me. "*You* are washing these sheets. There is no fucking way I'm touching them."

Grayson stifled a laugh. I focused on Riley's face, which had contorted into a more serious expression. Her fingers swiped up as she scrolled through her phone.

"Everything okay, gorgeous?"

Asher tried to look at her screen but she turned away from him, bringing it closer to her face. He grabbed her arm, guiding her back over to him. "No more secrets, little liar."

She sighed. "Ugh, fine."

We sat in the living room, after getting dressed and let Riley tell us all about what Corrin and Ike had discovered. She sat on my lap while she spoke with her hands and occasionally, I would feed her tiny pretzels in between sentences. Beau sat at her feet, giving us all judgmental looks as we settled down, but it was like he noticed how calm she was now that the tension between us was starting to dissipate.

"Well, do you want to go?" Grayson asked, twirling his shadows between his fingers.

"Even if she slams the door in my face, I kind of feel like I should at least try. She didn't like my mom, but why do all that to help her—help me – and then just disappear. It has to do with Chancellor

Fowler most likely and that's honestly enough for me to want to try." She opened her mouth for me to drop another salty snack onto her tongue.

Asher sat at the end of the couch, his elbow propped up on the arm. "Okay, so we can leave tomorrow. We'll get the wolf shifter to watch the dog."

Riley fidgeted with her fingers, chewing on her pretzel slowly. He narrowed his eyes. "What?"

"It's a girl's trip," she replied.

"And that's supposed to mean something to me?" he pressed, not looking away from her.

Riley let out an annoyed huff. "You are all very protective and I appreciate that, but Corrin and I have this. Based on her text, I think Jade is coming too. Mateo has the wolves keeping an eye on my mom. She has a hotel lined up for us to stay in overnight and it's pet friendly so we'll take Beau. I'll be back Sunday, I promise."

Asher gave her a skeptical look.

She crossed her arms over her chest. "Napa Valley is not super far. If I need you, I'm pretty sure you can get to me. Corrin helped figure it out, so she's who I want with me. I'm not going to let that fucking man scare me and run my life from afar. I've already planned to call my mom on the way, maybe get some insight from her." Riley shrugged, slipping off of my lap. "Actually, it doesn't really matter what you say since while we were all getting settled in here, I already texted Corrin to come by and pick me up in a few hours when she's done helping her mom."

Grayson cackled. "This whole thing was an update for us and you just planned to leave anyway?" She shrugged at him, sticking her tongue out.

I grabbed her waist, pulling her back against me. "That's not very nice, gorgeous."

She swatted me away, walking past Asher, who pushed against her shoulder, so she had to stumble back a few steps. "You have no fucking idea how badly I want to make your ass red from my hand right now."

She tapped his nose. "I think I have an idea, *sir*. Maybe you can do it in my dreams while I'm gone."

I placed my hand over my mouth to stop my smile. The amount of challenge in her voice had me wanting to take her right on our coffee table. She had so much fight and determination, despite the things that had happened to her. I was proud of her to say the least.

I walked around the coffee table and turned her to look at me. "You call if anything happens. Nightmares, Chancellor Fowler pops up, anything happens...you call us."

She got on her toes and rubbed her nose against mine. "I promise."

Chocolate.psd
Bar Mock-Up
ood Packaging Collectio

29
RILEY

I zipped up my overnight bag, sitting down next to it on River's bed. Beau jumped up on the bed, a book between his teeth. He dropped it in my lap, nudging his nose against my shoulder. I picked up the book, examining the cover.

You think I'll have time to read while I'm in Napa Valley.

He sighed. *For the car ride.*

I scratched underneath his chin. *Good thinking. Although, I have a feeling I'm too in my head to even pay attention to a book right now.*

But this one has cowboys.

A laugh erupted from my throat. *I didn't know you could read.*

He laid down and rolled over, so he exposed his stomach to me, his tail wagging between his open legs. *You also weren't aware you could talk to me either. We learn new things every day, Mom.*

I ran my hand along his belly, hearing the door open. Asher came in, leaning against the doorway.

"Your witch friend is here."

"She has a name."

He continued to stare at me, unamused. I challenged his stare and then when he finally conceded, he groaned. "Corrin is here. Better?"

I smiled a little. "Good boy, much better."

Hopping off the bed, I grabbed my bag which he immediately took from me, hooking it over his shoulder. Beau raced past him and barreled down the stairs. Asher stopped me from walking any further. "Don't call me that. I'm not your shadow wielder. I'm not your good boy."

I hummed, tapping his chest. "So what? Are you, my *sir*?"

"Is that what you want?" he questioned, leaning down towards my face.

I lifted on my toes and kissed his lips softly. Pulling away, I turned so I could walk backwards out of the room. "I believe in mutual respect, so if that's what you want then well, I'd have to say yes, that's absolutely what I want." I flipped my braids over my shoulder and hurried down the stairs.

The squeal that came from Corrin's lips was unnatural as she ran over to me, squeezing me hard. "Are you ready?!"

"Is this supposed to be a fun trip or an informative one?" Grayson asked, stuffing his hands in his pockets.

Corrin tapped her chin. "That's a mystery, but honestly, I can make anything fun."

Beau whined at her feet, circling her and looking at the front door. Asher came down the stairs, the minute I let Beau outside. Jade leaned against her car, sunglasses propped on her nose and a big smile on her face the minute she saw my familiar.

"Ah! *Mi amor!*" She got down to his level and scratched behind his ears.

We walked outside, Jade taking my bag from Asher and Beau jumping into the backseat.

"You call us the minute you get there." River said this like it was a fact.

"Call you when I get to the hotel or the mysterious woman's house?"

"All of it," they all said in unison. It stunned me to hear them agree completely on something.

Corrin and Jade giggled behind me, pressing their lips together and trying not to make eye contact with me when I peeked over my shoulder at them.

I shook my head, giving them each a kiss on the cheek before I rounded the front of the car to the passenger seat. River jogged over, leaning against the open window. "I mean it, gorgeous. I don't hear from you and I will find you."

"Just say yes to the hot man, please." Corrin pleaded, turning on her car.

I snuck a glance at the others standing on the opposite side of the car as if they were waiting for my answer as well. River waited patiently for my response. I ran my hand through his hair and Beau barked loudly.

"Yes, I'll call."

"That's a good girl." He leaned forward and kissed me quickly. "Take care of her. Both of you."

"You got it!" Jade answered from the back seat.

"YOU HAVE THE CUTEST TOE BEANS, DID YOU KNOW THAT?" JADE ASKED Beau who simply licked her cheek and panted.

Corrin looked in her rearview mirror at them and chuckled. She lightly shoved my shoulder. "Are you prepared with what you're going to say?"

I chewed on the inside of my cheek as I scrolled my phone. "Not in the slightest. How do you start that kind of conversation, while also just completely dismissing the fact that your brother went FBI level hunting to find her?"

"We can leave that part out." She shrugged nonchalantly, changing lanes. "She did some sneaky shit too, so really she has no room to judge."

"Well, when you put it like that..." I started to say sarcastically before my phone vibrated in my hand. My mom's name appeared on my screen.

I answered, putting her on speaker. "Hey, Mom."

"Hi honey, why is there an echo sound? Where are you?"

"Um, Corrin, Jade and I are driving to Napa Valley."

My mom was silent on the other side of the line. "Napa Valley?"

My eyes met Corrin's and then I looked in the back to meet Jade's. The wolf shifter widened her eyes at me as if to say, *well fucking tell her*.

"We are going to see Teresa Lowe. Or Teresa Fowler, or whatever."

"Riley!"

I reduced the volume on my phone. "It's all very spontaneous okay. I'm sorry I'm just telling you now, but mom, just listen to me."

"Riley, that woman wants nothing to do with us. I've told you, she didn't like me then and I'm sure she will think the same about you. I don't understand what you think you'll achieve. You are trying to separate yourself from that man, but it seems like you are just getting closer in a different way."

I rubbed the side of my head. "I know, I know. Mom, if she didn't like you very much then why was she involved in getting you my necklace."

"What do you mean?" She sounded genuinely surprised.

"I know you went to Samia to get my necklace made and she sent you to Evie Malcolm. She was a part of Celica, Mom." I explained everything I knew and she listened, like she always did, without interrupting me.

When I was done, she waited a moment before speaking, "I just trusted Samia since she was who everyone had always recommended when it came to dampeners and other things. Your father is the one who told me about her, since he'd learned some things from the students. When she said she couldn't help me, I was determined to find someone who could. Your powers would only get stronger and despite thinking that Erik was gone, I just didn't want to risk anything. I never interacted with any of the other witches from the coven, just him, so when Samia brought in Evie, I trusted her. She was sweet and wanted to help. I was just so determined to get you situated that I didn't see what was going on."

Corrin jumped in. "Riley's necklace was a super powerful tool that kept her magic in place for years. Teresa had to have known Evie was involved in something like that. She would have wanted to know what it was for and who, just in case any backlash fell onto the coven."

The sound of pacing filled my phone. "Understandable, I guess. Honey, I truly don't know why she would give the okay if she knew it was for me. Maybe she did have a heart somewhere deep, deep down. Or maybe she knew it would continue to keep me away from her..." She sighed.

I bit my thumbnail. "Mom, if you had such a past with Mystic Riegan, why did Dad work there? Why weren't you way more adamant about me not going, even if you thought Chancellor Fowler was gone?"

"Your dad had been working there and he loved it. He was always so proud of what he did and if anything ever seemed off to him, he told me he would say something. And you," she took a moment to consider her words, "your dad's death almost destroyed both of us and as nervous as I was, you were an adult. You were going to head off into the school whether I truly liked it or not. I really don't think explaining my past would have stopped you. You just might have been a bit more cautious."

"Probably not," Jade mumbled under her breath.

I gave her an annoyed look over my shoulder, noticing that Beau was throwing me his judgmental face.

"Are you really sure you want to talk to her?" my mom asked, her voice a little shaky.

Before I could respond, Corrin cut me off. "Don't worry, Mrs. Monroe. We've got her."

I gave her a small smile and she drummed her fingers on the steering wheel, dodging through traffic.

My mom let out a small laugh. "I'll have to take your word for it, but honey, please text or call me when you get there."

Jade stifled a laugh. "Wow, you sound like all of Riley's boyfriends."

"Riley's what?"

I choked on air and struggled to find words. "Umm...hey Mom, you are cutting out. I'll call you later, love you, always and always." I hung up and immediate laughter filled the car at my expense.

I leaned my head back against the headrest. "I'm happy you guys can enjoy a good laugh or two."

Jade leaned forward, placing her hands on my shoulders. "*Necesitas relajarte.* Breathe in, breathe out. Stewing in the car will solve nothing. Once we get to the hotel, we can figure out what the plan is."

"Thirty more minutes to go!" Corrin shouted, suddenly breaking behind a car that randomly decided to stop and pressing on her horn. She shook her head, while I reached for the dashboard. "I also had lots of fun making your little mind potion. I still can't get flavors to be super tasty, but it should help keep your beautiful brain safe for the trip."

"Thanks. I appreciate that and you."

She winked at me, immediately putting her eyes back on the road. Jade popped up into my periphery vision, causing me to turn my head and realize she situated herself onto the center console. "Mateo told me they're going to invite your boyfriends to Marth Moon. Is that to keep an eye on them on our territory? Probably. Anything goes down, there are enough people around to help." She poked my cheek and sunk back into her seat. "You guys are like a part of our family now."

Beau jumped up and licked my face. I wiped the wetness from my skin but found myself laughing just a small bit. My heart hurt for a moment, realizing that Marianne would have loved this. The car ride, the laughs, the unknown for what was ahead. I casually looked at Corrin and Jade, considering that even though I didn't have Marianne—I had them.

30
GRAYSON

I stretched out on the couch, peeking over my book as I watched River and Asher practice mental training. Or mental warm-ups. Or whatever the fuck they were doing. River would close his eyes and relax and Asher would use his magic, then Asher would smack River on the side of his head and tell him to focus when it clearly didn't work. I would have to press my lips together to keep from laughing.

This was solid entertainment since Riley was gone. I missed her and maybe it sounded pathetic to say that, but the minute she drove off, I instantly wanted her back. I heard a frustrated groan and looked over at the St. James brothers.

"Your bedside manner could really use some fucking work," River scolded, swatting Asher's hands away.

"Stop being a baby and focus."

"I swear if you tell me to focus one more fucking time, I'll punch you in the throat."

Asher scoffed. "I would love to see you try, baby brother."

River ran a hand roughly through his hair and shook his shoulders. "Whatever, let's just go again." He closed his eyes, taking a few soothing breaths.

Asher rolled his eyes but focused on his brother. His eyes narrowed, but his body was perfectly still and unbothered. His green eyes widened behind his glasses and he whistled. "Finally. You pushed me back. Not with the impact I would have liked, but I struggled to progress."

River fiddled with one of his earrings. "I'm flattered that you're proud of me." He started to get up from the floor, but Asher grabbed his arm.

"Where are you going? We aren't done."

River wiped a hand down the front of his face. "My brain is tired."

"Your brain is complacent. Sit your ass down and let's do this again." Asher tugged his brother's arm down, causing River to fall back onto the floor.

I kept my finger in my book to hold my place before saying, "You guys are so cute when you bicker. I should get a video for Riley."

"We should probably work on getting your mind prepped too," River suggested, sticking his tongue out at me.

"Since Riley isn't here to distract either of you, I think that's a perfect idea," Asher agreed, patting the space next to River.

My mouth fell open but grabbed my bookmark from the coffee table and placed it in my book before coming over to them and sitting on the floor.

"She distracts you too, by the way," River said, flicking his brother's knee.

Asher gave him a fake smile before smacking the side of his head again.

"Oh my god, it's finally break time. I feel like my brain is pure mush," I complained, rubbing my forehead.

Asher stared down at his phone. "Mmhmm, good." He clutched his phone until his fingers turned nearly white. He blinked up at us. "I'm going out for a little bit."

"Where to?" River asked, raising an eyebrow.

"Out," Asher answered plainly.

"Well, that's not suspicious at all," I said sarcastically, crossing my arms over my chest.

Asher begrudgingly handed River his phone. My best friend scanned the screen, quickly looking at his brother. "Dad contacted you?"

Snatching his phone back, Asher nodded. "If I ignore him, this just gets worse. Riley is doing what she can to keep Chancellor Fowler at bay, so I can do what I can for our own dad. Besides, he needs to answer for whatever the fuck he's doing when it comes to you guys. If the chancellor is making the rules, then clearly dad is out of line on many accounts." Asher went over to the entryway table to grab his keys.

"We'll go with you," River said, coming up behind his brother. I followed, prepared to face Oliver St. James with them. The man has fucked with too many people I cared about.

Asher swiftly turned around. "Nope. You stay here."

"I'm not a fucking kid, Asher."

Asher was already opening the door. "Well aware, but please just do what I say and stay put." He closed his eyes and then looked back at his brother. "I know you can hold your own, okay?"

I placed a hand on River's shoulder and squeezed. I felt the tension in his body start to soften. He waved his hand towards Asher. "Fine. I guess just be careful."

Asher reached out and ruffled his brother's hair. It was a move I'd never seen before, but I knew Asher cared immensely for River, even if it meant throwing himself into the fire just to keep him out of harm's way. River had always told me that he never really understood why Asher took a job at Mystic Riegan or why he always tried to keep a leveled relationship with their dad. Maybe, River was the reason for all of it.

It wasn't really my place to analyze, but as much as Asher could be ice cold sometimes, I could see the cracks in his exterior.

River leaned against the door, blowing out a breath. "What do we do now?"

I smiled at him, letting my shadows come out and move around his neck and through his hair. "Hmm, I don't know. My brain is exhausted so I don't think I can continue reading at the moment; I would rather not do anything that involves a lot of thinking."

River pushed away from the door, my shadows dissipating with his movements. "I might have an idea." He slid his hand down my arm, threading his fingers through mine. He kissed my knuckles and pulled me up the stairs towards his bedroom.

He kicked his door closed with his foot, shoving me against it and kissing me hard. He pressed his body into mine, his tongue exploring my mouth. I moaned against his lips, his hand grazing past my stomach and between my legs.

River rubbed the front of my pants roughly, causing me to groan and thrust my lower body forward. He gripped my shirt and pulled me away from the door, pressing his forehead to mine. He planted one more kiss to my lips, before starting to unbutton my pants.

"You cleared things up with Riley." He shoved my pants down along with my underwear. His fingers started to work opening his own pants. "I think I'll reward you for being such a good boy for our girl."

My heart thundered in my chest and I reached for him, aggressively kissing him. I clawed at his shirt, removing it from his body and helped him with my own. "Are you going to gag on my cock again?" My shadows roamed down his body and wrapped around his length, stroking him.

River bit his lower lip and shook his head. "You get to fuck me."

Blood rushed to my dick and I wrapped my hand around the back of his neck, pulling his face to mine. He gripped my cock in his hand and started to match the rhythm my shadows had on his own cock. Our mutual moaning filled his room and I could have come just like this, but I wanted what he was offering.

Before Riley, we switched it up sometimes, although I did like being on the receiving end more. River always naturally took charge, but he was never afraid to let me take the lead whenever the moment was right. I was eager to be inside of him and be intimate in that way again.

River lightly shoved me back and shuffled to his end table. He pulled out a bottle of lube and tossed it on the bed. I got in front of him, dropping to my knees and taking his cock into my mouth. The metal of his piercing hit my tongue as I sucked him off.

His hands went into my hair, flexing his hips. I started stroking myself, gagging sounds coming from my throat as he fucked my mouth. I licked the head of his dick, straightening up but keeping a hold of my cock, moving my hand in slow, methodical movements along my shaft. River watched my hands as if he was transfixed.

"Turn around."

River didn't look up. "I could…"

I chuckled, taking his chin in my hand and forcing him to look at me. "I'm good, believe me. Turn around and hand me the lube."

"So bossy," River joked, turning around and bending over. He handed me the bottle and I squirted some onto my hand, coating my cock. I drizzled some between his ass cheeks, using my fingers to massage it into his tight hole.

He stifled a moan when my fingers were inside. I stretched him, curling my fingers as I went. I went slowly, but not too slow because I knew he didn't like that. My other hand held his hip tight and I could feel him relaxing more and more, so I added more lube.

"Fuck, fuck, fuck," He mumbled, his head dropping down as his body started to become putty. "Just put it inside, for fucks sake."

I withdrew my fingers, taking my cock and sliding it over his hole. "Say please."

He groaned. "Now."

"Always topping from the bottom." I pushed the head of my cock inside of him, moving delicately. He tensed but then relaxed, taking deep breaths in and out as I moved. He was so tight and I had to pause for a moment to take in how good he felt.

He started to move his ass back, letting me know he needed me to keep going. I inched forward giving him more of me, then a little bit more. I started to pull out, then I pushed back in.

"Fuck, that feels good," he grunted out, falling forward on the bed, propping his ass up more.

I held his hips with both my hands, building up a rhythm. My shadow curled around his legs and started to jerk his cock again. "Your ass looks so perfect filled with my cock."

Too bad our phones are too far away so we can't send a picture to Riley. He thought to me. I started moving faster at the idea of her seeing this. His cock twitched in my shadows grip while I fucked him.

"So tight. You're going to make me come, aren't you?" I gripped his shoulder, hitting him with shallow thrusts. His legs were shaking, but he kept meeting me with each pump of my hips.

My spine tingled and I knew he was so close. I pulled him up by his shoulder, so his back was nestled close to my chest. I kept moving inside of him and working his length.

You plan to make a mess all over your bed? I asked him in my head.

Only if you plan to fill me up. He volleyed back.

That was all it took and I pumped harder, his breathing becoming rougher. I held onto him tightly when I came, releasing everything I had. I replaced my shadows with my hand around his length, continuing to stroke him until I felt hot liquid on my hand and saw it land on his comforter.

I placed my forehead on his shoulder, kissing his skin. I eased out of him, teetering backwards since my legs felt like Jello. River turned around to watch me lick my hand clean and he ran his tongue along his top teeth.

"I'll be right back." I pecked his lips and left to head to his bathroom.

I came back to him sitting on the edge of his bed, still completely naked and typing on his phone.

"What has you so invested?" I asked, picking up my clothes.

"Mateo. They invited us to Marth Moon."

I tugged on my pants. "Does that include free beer?"

River laughed, throwing me my shirt. "Jade is with Riley, so clearly Mateo needs to keep an eye on us. I swear those wolves are worse than my overprotective brother, but they've been good to our girl. I do like the way you think though."

I shrugged, watching him walk past me to the bathroom. "What's the worst that could happen?"

31
ASHER

"What do you want?" I barked, slamming my dad's office door. I didn't see my mother anywhere when I came inside, telling me he must have sent her out. He treated her to nice things like spa days to keep her occupied, which from the outside looked sweet, but I always knew better.

"A hello is the polite way to greet anyone." He shook his head as if he was upset by my lack of respect.

Chancellor Fowler sat in my father's office chair, his hands folded together and planted on the desk. "Lucky for you, my daughter has been compliant enough where I haven't needed to force your hand."

I ignored him to focus on my father. "Did you bring me here to gloat about what you've been doing?" I walked up to the desk, slamming my hands down on it and staring at Chancellor Fowler. "She is joining Celica, she is inching closer and closer and you still let him fuck with my brother's head and meddle in Riley's dreams? She said you claimed you would ease up and yet, it seems you can't keep your fucking word."

Chancellor Fowler reared his head back, giving my father a menacing look. He pushed back the chair, moving his hand in front of him. My dad was thrown back against the wall while he clawed at his throat. "Oliver, what the fuck is he talking about?"

Gasps of air were coming from my father's lips, so the chancellor loosened his hold. "It was nothing. I wasn't harming her. *I* wasn't doing anything."

"River was right. It wasn't you. You tasked others to do it for you," I stated.

Chancellor Fowler walked up to my father, pressing his finger into his chest. My dad winced at the pain, knowing the pressure was digging further into his skin than he would have liked. "I offered you power and what? I'm not moving fast enough for you? My daughter is off limits and I will remind the people working for me that they do not work for *you*." He moved his hand back, my father's back arching off the wall and then threw his hand to the side. My father's body was flung to the right, hitting the other wall. "You do whatever you will to your own son, but my daughter, my rules. You infiltrate her mind, you mess with her everyday life without my consent, and I will kill you. I will break every bone in your body without even touching you and I will do it in front of your precious wife and then guess what? I'll kill her too."

His words came out casually, but I could hear the venom at the end of every sentence. He sat back down in the office chair as if nothing happened while my father tried to clutch the wall to stand back up. Chancellor Fowler gave him a bright smile. "Are we understood?"

My father glanced at me, his eyes filled with malice, but he nodded.

"Perfect." Chancellor Fowler placed his attention back on me. "Now, Asher, is there anything else you'd like to inform me of?"

I opened my mouth to speak but clamped it shut. I didn't actually come here to assist him in anything. "No, not at all."

"Hmm. You do bring up an interesting concept though."

I raised an eyebrow at him.

"Let me ask you a question, Professor. Did my daughter immediately think you caused her nightmare?"

I looked down at the floor, not answering him.

He clucked his tongue. "Interesting indeed. Trust is a funny thing. It's always spoken about and having someone say they trust you is very different then actually believing it. Maybe your magic isn't truly needed at all. The idea that you *could* do those things and that your brother's own mental state is at risk is enough for her to always be on the fence."

"She doesn't..."

He kept going. "One foot always out the door, even though on the outside she'll dote on you and have this supposed connection, but she'll blame you instantly for things you didn't do all because she'll never really trust you...not completely anyway. Not like she does your brother."

My chest rose and fell, but I tried to control the beat of my heart. The look in her eyes when I'd shaken her out of that nightmare and the way she wanted to get away from me had the things he said hitting me all at once.

"You're wrong." I tried to say it with conviction, but the tone of my voice betrayed me.

"I almost think she trusts the shadow wielder more than she trusts you," my dad's voice chimed in.

"You shut up!" I yelled.

Chancellor Fowler tsked. "Don't blame yourself. Riley's eventual tumble into my arms will be of her own volition. I will always protect my daughter, Asher. Unfortunately, what happens to your brother is not my responsibility as long as Riley keeps moving in the direction she's headed. A little mental tussle won't kill the little telepath, so while I don't completely condone what your father did, I can't very well tell him how to discipline his children." His shoulders moved as he chuckled at my brother's expense.

"Discipline? River hasn't done anything to you!"

"Ah, but it just shows what can happen to him. Which has always been my point." My father got up behind me, knocking his shoulder against mine as he walked past. "You should be happy I had someone else do it. You would hate for me to take over."

"I actually just hate you, plain and simple," I spat back.

"Oliver, were you doing those things to your son for Riley's sake or your own personal vendetta?" Chancellor Fowler asked, looking bored.

My father shrugged. "It was for me. It has been a minute since I gave that boy a little nudge, but this time it didn't come from me. Not directly anyway. If things happen with Riley that end up in Erik's favor then it's a win, but I always seem to have to pull your brother down from his *I can do whatever I want attitude*. That is your fault. You coddled your own brother and now anyone can mess with him. You made him weak."

"I protected him!" I shouted. "I protected him from you! You tried to make us fucking entertainers for your friends, feed us magic enhancers before fucking puberty. I didn't coddle him!"

"Protect?" My father let out a loud laugh. "Your brother is right here and so are you. You both have never left me, son. And soon, you'll be just as powerful as I've always planned for you to be." He glanced over at Chancellor Fowler who nodded at him.

"He is at this school because you and mom wouldn't leave him alone about it. I'm here *because* of River. I needed to be a fucking buffer..." I let the words fall away because it didn't matter.

Our dad getting someone to break into River's mind was one of the first times I couldn't help him myself. I had always been there to make his pain go away or even just ease it, even if he'd suppressed so much of it.

My magic was startled awake by my brother's cries. It was like a rumbling in my head and the immense sadness that entered my mind had my heart breaking. I woke myself up, but my mind was still attached to his dream. I stepped into the darkened area he found himself in. It was cold wherever he was and I couldn't see a fucking thing.

I heard his crying and everything around me vibrated. I couldn't see him yet, but I felt his presence, so I kept walking. The cries got louder and louder, eventually I called out his name. I heard a hiccup. I called out again.

"Asher?"

I felt relief wash over me. "It's me, just keep talking."

"I can't see anything. I'm scared." His voice was trembling and shaky.

"I'm coming, okay?" I got up from my bed, throwing open my door while my dream self searched for him. I'd gotten much better with staying in reality while also being in the dreamscape.

I opened River's bedroom door slowly. He'd kicked off his covers and was huddled in the fetal position, tears staining his cheeks. In his dream, I saw movement. I ran over to it, nearly throwing myself at my brother. He was cold and I couldn't see him all that well, but I knew it was him.

"Hey, hey, it's me. I'm here." I brought him closer to me.

"A-are we in my head?" he asked, his teeth chattering.

"Yes. It's going to be okay. Is this about dad?"

River didn't respond but I knew the answer was yes. He was always the problem.

I got on River's bed, pulling his sleeping body in my arms. I pulled the covers over us and combed my fingers through his hair. In his dream, I did the same.

"I'm going to make it better. Like I always do." I filled the room with a warmth that could banish any kind of cold and created a brightness that I knew would put a smile on his face. When the room was filled with light, I looked down at him, watching him take in the change. I let calming smells

enter the space and he inhaled. "Now you can go to sleep. Forget what made you upset and rest."

River's head felt heavy against my chest. "Will you stay with me?"

"I always do."

His dream self started snoring softly and in reality, his tears had stopped and his body settled. I didn't leave until much later, but like all the other times, he wouldn't remember this. I never wanted him to.

"My daughter's on a little trip, hm?" Chancellor Fowler inquired, pulling me from my thoughts.

"What?" I asked, looking between both of them. "How do you..."

Chancellor Fowler waved his hand dismissively. "I don't mind where she's going. I'm hoping she gets all the answers she wants, actually. It will all work out in my favor, don't you worry. Things have to get worse before they get better, right?" He sighed, smiling up at me. "You should be happy you won't need to meddle in her mind; I apologize for even putting that kind of stress on you. I should have known how my own daughter would react, how her mind would work. That one is on me. You can sit back, keep that brother of yours and his friend in line. That is something you are willing to do, yes?"

"How do you know where she's going?" I asked, actually getting to finish my question.

He pressed his lips together and smirked at me. "It is amazing the information people are willing to give up, what they are willing to do for the people they care about. Believe me Asher, you aren't the only one with a family of sorts to protect."

Chocolate.PSD
Bar Mock-Up
Food Packaging Collection

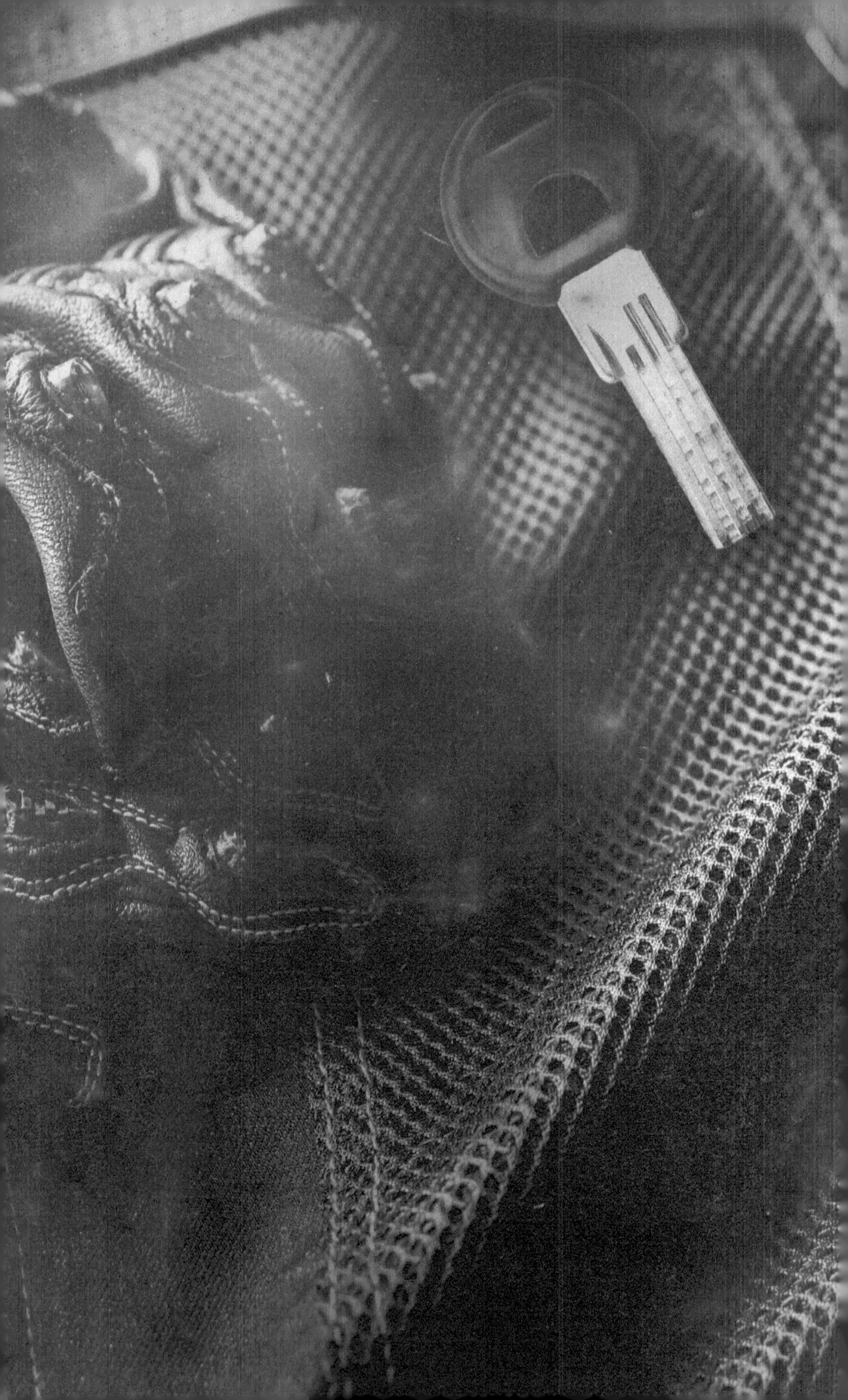

32
RIVER

I could count on my hand the amount of times Grayson had ridden on the back of my bike, but any time it did happen made me smile so hard that my cheeks hurt. When Riley was back there, she would press her entire body against my back and wrap her arms all the way around my middle. I could practically hear her heart beating rapidly in her chest, even over the noise of the motorcycle.

Grayson simply held onto my sides, going sans helmet because he liked to claim he was a *rebel*. That just meant I took it easy on turns and didn't go my usual fast speed all because he wanted to, I don't know, feel the wind in his hair or some shit.

I turned off the engine when we got to Marth Moon, the smell of the marth instantly hitting my nostrils. I inhaled, letting the scent overwhelm me in the best way. It had been a little bit after seven when we left and Asher still wasn't home. Cars were piled close together in the gravel lot and the sign over the door was lit up in neon yellow.

I tucked my keys into my pocket and Grayson walked in step with me while we passed by smokers and plenty of patrons already a little too wasted to flirt properly. I opened the door for my best friend, following him inside.

"*Amigos! Entren!* Finally!" Mateo yelled from behind the bar.

A few people looked around, focusing their eyes on us but then looked back at Mateo. All the stares ceased as if their friendly demeanor towards us was good enough for them. I recognized a few faces from school, but mostly everyone was a stranger to me. That didn't deter me; there weren't many people that disliked me, so turning strangers into friends wasn't much of a challenge.

We sat on the barstools and Mateo started preparing two glasses.

Grayson pointed towards where they tilted one of the glasses towards a spout. "Pretty sure we haven't even told you what we want."

Mateo chuckled. "That doesn't matter. I already know what you want." They tapped the side of their head. The button-down shirt they wore had half the buttons undone and their sleeves were rolled up to their elbows. Small stains already decorated their clothes.

They placed one of the glasses in front of me and started filling the other. I picked up the glass filled with the deep brown liquid. I brought it to my nose, sniffing. It smelled like utter perfection. I waited until Grayson had his and we clinked glasses.

Mateo threw a hand towel over their shoulder and watched us while we took a sip. Their eyebrows raised expectantly.

"Well fuck, that's good," I complimented, taking another drink. "Are you sure this isn't your partner's witchy touch that makes it so perfect."

Mateo shrugged. "*Mi amor* is very helpful and yes, she is perfect. She is much prettier than me, so I am fine with her receiving more credit." One of the groups behind us started getting loud and a deep growl came from Mateo's chest had them settling down. "*Cálmense, idiotas.No tengo miedo echarlos, por el amor de Dios.*"

Grayson had already downed half his beer. "Are you babysitting us?"

The wolf shifter moved to the side for another bartender to come behind them. "No, not really. Your lady is away, so I assumed you two would either be mopping around or fucking around with each other. I am hoping you have already done the latter because our bathroom is off limits for that kind of activity." They winked at us. "Well, it is off limits to *you*. Me, on the other hand, I can do whatever the fuck I want."

I licked my lips, letting them take my glass and refill it. "You don't have to keep watch on us, you know? I have a healthy assumption your pack leader doesn't love that you are just delegating wolves to do menial tasks."

Mateo shook their head, wagging their finger at me. "Corrin loves Riley. And I love Corrin, so it's an instinct to keep whoever she loves protected. Dante knows what's happening and he's—he hasn't made too much of a fuss. He's been busy anyway, always on his phone."

"Dante?"

Mateo wrinkled their nose. "The alpha. He wasn't a super fan of Corrin helping out at first, but clearly the beer is much better, so he hasn't opened his mouth about her coming and going." They started to wipe down the counter. "He leaves me and Jade to help out with this place so it's basically ours. Our parents are a friend of his, so he's like family, but I only speak to him when I have to. It's complicated."

I clucked my tongue. "I know a thing or two about complicated relationships. I think we all do." I peeked over at Grayson who glanced at me from over his glass while he took a drink.

Mateo rapped their knuckles on the counter; tiny dark curls fell into their forehead. They opened their mouth but stopped to glance over our shoulders. "*Por fin!* Now it's a party."

Grayson and I looked behind us to see Ike walking out of the bathroom. He gave us a tight smile, sitting on the barstool next to me. He nodded at Mateo who started to make his drink. "I profusely apologize about my very abrasive twin sister who can't seem to keep her nose out of things that don't involve her."

I hummed. "I mean, you can always say no when she asks for your help."

Ike tilted his head from left to right, thanking Mateo for his drink. "She's my sister, so I complain about her, but I'll never say no to helping her. Especially when Ted got a broken wing and she healed it." He looked down into his drink, mumbling, "and she never lets me fucking forget it."

"Ted?" Grayson inquired.

"His familiar. A pesky *pajaro* that almost pecked me in the eye," Mateo explained, throwing a glare in Ike's direction.

Ike waved his hand dismissively. "Anyway, you don't have to be a telepath to hear the whispers about your girlfriend."

With my dampener I couldn't use my powers on campus, but I didn't need to. The looks that were thrown in Riley's direction right before she had left with Corrin were enough to know what people were thinking. And the minute I could hear, I just shut it out.

"She's handling it well enough from what I can tell. And joining Celica is a...choice. Chancellor Fowler must be pleased with himself." Ike's voice was full of disgust towards the man.

Grayson huffed. "He told her he'd back off if she did. Any small things to keep her close."

I ran a hand through my hair. "Who knows, maybe Riley will discover something massive while she's gone."

Mateo snorted. "You, my friend, are very cute when you are optimistic. I am happy Riley is going to be there with *mi amor.*"

"It would be odd if Chancellor Fowler doesn't have his hands in more things or have gotten to people much closer to Riley. You guys are one thing, but I mean he seems like a guy who finds his way to get people to his side. The way he just wrapped up Riley's dad's death, I mean...." Ike started, but a group of men and women came in through the back door and the air in the room became tense.

I flicked my eyes to Mateo who had their eyes trained at the door, following the group. Their body was relaxed but it was almost like they had trained their body to react that way for this very moment.

The man at the front, clapped hands with one of the people sitting down, giving them a toothy grin. His hair was a dark brown, meeting right at his chin in spiraled curls. His skin was brown, the same as his eyes and he had a scar that sat just above his lip.

He stared at me intensely and I hated that I had looked away, but even though his eyes were just a normal brown...there was something about them.

Mateo cleared their throat. "Dante."

Dante tipped his chin up to Mateo. "Good night?"

Mateo swept their hand towards the room. "Clearly."

Dante huffed, snapping his fingers. "That attitude of yours can fuck off. I can easily take this bar away and you'll be forced to find something else to fill your time. *Como suena eso?*"

I could feel Dante's presence behind me and it was heavy. It felt almost like my dad's and I wanted to get it the fuck away from me. I understood alpha's gave off an aura, but the way Dante displayed it was too much and it didn't feel natural. I was damn near forcing myself not to get into his head because I knew it was a place I didn't want to be.

Mateo sucked their teeth, but rolled their eyes, muttering, "You wouldn't have any customers if it wasn't for me, *cabrón.*"

Dante smirked, granting us his attention. "And who are your friends?" He nodded towards Ike. "Well, I know you, but I don't know—" he wagged his finger at us, "you."

Grayson ran a finger over his top lip. "I'm Grayson and this is River. We just came to have a drink, that's all. No trouble." He sounded clear and casual, then again, if Grayson really wanted to, he could cloud this entire room in shadows and get us the fuck out of here.

Dante pursed his lips. "Of course, no trouble. Magic wielders respect my establishment, and you all are welcomed here at any time."

"How do you know..." I started, but he scoffed.

"Well, I know you aren't fucking human that's for sure." He gave me one of his toothy grins and looked at Mateo again. Another wolf shifter came up, grabbing his arm and whispered in his ear.

Mateo cocked their head to the side. "Ariella, what are you doing here? You are supposed to be watching Mrs. Monroe's house."

Dante reared his head back. "I pulled her off. I let you delegate every now and then, Mateo, but you don't tell this pack what to do. When I want them back at this bar, they come. Besides, our job is not to play fucking *guardaespaldas*." He walked around the bar and stepped up to Mateo, who straightened their spine. "We are about to come into a lot of power pretty soon and I need the pack united. Ariella will go back out when I tell her too, but for now, I think that woman will be just fine. Trust me."

My ears perked up.

Mateo shrugged past him, walking around to our side of the bar, shaking their head. Dante grabbed their shoulders roughly, turning them around. "Hey, I let your sibling go to Napa Valley with that girl. I could have said no. We are *family*, Mateo."

Family. That was such an odd word. It seemed like everyone that used it had no idea what it even meant anymore.

Mateo's eyes started to flicker to a golden color but then returned back to normal. Their hands balled into fists at their sides. Dante got his phone from his pocket and put it to his ear. He started to walk out. "One of my wolves is with her, yes. I'll send Ariella to brief you on everything about the other." Dante clucked his tongue. "No, they're friends, she won't be harmed. I'll let you know when she's back."

Grayson and Ike both looked at Dante's back as he walked out the door.

Mateo's eyebrows furrowed, blinking their eyes over to me. He whirled around, grabbing the one named Ariella by her bicep. "What the fuck is he talking about?"

She widened her big brown eyes, startled. "I-I..." she stuttered.

I stalked over to them. "Who are you briefing?" I got closer to her and so many snarls echoed in my ear. I looked up to see the wolf shifters pining their gaze on me.

Ike and Grayson stepped up behind me, but Mateo created a space between us and their pack. They stared down at Ariella. "Who is he talking to, Ariella?"

She narrowed her eyes at me, but blinked over to Mateo. "I don't know. Dante asked me about that girl's mom and I told him what I'd observed. The last I heard when I was there she was talking to her kid on the phone, something about a coven, someone named Teresa..."

"He's gotten to the wolves," Ike explained, running a hand over the back of his neck.

I heard my name but my feet took me in the direction of the front door. I shoved it open, pushing past a few people and looked around, finding Dante still on the phone. I fast-walked over to him, ripping the phone from his hand, throwing it on the ground and shoving my foot down on top of it.

"You're working with Chancellor Fowler?"

He turned on his heels to face me. "Excuse me?"

I pushed my palms into his chest and grabbed his shirt, pulling him into me. "I didn't fucking stutter. You're working with that man and all he's done is caused so much fucking pain. He knows exactly where Riley is going, doesn't he?"

Dante took my wrists and squeezed. The amount of strength he had caused me to let go instantly. "Your tone could use some work, kid." He licked his lips. " I don't want any trouble, but he has offered my pack, my wolves much more strength, much more power just for some simple information. How can I pass that up? Mateo is the one that placed them in the perfect position."

"Is that all any of you care about? Fucking power?" I asked, thinking about my dad and his motivations. "Have you even asked your pack if that's what they want? They don't even know what they're doing, who you're answering to."

Dante chuckled, tilting his chin up. "They don't have to. I keep them safe and out of harm's way. That is what a leader does, boy. Witches' business is not my own, whatever they want to do with their own kind is not my problem." His eyes flicked to a reddish color and he cracked his neck.

I heard the sound of feet on gravel, noticing Grayson and Ike, slowly making their way to me.

"You have no idea what that man is capable of! That power you want, he's getting that from his own kind. You'd be gaining power that's been siphoned. It was stolen. I thought wolves had some kind of honor!" Ike yelled over the commotion that was flooding its way outside to the parking lot.

Dante growled over the metal magic user and bared his teeth. "Watch your mouth. You wouldn't need to worry so much if your sister had just kept her nose out of things. Don't worry, I've been keeping him updated on her as well, especially since she has her witchy fingers in the workings of my bar—" He started to continue on but Ike had reached his hand out and used his powers to rip a hubcap off one of the cars, contorting the metal into the likeness of a fist and punching Dante clear across the face. Some of the skin of his cheek had split.

Dante held the side of his face, while Ike let out harsh breaths. "Anything happens to my sister and I'll fucking kill you."

I started to step forward, but Grayson grabbed my shoulder, forcing me to stop as we both watched Dante take in breath after breath. Each exhale started to be guttural and more like a rumble. I had never witnessed a wolf transformation before, but if I had a weaker stomach, I would have vomited with how his back arched in an unnatural way. His fingers elongated and broke. Hair started sprouting from everywhere and the spirals at his head fell away while his head and face morphed more and more into a wolf.

Red eyes stared us down as he thrashed and got on all fours. Sharp teeth glinted from the streetlights and steam came from his nostrils. My hands shook from the way he dragged his claws on the ground and the resounding howls that were heard behind us just told me his pack wasn't about to help us, yet they weren't going to interfere with their alpha's business.

Erik told me that girl is his daughter. He wants to protect his family. And I want to help mine. I'll make sure to tell him you fought valiantly, so he can let her know what a hero you and your friends were. I heard him in my head and then he lunged.

His paws slammed against my chest, sending me back and slamming my body against one of the cars. Grayson started to run over to me, but Dante's tail swept him back. Grayson stretched out his hand, tendrils of black swiftly wrapped around Dante's legs. My best friend moved his arm back and the wolf tumbled forward, creating a cloud of dust and debris.

Dante shook it off, snarling at us, drool coming from the sides of his mouth. He ran towards Grayson, getting a dark shadow thrown at his face and he snapped his teeth at it. Ike ripped a bumper from one of the cars, molding it into a moveable metal rope and threw it over towards Dante, lassoing him around the neck. Ike pulled, right before the alpha could catch Grayson with his claws.

I swallowed hating this part of my powers and that I even knew how to use it but I found Dante's dark mind and pushed on it. His head twisted, red eyes finding mine as he tried to claw at the metal rope around his neck.

Stand down, Dante.

He growled, running his claws into the gravel, pieces flying everywhere. I pushed harder against his head and he whined with the way I put pressure on his mind.

Never. He thought back to me, letting out a howl that rattled the gravel at my feet.

I was about to send more of my powers to him, but a claw sliced right at my side and I flew backwards. I got up on shaky legs, finding purchase on the hood of a car, holding my side and noticing my entire palm coated in blood.

The blow caught Ike off guard and another wolf took his rope between their teeth and pulled, sending him flying forward. Grayson threw his hands back and then thrusted them forward, sending massive black wisps around us, which caused the wolf that was darting towards me to lift off the ground and crash back down with a thud.

Dante shook his whole body and licked his teeth. *I'll kill you slowly for trying to make a fool out of me in front of my pack.*

A threatening growl came from near the side of the bar. It was possessive and the wolf that appeared only had its eyes on Dante. The alpha huffed and turned so that it was face to face with the other wolf. All the other pack members backed off but stayed alert. The new wolf bared its teeth and Dante didn't hesitate to run towards it. They got on their hind legs, biting and clawing at one another.

"Is that..." Grayson sighed, struggling to stay on his feet.

"That's Mateo," Ike finished, his hands shaking. I noticed the rope burn on his palms.

I watched as Dante pinned Mateo down, snapping his teeth close to their neck. Mateo struggled to get up, their eyes shutting harshly as if Dante was in their head. I wanted to help, but my vision was getting blurry and I needed to maintain some sort of upward balance, so I remained against the car.

"Grayson, do something!" I managed to get out, before coughing.

My best friend created a ball of dark shadows and threw it in Dante's direction. It hit the wolf in the back of his head and he turned to look at Grayson, his red eyes much darker now.

That was all Mateo needed. They pushed their paws up, throwing Dante off of them. Before the alpha could get his bearings, Mateo ran into him, using their head to flip Dante over, his body skidding across the gravel. Mateo jumped on top of him, licking their canines before devouring the side of Dante's neck.

Audible gasps settled around us and then silence. I heard human breathing and just over a car or two, Mateo's head popped up. They turned in my direction and their face was covered in blood. Their eyes were also...red.

Pack members that were still wolves focused solely on Mateo, while one of the members came bursting out of the bar with a towel. Mateo became clearer in my view, wrapping the towel around their naked body.

The bar patrons looked on, stunned, and Mateo's chest rose and fell as they examined their pack members. They licked their lips, instantly wiping their mouth and seeing the blood. "This pack does not make deals with people who threaten to hurt the ones we care about! Is that clear?!"

The wolves and non-shifted pack members looked at one another. One by one they all nodded and lowered their heads.

I eyed Ike who had his eyebrows raised. "What's happening?"

Ike delicately touched the wounds on his palms. "Mateo killed Dante. They're the alpha now." He whistled. "Corrin is going to be even more insufferable now."

Mateo started to walk over towards us and my phone buzzed in my pocket. I was surprised it had survived this fight. I pulled it out of my pocket slowly, seeing Riley's name on my screen.

I hissed when I brought it to my ear, the movement creating pain in my side. "Hey, gorgeous." I tried to sound normal, like a giant wolf hadn't just tried to kill me or that I wasn't bleeding out of my side.

The other line was silent.

"Hello?"

I heard sniffles and then a small cry. Deep breathing filled my ear and then another tiny cry.

"Riley? What's wrong? Answer me, baby."

Grayson swiveled his head to look at me, leaning in so he could try to hear.

Silence again and then her voice sent my heart into a spiral. "R-river, can y-you please...." She started and then stopped, her voice becoming too shaky for her to continue. She tried again. "I-I don't know w-what I d-did. R-river please. I n-need you."

33
RILEY

"Did we really have to leave Beau at the hotel?" Jade asked, continuing to look at the back window, even though we were miles away from the hotel.

"Yes, Jade. We are already bombarding the woman, we don't need to also surprise her with a dog," Corrin explained, laughing.

I watched the houses go by, trying to clear my head and consider what I planned on saying. This was probably making the top three wildest things I've ever done, right alongside having a foursome. I would much rather be in the middle of a foursome right now than doing this if I was honest. I'm sure the boys would love that as well.

Corrin looked at the GPS on her car's screen and then back at the road, turning on her blinker to make a right.

All the houses looked relatively normal, though I didn't really know what I was expecting. I didn't know anything about this woman. I didn't know how she lived or what her day-to-day activities were. She could slam the door in my face and I couldn't say much about it. Fuck, now I really wished I was back in the foursome.

"Is it this one?" Corrin asked no one in particular, driving slower.

Trees covered a good portion of my vision, but a medium-sized one-story home stared back at me. The front yard was massive and looked like it was being well taken care of. There was a stone path that led to the front door and simple rectangular windows that would have let me see inside if the curtains weren't closed.

Corrin pulled into the driveway and I swiveled my head towards her. "Park on the street."

"Why would I do that? There is a perfectly good driveway right here." She rolled her eyes, putting her car in park.

"I don't know. Parking in the driveway seems way too comfortable."

She shrugged, opening her door. "Too late. Already did it."

I groaned, getting out and shaking out my nerves.

I pulled on the sleeves of my shirt, cupping the ends with my fingers. Once the front door was the only thing in front of me, gathering up the courage to knock was proving difficult.

"Allow me," Jade offered, placing two hard knocks against the door.

I was about to say fuck it and run back towards the car when a lock turned and the door slowly opened. The woman from the picture Corrin showed me appeared. She had aged a bit, but there was still a youthfulness to her features. Her skin was light brown and her curls were pushed back with a scarf she'd tied around her head.

"Can I help you?" she asked, scanning each of us quickly and looking confused.

I felt both of my friends' eyes on me and I took a deep breath. So many variations of things I could say came to mind, but nothing left my mouth. Teresa looked at me expectantly, then her eyes shot to my necklace. Her head tilted to the side and her mouth second by second began to form an O shape.

Her brown eyes found mine. "You're Jillian's daughter." She said it more like a statement, no inflection indicating that she was asking me anything.

"Yes."

She gave me a small smile and moved away from the door, motioning for us to come in. I hesitated but stepped over the threshold. The house was much bigger inside, the wooden floors looked like they had just been cleaned and various amounts of art decorated the walls.

Jade and Corrin stayed close by, gawking at the house along with me.

"Have a seat. Would you like anything to drink? Water? Tea?" Teresa offered, pulling at her cardigan.

I awkwardly sat on the couch in the living room. "Umm, water."

Corrin and Jade shook their heads, keeping an eye on her when she walked away.

"Well that went...better than we hoped," Corrin said, giving me a thumbs up.

"Nothing has even happened yet."

"Mm, true, but she let you in after knowing who you were so that's progress." Jade bumped my shoulder when she sat down next to me.

Teresa returned, handing me a glass of water and sitting down on the opposite couch. "I have to admit, I'm a little taken aback."

I took a long sip, placing the glass on the coffee table. "You and me both. I'm actually really rude, this is Corrin and Jade. My friends."

They both casually waved and Teresa gave them a friendly smile. "You must know who I am if you came all the way here."

"I do. I won't bother you if you don't want to talk about it, but I just have questions that I'm hoping you'll answer. And maybe when we're done, you'll be willing to help me with something."

She pressed her lips together, placing her hands in her lap. "We are family, so I suppose that isn't asking too much."

I interlocked my index fingers together, fidgeting. "Hmm, well... I..."

"You're probably wondering about your necklace?" she asked, crossing her legs.

"That's one thing, yes."

She sighed. "When Samia called on one of the coven members for that kind of help, I was intrigued. When I learned it was for your mother, well, I was even *more* intrigued. We have a—" She cleared her throat then cracked her neck, "—complicated relationship."

Jade side-eyed me but kept quiet.

"You let Evie do it. You allowed her to help create my necklace, even though it was for someone you didn't like?"

She drummed her fingers on her knee. "It was for you, not your mother. There is a big difference. I knew Evie could do it, so it was also a way for her to show her skill. I needed my witches to be top notch. You are aware of that, I'm sure." She glanced over at Corrin, who audibly gulped.

Teresa gave her a sly smile. "I don't remember all faces, but I do remember most and I do know you are one of ours."

Corrin blinked, her eyebrows turning inward. "Did you kill your husband?"

I choked on air, staring at her. Jade snorted, covering her mouth.

Teresa didn't flinch. "Why would you ask that?"

Corrin licked her lips, smacking them. "Just curious. The school has archives, and I just wanted to clear some things up. Riley is curious about it too."

I rubbed my temple but didn't stop her. She wasn't wrong...I *was* curious.

Teresa leaned back against the couch. "My husband had a wandering eye. Our marriage was never about love, but our son was the only thing that connected and united us. Phillip was a weak man, but Erik loved him. We wanted what was best for our son. That was where our similarities ended."

"That doesn't answer my–" Corrin started, but I grabbed Corrin's knee and squeezed hard enough that I'm sure she felt a bit of pain.

"If that's a sore subject, I'm sorry to bring it up..." I began to apologize, but she cut me off.

"His death was such a tragedy to that school. I tried my best to make the transition of the next chancellor easy, but it destroyed my son...amongst other things." She looked at me, but it was almost like she was looking past me.

I stuck my tongue in my cheek, taking a moment before speaking. "I'm going to just assume you were fully aware of when he came back from his disappearing act and was the Chancellor of Mystic Riegan?"

She blew out a breath. "Of course. That moment made me so proud, finally being the person his father never was. He was going to run that school better than Phillip ever did."

"My mom told me you and Chancellor Fowler didn't get along."

Teresa stared at the rug underneath her coffee table for more than a few seconds and I shifted on the couch. She ran her hands along the tops of her thighs before getting off the couch. "Would you excuse me a moment?"

"Sure," I answered quickly.

"Bathroom?" Jade asked, grabbing her mass of curls and moving them over her shoulder.

Teresa pointed around the corner, waiting as Jade followed her instructions. Chancellor Fowler's mother disappeared into her kitchen and I let the heaviness I felt in my chest ease up.

"I shouldn't have fucking said that," I whispered to Corrin.

"We'll get nowhere if you play it safe. And that means maybe making things a tiny bit uncomfortable."

"A tiny bit? Corrin, I basically told her that I know her son didn't like her that much. Also how the fuck do you just blurt out a question about her murdering her husband?"

She pushed out her bottom lip, not looking sorry at all. "Hmm, yeah, well can't take it back now. Keep moving forward."

Teresa walked back into the room, now choosing to sit on the arm of the couch. "You caught me off guard with that, I'm sorry."

I shook my head. "No, I shouldn't have brought it up like that, but it's just odd to me that he took your maiden name later on."

She hummed. "We had spoken about it and thought it best he move on from his father as much as he still adored that man. He needed to build something new for himself."

I tucked one of my braids behind my ear. "Mrs. Lowe..."

"Call me Teresa, dear."

"Okay, Teresa. You were around the time my dad died, so I have to ask..." I rolled my lips together, "did you know that your son was responsible?"

She narrowed her eyes at me, but there was no indication that she was hurt by my question. One of her eyebrows shot upward. "Freak accidents happen all the time."

"Accident? No, no. He admitted to me that he did it. I want to know if you knew, if you found out that your son killed my father, so you left?"

Teresa shook her head, placing her hands on either side of her skull. "Of course he admitted it. Always so obsessed with you and that woman." She wasn't looking at me, but she was talking to herself. "I thought maybe him leaving and just getting away would be good for him; he came back and wanted to be a leader, he wanted power, and I had the son I always deserved again."

I caught Corrin's eye and she quickly nodded towards the door. Jade walked around the corner but stopped when she saw the concerned looks on our faces.

"Teresa...we've caused you a lot of stress and I think we should be going." I started to get up from the couch, Corrin following close behind.

"I don't hate you sweetheart, I really don't. Your mother was going to make my son weak. He wanted to leave, he wanted to rid himself of his own family and make a new one and that kind of over-bearing love scared your mother. She left him and that was the happiest day of my life." She turned her head so she could look at me. I was halfway to the door, but her stare caused me to stop. Jade hustled over to us and Teresa never acknowledged her. "He blamed me for it. I got rid of his cheating father so that that man's feeble heart wouldn't taint my son. Your mother made Erik's heart just as vulnerable, and it made me sick."

I was inches away from the door when my feet wouldn't move. Corrin tried to shift sideways, but nothing happened. Jade tried to move her legs, but it was like there was force keeping us here.

"Erik knows you. He wants you back and I can't have that. He was so much better when it was like you didn't exist." Her face was still so content and sweet as if all the insanity lurking in her brain was hidden deep, deep down. "He needs to go back to that place. I need to make it so that you stay gone."

Jade's body lurched forward, a growl coming from her throat. She was thrown to the side so swiftly that her body flew through the glass of the back door that led to the backyard. Corrin was swept off her feet and lifted up, thrown against the wall. Her head made a hard thump before she slumped down towards the ground.

I screamed; my mouth instantly being shut by Teresa's magic. I clawed at my mouth, wanting to force my lips apart but I couldn't. My powers twitched within my veins and I lifted my arm to try to protect myself, but my wrist twisted painfully.

"Oh, sweetheart, Erik gained those telekinesis powers from me. It's so cute that you think you have any use for them here." The pain she was inducing had my mind jumbled and I couldn't think straight. I heard a snap and cried out, realizing that she'd broken my wrist.

I grabbed hold of my broken bone when a force surrounded my neck and then pressed against my throat. My airway was becoming smaller and my breaths shallow. I used my good hand to touch the front of my neck, using my nails to rake down my skin, knowing that nothing I did would help me take in air.

My body was flung off to the side and the impact of the wall sent a pain shooting through my side. Teresa quickly shuffled over to me, kneeling down so that she could take me by my braids and pull my head back. "I didn't think Jillian would come back. I thought she would stay away, keep you far from everything. She couldn't do a simple fucking thing, so I made it easier. I let Evie make that necklace so that the magic you got from *my* son would cease to exist. He could go about his life and not think of you. He was starting to forget about you both." She yanked my head back more and I felt the sting in my scalp. "He stole from those witches because he liked the high it gave him. You don't need a witch's particular power, just the strength that comes with it to enhance your own. That man your mother was with should have never angered my son. He deserved what he got, but now Erik is fixated on you. And I can't have that."

She kept my hands at my sides, as she squeezed her powers against my neck, choking me. "He wants to give you this legacy and you don't deserve it. Your mother doesn't deserve it. You don't deserve his magic." Her magic pressed against my chest and a weight barreled down, making it even harder to breathe.

"P-please. Stop," I choked out, trying to kick my legs out.

She slipped her finger along the chain of my necklace, grabbing hold of it and yanking. The sting of it slicing my neck was quick as she held Asher's gift in my hands. "I should have made you harder to find. I should have just killed you both when I realized you were back, ended this problem right then and there."

My vision was blurry and my head was swimming with pain. I felt myself going under.

Quick footsteps sounded behind Teresa. Corrin jumped on her back, tucking her arm under her neck and pulling back. Teresa let out a choking noise as she reached behind her to try and subdue my roommate. They tumbled backwards and I was released from Teresa's hold.

I rested my hand on my chest, the pain that vibrated there making it hard to breathe.

Teresa tossed Corrin aside, curving one of her fingers in a 'come here' motion and a knife came flying past my head. Teresa willed it to head straight for Corrin when the sound of more breaking glass and a loud rumble sounded. A wolf came running towards us and knocked Corrin out of the way, taking the knife to the shoulder.

The wolf whined, but stood tall, even when wounded. Its eyes pierced into mine as it stared at me and I instantly knew Jade's determination anywhere. Her whines grew louder when the knife started to twist and her large wolf head was slammed against the wall. Corrin tried to run at Teresa and was tripped. Chancellor Fowler's mother used her powers to drag her through the living room, letting her body hit various pieces of furniture as she went.

Tears stung behind my eyes and I just wanted this to stop. She was no better than her son. She was honestly worse. It was hard to swallow, and seeing straight was difficult, but I used my magic to grab at her hair, roughly ripping her away from Corrin. Different pieces of furniture dangled in mid air around me as I lifted them up. I sent end tables, picture frames, vases, anything I could get my eye on at her. She dodged them, getting hit by a vase as it shattered around her.

"You have learned nothing," she taunted, staring at me as I felt that familiar weight coming near me, attempting to suffocate me.

Then it stopped. It was gone within a blink and Teresa started choking. She was reaching for her neck, taking in any small gasp of air that she could. I kept looking at her, my heart beating faster. The area around me blurred and all I saw was this person that threatened my friends, threatened my family, my life.

I felt her own power trying to push against me, overpower me, but I pushed back harder. Corrin shuffled over to Jade's wolf form now that Teresa was occupied. The chancellor's mother fell on the ground, trying to get words out to spew at me, but all I did was force her hands in front of her face. The same hands that touched my necklace and ripped it from my body.

The sound of breaking bones, each and every one resounded in my ears. Her fingers bent in odd ways and her cries were masked by the lack of oxygen she was getting. I felt nothing when I watched her. The smell of burning flesh filled my nostrils, but I didn't feel hot.

Burn marks appeared on her skin, red welts developing on her body as she shook from the overwhelming pain. Blood seeped from the wounds and her brown skin had a red hue all over. The blood that came out looked as if it was boiling.

Her wails echoed and I wanted her to shut up. Just stop. I focused one last time and the sound of her intense gasps were sharp and then I cinched my power around her neck, pressing hard until the sound of her neck snapping had the tight feeling in my chest unwinding.

I blinked when it was over, the silence surrounding me like an uncomfortable blanket. Corrin and Jade were both looking at me, concern in their eyes. Jade had returned back to her human form, not paying any mind to her nakedness. The knife that had been lodged into her shoulder was now on the ground, covered in blood.

My vision was vibrating and I noticed I was shaking. There was a dead body in front of me. I did that. I...

I did that?

I focused on the blood, my mind transporting itself back to that place I didn't like to go. Teresa was now Marianne. Her body unmoving and red liquid surrounded her, coating the ground. My stomach turned thinking that that would make me Chancellor Fowler, using my powers in ways I shouldn't. I felt no remorse for what I'd done. Should I?

My eyes got glassy as I considered everything, tears starting to stream down my face. Every time I opened and closed my eyes, the setting would change. I was in Teresa's house one minute and then back hovering over Marianne's dead body the next. I looked down at my hands, blood coating them and I couldn't shake it off.

I didn't want to be here anymore. I wasn't a murderer. I didn't do this.

I just wanted to protect my friends. I wanted to protect myself.

I saw movement as Corrin walked back into the house. I hadn't even realized she left. She handed Jade something. It looked like clothes. She headed over to me slowly, picking up something from the ground along the way.

Corrin hunched down next to me, placing her hand on my arm, but I shrugged her off. She let out a breath. "Riley... can you look at me?" She hovered her hand over my broken wrist and used her powers to stitch the bone back together. It was mildly painful but I didn't let it show.

I heard a phone buzz and Corrin cursed under her breath. She took it out and looked at the screen. Out of the corner of my eye, I saw that it was her mom.

She hit ignore, giving me her attention again. "Riley, we have to go. We have to go now."

"Mari–Marianne."

"Marianne? Your friend? What about her?"

I opened my mouth to speak, but forming words was hard. I frantically licked my lips and tried again. "H-he kill–" My voice cracked and I took a deep breath, staring right at Teresa's body. "He killed her. Right in front of me. So much blood and I couldn't save her. I couldn't save my dad. I wanted to save you guys." I closed my eyes and tears doubled over, sliding down my cheeks. "Does this make me a bad person?" I blinked over to her and Corrin was looking back at me, her eyes glassy as if she wanted to cry herself.

She tentatively touched my head. "No, Riley. I'm so sorry about Marianne. I—I know you cared about her, but that man killed her for no reason. You did this out of self-defense. You are not the bad guy."

I nodded, towards the ground. "W-we have to call the p-police."

She hummed. "Okay, we can do that from the car. We need to go back to the hotel and clean you up. I need to clean up Jade as well."

"N-no, w-we need to d-do it now." I heard the vibration in my voice.

"Riley. No. We need to get you away from here. This is all too much for you right now" She let her fingers touch my wet cheek. "We will call. I promise. Please come with me."

I moved almost robotically when I started to get up. My mouth opened but all that came out were sobs and Corrin grabbed my shoulders and pulled me into her. She spoke into my hair. "I'm so sorry any of this happened to you."

I felt immobile when they got me into the car, buckling my seatbelt. Jade kept telling Corrin she was fine as she put pressure on her arm, blood trickling down past her elbow. Her face gave it away that she was in pain, but she didn't speak about it. Corrin gripped the steering wheel tightly, then adjusted her glasses on her face and shook her shoulders before putting the car in reverse.

I let out shallow breaths, tears continuing to move down my face. The house got further away and with one hand Corrin grabbed her phone and dialed 911. I looked out the window, trying not to scream. I could have passed out at this very moment, but I was terrified that I would be back in that room with a man who claimed to want me to have all the power in the world, but now I'd used that power for... this.

Shakily, I took my phone out and dialed the one person I wanted to talk to right now.

He answered almost instantly, but I couldn't speak when I heard his voice. The smooth sound of it, the comforting tone, it made me want to cry even harder.

"R-river, can y-you please...." I started, but it was so difficult to get my words out. I noticed Corrin had hung up the phone and I swallowed the lump in my throat. "I-I don't know w-what I d-did. R-river please. I n-need you."

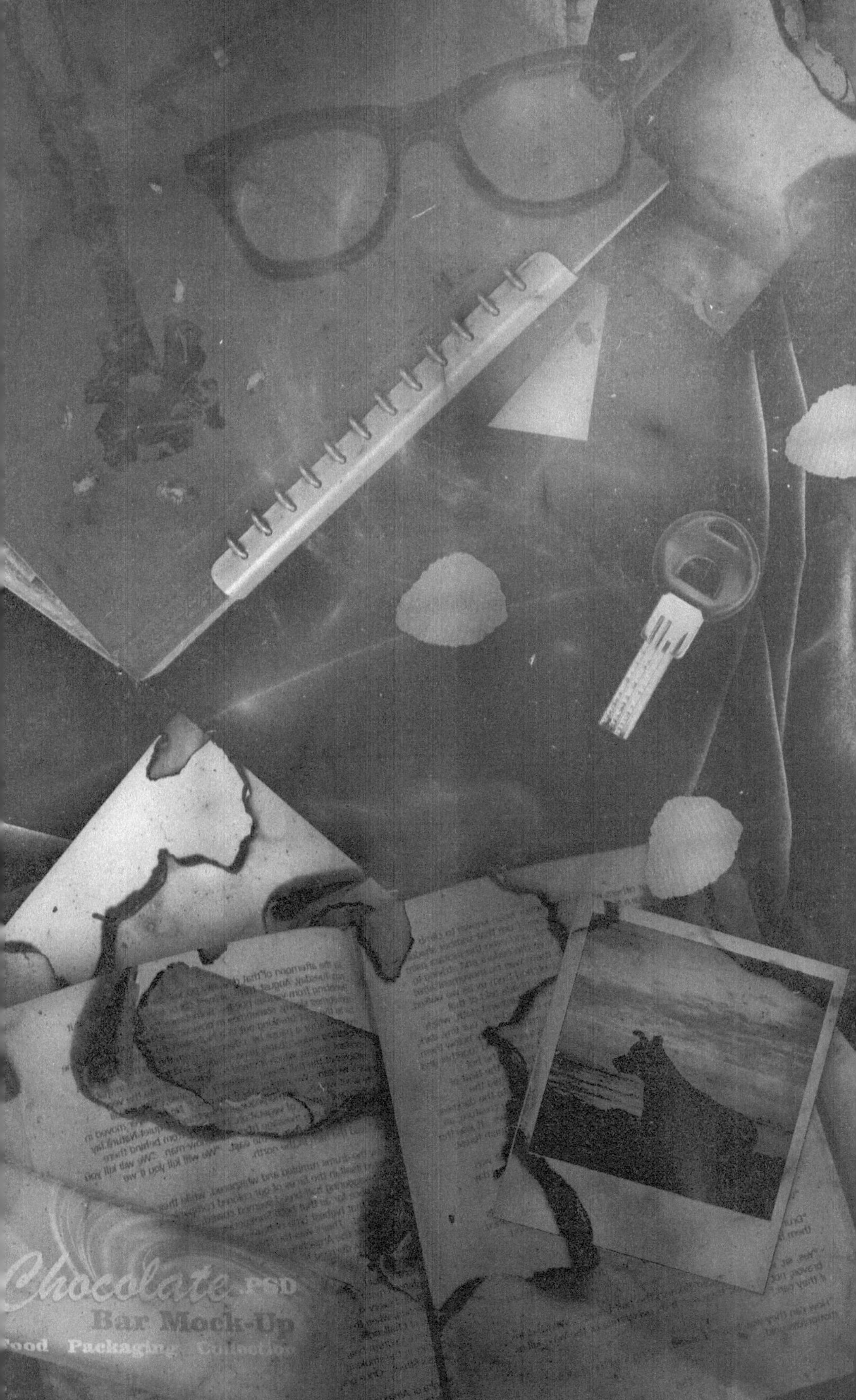
Chocolate.psd
Bar Mock-Up
Food Packaging Collection

34
RILEY

I heard Jade hiss from the other side of the door. Before I'd closed myself in the bathroom, I saw her sitting on the edge of the bed, her arm covered in bloody lines. I knew Corrin would heal her wound as painful as it might be, but what I did couldn't be fixed and I didn't deserve that anyway.

We'd stumbled into the hotel lobby, the front desk attendant remembering us and immediately yelling at Corrin. They scolded her about noise complaints from our room, the continuous barking and how if we didn't get our shit together they would kick us out and charge for any damages caused. Even in pain, Jade moved in front of us and growled at the attendant, saying in the most lethal voice I'd ever heard to leave us the fuck alone.

The attendant audibly gulped and motioned for us to go ahead.

Beau threw himself in my arms when we'd gotten into the room and he'd definitely made a mess of the beds and deep claw marks were on the other side of the door. Pillows were thrown everywhere, and the mattresses were askew. It almost looked as if he'd created track marks into the carpet. He was at my feet now, while I sat on the bathroom floor, leaning against the tub.

I felt like my heart was going to explode from my chest and I kept flexing my fingers out and creating fists as if I had no feeling in them. Beau put his head on my knee, sighing.

Are you going to tell me what happened?

I shook my head. *No.*

I'm a good listener.

A tiny smile escaped my lips. *I know. I just don't want to say things out loud right now. Can you understand that?*

He blinked at me, his ears twitching. *I understand.* He got up and walked over to me, nudging his face against my shoulder. *I was so scared.*

I reached up and scratched under his chin. "I don't like scaring you. I just need to figure out how to breathe normally right now. I just feel like everything was going okay and then..."

A loud pounding noise sounded at the door. I heard the door open and multiple voices.

"Where is she?" My heart stumbled within its tense rhythm when I heard River's voice. Beau's head cocked to the side and his tail thumped.

The bathroom door flew open and my boyfriend looked down at me, his green eyes exploding with this kind of wild protectiveness. "How did you find me? I hung up so quickly and didn't give you..."

"Corrin texted me your hotel when you checked in." He was down on the floor with me in seconds, scooping me up into his arms and cradling me in his lap.

I let crying screams rip from my throat the minute the heat from his body took over. I tugged on his shirt and threw my head against his chest. He kissed my forehead over and over again. "Hey baby, I'm here. I'm right here."

I didn't realize Grayson was there as well until I felt another body. He sat on his knees, rubbing my arms and back, his shadows coming out to almost lull and calm me. I peeked out from River's chest, receiving a comforting smile from my shadow wielder. Corrin and Jade stood in the doorway, letting me take my time before I spoke.

"I'm s-sorry."

They both shook their heads.

"Absolutely not. That lady was crazy and I should have never thought this was a good idea, but—" she slipped her fingers into her back pocket, pulling out my necklace. "I thought you might want this back."

Grayson took it from her and he placed it in my open hand, letting his fingers wrap around my own.

"What the hell happened?" River asked, cradling me closer.

Jade and Corrin looked at each other and then back at me. I cleared my throat. "Can we have a minute?" My friends hesitated for a moment. I appreciated them, I really did. "I'll be okay."

They closed the door behind them, leaving me alone with Grayson and River, along with a watchful Beau. I licked my lips pulling away from River and sitting up so I could easily see both of them. "Asher didn't want to come along?"

River kicked Grayson's leg when he snorted. "We told him where we were here and he sent back a very loud and angry voice message." He tucked one of my braids behind my ear. "He's at the house making sure you have whatever you might need when we bring you home and likely awaiting our message that you are in one piece."

"Now tell us what happened," Grayson coaxed, softly.

I wiped under my eyes, tears still threatening to fall. "Umm, we were just talking to her and then it got weird. She started saying all these things about my mom and Chancellor Fowler...I just wanted to leave. I didn't want a p-problem." I was starting to stutter when I felt the tightness in my chest return.

"You are here now, you're out of there. Why are you crying?"

River asked, curiosity in his voice. "Are you afraid she'll come looking for you? Tell Chancellor Fowler?"

I ran a shaky hand along the back of my neck. I shook my head, reaching out for the top of Beau's head, which he presented to me instantly. "That won't happen."

Both men glanced at each other and then back at me but remained quiet.

"I, umm, she tried to k-kill me."

"WHAT?!" they shouted and I flinched.

I swallowed the lump in my throat. "She t-tried to kill a-all of us. I didn't have a choice, right? I couldn't l-let her do that. She never wanted to h-help my mom. She wanted me to disappear and k-keep her s-son focused and powerful. I had to do s-something. I d-didn't know what was happening. M-maybe I did. M-maybe I'm a bad person..."

"Slow down, Riley. You aren't a bad person. She tried to hurt you," Grayson said, rubbing my arm.

I vigorously shook my head, rocking myself against River's lap. "That doesn't mean I hurt her back. That doesn't mean I become a murderer." The word fell from my lips so smoothly that I almost didn't realize I'd said it. Once it was out a sense of dread washed over me.

"Murderer? Riley...you killed her?" River whispered, turning my head so he could look directly at me.

I sniffed, my lip quivering. The visuals of me choking her, breaking her fingers, boiling her blood....I didn't want to do something like that. I never thought I could. "Y-yes."

"Baby..." He moved his thumbs over my cheeks to clear my tears, but they just kept falling. He brought my face towards his lips, kissing my cheek. "I'm so sorry you went through that."

"Defending yourself does not make you a bad person." Grayson turned my face so he could speak his words directly at me.

"This will only make things worse with him. He might not have liked her, but that was still his mother," I explained, placing a hand on my chest and clutching my necklace in my palm. I opened my hand, letting the chain dangle between my fingers before I secured it around my neck again.

River hummed. "Chancellor Fowler knows you're here. He's probably waiting to see how it plays out, or maybe he already knows. Did you take Corrin's potion to attempt to protect your mind?"

I nodded, remembering its nasty flavor. "Wait, he knows I'm here."

"We'll explain later. Let's take you home," Grayson offered, starting to get up from the floor.

I pressed on River's stomach to balance myself and he hissed. I pulled back quickly, then tentatively pressed my fingers to his side feeling gauze there. I moved off of him and lifted up his shirt. A large piece of gauze was taped to his side, red coloring already seeping through the material.

"What the fuck?!" I yelled, whipping my head around to stare at Grayson.

"That's a long story for when we are home." Grayson reached down for my hand so he could help me up. I let him pull me to my feet, but then I ripped my hand away.

"No, you are telling me now. I watched her bleed and I broke her bones, Grayson. I tried to protect my friends and now this is happening when I'm not around. Don't shield it from me, just fucking tell me," I demanded, poking my finger into his chest. Beau huffed next to me, his tail high and alert.

Grayson looked over my shoulder at his best friend. "She has a point." River sighed, pulling his shirt down before getting off the floor.

I moved past them to the door, opening it. "Let her heal you while you explain and I can focus on something else."

Jade and Corrin had decided to drive back themselves while Grayson shadowed the rest of us back to the house. We landed right in their living room and Asher came running around the corner.

"Thank fuck," Asher announced, moving to the side for Beau to race up the stairs to River's bedroom. "You can't just fucking send me a text with vague shit and think it's okay. For fucks sake, River, a wolf fight? And then you leave me with 'Riley's in trouble, but she sounds fine', what the actual…"

I rushed over to him, pulling his face down and pressing my lips to his. Asher didn't have room to speak, but the minute our mouths met, he didn't seem to want to. I broke the kiss, speaking against his mouth. "Your care for me is showing."

"Are you okay?"

I placed my palms at his chest, breathing in and letting his scent envelop me. "No."

Asher pulled a small item from his pants pocket and presented it to me. It was my dampener ring. He took my hand and placed it on my finger. The irony of realizing what having it would have meant for everything that happened wasn't lost on me. If I hadn't been able to take it off, I could have died. Without it, I now had blood on my hands. It was blood that never touched my skin, but I felt it. Marianne's blood, my dad's blood—those weren't my fault, but I felt drenched in so much spilled blood that I could hardly breathe most of the time.

"Thank you," I said in a small voice.

River cleared his throat, coming up to us. "Corrin said you never actually showered when you got back. Let's go, gorgeous."

They all moved around me like some sort of prestigious bodyguard service. Each of them taking my stuff, removing pieces of my clothing and turning on the shower. They left me alone but claimed to be close by if I needed them. I didn't want to be alone for long, so I kept my shower short and came out as refreshed as I could be. No amount of scrubbing was going to remove my thoughts and the way I currently felt about myself.

"Are you hungry?" Asher asked, crossing his arms over his chest. His simple black t-shirt tightened around his arms and his slouchy gray sweatpants sat low on his hips.

"No," I answered, not really in the mood to attempt to put food in my mouth.

They all looked tired and I assumed for different reasons. I'd gawked at River when he explained about what happened at Marth Moon. Corrin had to refrain from squealing when she discovered her partner was now the alpha. Chancellor Fowler had his desperate claws in everything. He wasn't always around, but he was always watching and I wasn't surprised. Maybe things would be easier if I just submitted. If I was the obedient daughter in all things, like he's wanted me to be.

That idea made me want to throw up.

"I think bed is a good option," I offered, nodding towards River's room. I started to walk but then a hand gripped my bicep and pulled me past the door. I looked up to see Asher steering me towards his room.

"Is this a sleepover?" Grayson joked, trying to lift the mood.

"Don't call it that," Asher said, closing his door when we were all inside. He focused his green eyes on me. "You sleep in here tonight. And I suppose the rest of you can as well."

"So, a sleepover," Grayson repeated, winking at my boyfriend's brother.

I heard rustling from outside the door and then a body slamming into the wood.

You don't want to come inside? I thought to Beau.

I cuddle with my mom or mom and River, not mom and three other people. Even if they want to make you happy. I could have sworn I heard him sigh from outside.

River came over to me, wrapping his arms around my body. He kissed my forehead. "You need anything, you tell one of us, okay?"

"I will. I just really want to sleep." I padded over to the bed, the sheets cool against the exposed skin of my thighs. I watched the guys mentally decide how they wanted to lay in bed. Asher removed his shirt, tucking himself into my right side, while River let Grayson snuggle into my left side before he snuck in behind Grayson, spooning him.

Asher took off his glasses and reached over to cut off the light from his lamp, shrouding the room in darkness. I didn't know what it was but something about this sleeping arrangement had my heart beating at a normal rate, the anxiety that consumed me mellowed out and the sleepiness I tried to push aside overwhelmed me.

I trailed my hand over to Asher's. It was laying palm up on the pillow and my fingers traced over his until they interlocked. I tried to pull away, but he kept my hand hostage. I stopped trying to escape and found myself cuddling into him, hoping that he might fill my dreams with something happy and falling asleep.

WHIMPERING FILLED MY EARS AND STARTLED ME AWAKE. I WOULD KNOW Beau's cries anywhere. I had to slowly pull the covers down and shift over Asher's body. I had one leg over when I felt his hands at my waist.

"Where are you going?" he whispered in my ear.

"Beau is crying and I want to comfort him."

"You coddle him."

I rolled my eyes, grateful that he couldn't see. "He's my familiar. It's my job to take care of him, so let me do that." I could feel his erection pressed against me, but I was more concerned with what was on the other side of the door.

"Right back to bed, got it?" Asher scolded, letting me go.

I walked over to the door, opening it up to see Beau circling. I gently closed the door behind me and crouched down to his level. "Hey buddy, what's wrong?"

Beau stomped his front paws, turning and then dashing down

the stairs. I raised an eyebrow, turning to look at the door that led to Asher's room. I considered getting them up but decided against it. I followed Beau and realized he was at the front door. His tail was curved upward and stiff. There was a small light from the kitchen that illuminated a part of the entryway, so I could see that the short hair on the back of his neck was up.

What's going on? I thought to him, confused.

He didn't reply, but a growl came from him and he bared his teeth. I nudged him back from the door and pulled it open, peeking out. I didn't see anything except the trees that swayed just a little from the wind and the sound of cars filled my ears. I almost closed the door back completely when I felt a shiver go down my spine.

There was this feeling like I wasn't alone and I looked down at Beau. He was still staring directly at the door, unmoved. I stuck my tongue in my cheek and pulled the door open again, stepping fully outside to get a better look. If I was reading this part of one of my books, I would consider myself very stupid right about now, but trying to move on and pretend wasn't working for me anymore.

That feeling I had persisted but standing here wasn't proving fruitful, so I turned to go back inside. And then the feeling hit me harder than before when I felt a presence behind me and the sensation of feeling trapped seemed to want to devour me whole.

"You've been a busy girl. Doing what I should have done years ago. I've never been prouder to call you my daughter."

35
RILEY

I reached behind me for the doorknob but he tsked. Chancellor Fowler shook his head quickly and pointed over my shoulder. "Calm that anxious familiar of yours. I'm not here to hurt you."

I swallowed and kept looking at him but spoke to Beau in my mind.

I'm okay, buddy. Just stay there and don't be too loud.

I could feel his frustration. *I don't like this, Mom.*

I know. Please do not wake the boys, just stay quiet.

I had to take his silence as his compliance to my request.

"Why are you here?"

Chancellor Fowler shrugged, placing his hands in his pockets. "I came to check on you. What happened must be taking a toll and I want to offer my advice, if you'll receive it."

"I won't."

He sighed. "Always so stubborn. I bet you never thought you were capable of so much anger. Enough to do what you did. I made sure that mess you made won't be a problem for you. The things we do for our children."

My mouth went dry as I thought back to Teresa's limp body and a cold shiver went down my spine as the sound of cracking bone echoed in my ears. "I hate what I did. I'm not celebrating it, it didn't make me feel good. I'm not a fucking monster."

He started to pace in front of me, casually looking at me. "I hated myself the first time I took a life as well. It leaves a dark mark on our soul, knowing that you are the reason another person is no longer breathing. I was distraught."

"So, you regret what you did to Marianne, to my father?"

He cracked his neck at the mention of my dad, then he let out a laugh that was so forced it made me cringe. "I never wanted to hurt your friend, but you left me no choice. Thomas was in the way, so his death was inevitable. All that carnage brought us closer, and I will never apologize for that. This death is no different. Causing pain and death gets easier, it gets better."

My eyebrows furrowed. "She was your mother."

"You think of me as a monster, but that woman was so much worse. Never loving my father, killing him and speaking such vile things about your mother, it was infuriating. I had so many plans to end her life, yet I never did. She'd dug her claws into me, especially when your mother left me and I let her. I only have myself to blame. I let her stay with our coven because it got her out of my hair, but once she realized you were going to be back in the picture, once Thomas was no longer an issue, well, she was back to her old ways. Her leaving was the best option and it let me focus on finding you. She should have been grateful I didn't just crack all her useless bones then." He placed a hand on his cheek, shaking his head as if the fact that he didn't do the things he said was a missed opportunity.

"Even if your mother never comes back to me, I'll at least have you." He started to step in front of me and reach out his hand to touch my cheek.

I backed up, swatting him away. "You've been spying on her, on all of us. You are still using people and I thought we had a deal. I join Celica and you back off."

He made a fist and dropped his hand. "I haven't harmed anyone, Riley. I simply made a deal with some wolves. Dante could have said no and he didn't. I have nothing against those creatures and they want what everyone wants." He leaned down to be near my face. "Power."

"That's not…"

He hummed, starting to pace again. "Your little friends caused destruction, not me. You went to my mother and needed answers, resulting in you using your glorious powers to kill her. I had nothing to do with that. Anyone is capable of heinous things, Riley. I do understand wanting to make me your villain, and that's okay. I'm sure Lena would love to hear all about your troubles."

I closed my eyes and opened them again, pushing down my frustration. "I told you I'm not meeting with your fucking liaison. Why are you not more worried that I won't tell her everything about you?"

He laughed, his shoulders moving. "Lena works for me, dear. Thomas's employment may have fallen through the cracks, but Lena understands how things will work. She's been a friend of our family for quite a while. We need to keep your emotions and power in check if you are to succeed." He lifted his eyes up to the house, wrinkling his nose. "You can't achieve anything while you are in this house. Those boys can teach you nothing. Some relationships can hold you back, Riley. They can feel safe and sane, but you will never reach your full potential if you play it safe."

I didn't care about hearing this. I didn't want to look at him, I just wanted him to leave. I turned to go when he grabbed my wrist, swiveling me around so I was only a few inches in front of him. "You are wondering how you could do something so vile? I went to her house and saw the masterpiece you made of her. I saw the power you had, and you are willing to just let it sit there and…fester? Look me in the eyes right now and tell me that you haven't let your power out to hurt someone you *actually* care about."

I opened my mouth, but no words came out. I could have lied and spat 'of course not' right in his face. I couldn't find the will to lie because all I saw was the way my mom's eyes widened when my power collected around her throat, when I let my angry and vulnerable state become too much and I lashed out at her.

My emotions were all over the place with each scenario. Teresa had tried to kill me, she had tried to hurt my friends, so I removed her from the equation. My mom had lied to me for good reason, but I'd been hurt and I'd made a bad decision. I'd caused pain for different reasons, but I was still the catalyst.

Chancellor Fowler chuckled, letting go of me. "Hmm, your heart is so good. Your regret for things is quite mundane."

I pressed my finger into his chest. "All these people want to do is help me and you *want* them to see me as the bad guy. Your own mother helped make my necklace, she helped hide me, despite her dislike for my family and for that I am grateful to her. I'm sorry you never had understanding friends or parents that wanted to protect you but stop projecting your fucked up childhood on me."

He squinted, taking in my words. His shoulders stiffened at the realization but then he shook it off as if none of it mattered to him. He used his powers to move my hand back and forcefully place it at my side. "I've been very nice to you, Riley. I've provided you with a lot of freedom to do what you will and I've tried to make sure Oliver doesn't harm your toys too much. I can't very well tell the man how to handle his business. He will not touch you, but he is more than happy to make his sons pay for their insolence. I can completely let go of their father's leash and let him run wild, disregarding your feelings. I've been dying to have a talk with your mother as well, now that I've been told by the wolves that she's doing so great. Your lack of respect could cause them great pain, so I suggest you don't speak to me like that again."

He looked around his face for some kind of crack in his exterior, but I saw nothing of the sort.

"Be a good daughter and go see Lena on Monday as planned. We will work through this mess and get to a good place. And then we can talk about moving you into the house."

"Excuse me?"

"Family has to stick together. These boys, all these little friends you've collected, they aren't your family. They will not be able to protect you from yourself."

I scoffed. "As someone who likes to call themselves my dad, you have very little faith in me."

His expression turned sad. "I do. I have the utmost faith. I just don't want to see you so defeated and distraught if the next person's neck you crack just so happens to be your little witch friend. Or maybe your boyfriend with the weak mind."

"Don't fucking…"

He held up his hands in surrender. "I'm threatening no one. I'm just speaking things out loud. I won't mourn their deaths like you will." He backed up looking at the sky and noticing the morning was just on the horizon. "Oh right, I forgot to mention, the wolves at Marth Moon, pity that was but they were a part of my plan. I did tell your shadow wielder that if they tried to get the upper hand on me again that there would be a price. The wolves are now sworn to your precious friend's partner, which puts me in a bad position. One of those boys will have to pay for meddling in my affairs."

My eyes widened and the words flew out of my mouth faster than I was ready for. "Fine, fine, I'll go see Lena. I'll do whatever, just don't—"

He finally touched my cheek, raking his knuckles across my skin and it felt like razor blades. "Shush. You *will* go see Lena but that doesn't change what has to happen. Disobedience breeds consequences."

He walked away at my stunned silence, turning at the end of the driveway. I rushed after him, but when I got to the street, he was gone.

36
ASHER

I watched as River and Grayson sat on the couch, watching TV and occasionally glancing over towards the stairs. River was laying down with his back against the arm of the couch, his legs resting on top of Grayson's thighs. Grayson doted on my brother as much as they both doted on Riley.

Most of the day had passed and it was dark outside now, letting me know that Riley had spent pretty much the entire Sunday in River's room. From the little bit I'd overheard, she'd had conversations with her mom, Corrin and Beau. I felt her body move against mine when she came back to my bed. She hadn't said anything, but there was something different about her. She went back to sleep quickly, so I didn't think much of it. And I hadn't really gotten the chance to ask since she'd gotten up, grabbed a breakfast bar and trapped herself in River's room.

She'd witnessed something horrific yesterday and unfortunately, was also the cause of that incident. I didn't know what that was like and I didn't want to pretend like I could help her when I couldn't. If she wanted to be alone, then that was fair. It didn't mean I had to fucking like it.

"You both have been rotting on this couch for hours," I pointed out, sitting on the arm of the couch.

"I am recovering from an injury. And what else are we supposed to do while Riley is having her alone time?" River asked, reaching towards the coffee table for the remote.

He started changing the channels, so I grabbed the remote and threw it onto the adjacent chair. I sat on the coffee table, facing them both. "She might not know what to do, but this whole mess is getting far too fucked up. She dives into the coven tomorrow and I remember you—" I glanced at Grayson. "—offering those shadow skills to watch her."

"I'll do whatever keeps her safe." Grayson crossed his arms over his chest, leaning back against the couch.

"I talked to Mateo earlier today and they'll be on alert in the surrounding area. Not too close to cause suspicion but just enough. Corrin is with her, so she'll have someone directly by her side. Ike is doing some digging on Chancellor Fowler's old house. Based on what Mateo told me, that might be the place he had you take Riley." I nodded over to Grayson.

"I've only even been in that room and the basement area that he kept the witches in. I was always in and out. I couldn't even tell you what street it's on or if it's even in the surrounding cities. I would assume with how close his family ties are to the school that they have to be close enough." He nodded at his own words as if the more he spoke, the more they made sense.

I reached out and patted his shoulder, continuing. "Jade will be keeping an eye on Riley's mom. Despite Mateo being in charge now, I only really trust her with that task. She has a pretty vicious vendetta against Chancellor Fowler. I mean, we all do now."

"Getting stabbed by the guy's mother will do that to a person," River offered, delicately sitting up. I narrowed my eyes at him and he waved me off. "I'm fine, okay. There is a little scar and some residual pain, but nothing I can't just shrug off. Your caring makes me all tingly inside though, so keep it up."

I rolled my eyes. "Now you—" I pointed at River, "need to lay low with what already happened and how eager dad is to get ahold of you."

"I'm sorry, you want me to just let everyone else help my girlfriend while I what? Just sit on my ass?"

I rubbed my forehead. "No, River. The best thing you can do is not place yourself in a position that would put you in more trouble."

"And what are you planning to do, hm?"

"I still have to teach classes, so I'll keep an eye on her there and do my best to intercept dad. Riley is seemingly doing what she needs to based on Chancellor Fowler's wants and needs, so I'll just boost his ego by playing along. Riley has been doing a lot and it's time we started pulling our weight."

"Yet, you won't let me," River complained. "I don't even know why I'm listening to you. It's not like you can force me to stay put."

"Hmph. I can't, but it's in your best interest. Just like instead of watching TV, we should work on your training some more. I really need to have a fucking talk with some of the mental magic teachers if your mind is this vulnerable."

Grayson put his hands up between us. "Okay. We are all very on edge and determined to make sure our girl is taken care of. I don't really enjoy sitting here and basically listening to you both shout about how much you love each other and love her because its fucking exhausting."

I opened my mouth to protest his insinuation, but he wagged his finger at me.

"Oh no, we will get into those feelings of yours later, professor." He gently moved River's legs off of him and gave him his attention. "Right now, maybe your best bet is to just—"

"How about I get into Chancellor Fowler's head. Just keep his mind in check. I can do that just fine and he wouldn't even know it's me."

"River...that's a dangerous option. What about if dad..."

"I know how to infiltrate mental conversations, so the teachers taught me something in case you were wondering. Dad is really good at focusing on one thing but mentally doing something else. I wouldn't even be near dad's mind, just the words he lets float in the mental space while telepathically speaking. It's just another safeguard for everything we are trying to do, that's all."

I worried my bottom lip but conceded. "Fucking fine. Can you do it from the house or is your telepathy not good with long range?" I asked, sarcastically.

River gave me his middle finger and the sound of a throat clearing had us all looking at the entryway. Riley gave each of us a small amount of eye contact before sighing and stepping further into the room.

"Hey, gorgeous. How are you feeling?" River asked, immediate concern in his voice.

She moved her braids over her shoulder and started picking at the ends. "Fine. I started and finished a book, so I guess that's progress."

"You've been tucked away up there for a while now, *aking sinta*," Grayson said, his voice soft and soothing.

She gave him a stiff smile. "Sorry, I didn't mean to ignore you guys. I needed to talk to my mom and then Corrin got my mind off things by telling me how much Jax fucked up her bedroom when she was gone but got over it by gushing about Mateo being way sexier now than they were before. It helped for the most part." She let out a half-hearted laugh.

"And what did your mom say?" I asked, getting up from the coffee table and walking towards her.

"She was more concerned with how I was. Then yelled about how messed up Teresa has always been and she hates herself for being happy that she's gone, but her heart hurt that I had to be the one to..." Her voice trailed off and she shook her head, moving one of her braids from her face. "I fucked up, I know that. I need to just keep this dampener on, so I don't create more of a mess."

"What? Riley, no. What did you expect to happen? She was coming after all of you." River tilted his head to the side.

She gave a small shrug. "I could have just broken a bone, something simple. I didn't have to do...*that*." Riley placed her hands on either side of her head and let out a heavy sigh. "Anyway, you guys sure have been busy planning things it seems."

"Professor St. James has been planning while we have just been listening." Grayson slung his arm over the back of the couch.

"Hm, well don't bother with any of it. I would rather you guys just stay away from it all."

I furrowed my brow. "That is really hard when we're in it. Even if we didn't know you, our dad is still very much involved."

She fiddled with the ends of her long sleeve shirt. "Your dad will stop messing with me and all of you if we just, I don't know, keep a distance. I can move back in with my mom and I'll have Corrin and Mateo and everyone else. It's not a big deal. You don't insert yourselves in things and everyone is better off."

"What the fuck are you talking about?" River pressed, getting up from the couch.

"I can figure this out on my own."

"No one is asking you to," River argued, his voice raising.

She kept her eyes on him, but they were becoming glassy. "No one is asking you to do *this*. Any of this. You are asking to get hurt, to lean into his threats rather than run the other way and let me handle this."

I grabbed her shoulders and forced her to look at me. Her brown eyes were so beautiful in her obvious sadness. It was odd to look at it that way. "His threats are from a desperate man and men like that have weaknesses. He dropped nearly everything the minute he realized he could have you back. No matter how much power he thinks he has, you are his weakness."

There was a part of me that wanted to say that she might be one of my weaknesses, but it didn't feel like the time to confess something like that. I didn't even know if I believed it. I really thought the only thing I would ever wholeheartedly care about was River, but that was a heavy miscalculation on my part.

"You actually want to risk a lot for me? What about your mental state?" She looked at River. "Your parents?" She glanced at Grayson. "And we both know you care about your brother and there might not be an option for choosing both sides anymore." She placed her eyes back on me.

I licked my lips, pushing my glasses up when they'd slid a little too far down my nose. "It is quite easy to care about two people at once. You always have a choice, but in your case, ending someone else's life to defend your own was a necessary means and any idea of choosing something else wasn't a priority, but for me, there *is* a choice and I choose to care about you both. There is no other choice. That *is* my only option."

It was almost like she stopped breathing for a moment, and her fingers touched her necklace.

"My mental state is fine, baby. But if you're that concerned I'll let Asher torture me with more mental exercises," River said, coming up and caressing her cheek.

Grayson sidled up next to him. "I'll see if Mateo can delegate some wolves to watch over my parents. I think it might be nice for my dad to chat with some shifters."

"Why are you so against this now? You didn't mind the mild planning and discussions before." I raised one of my eyebrows, suspiciously.

She pressed her lips together, giving us a tiny, forced smile. "I'm just in my head, that's all." There was a small moment like she wanted to say something more, but she pushed it away. "Just clue me in on whatever tomorrow morning. I'm just going to go to bed." She turned away after giving us each a quick kiss on the cheek.

I watched her get up the stairs and immediately started to follow her.

"So, we aren't doing mental exercises?" River asked, but I ignored him.

The door was ajar so I let myself in. She was on the floor with her back to the bed. Beau was curled up on the comforter, his head resting against the side of the bed so he could look at her.

"You want to tell me what's going on?"

"What do you mean?"

I got down on the floor and sat next to her. "You were slightly off when you got back into bed last night, so I would love to know how checking on your dog caused that."

She brought her knees to her chest. "We said no more secrets..."

"I'm so happy you remembered that." The sarcasm in my voice rolled off my tongue.

"Chancellor Fowler was here last night." She spoke directly to her knees, never giving me any eye contact.

"WHAT?!" I almost leaped off the floor, but her hand found where I rested mine on the ground.

"It wasn't for long and he was spouting all his normal rhetoric, but he plans to hurt River or Grayson for messing up his plan with the wolves. They removed one of his assets and he wants retribution. Maybe he's bluffing. I don't know, Asher."

"Then we can have Ike or another wolf stay here with River, so they can tell us if something goes wrong. Grayson will be close to you, so we'll know. We can make it work, so please don't push people away."

She squeezed my hand and I found myself not wanting to let go. "I just don't know how much more I can take, knowing I'm the surrounding factor. It's not fair to anyone. You could fight for me and you'll get hurt...I could end up hurting you if I'm not careful. Look what I did to..."

"Stop. Just stop with his mother. You have remorse. So much fucking remorse for this person who wanted you removed from this world and yet, you still think you're a problem. You are actually too good, little liar." I traced a circle on the top of her hand.

She took in a shaky breath. "You knew my dad, right?"

"I did."

"Sometimes I wish I had the power to go back in time, you know? Tell him not to leave the house or something. Chancellor Fowler keeps pushing to try to be this parent and I'll never see him that way. Not because he's a literal monster, but because I already have a dad —had a dad, I mean." Her voice broke for a moment, but she kept going. "He also told me that I was too good for the world, and he wished that I didn't have to ever face the bad things so I could keep my confidence and positive outlook." She chewed the inside of her cheek, while her tone wavered as she spoke.

She was looking at me now, her bottom lids wanting to overflow from the tears filling them. "One of my favorite places to go was the San Diego Zoo, so rain or shine if I was feeling bad, he would take me there if he was able to. There was a time during my senior year that I didn't know what I was doing with my life. Mystic Riegan was always an option, but I just wasn't sure. He didn't ask me much about anything when we walked around, but at one point he looked at me and said, 'Riley I...'" She stopped talking and closed her eyes, lifting her face to the ceiling. It looked like she was mentally counting to ten before she gave me her attention. "He said, 'Riley, I don't think I've seen a more genuine smile than when you are right here. I don't care what you do after high school, but make sure it makes you smile just like this and I'll be h-happy no m-matter what.'" She pressed the heels of her hands to her eyes, her shoulders shaking from crying. "I miss him and this entire mess makes me think of all the other people I could lose. I've already lost Marianne; I just can't go through that again. I don't really know why I'm telling you this."

I looked off to the side, trying to find the right way to say what I wanted. "I don't either but I'm...happy you did. Did it make you feel better?"

"I think so. It doesn't change what's happening, but at least you weren't a total dick and told me to just suck it up."

I used my thumb to wipe under her eyes. "I'm sorry about the things I said about your dad before. Before everything with *us* happened. I think I was just...a little..." I cleared my throat deciding that if no secrets is what we all decided on, I shouldn't break that kind of trust. "Riley, I was the one who met with your dad the night he died. I'd already left campus before everything happened with Chancellor Fowler. I didn't mean to keep him so long, but he was a good man. He'd seen a few interactions with my father and well, we talked from time to time. It wasn't a particularly good day and I wanted someone to vent to and he was there. I think I...I just didn't want to consider what would have happened if I would have stayed and kept talking to him. Chancellor Fowler wouldn't have felt the need to speak to him. I'm just—sorry." The words came out so fast and I didn't know if I had said them too fast or if I was even speaking in complete sentences.

She threaded her fingers through mine. "Thank you for telling me. We both have a lot of regrets, but that won't help us win this." She squeezed my hand and I felt the sensation throughout my entire body. "Did you tell him about just your dad or did you talk about River?"

I felt Beau's breath near my face and I side-eyed him to shift away from me. I was starting to like the familiar, but not that much. "Really just my dad, but River came up a few times. Thomas was really easy to talk to and sometimes things just came out. My father didn't have money growing up and he was adopted by humans who never really appreciated his telepathic ways. He met a well-off man at a part time job that grew fond of him and also had telepathy of his own. He helped my dad harness his powers and when he turned eighteen, he left home to live with this wealthy man who gave him all the things he could ever want...he even wrote my dad into his will."

My jaw ticked. "My father was taught that your own power was important but creating more, gaining more kept you ahead of the rest. It made you the best. And showing off the fact that you have surmounted so much power was important. It made sure you were talked about, kept at a level of superiority. When my parents met and got married, my father wanted to give her all the things and when his *benefactor* died and left him everything...I'd already been born, but I hadn't ascended into my own powers yet, so he waited. He waited for me, he waited for River, and let's just say he took the showing off portion too far."

"Asher..." she started, but I shook my head.

"I always wanted to make my dad proud, but at some point, it always felt like it was never enough. I didn't want to go into strangers' dreams and meddle just to prove how strong I was. I didn't want to take elixirs that his witch friends would make to try to improve my powers. I was a fucking kid, but when he didn't have me, he moved onto River and that's when I needed it to stop." I found my voice drifting off into the place I didn't like to go, back with my brother and his scared helplessness that I always tried to fix. "Our dad was worse on him all the time. If I said no to things, I got scolded, but when River did it was like the world was ending. He was never a fan of how River latched onto me...well, until he learned how to fight for himself. Before then, I fought for him.

I, umm.... I may seem hard on him, but I've always wanted the best. Not in that weird pretentious way, but I just wanted him to be happy but safe. I got into his dreams all those years ago because what my father was, what he *is*, haunted his dreams. I just wanted to make it better. I'm a hard ass, but I could have gone to any school, yet I chose Mystic Riegan to be closer to him, to keep an eye on my father. I've tried my best, Riley, I really have."

She cupped my cheek and stroked her thumb on my cheekbone. "You are a good brother, Asher."

"Yeah?"

She nodded, scanning her eyes along my face. "Mmhmm. I'm going to assume he doesn't...know or remember all the more invasive things you've done?"

"He doesn't. I think he chooses to block things out and that includes everything I helped him with. We bicker now, but there was a time I was like a shield for him and he loved it." I ran a hand through my hair, but kept my other hand locked with hers.

Her hand was warm against my face. "We all love your brother. You, me and Grayson, and we'll protect him. What you've done won't be for nothing."

I leaned into her touch. I didn't know why, but it felt like the right thing to do. It felt good. "And we'll protect you. That's it."

"Your caring is showing again," she teased, sniffing as the last of her tears fell past her chin.

I grabbed her wrist and leaned my face down, kissing her. Her lips were soft and inviting, opening up for my mouth. The kiss was slow and our tongues were lazy as they moved together. I pulled away and kissed her forehead, saying against her skin, "You're ours to protect."

37
GRAYSON

I was looking over my shoulder more frequently, not exactly sure what I was afraid of. Everyone knew the plan and I kept checking my phone to make sure I had the time right. I bounced on my feet while I waited outside my last class. I knew Riley would be coming this direction anytime now and in about an hour she would be headed to the Celica meeting and I would be monitoring, just like Asher wanted.

I wasn't going to encroach on Chancellor Fowler's plan and cause more problems, but I was more than happy to watch over her. And if something did pop off then I wouldn't hesitate to ruin anyone who threatened to hurt her, but for now, I would stay in my shadows and let her deal with things until she really needed me.

I saw her before she saw me. She held onto both straps of her backpack and walked with her head down, like she was trying to avoid eye contact with anyone that passed by. This school could be brutal with the way gossip traveled. I met her halfway, gripping her arms and startling her.

"Hey, it's just me." I let out a short laugh when she let out a breath of relief.

She looked over her shoulder, letting out her own awkward laugh. "Were you waiting for me?"

I nodded. "Well, yeah. That's the plan."

"Mm, I'm pretty sure the plan is for you to look on from afar, not literally shadow me."

I wrapped my arm around her shoulders, keeping her moving forward. "I like a hands-on approach, *aking sinta*."

Riley molded into my body as we walked, seeming to find comfort there. I could have kicked my feet with how happy I was with that, but I needed to focus.

"So, you came from a different side of campus. Isn't your last class on the east side?" I asked, turning us so that we could make our way to the parking lot.

"Uh, yeah, it is. I had a meeting."

I stopped walking, forcing her to stumble before regaining her footing. She looked up at me with confusion.

"Meeting with who?"

"The new human/magic liaison."

I scratched the side of my head. "We didn't know you had a meeting."

"I didn't know I needed to inform you of my schedule. Regardless of what's going on, I am still very much allowed to do what I want."

I put my hands up in surrender. "Okay, okay. I'm sorry it came out like that. I just meant, well, I was just nervous it was another surprise Chancellor Fowler meeting." She'd told us all about his crack of dawn intrusion at the house and his ominous message.

She sighed, pressing her lips together. "Sorry. I didn't mean to snap at you. He wasn't there, but he might as well have been."

I cocked my head to the side, confused.

"Celica, this meeting, it's all his stipulations. Submitting to him makes my fucking skin crawl, but as much as you all want to see me safe and secure, I want the same thing for everyone else."

I pulled her into me and she wrapped her arms around my middle. "Sending you to see the person who took over your dad's old job is fucked, but I don't really see how that helps him."

"Lena is one of his. She's another person to keep an eye on me. Unlike my dad, she isn't human. Her powers lull you so you're a little bit more susceptible to help and opening up. Even if I wanted to spew out all that I know about him, it wouldn't matter."

"How did it go?"

"It went. It was like I felt comfortable there, but I also knew I didn't want to talk to her. I did some research on her powers on my phone and it's like it can be an offset of River's. It's not necessarily mind control, but it's almost like she's trying to eventually condition you to believe something. She kept trying to get me to talk about my dad, my powers, everything, but lucky me, I'm far too stubborn for one session to work."

"That's my girl," I praised, starting to walk again.

Corrin was waiting for us by her car, leaning against the hood and typing away on her phone. She looked up, her eyes widening when she saw us. She turned her phone so the screen was facing Riley. "Jade sent me a picture of her and your mom. She said something about how she makes really good cookies, so now if anyone fucks with her, she'll be even more inclined to rip their heads off."

Riley's lips lifted a little at the mention of her mom and her safety. It had me thinking about my parents.

Corrin grabbed Riley's hand, gently pulling her over to her side. "She is mine now, shadow boy. You know where the meeting is, so don't be late. Mateo will be around as well, so if you hear some heavy-ish breathing, don't be alarmed. You just have an *alpha* on your ass."

"You really love saying that don't you. *Alpha*," Riley mocked and it was nice watching her be casual and playful.

"Oh, fuck yeah. I've been telling them that they deserved it far more than Dante ever did. I'm glad that fucking prick is dead."

Corrin walked around to the driver's side. "Jax told me he would piss on his grave if I let him."

"Morbid much," Riley scolded playfully.

I cut into their conversation. "I'll let you know when I'm there, okay?" Riley looked at me, raising an eyebrow. "I have to do something first, real quick, and then I'll be at the meeting spot."

She started to open the passenger door but stopped to scan my face. Skepticism was written all over it, but I knew she wasn't trying to come to a malicious conclusion.

"I'm checking on my parents, that's all. I know Mateo has wolves on them, but still."

Riley gave me the cutest smile I'd ever seen and opened the car door all the way. "You're a good boy, Grayson." She let those words linger as she got inside the car.

I heard Corrin giggle before the sound of the engine running drowned them out.

I took my ring off, washing the feeling of Riley calling me a good boy away for now and shadowing home.

I stood in the kitchen entryway and watched my parents bicker over how long something had been left in the refrigerator for. My mom took a whiff inside the plastic container and wrinkled her nose, scolding my dad. I cleared my throat and my mom's shoulder's lifted dramatically, flinching and my dad had to catch the container before it flew out of her hands.

I had to catch myself before a loud laugh erupted from my throat.

"Grayson! *Bakit di ka man lang nagsalita*! You know not to scare me like that!" My mom wagged her finger at me before letting the knowing smile return to her face and coming to hug me.

My dad chuckled. "If I was him, I would shadow all over the

place." He patted my arm and pulled me into another hug after my mom was done.

"What brings you home? Is something wrong at school? Are you hungry?" My mom questioned, looking like she was prepared to make me a whole meal.

I bite my lower lip, moving towards the stove and shooing my mom's hand away from the knobs. "Um, can we sit down? There is something I need to tell you."

"Is this about your shifter friends?" My dad asked, walking to the living room. "We were going to call you, but we all got to chatting and I forgot. You know I don't shift anymore, but it was nice to hear them speak about their adventures while your mother forced them to eat."

My mom smacked him on the back of the head when they sat down on the couch. "*Wag kang magsinungaling.* I forced no one. I suggested they get something to eat, like a good host."

I sat on the other end of the couch, nervously running a hand through my hair. "It does have to do with them, but it's more than that."

I felt sweat prickle at the back of my neck and I knew the nerves were starting to kick in. My parents were two of the most under-standing people on the planet. They were concerned with my educa-tion and what I wanted to do with my life, but not so much that I felt suffocated. I never even told them I was bisexual. They were always curious about my love life, but not enough to infiltrate and interro-gate me. I'd introduced them to boyfriends and girlfriends, and they never batted an eye...they just asked me if I was happy.

I didn't know what exposing my bad decisions would do to our relationship. I didn't know if they would view me differently. I'd decided to hurt people over a scholarship, but also for their safety, but knowing them they would scold me for endangering others.

"*Bakit ka nanginginig?* What's wrong, Grayson?" my mom asked, worry lacing her tone.

I pressed my lips together, hard. I wasn't sure where to start, but somehow when I opened my mouth, the words just flooded out.

I blew out a breath when I was done, refusing to look at either of them. They'd asked no questions during my explanation, but their eyes gave them away during certain parts. I barreled through even though every part of me wanted to leave this house and never look back. I wasn't sure how I was going to handle it if they thought of me as a bad person.

I felt my mom's hand on my thigh. "Grayson, *tumingin ka sa akin*"

I peeked over at her, preparing for the worst. Her face was neutral and no look of shame could be found.

"I know your father and I are honored you care so much for us." She rubbed her lips together. "But we did not raise you to think that putting others in harm's way was a good trade for our safekeeping."

She sounded disappointed and that was so much fucking worse than anything I could have imagined.

"I'm sorry, Mom. I-I don't know what else to say."

"Did you apologize to Riley? Have you made that right?" my dad pressed, leaning forward.

I nodded vigorously.

"And how is she? You've said a lot and I don't even think I could handle all those things at her age. Her father, her friend, the chancellor being her...oh, Grayson, is she alright?" My mom's lips moved a mile a minute.

It warmed my heart a little to see my mom care about Riley as much as I did. "She's about as good as she can be. She has a lot of support." I licked my lips "Everything felt like my world was caving in and maybe that sounds dramatic, but he put me in a corner. Now the logical response would have been to tell someone, but in the moment I just..."

My mom cupped my cheek. "I know, honey. Grayson, please tell me that you are not involved with that man anymore. No more hurting people."

"I'm not. We're actually trying to fix everything, hence the wolves monitoring you. Your protection is imperative to me and it always will be. *Nagkamali ako at gumagawa ako ng paraan para maayos ko ang aking mga kasalanan*"

My dad shook his head, slapping his hands on his knees. "He needs to be dealt with. He can't manipulate a young boy into doing his dirty work. He can't just..."

I stood up, causing them to tilt their heads up to look at me. "For now, he can. *Nakakatakot siya*, Dad, but we've got this. Can you please trust me?"

My mom got up from the couch and puffed her chest out, almost trying to size me up. "You just told us an entire story about how you've been keeping things from us and now you want us to trust you to take on a grown man who's been basically...what's the word..." she snapped her fingers and looked at my dad who shrugged. Her eyes lit up when she had what she wanted to say. "Stalking his daughter, and trust you to make everything better?"

I searched around the room for a good, solid answer to her very valid question. "Yes."

They both sighed, knowing that no matter what they said, I'd continue to do what I wanted. I plucked my phone from my pants and checked the time. "He manipulated more than just me and I can't stand by and let that continue to happen, okay?" I walked around them to head for where I left my shoes.

"We can't stop you, but I will be a nervous wreck the whole time. Give me Riley's mother's number. I need someone to discuss the actions our children are taking." She pointed to my phone and I did what she asked. I leaned down to kiss her on the cheek.

"I'm sorry for not telling you the truth. I just don't like burdening you with things, especially when you've already done so much for me."

My dad huffed. "You burden us even more when you keep your mouth shut. You worry about us, hell, we worry about you. *Anak ka namin*. End of story."

I gave my dad the biggest hug and then pulled away, letting my shadows wrap around my legs as I prepared to leave. "I love you guys. I'll be safe, I promise."

"*Pssst.*" That sound coming from my mom's lips grabbed my attention. It always did, even when something else had my sole focus. She grabbed my shoulders and made me bend down so she could kiss my forehead. "Your scholarship is as important to you as it is to us, but if you'd gotten it taken away, we would have figured something out. We should have known something was up when it all happened and that's on us. School is important, but so is your well-being. We've always known that and I hope you know that now too."

I held in my emotions, not because I didn't want to cry, but because I needed to be vigilant for Riley's sake. "I love you a lot, Mom. Please do what the wolves say if it comes down to it."

She wiped small tears from underneath her eyes and waved me off. "I'm still your mother. Don't tell me what to do. *Tulungan mo ang girlfriend mo*"

I landed behind a tree and when I looked around it, the witches were farther away than I'd hoped. I couldn't hear much of what they were saying but I spotted Riley and Corrin the minute they walked up. I started to muster up my shadows so I could move closer, but I heard a cracking branch and looked over my shoulder.

Red eyes appeared from beyond some trees, and I sighed a breath of relief knowing it was Mateo. A noticed a few other yellow eyes that came and went as I scanned the area around me but at least I knew they were there. I shadowed closer to where the witches convened. I leaned against a tree and watched Riley from afar. As if on cue, she looked over in my direction. She looked like she was staring right at me, but she couldn't know my exact location, could she?

She tilted her head to the side and tucked one of her braids behind her ear, looking away. Some of the other witches came over to greet them, one of them far too cheery for my liking. I watched them talk and it looked casual, but not exactly friendly. Corrin stepped in between Riley and one of the other girls. A cluster of other witches started to come over, curious on what the issue was.

A taller female, which I had to assume was the coven leader, started putting their hands up and talking to Riley and then turning her head to speak to the other one.

Wait. I recognized that other girl. She was the one from Leif's. The one that I think tried and failed at hitting on my best friend.

My fingernails dug into the bark of the tree trunk as I leaned in, trying to focus my eyes on what I was seeing. I was still a little too far away to hear anything, but I honestly didn't need to. My eyes widened when I noticed this girl get in Riley's face and Corrin had to push her away.

The girl came back with a force and Riley started yelling back while Corrin kept trying to grab her arm and lead her to another area. I watched as Riley fidgeted and rubbed her hands together, but what I didn't notice was her slip off her dampener.

In a matter of seconds, the other witch was clutching at her throat, falling to her knees. Her body was shot back, through the crowd of witches and slammed into a tree. If Riley was apologetic or stunned by any of it, her face didn't show it.

38

RILEY

My dad's office had been completely changed and the longer I sat in here, the more I wanted to rip the wallpaper apart and flip the desk over. I would relish watching all of Lena's ugly figurines break into a million pieces on the ground. I looked down at my phone and saw multiple texts from the guys.

RIVER

> If you get uncomfortable just leave. I'll come pick you up. Asher might not love it, but it's better to ask for forgiveness than permission.

I stifled my laugh, not wanting to alarm the liaison while she shuffled some papers, getting my file together.

GRAYSON

I'll be waiting for you later, okay? You want out of this meeting and I'll shadow you out of there. Fuck the school rules.

A small smile crept onto my face.

ASHER

You know how to be sassy and annoyingly frustrating so just do that and I'm sure Lena will regret ever having to meet with you. You are so much stronger than you think.

My eyebrows furrowed with my mixed emotions. Corrin had messaged telling me that everything was in place and I should just go about my school day as normal. I'd gotten three calls from my mom, all of which resulted in her trying not to cry. She trusted me and I had been surprised that the minute I'd blurted out that I'd killed someone, she didn't make a sound.

It was almost like she knew something like that was inevitable, but her soothing words to me about how yet again none of this was my fault, echoed in my head.

"Okay, Riley, sorry about that. I just wanted to make sure I had everything I needed." Lena smiled at me with all her teeth and she already had me on edge. She scanned her eyes down the paper in front of her. "How are you settling with your powers?"

"Fine," I said, looking right at her and swiveling my dampener ring around my finger.

"I highly doubt that based on what I've been told. No mishaps or confusion?"

I scowled at her. "Nope."

Lena hummed, looking down at her papers again. "I'm just trying to help. Based on what he's told me, you recently gained your powers again, so I would assume you've had some trouble."

I narrowed my eyes. "Some trouble? Is that what he's calling it?"

She blinked over at me, innocently. "He's concerned about you. The fact that the chancellor is hiding the fact that you're his daughter is quite nice of him. I am sure you're trying to maintain as much of a stable existence as you can, but that kind of outing would make it harder."

"Are you trying to get me to give him some kind of sympathy?" I asked, leaning back against the couch.

She pursed her lips. "Well, of course not, but cutting him some slack could be good for you. He understands your powers, things those boys could never understand."

"How the fuck do you know about them?" My shoulders tensed as I tilted my chin towards her.

"Of course, they aren't in your file, but Chancellor Fowler made sure to let me know everything I needed to before our meeting. We don't have to talk about them if you don't want to." Her voice was calm and collected. I felt something change in the air just a bit, like an overwhelming sense of peace.

The feeling was abrupt and my body started to relax but the sudden difference felt foreign. I rolled my neck and tried to shake it off. I took in a breath and focused on her. Her expression was one that exuded patience, like she was happy to wait for this rush of relaxation to take me over.

"The fuck are you doing to me?"

She sighed. "I felt you getting a little hostile so I just made it better. I want to be your friend, Riley. Your father won't be happy with me if I don't make sure you make progress here."

"He's not my..."

"I've been told you are having your first Celica meeting today, that must be exciting. Getting to know your fellow witches while you are struggling to figure things out will be very helpful. Are you nervous about seeing them? Anxiety is quite common when presenting yourself to new people."

"What the actual fuck are you—" A wave of that feeling hit me again and I wanted to slump back into the couch. Her words were sounding more appealing, and I could have been lulled to sleep by them.

"I think it might be best after the meeting for you to start coming to see me maybe twice a week, just until you are fully in a routine with them. Also, as long as your lips are sealed, so are ours. The coven doesn't need to know how much superiority you have over them. Being humble is a wonderful attribute."

I rubbed the side of my head. "Yeah...I guess..."

"So, let's talk classes. I see you're an English major. How is that going?" She smiled at me again with all her teeth and I almost wanted to smile back, but I looked off to the side.

I zeroed in on the window, an influx of memories flooding my mind. I remembered taking the potion Corrin had made, I'd seen what I now knew was Chancellor Fowler pushing my dad out a window and I heard Corrin screaming for me while I tried to focus. This office may have changed, but that window and what it represented didn't. I blinked, shaking my shoulders.

I gripped one of my backpack straps and started to get up, right as Lena went to repeat her question to me. "Riley, our session isn't over."

I shook my head, the weight of the soothing feeling leaving my body in waves. "Yes, it is."

"You need to stay and talk," she insisted, her powers trying to pull me in and the need to go back to the couch and rest was strong.

I waved my hands in front of me as if I was slapping away the mood she was trying to set. "I'm *done*. This meeting was a stipulation, and now we've had it." I tugged my backpack over my shoulders and leveled my gaze at her. "Try to keep me here and you'll see how fast this ring comes off and how easily your spine snaps in half." I had no idea where that had come from but I wasn't taking it back.

Lena didn't look alarmed, but she lifted her chin towards her door. "You really are your father's daughter."

PRESENT

Corrin pulled me along through the woods, realizing how much I was starting to dread the idea of having to face this head on.

"Listen, no one is in the dark about things, Riley. We know where everyone is and they're accounted for. Lighten up. I've got you." She squeezed my arm and gave me a hopeful smile.

I attempted to give her one back, but I could feel how strained it was. I heard laughing up ahead and eventually a large group of people came into my view. I felt a chill down my spine, but not so much that I needed to be on high alert, but like I was being watched and protected. I glanced over, past Corrin, in the direction I would have bet money that Grayson was.

I didn't see anything, but I knew I was right. I looked away just to be met with three witches walking up to us. I wasn't intimidated but I had a feeling they wanted me to be.

"Seth, Geena, Olivia," Corrin said, casually pointing to each of them and then looking back at me. "This is my best friend, Riley. She's new to the coven..."

"Oh, we know." The girl in the middle, Geena, crossed her arms over her chest and gave me a once over.

Corrin clucked her tongue and pulled at one of her tight curls. "Right. I'm sure Jamie already filled you guys in." On the car ride over, Corrin had told me as much as she could about her coven, including the interim coven leader, Jamie, who she liked but didn't really think twice about disobeying her orders if need be.

Geena quickly snuck a glance over to the girl at her left, Olivia, before giving me her eyes again. "Mm, that's not it. We were at the meeting when you went berserk. What a way to show off your powers, truly what a show."

I almost started looking around to see who she was talking to. I hadn't even said a word to them and she already had some kind of attitude towards me. "I'm sorry, is there some kind of issue?"

Corrin stepped between us and laughed awkwardly. "It's Riley's first day so just lay off, okay?"

A tall female approached us, a curious look in her eye. "Everything's okay over here. We are about to begin." She smiled over at me. "Ah, Riley, yes? I'm so happy you could join us."

"Keep an eye on her, Jamie. Undisciplined witches are the fucking worst," Geena snickered, biting her bottom lip.

"What is your problem?" I demanded, pointing my finger at the witch.

Jamie raised her hands up, trying to diffuse the situation. "Riley, Geena, let's just both calm down and discuss whatever this is *after* the meeting. This coven is a family, remember?" She sounded so secure in her response, like she knew this was the most educated thing she could say at the moment.

Geena sauntered over to me, getting way too close for my liking. "Yes, and family protects each other, which is why you being here doesn't really sit right with me. Simply being a witch doesn't grant you access to Celica and based on what you did. I'd think you need more education in your own skills, but here you are putting us in danger." She tsked, her lips coming together in a smirk. "Focusing on this rather than that delicious boyfriend of yours would do you good."

I could have sworn my fucking eye twitched at her mention of River. What the fuck did he have to do with this? "I'm here to maybe get help with said powers you seem to be so scared of. You don't know me so why the fuck are you bringing up any aspect of my life right now?"

Corrin took Geena by the shoulder and lightly pushed her away from me. "Geena, back off. Fuck."

The other witch shrugged her off. "You caused that big scene to what? Get attention? You're in now, so what do you plan to do?

Dazzle us all with your connection to Hecate? As if the goddess would even show you the time of day." She got close to me again, but this time her face was inches from mine. She was goading me and I hated to say that it was working.

"Attention?!"

She poked her finger into my shoulder. "Trainwrecks like you will give a bad name to this coven, no matter how hard you work. Stay, go, it doesn't really matter to me, but you'll always be looking over your shoulder, knowing that none of us actually trust you!"

"It's so fucking ironic that you think you know this coven so well!"

"Riley..." Corrin hissed at my side.

I twisted my dampener ring around my finger. I tried to control my breathing, but I was too irritated, too pissed off. Fucking Lena, Chancellor Fowler and now this random bitch who decided that starting a fight with me was a smart move.

Geena snickered. "How about you give River a free pass to spend his time with someone who doesn't become the school pariah in less than a month. The poor guy deserves so much better than a lackluster witch. You must be *incredible* in bed because everything else is well," she moved her eyes over me as if she was unimpressed, "less than desired."

She reached up and tapped my nose with her finger and everything in front of me vibrated. It was like my whole body was shaking. My ring shifted down my finger, the transition smooth and powerful with the way I meticulously tucked it into my front pocket.

Geena started to laugh, but the sound was caught in her throat. Choking sounds came from her, her fingers digging into her neck. She tried to gasp for air but just ended up on her knees, clawing at the ground and eventually looking up at me, an accusatory stare on her face.

Her friends tried to help her, but I didn't care. I flicked my eyes up to the tree that was beyond the crowd of people, and I watched her body lift up from the ground and get propelled backwards by an invisible force. My invisible force.

I felt Corrin grip my arm, but I yanked away from her, shoving my way through the crowd.

"Miss Monroe!" Jamie yelled behind me.

I finally made it over to Geena who was crumpled on the ground, attempting to pull herself up. I pressed on her legs, keeping her grounded. She reached for her own dampener ring, but I pinned her arms to her sides.

"Tsk, tsk. What was the word you used? Lackluster?" I said the word with a flourish before I forced my power onto her left leg and heard the resounding snap of bone.

"Riley, stop!" I heard Corrin yell, but I ignored her.

"Stay back! Miss Monroe, stop what you're doing." Jamie demanded, as if her words meant anything to me. All I saw was red.

Suddenly, branches from the tree Geena was pressed against wrapped around me and started to rip me away from her. They dug into my arms and chest. I whipped my head around, seeing Jamie move her hands in a fluid motion. I scowled, feeling heat rise in my body. Tiny sparks of flames scattered along the branches and those small flames became larger, wrapping around me. The tree branch burned and eventually fell away. I flicked my hand back sending Jamie sailing backwards.

Collective gasps and screams echoed but I didn't hear them. I was tired of everyone trying to undermine me. I was tired of feeling like I had control just for the rug to be pulled out from under me. I was tired of all the surprises I didn't fucking ask for. Geena wasn't worth any of my effort. River would never want her and she was just a mean girl with nothing better to do than to put me down.

I *knew* all of that. Yet, I felt flames leave my fingertips and hit her jeans. I didn't want to stop it. My other hand touched the ground and a trail of red and orange flames followed along the leaves and dirt, creating a separation between me and them.

"You have no idea what I'm capable of," I gritted through my teeth. Geena writhed on the ground, the fire burning through her jeans and likely starting to hit her flesh.

A disturbing sensation hit my mind. It felt like someone was rifling around in there and I couldn't stop it. Different memories of mine were brought to the front. Marianne's bloody body. The vision of my dad falling out his window and the agony of me watching it. The hurt I'd felt with my mom, Grayson, even fucking Asher. My brain felt violated and like whoever was doing this was searching for something. Wait, they weren't searching. They were picking and choosing, plucking different memories and it made the flames worse.

I took my hands away from Geena and landed on my ass, shuffling backwards, needing it to stop. Pieces of my mind were being trifled with and I wanted to dig my fingers into my head to make it stop. This had happened to those witches Chancellor Fowler took, which meant whoever helped him was...here.

A loud howl penetrated the air and paws scraped along the ground. Beyond the flames I saw red eyes, which looked past me. I knew Mateo was looking at Corrin, almost like even as the alpha, they wanted her direction on what to do.

Mom! Tell them to open up the door. I need to be with you! I heard Beau in my head, but he was too far away right now. I tried to tune him out.

"Holy fuck! Wolves!" a witch cried.

"Did she bring them here?" another one speculated.

Riley, what the fuck is going on? Answer me, please! River's voice in my head caused my breathing to stutter. Beau only acted up when I was in trouble and River was with him, so of course my boyfriend would think using his telepathy was necessary.

I—I.... I tried to think back, but my mind was too chaotic, it was too wild to concentrate on communicating.

"Fucking Seth, do it!" Someone screamed. I didn't know what was happening until a layer of water fell over us, cold and heavy. Seth must have had the power over water. It shook me to my core and I shivered, the memories going dormant and my mind becoming quiet again. I heard Geena's whimpering cries, clasping my hands over my mouth, trying to piece together everything I'd done.

I needed to get out of there. I needed help. I needed to leave.

Before I could gather my bearings, a shadowy figure embraced me and wrapped up in its wisps of darkness. The black smoke was one I knew and the last thing I saw before Grayson shadowed me away was Corrin's face.

For the first time since we met, she looked scared of me.

Chocolate.PSD
Bar Mock-Up
Food Packaging Collection

39
RIVER

"This card game isn't really going to work since you talk about what you're holding in your head," I explained, placing my cards on the coffee table and getting up. Ike had been here for over four hours, and I liked the guy, but he really needed to learn how to lighten up.

"I thought we said no powers?" he scolded.

I shrugged, pulling my shirt up and inspecting my healed wound. The scars were deep and raised but I couldn't feel the pain as intensely as before. Corrin's healing powers were top notch and I'd told her so when I saw the wound start to heal itself right in front of my eyes. "You agreed to that. I did not. Any news from your sister?"

Ike got his phone out, scanning the screen. "Nothing since she said they were on their way to that meeting."

"Is there a reason you didn't join Celica with her? As much as you both bicker, you also equally talk about how much you care, so..."

He leaned back on the couch, running a hand over his freshly shaved head. "Not for me. Corrin is a fan of group projects and all that. I'm my sister's keeper to an extent. Also, she would annoy the shit out of me if I followed her to the coven. She likes to have her own thing with her own group of friends and I'm the same way. Besides, she likes to explore her magic and be all smart science girl. I don't really like to use my powers all that much."

"Except for when you are helping take down alpha werewolves?" I joked, watching him put the cards in a nice little pile.

"I do what I can. I'm a nice guy, sue me."

I chuckled, turning up my powers and finding Chancellor Fowler. I was careful when I moved through his head, but I didn't need to work that hard since nothing was happening. He hadn't tried to have any mental communication with my dad and a small part of me was happy about that. It was a little selfish that a piece of that happiness had to do with myself and not with Riley.

I was committed to this and whatever it would bring but I was also a little on edge with being so potentially close to my dad's mind. I'd told Asher I would be fine—and I was— but that didn't mean the man didn't make me just a tiny bit nervous.

"Jade gave an update that Riley's mom is okay. She's apparently asking a million and one questions about her daughter. Putting Jade in charge of her was a bad idea. It's just a matter of time before she word vomits every single minute detail about Teresa's death," Ike said, scrolling through his texts.

"Riley already told her mom."

"Yes, but did she give her mom all the gory details? Because Jade is known for leaving no detail unturned," Ike explained, shivering as if he just remembered something he would rather forget. "I'm about to order food, do you want—"

I put my hand up to stop him, when I heard an unfamiliar voice speak to Chancellor Fowler.

She's here with her friend. She looks fine, nervous but just fine. I thought I was done doing this?

Chancellor Fowler chuckled in his mind. *You're done when I say you're done. You should be happy, I don't ask you to do more. How about we let all your witch friends know you're the reason why their minds felt violated some time ago. You use that little memory magic of yours for good, but who says they wouldn't believe that you use it for other things. Is that what you want?*

No. Don't. I don't know what else you want me to do?

The chancellor was silent for a minute. Ike started to speak again but I waved him off, moving into the kitchen. The other voice spoke again.

Wait, something is happening. I think there might be a fight.

Between?

Your daughter and another witch. Should I try to stop it? The coven leader is a joke...

Chancellor Fowler hummed. *No, just observe.*

Riley just threw her against a tree and she's not stopping. I really think I should.

The energy in Chancellor Fowler's mind grew as if he was excited about whatever was happening. I had to keep my focus, so I placed my hands on the counter and closed my eyes, keeping my mind steady. I couldn't cause too much commotion, or he would notice someone else was eavesdropping. The key to good telepathy was being smooth about your infiltration, as if nothing was amiss.

No, don't you dare try to stop her. Chancellor Fowler insisted.

What the fuck was going on? This Celica meeting was meant to be simple, but what was Riley doing? My mind nearly short circuited when they mentioned something about a fire. I needed to be there, but I knew there was only one way for me to do that.

Fine, I'll do it. After this we are done. The other voice said and I realized I'd missed what Chancellor Fowler had asked. Fuck.

Loud barking started and the sound of Beau's paws scrapping against the floor echoed in my ear. His barking pounded against my head and I looked off to the side to see him practically ramming his body into the front door.

"Hey, buddy, calm down. River, what the fuck is going on?" Ike asked, trying to handle Beau but the pitbull wiggled his way out and kept running around.

The issue with Beau had me rubbing my temples and trying to maintain my powers. I searched for a moment and finally found Riley's mind. The minute I was in, I pressed my fingertips into the counter because fuck, was it painful in there. I wasn't an empath, but that level of mind fuck hurt even me. I saw the memories fly by and her internal thoughts of begging it to stop. The heat that she could create was increasing with every passing memory and I knew she wasn't doing this to herself.

Someone else was in here and I would bet all the money I had that it was the same person who'd gotten into my own head. They must be a hybrid magic wielder just like Riley. I pushed my way through the madness and spoke to her.

Riley, what the fuck is going on? Answer me, please!

I knew she was trying and then there was a shift in her mind, like whatever was there was gone. They must have gone back to talk to Chancellor Fowler. If Riley needed me, she could call out for me, but if they'd left her mind, maybe this entire mess would settle down.

I raced my powers back to Chancellor Fowler and I landed in the middle of whatever they were talking about. I saw Ike out of the corner of my eye struggling with Beau and I would help him in a minute, but I just needed to...

I know it was him. I've been in his head before, I'm sure of it.

Chancellor Fowler lulled his mind a bit. *She will be quite upset with me for this, but I did warn her. Let him know what to do and shield your mind, since we have a little watcher.*

I can do it. I did fine last...

I could practically hear the chancellor tsk. *No you said you were done and I respect that. Just do what I say and let the man have his fun.*

I pushed myself out the minute I felt him look at me, even though he couldn't actually see me. I pressed my hand to my chest, feeling my heart beating rapidly. I looked over to Beau and Ike, noticing the familiar had settled down, but his body was still shaking. Ike had his arms wrapped around him while he sat on the floor.

"River, what the fuck?"

"It's Riley...I don't know. Something happened at the coven meeting."

Ike's eyes widened and he fumbled for his phone, likely to check if Corrin had written anything.

I'd left my phone on the kitchen counter earlier in the day and saw it buzzing. A phone call from Asher was coming through. I went to pick it up when an intense grating sound hit my head. It sounded like nails on a chalkboard, but then it felt like my brain was getting pulverized with a mallet. I gripped the side of my head, trying to build up the walls around my mind. Inch by inch a shield was created but it stopped. I couldn't keep going or maybe I wasn't strong enough to keep pushing back.

The shield reverberated as if something was barreling through. It pulsed and I felt my knees hit the floor of the kitchen. The wall I'd tried to build exploded around me and I quickly tried to create another, but each time was weaker and easily destroyed.

Oh, River. You've learned so much, but it will never be enough to keep me out.

"No, no, no," I whispered to myself, continuing to try and fail at helping myself, helping my mind.

Disobedience breeds consequences, son. It won't hurt too badly.

I slammed my fist against the floor and the feeling I dreaded started to claim my body, my mind...everything. He was starting to take over and I wanted to push back, but he was already in. That familial tie was strong even if I had every reason to want to shred it to pieces. I gritted my teeth, nearly biting my own tongue from the sheer will to not obey him.

I regretted not pushing myself more to be able to take him on. Despite being shielded by Asher, I should have done my due diligence. I knew that.

Ike ran over to me and an anxiety-ridden Beau licked at my face, whining. "River, talk to me. What can I do?" He sounded desperate and I wanted to tell him there was nothing he *could* do.

I heard what my father wanted and my own will kept attempting to intrude on his control. He was stronger and he always had been. I got up from the floor, feeling myself move like a robot.

"Where are you going? What did you hear?" Ike pushed, grabbing my forearm.

I whirled around and slammed him into the kitchen wall, his eyes grew with shock. His expression quickly morphed into panic when he looked into my eyes. If he realized something, I wasn't aware because I didn't *feel* anything. I pulled away heading towards the entryway table, grabbing my motorcycle keys.

Beau bit at my heels but I ignored him, like I ignored my own pleas to stop myself.

I left my helmet behind as I slammed the door behind me and got onto my bike. I heard the engine revving and all I could think was *he was going to make this hurt*. This would hurt everyone.

I backed out of the driveway and headed down the street, not really knowing where I was going but the fact that I needed to keep driving was my only thought. He was leading my directions but never showed me the destination, even though all that came to mind was one word: pain.

Chocolate PSD
Bar Mock-Up
Food Packaging Collection

40
ASHER

Riley hadn't looked all that focused in my class and I didn't blame her. I went through the normal motions but always kept her in my sights. Her witch friend would whisper to her and she would answer back, but nothing about her expression ever changed. A simple coven meeting held so much unknown for her.

I had a plan in place. Precautions. I kept telling myself that everything would be just fine and the fact that I was even letting my confidence falter was some kind of mistake. I tapped my pen on my desk remembering how she'd let Corrin go ahead of her and waited for everyone to filter out. She'd slowly made her way around my desk and waited just a quick moment before kissing me.

It was a desperate kiss that told me she wanted everything to be fixed, she wanted to rewind all of this and go back to when things were easier. I pulled away knowing that things stopped being easy the minute we'd decided the four of us being a 'thing' was feasible. Her lips had pulled into a small smile before leaving.

I'd checked on River multiple times throughout the day, even though he occasionally updated me through his telepathy. Chancellor Fowler had been quiet, surprisingly. That made me nervous but not enough to call this whole thing off. Villains had to take a moment of rest at some point, right?

Two more classes, an hour spent in my office planning coursework and finally I headed straight to my car.

I didn't know my father's schedule completely, but I least knew how Mondays went. He had a bunch of emails to get through in the morning, various meetings throughout the day, lunch with some of the other deans and then back to whatever the fuck he did in his office the rest of the day. Eventually somewhere between five and six o'clock he went home.

It was slowly getting dark when I pulled up. The sun hadn't completely set, but it was descending towards the trees little by little. I walked into the house and was met with my father coming down the stairs.

"Asher, I'm surprised you're here," he acknowledged, looking me up and down.

"Well things change."

"And your brother wasn't in his classes today. Do you know anything about that?" he asked, gruffly.

"He wasn't feeling good, so better safe than sorry." I bit the inside of my cheek. "I did want to talk to you about him. I thought it might be better if we did it away from the school, just you and me."

"You're finally ready to have a civil conversation?" My dad rolled up the sleeves of his button down.

I grinded my molars together. "You call threatening both of us and everyone else, civil? Is that what all those other times we've spoken were to you?"

He raised one of his eyebrows. "Even you know I could be far meaner, but I am choosing not to be. Chancellor Fowler is not a bad man, Asher. He wants his family to be stronger than ever, and so do I. I don't understand your aversion to that."

I nearly choked on how flippant he was being about everything, but I couldn't say I was surprised. "You and I will never agree that he is a good man in any way, but I talked to him. River, that is."

He hummed, turning to walk towards the back of the house. "Did you now?"

I followed behind him, stepping outside when he opened the back door. "As much as I don't appreciate your heinous version of discipline when it comes to him, his safety does matter. Not that I think you really care much about that, but I did tell him that letting Riley do what Chancellor Fowler asks was for the best." The words rolled off my tongue with ease, but they tasted bitter and awful. "I need to look at this logically and Riley will be fine, but River has you as a parent, so he doesn't have the same protection as she does."

"As a parent, you want the best for your children and even as adults, they tend to forget where they came from, so they need to be forced down a peg by any means necessary. He wants to learn lessons the hard way, you both clearly do, but it seems like you are finally being the older brother I knew you could be." He spoke like everything he said was fact and maybe I'd inherited that need for control from him, but at least I knew when it was enough. I never wanted to truly hurt anyone for the sake of myself.

"He doesn't like it, but as long as Chancellor Fowler sees she's doing what she needs to do then they'll be fine. Their relationship can be maintained, right?"

He ran his finger over his bottom lip, eyeing me. "I believe so. The shadow wielder too, if that's what Riley wants. And you want no part of a relationship with her?"

"Excuse me?" I asked, furrowing my brow.

"Let's not play dumb. It's not becoming of someone with your education. Besides, someone who fights so hard for a person they claim is just their student is fooling themselves."

I bit my bottom lip so hard I thought I tasted blood. "No, I don't want to complicate things more. Eventually if all goes well, River will graduate, move out and take her with him. Riley can try to have some kind of relationship with him or whatever that looks like and she won't be my issue."

My dad nodded, looking up at the sky, watching as the sun kept slowly hiding behind the trees. "I could persuade Chancellor Fowler to take out his efforts on the shadow wielder instead."

I waved my hands in front of me. "I wasn't saying to go after Grayson in light of River not being an option."

He looked at me as if I had three heads. "My boy, your brother and his friend still need to learn a lesson, and he hasn't quite decided which one will get the brunt of it, but I suppose you've made the choice easier." He grabbed my arm and squeezed. "I am so very happy you've come to see my side of things. You'll learn to love the feeling of power once this is over and that girl does right by her father."

He got his keys from his pocket and walked past me towards the door. "Stay awhile. Your mother is in the master bedroom; she'd love to see you."

I caught the door before it closed, falling into step with him. "Where are you going?"

"If you must know, I'm meeting with Chancellor Fowler."

"You're going back to the school?"

"I never said that." He stopped, turning around and scoffing at me. "Would you like to come with me? I'm sure he would love to know how cooperative you're being, but of course, that means that you would be in league with us and that means unbridled loyalty."

That made me uneasy. "Are you going to his house?" That was likely the place Grayson had shadowed Riley to.

"It is quite nice. His family clearly did well for themselves. Are you coming or not?"

My first instinct was to say no, but then again, I would rather *I* get physically close than anyone else. "Sure, that sounds—"

My dad held his hand up, silencing me. His eyes looked far away, the same way River's did when he was using his powers. His lips curled up into a snarl before he gave me his attention. "Do you take me for a fool, Asher?"

"No..."

"Truly, do you? Your brother may be under the weather, but he seems to have no issue fumbling around in Riley's mind and possibly Chancellor Fowler's?"

"I don't know what you're talking about?"

He laughed, holding his stomach. "He couldn't just sit back and let things be as they should. He's bold, I'll give him that, but clearly not smart enough to not get caught. He just had to tend to that girl, didn't he? Clearly, your brother is going to have to learn things the hard way. And no I don't mean that little mind game that happened at the university."

I ran in front of him, confused and thrown off guard. "What are you going to do?!"

"*I* won't *do* anything."

He shoved me to the side, heading out the front door and towards his car.

"Dad, just leave him alone. I'll talk to him, okay?"

He huffed, unimpressed. "Like you *talked* to him before? I should reprimand you for lying to me, but you'll take on your brother's pain just like you've always done."

He opened up his car door and I slammed it closed before he could climb inside. "Dad, I've never asked you for anything. Just please, stop."

He grabbed my shirt and tugged me closer to him. "Pleading is for the weak. Get out of my way or I'll make sure Erik takes his frustrations out on everyone you've grown to like or care for. Your girl will end up with only you and you know what happens when there is no one left, Asher. Resentment. Is that what you want?"

My mouth dropped open and for the first time, my bravado was gone. My mouth was dry and all I wanted to do was call Grayson to check on Riley and find my fucking brother.

He slapped my cheek and got into his car, slamming the door and getting out of our driveway so quickly that I'd only blinked before he was gone. I went into my head, searching for my brother, but every time I tried to talk to him...I was kicked out.

I looked up towards our house and saw my mom peeking out through the curtains of their bedroom. She loved us but she was a coward. I kept trying and trying to get mentally get to River. I'd worked with him, but it wasn't enough. Dad was too pissed off and River was so vulnerable when it came to Riley.

I tried again and my head hurt from the resounding hit that connected with it, like something was kicking me out and making it count. Sweat percolated at the back of my neck and I raced to my car, every breath getting harder to take in. I fumbled around for my keys, finally getting my car started and racing down the street.

I swerved around a car, practically running a red light. My phone lit up with a text from Grayson. I picked up my phone with one hand, keeping an eye on the road as best I could.

GRAYSON

Riley SOS. I brought her to the house. Ike is here but River isn't. He doesn't know where he went.

I got another text from Mateo, having to slam on my brakes when I realized the car in front of me had stopped.

MATEO

Corrin wants me to take her to your house, but I don't know if I should. Is Riley okay? What the hell happened out there?

I wish I fucking knew. I slammed my hand against the steering wheel. Fuck, fuck, fuck.

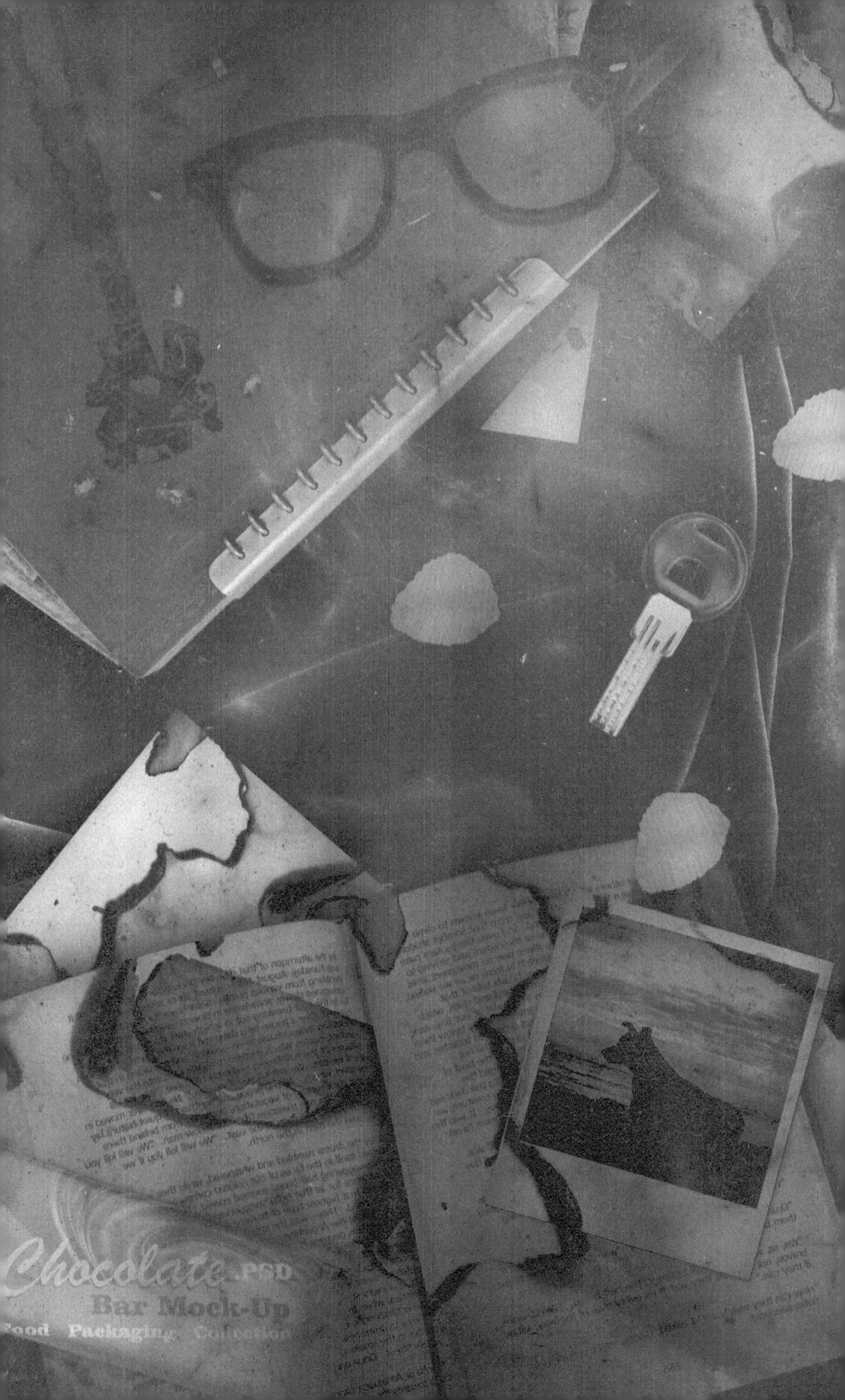
Chocolate .PSD
Bar Mock-Up
Packaging Collection

41

RILEY

I was shaking so hard my bones hurt from how tense I felt. I was cold and wet, a wave of vertigo threatening to wash over me. I didn't regret standing up for myself, but I instantly regretted how I went about it. Bones cracking, flesh burning, it was all so intense in my mind and I couldn't get it out. Every time I blinked, the moment my eyes would close, I would be back there. It was almost like this took the place of my haunted memories of Marianne and Chancellor Fowler's mother, yet those were there too, just lurking in the background.

"Riley, where is your ring?" I heard Grayson ask when I finally was able to focus.

"What?"

"Your ring, baby, where is your ring?" He brought his fingers to my cheek and asked in a softer tone.

"P-pocket," I stuttered out, trying to collect my bearings. I realized I was on the couch and laid back against the cushions, a blanket thrown over my body.

Grayson dug his fingers in my front pocket, pulling out the metal ring and placing it on my finger. He moved my braids out of my face and kissed the side of my head. "Just relax, okay?"

I nodded, starting to look around, feeling a furry presence next to me. I reached my hand out to pet my familiar, who snuggled his face into my palm. His tongue licked me, shuffling his way into my lap.

"Where the hell is he?" Grayson exclaimed, throwing his hands up.

Ike groaned. "I don't know! He was having a whole moment in the kitchen and then when I tried to help, he came at me and then he left. He took his keys."

"And he never spoke about where he was going?"

"No, he didn't do much talking at all. He looked dazed, like he wasn't himself."

Grayson ran his hands into his hair. "Oh fuck, fuck, fuck."

Ike forced Grayson to look at him straight on. "What about my sister?"

"Corrin is fine. Everything was clear when I got to Riley." Grayson was about to open his mouth again, but Ike brought his phone screen up to his face and walked away, placing it to his ear.

"Grayson," I called, his shoulders relaxing when he turned to look at me.

"Yeah?"

"Where's River?" We were back at the house, so he had to be here. That was the plan.

I watched his Adam's apple move as he swallowed. "I—he—" He looked from me to the doorway as if River would just walk right in at this very moment.

"Grayson, what's going on?" Beau lifted his head up, his ears perking. *River's not okay, Mom.*

"What?" I asked my familiar, waving Grayson off when he tried to respond.

It wasn't him. He's not okay.

"It wasn't him?" I repeated, looking down at the ground and thinking this over. He'd been in my head for just a moment during my absolute meltdown. The person who'd fumbled my memories had vanished and now so had River.

Chancellor Fowler's words came back to me like a gut punch. Disobedience breeds consequences. And he had yet to make good on his threat, but maybe this was it...

"Corrin is fine and Mateo said she's worried about Riley," Ike said, walking back into the room. "He's calling Jade and filling her in."

She was worried about me? That can't be right. The way she'd looked at me told a different story.

"Have you tried to call him?" I cut in, moving Beau off of me and standing up. The feeling of my wet clothes sticking to my body wasn't a bother to me anymore.

Ike tilted his head to the side, a little confused until he realized I was asking about River. "Oh, I've tried to call him, text, all of it."

The front door flew open and Asher ran inside, swiveling his head around and placing his eyes on me. He came over, tentatively tilting my chin up. "Are you alright?"

"Coven aside, yes, but where's your brother?"

Asher's eyes grew sad. "I don't know. Wherever he is, he's under our dad's control."

My heart started to speed up and I started to feel like I couldn't breathe. What was he going to do? This was all because I couldn't figure my shit out, because I was so fucking difficult. This was all because they wanted to help me, because there were parts of all of them that cared about me enough to put themselves in danger.

I was the reason my mom decided to leave, albeit I wasn't even born yet, but still. I'd decided that I needed to look further into my dad's death and step foot on that campus. I'd put all these people who called me their friend on the chopping block, for what? Things had just gotten worse and worse and all I had was more pain to show for it. Me and the guys had fixed things, we were united again, but now it was falling apart.

Because of me.

"Hey, Riley, look at me. We'll find him. I just need to—" Asher stopped talking, taking out his phone and squinting at the screen. He immediately put it to his ear. "Hello?"

He didn't move from in front of me, so I planted my feet and refused to leave my spot as well. Grayson and Ike crowded around us, waiting.

"Yes, that's me. Wait, what? When?" Asher placed his fingers over his forehead, slowly rubbing back and forth. "Okay, okay, w-what happened? Okay, yes, I'll be right there. Yes, thank you." He tried to sound calm, but his voice shook right at the end.

"Asher?" I asked, reaching out and touching his elbow.

He flinched as if he was suddenly out of it. Shaking his head, he nodded absentmindedly, looking at each of us. "We need to go to the hospital. Now."

Chocolate.PSD
Bar Mock-Up
Food Packaging Collection

42
RILEY

I immediately burst out in tears when we were led into his hospital room. Asher had originally gone to speak to a nurse at the front desk, practically leaping over the counter when she wouldn't instantly let him see his brother.

The security guards eyed him carefully as he calmed down and eventually someone came out to talk to us. It had all seemed so cut and dry to them. He'd been riding his motorcycle, sans helmet and crashed it into a tree. He had a broken arm in two places, shattered his knee, had fractured ribs and a head contusion. Every new piece of information made my stomach turn. Healers could only ever do so much. The more wounds a person had, the more it took a toll on them as magic users. Their magic would be useless if they didn't have the strength to keep providing it. Some things were better when healed by medicine from both humans and healers alike.

A healer was in his room when we stepped in, cleaning up some of the smaller cuts and bruises around his chest and face. He gave us a small smile before heading out. I had promised Ike I would let him know how River was doing, which led to my mom calling me on the way over here since Ike had spilled the news to Jade, who for some reason told my mom.

I wasn't in the mindset to call her back right now. I didn't even know how to form a correct sentence at this point. We circled around his bed and I grabbed his hand, still feeling the warmth it always gave me. His chest moved up and down, his eyes roaming from behind his closed lids. They'd given him something to help the pain and fall asleep, which I appreciated because the way I only imagined him in agony from his impact with the tree was unsettling.

Asher held onto the bed, his fingers turning white from his grip. His head was down, but with the way his long sleeves were rolled up, I could see the muscles in his forearms tensing. Grayson rubbed my back in soothing motions which helped but not in the way it used to.

"I can't get into his mind to try to see if he'll talk back to me," Grayson said softly, his voice almost like a whisper.

"What they gave him probably dulled everything," Asher explained, looking up at us, his eyes a little glassy but he had his lips pressed together as if he was trying to keep all his feelings tight and put together. "It would be pointless for me to even go in there right now."

I leaned down, brushing some of his hair from his forehead and kissing River on the forehead. There was enough damage to severely hurt him....to hurt me. I looked down at his body to see his leg elevated and beyond that the sterility of the room. I wanted him back in his own room, with all of his things and memories we'd collected throughout our relationship.

"When will the sleep medication wear off?" Grayson asked, walking over to Asher.

My boyfriend's brother cleared his throat and yanked off his glasses, gripping the bridge of his nose. "Tomorrow morning, I think, but they are going to monitor him for his head contusion. They want to make sure he, uh, does wake up." He sniffed and put his glasses back on.

I crossed my arms over my chest and hugged myself, taking in a shaky breath. "Tell them about your fucking dad, Asher."

"And say what, Riley? It won't do any good. They might look into him, but it's our word against his and well, he's Oliver St. James. It may not mean something to you, but it does to a lot of people. I don't like it but telling anyone will cause a bigger mess. It will just piss him off more." He gently ran his hand through River's hair. It was the caress of an older brother who cared deeply but only knew how to show it in a certain way. It made my heart hurt. "I won't cause him or anyone else more pain."

I looked off to the side, chewing on my lower lip. I was tired, my body was tired, but I was so fucking done. "I caused it," I mumbled.

"What?" Asher and Grayson both said in unison.

I shook my head, giving River one last look and turning on my heels to exit the room. I heard footsteps behind me and a hand grabbing my arm.

"Riley, where are you going?" Grayson's dark eyes took my hand and let his fingers intertwine with my own.

"I just need some air."

Grayson looked over his shoulder, seeing a nurse come into River's room. "If you're worried about what about happened at Celica, we'll figure that part out—"

"I'm pretty sure Chancellor Fowler took care of all that. If he was aware of what happened, there is a high chance he's ecstatic over what I did."

His eyebrows turned down. "Okay, well then let's sit down. Or we can get you something to eat...I'm sure they have snacks here and I'll pull up an audiobook on my phone and we can listen together—"

I interrupted him again, even though he was being incredibly sweet and turning him down gutted me. "No, I need to let my mom know what's going on, update Ike and all that."

"I can explain things to Ike, you don't need to worry about that right now."

I shook my head. "I just need to not breathe hospital air right now, okay?"

He let out a sigh of defeat. Leaning down and placing his forehead to mine, he whispered, "It will be okay, *aking sinta*. I promise." I tilted my head up to kiss him, pulling away and walking in the other direction.

I stopped. This is what Chancellor Fowler wanted. This pain I felt, this dread of thinking I was the catalyst of my loved ones destruction…he wanted all of this. River was a low blow, but he'd warned me. I needed to make a decision, make my own plan and I needed to do it now.

I turned on my heels and walked back over to Grayson. He smiled at me as if he assumed I'd changed my mind. "I need you to take me somewhere."

He cocked his head to the side. "I'll need to get Asher's keys, but sure."

"No, Grayson, I need you to shadow me somewhere."

He rubbed the side of his neck, clearly not liking where this was going. "Where are you trying to go?"

I threw a chunk of my braids over my shoulder, straightening my spine when I said, "Chancellor Fowler's house."

His eyes widened in shock, his voice lowering as he pulled me away from River's door. "Why the fuck would you want to go there?"

"I just do. You're the only one who can. You don't need Ike to find an address for you because you've been inside. Get me inside."

He pressed his fingers into his eyes, rubbing. "Is that supposed to make me feel special? What happened to no more secrets?"

I shrugged. "This isn't a secret. I'm blatantly asking you to take me. What happens from there, I'm unsure."

Grayson nearly choked. "So, you want me to take you there without any sort of idea how you plan to proceed. What even is this plan, Riley?"

"I DON'T—" I started to shout but looked around to see some of the staff starting to look at us. I took in a deep breath and collected myself. "I don't know. He's always finding me, coming at me, talking to me. It's time I did the same to him. I don't know the end result, but I'm asking you to do this one thing. I'm not telling you to keep it a secret but just let me do what I need to do. River is my last straw."

Grayson focused on my eyes and I could clearly see when he noticed nothing but determination there. "Regardless of being truthful, Asher is going to kill me."

43
RILEY

We landed in that same room I found myself in a while back. The same couch, the same fireplace, the same bar cart where Chancellor Fowler had elevated the glass pieces to strike Marianne. I shuttered, quickly letting the memories subside. The fireplace wasn't illuminating the room, so a few sconces surrounded us with light.

I heard the sound of coughing from behind me and I looked over at Grayson. He held his hand to his chest, another cough erupting from his throat.

"What's wrong?" I asked, rushing over to him.

"I don't—I don't know. My heart is going really fast and—" He started to walk forward but he lost his footing, catching himself before he fell over. "And everything won't stop moving."

I grabbed his hand but it was clammy and cold, like the warmth was being drained from it. "Grayson what's going on?" I took his face and turned it to look at me. In a matter of seconds, his lips looked dry and his body was wobbly within my grasp.

I wasn't strong enough to hold him up, so we both fell to the ground.

"The room needs to stop spinning," he pleaded, trying to clear his throat.

I heard a door open and multiple footsteps echoed in my ears. A voice that made my blood go cold filled the room.

"Your little shadow wielder having some trouble, sweetheart?" Chancellor Fowler bent down next to me, watching as Grayson struggled to breath and how the color started to drain from his face.

"What are you doing to him?" I seethed out.

His face turned innocent. "I'm doing nothing." He lifted his chin towards the girl who casually sat on the couch, tucking her legs under her thighs. "Fluid manipulation is a wondrous thing. Slow, draining and extraction and then as you can see the dehydration sets in. No one barges into my home unless I want them to and I need to take precautions."

I held Grayson closer to me. "Make it stop."

"You aren't here to do anything stupid now are you, Riley?" he questioned, curious.

I shook my head erratically, my heart speeding up.

He narrowed his eyes at me, reaching up to touch his knuckles to my cheek. I made no move to lean into it, but I didn't shift away. His eyes shifted over my shoulder to the girl on the couch.

Grayson tried to swallow over and over, each time seeming to get easier and his skin grew less cold. He had his eyes closed still, but he was instantly looking better.

Chancellor Fowler grabbed my arm and lifted me up, leaving Grayson to fend for himself on the ground. He placed his hand on my shoulder and leaned down to be eye level with me. "Not that it's never a delight to see you, but why are you here?"

"You hurt him."

He pushed out his bottom lip as he considered my accusation. "You'll have to be more specific."

"I don't need to be so just stop."

He sighed, stepping around me. He moved his hand around, using his powers to lift Grayson from the floor and throw him onto the other couch. "You mean your little telepath. I didn't do that, his father did. Horrible accident, so I heard. He's alive so you should be grateful."

"Your entire thought process was that you never wanted to hurt me, but everything you've done has proven otherwise. Everything that you do makes me the sole reason why everyone is in pain, scared or dead."

He licked his lips, tilting his head to the side. "Are you here to scold me? Would you like me to apologize? What you did in those woods, what you did to my mother, all of it was your own doing. You can't keep your emotions in check, you can't handle a little push and shove...that is not on me, sweetheart. Your powers are tempting. It's so easy to let them out, know how much strength it gives you and in turn you use that strength to make people submit." He pinched the bridge of his nose as if I was exhausting him. "What I am sorry for is not being there for you and helping you with that magic. I'm sorry I wasn't more vigilant when it came to my own mother and the fact that she helped Jillian smother your powers into that abhorrent necklace."

He sauntered over to me, letting his fingers grasp the jewelry around my neck. "This dupe around your neck might comfort you, but you can't go back now."

"I know," I spat back, planting my feet to stand my ground. I knew what I had to do and no one that truly cared for me would like it, but...it was my best shot. "I want you to leave them alone. The wolves, my friends, the guys, everyone. Leave my mother out of it, leave everyone's families *out* of it. Stop manipulating people to do your bidding. Tell Oliver to back off," I stuck my finger into his chest. "And stop stealing from the coven. Just *fucking* stop."

His eyes sparkled with intrigue. "And why would I do that, hmm?"

"Because you'll have me."

He reared his head back, bringing his hand to his chin. "Finally admitting you need me?"

I wrinkled my nose at him. "No. But I know when I've had enough."

"Riley..." Grayson slung his arms over the couch, lifting himself up. He looked at me confused and alarmed. "What are you doing?"

My insides hurt but I would find a way to fix this. I just needed to be away from them; they needed to trust me.

I cut my eyes to Chancellor Fowler. "Do you have a way to get him back to the hospital?"

He rubbed his hands together in delight. "Of course I do. Riley, I don't want you to think you can't see these boys. I want you to be happy. But you know I don't tolerate meddling in my plans, so if they think..."

"They won't," I snapped, walking over to Grayson who sat up on the couch and grabbed my hands when they were in reach. I leaned down to kiss him, speaking against his lips softly for only him to hear. "Please trust me. Be as normal as possible and don't do anything. Not yet." He pulled back slowly.

Chancellor Fowler snapped his fingers, addressing the girl on the couch. "Laura, would you mind?" He waved his hand towards Grayson, and the girl quickly left the room to fetch whatever he'd silently asked for.

"We'll have to figure out next steps. Obviously, the coven is dealt with. That girl that bothered you is none of your concern any longer and we'll need to move your stuff here. I'm sure you'll want that familiar of yours. I'll have to introduce you to mine and teach you how to keep them out of your hair unless you need them. Despite her secrets, I would never keep you from your mother, so we will work that out so you two can see..."

His ramblings went on and on, but none of what he said really surprised me. I cut him off, his incessant talking grating on my ears. "And you'll do what I asked?"

Chancellor Fowler stood in front of me, cupping the sides of my face in his hands as if I was his most precious possession. "Yes. I promise. I will leave them alone. None of it really matters anymore." My shoulders stiffened when he leaned down and kissed my forehead.

Footsteps sounded and we both looked to see a tall man come over.

"Take him back to the medical center." Chancellor Fowler nodded over to Grayson.

My shadow wielder got up from the couch and started backing away from what I only assumed was another shadow wielder.

Chancellor Fowler scoffed. "He isn't going to hurt you. I promised my daughter, no more." He sounded proud to be able to say that, knowing that in his eyes I'd submitted fully with no ounce of backlash in sight.

Grayson looked right at me the moment I turned around to see him and I mouthed, "Trust me."

He gave a few small nods as if he understood and let himself be shadowed away. I took in a shaky breath, "This doesn't mean I've forgiven you for the things you've done."

Chancellor Fowler hummed. "All in due time. Come, let me show you your new home, while I send someone to go get your things."

44

ASHER

I finally took a minute to step out of River's room. I was tired as fuck and based on what many of the nurses said, he would be okay. I didn't see Grayson or Riley which was odd, but I couldn't think about it long when I heard rattling inside River's room. I hustled towards the bedside table, seeing his phone light up.

The name on the screen was Riley's mom. I hesitated, but picked it up anyway.

"Hello?"

"River?" she asked, her voice wary.

"Uh, no this is his brother."

"Oh, umm Asher, right?"

I nodded and then realized she couldn't see me, so I answered.

"Maybe you can help me figure out why my daughter hasn't answered me. She likes me to think she has a lot of things handled, but I'm allowed to be worried. I'm over here pacing and all I would like is some confirmation that she's alive and well. Not from her friends, but from her."

I looked up at the ceiling, not having the patience for this and my brother's dilemma, but I took in a breath through my nose. I would be the same way about River if I was in her shoes, so I couldn't fault her. I also didn't know how to answer her. The good part was Riley was alive but the bad part was I hadn't no fucking idea where she was.

"I understand, Miss Monroe. Give me a minute, okay?"

I stepped out of the room, clutching River's phone between my shoulder and my ear. I pulled out my own phone and started to send a text to Grayson, but then I saw him. He was getting closer as he walked down the hallway. He looked nervous and I hated it.

I tucked my phone away, putting Riley's mom on mute before meeting Grayson halfway. "Where the hell have you been?" I searched around him. "Where's Riley?"

"Don't yell at me," he scolded, walking towards one of the walls and leaning back against it.

"I'm not yelling at you. I *could* yell at you. Would you *like* me to yell at you, Grayson?" I got closer to him, clutching my brother's phone in my hand.

He put his hands up to stop me. "No, not right now. When I tell you something, that's when I need you to not yell at me."

I gave him a confused look. Grayson let a heavy sigh leave his lips. "She's with Chancellor Fowler."

I couldn't stop myself before I grabbed a handful of his shirt with one hand and pulled him forward, just to throw him back against the wall. "What the fuck did you just say?"

"Asher, wait!"

"You did this again?! Fuck, I told her to try to let your stupid ass back in and fucking forgive you, but you go and do this!" I shoved him back against the wall again. "You are so lucky we are in a hospital because I could fucking kill you right now."

Grayson's shadows came out and put pressure on my chest, shoving me back hard enough so that I hit the other wall. One of the nurses looked over her desk, eyeing both of us and we lifted our hand, trying to look innocent.

"It wasn't me. Riley wanted to go."

I blew out a breath, almost laughing. "That sounds ridiculous. You really think I'm believing that."

He shrugged. "She begged me and I didn't know what she planned to do, but I wasn't going to let her go off and find, I don't know, a more dangerous way to find him so I took her."

I looked down at River's phone, seeing Miss Monroe still holding on the other line. "Okay, so she's with him, when do you go get her? Are we going to have to barge in there together?"

Grayson's eyes dropped to the floor. "We don't. We don't do anything. She made the decision to stay for us, for everyone." He looked towards where River's room was. "I don't like it and again, I promise you I didn't know. I think she has her own plan, Asher."

I turned around and ball my empty hand into a fist and punched the wall. "I can't fucking deal with this right now."

"She told me to not do anything. To wait." His voice dropped to a whisper. "She wants us to trust her."

"She wants us to—" I ran my hand through my hair, nearly forgetting how to breathe and letting out a very long breath. "She's so agitating, fuck."

"I have a feeling her stuff will be gone from the house when we get back and probably so will Beau. Chancellor Fowler, in a weird way, doesn't want to upend her life, but he does want to be the person she constantly comes back to. We can be a part of her world, but can't interfere with, you know..."

"Yeah, I get it. My father wanted me to choose between River or Riley and Riley ended up just choosing for me anyway."

"Maybe we follow Riley's lead, as painful as it may be. And she'll let us know when she needs us."

I brought the phone up to Grayson's face. "And what am I supposed to tell her, huh? The man she ran away from finally has what he wants."

He took the phone from my hand, keeping it away from me when I tried to get it back. "I'll talk to her. Just go back to River. I'll be there in a minute."

"Thanks." I gave him a stiff nod and jogged back to River's room. He was still very much asleep and I sat down in the uncomfortable chair in the corner. My knee bounced up and down with developing anxiety.

How the hell was I going to explain this to him when he woke up?

I pulled out my phone, starting to email the department chair about how I wouldn't be in for a few days, but I stopped. I deleted my draft and pulled up my contacts. I found the number I wanted and hit the call button.

She picked up quickly, her greeting a bit exasperated.

"Hey, Corrin."

"Riley just texted me. Very long conversation, but breathe easy, Professor."

I sat up straighter in the chair. "She what?"

"We are going to talk more on campus later. Well, me and her, not you."

"I do trust her...I just...ugh. What is she up to?"

She hummed. "I'm unsure of the grand plan but I have some science magic to make in the lab." She got quiet for a moment. "I'm sorry about your brother. Full recovery, I hope?"

"Yeah, as long as he wakes up without issues tomorrow."

"Focus on that." It sounded like she took the phone from her ear to speak to someone else, then she was back. "I do have to go, but trust your girl, Asher. It's a really attractive trait in a person if you didn't know."

Chocolate PSD
Bar Mock-Up
Food Packaging Collection

45
RILEY

I was never good at acting and was told so when I tried out for drama club in high school. It didn't hurt my feelings and I moved on to something that did pique my interest. I started reading books and I read about women who knew that they deserved to be happy and safe, that the people they cared about deserved the same. I was always so intrigued by the things they faced and all the courage they had, even though I never considered that I would ever be in a position where my happiness and safety—and everyone else's—could be at risk.

I *acted* like I appreciated the random "helpers" Chancellor Fowler sent. I put on the most forced smile I could when I got back to my room and all my stuff was there. The only thing I didn't fake was the soft sob I let out when I heard Beau's growling and opened my door to catch him mid lunge.

I would go to school like normal and act like an everyday student, let Chancellor Fowler think he's got a daughter he can mold in his image. I stroked Beau's head as I thought about how if I went too deep, what happened to Teresa and Geena might be who I am.

It wasn't.

That didn't mean he needed to know that.

I'd noticed the people standing around the back gates of the house and the front, committing that fact to memory. Chancellor Fowler had said goodnight to me, answering his phone and instantly sounding aggravated. I heard the name Oliver, following him silently.

"Yes, you'll get what you want. You know when to be here, so don't be late. I'll make good on my word, but Oliver, you've made it so one of your sons can't leave the hospital, so I'll have to get them their power by a more long-distance means."

It was quiet which told me he was probably trying to listen.

Chancellor Fowler started laughing. "Oh, so now you're being greedy?" I heard him sigh.

"I'm honestly surprised you ever thought to share with them in the first place. If my daughter cared about power then I would insist they be stronger, but she has her mother's heart, so if you want to be incredibly selfish then so be it."

I backed away and headed back to my room.

The idea that Chancellor Fowler had any sort of distaste for selfishness was laughable, but now I had something to work with. He wanted me to be this force but understood I would never fall head-first into the madness of undying power. At least he fucking understood something about me. Things would have been easier if River and Asher were brought here, but the fact that Oliver was diverting from the original plan didn't ruin anything for me. I just had to pivot a bit.

I'd been told I'd be taken to and from the university, but with one sad look and a soft voice, Chancellor Fowler agreed to let me see my mom tomorrow after school. I needed her to know face to face that I was going to fix this. I got out my phone and looked at my text thread with Corrin. She spoke to me like we were still friends, like she still cared. I wouldn't be completely sure until I actually saw her and could see her facial expressions and body language.

The window to my right showed tiny sprinkles of light, telling me that it was early morning and the more I thought about it, the more tired I became. I didn't need to be the best actor; I just needed to be good enough for Chancellor Fowler to keep thinking he'd won. Unlike him, I didn't need to manipulate people or promise them outlandish and harmful things to get what I wanted to instill fear.

I just needed the people who trusted me enough to follow my lead.

Chocolate psd
Bar Mock-Up
Packaging Collection

46
RILEY

I tugged my backpack higher on my shoulders and headed for the library. I looked at nobody and headed straight for the same spot Corrin and Ike had found me in before. I turned down the aisle and found my best friend on the floor, scrolling through her phone.

I rapped my knuckle against the wood bookshelf, gaining her attention. She scrambled to get up, throwing her body at me.

"Oh my god!" She hugged me tighter and then pulled back, punching me in the arm.

"Ow! What was that for?"

She frowned, then punched me in my other arm. "Oops. Sorry I meant to do it twice. One was for leaving me dazed and confused after that coven meeting and the other was for ever thinking I was afraid of you."

"I never said that."

Corrin rolled her eyes. "You didn't have to. Ike is smarter than he looks and he assumed the worst. Let's get one thing straight, the last thing you will ever do is scare me. Well, not in that way at least. I was alarmed at what that whole mess would do to you, but not for a second did I think you would ever actually hurt me." She shook my shoulders. "I didn't appreciate you leaving me on read and allowing Ike, Mateo and everyone else to be the bearer of information."

I walked around her and let my back hit the wall, sliding down onto the floor. "I didn't know what to do after that and then everything happened with River. I didn't even get a real chance to talk to my mom. I promise you are not the only one who is severely upset with me."

Corrin sat down next to me, adjusting her glasses. "Well, help me understand what you're doing now. You told me that you're living with Chancellor Fowler? Like he thinks you'll be one happy family?"

"Something like that."

"And your guys have no play in this?"

I shook my head. "Not yet. Chancellor Fowler still owes River and Asher's dad a healthy dose of power. I have a big hunch it's happening during the next moon gathering, so he can siphon and then give it to Oliver."

"And the next moon gathering is in two days," Corrin confirmed, checking her calendar on her phone.

"Exactly. I heard him on the phone with Oliver and that might be my only shot to knock them both out in one go. He invited him over to the house."

Corrin made a disgusted face. "I'm going to make a highly educated guess and say you aren't planning on taking him down all by yourself? Because you have your boyfriends up in arms thinking you've gone insane."

I let out the smallest smile I could muster. "No, of course not. But they can't come busting in like I know they want to. The condition was I can 'keep' them, but they can't interfere, hence River in the hospital."

"So, they need to be good boys and stay put."

"Precisely, well, until I'm ready."

"And you wanted me to do some witchy science things for you? Tell me more." She scooted closer to me, our shoulders pressed against each other.

"How good are you at making sleeping potions?"

Corrin tapped her chin. "Depends."

"I need it to be strong and it doesn't have to be a liquid, it can be a powder."

"You want me to make something like what Oliver used to knock us out in your dad's office?"

I rubbed my lips together, wondering if I was asking too much. "Actually, yes."

Corrin grinned over at me, her dark skin glowing with delight. "Your wish is my command. Is this for Oliver? Because I would love to throw a whole pound of that shit in his stupid face."

I patted her knee. "No, it's for the people Chancellor Fowler has watching the back gates. All you need is one opening."

"One opening and all the metal weapons my brother can make or that I can carry." She poked my side and then gave me a serious look. "Have you talked to your guys today?"

"Asher texted me and said he would update me about River. As you know he wasn't happy with me, but there really isn't anything he can do. Grayson is the opposite and texted me good morning and that he's ready whenever I am. The contrast is astonishing."

"Hmph. Astonishing but not surprising, I'll say. Mateo and Jade are also ready whenever you are." I glanced at her and she gave me a knowing look. "You aren't getting rid of us. You could break a million obnoxious girl's legs and I would still love you. I choose to believe that despite Chancellor Fowler biologically being your father that Thomas was the real deal. Just remember that whenever you think you're a bad person." She rested her head on my shoulder. "You want to rid this university, this world of a man who wants to treat you like property all because you share his DNA? Sign me up."

I dropped my head on top of hers, feeling the sting of tears hit my eyes, but I didn't let them fall. "You can tell me no. You can tell me you love me but you're done and this is too much. I'll understand. I went with Chancellor Fowler to cease all the insanity. You can make the powder or potion or whatever and give it to me. I can do it myself. I can't stop the boys from helping because they will do it no matter what."

"And you can't stop me either. We're all adults, Riley. We might make dumb decisions and fumble around trying to fix them later, but at least we're *trying*. The fact that you did what you did tells me you're worth trying for because you want to help more than just yourself."

I lifted my face up, dabbing under my eyes where a few tears escaped. "I'm happy I met you," I admitted.

"Me too." She squeezed my thigh. "Now, tell me all about this moon gathering plan. Start to finish."

47
RIVER

Being in my own head sucked. Not being able to wake up and end said loneliness was even worse. The wild part was that I wasn't technically alone. I could hear the beeps of machines, the chatter of people and whatever was playing on the TV. The art of opening up your eyes and seeing a new day was something people took for granted, because the moment I realized I couldn't do it so easily had me wanting to scream. My eyes were one thing, but my mind was another.

It was like I was on drugs with the way I fumbled around in my own head. I couldn't turn my powers on, nor could I even attempt to let anyone else in. My brain felt like it was drunk. I felt pain in my physical body but the act of trying to remember what happened was pointless at the moment.

Little by little whatever was holding me back lifted. I could stretch my telepathy legs and it felt good. There was a hand touching mine, a hard squeeze and then I heard two people talking over me.

"It should be wearing off, so you are welcome to try. I wouldn't push too hard."

Asher's deep voice made its way into my ears. "But it could help him wake up?"

Who I assumed was the doctor answered, "It could, but that's not my official advice."

Footsteps sounded and disappeared, while Asher's hand moved into my hair, brushing pieces of it away from my forehead. My eyes felt glued shut and even though I was in an awakened state, I still felt trapped in some kind of subconscious lockdown.

Something pushed against my head, letting itself in and moving around as if it had been here before. I stood in that empty space in my head, waiting. Vertigo hit me and I leaned against the walls of my mind. I pressed my hand to the side of my head, the feeling passing. Whatever medicine they'd given me must be wearing off in the worst way possible because this was fucking awful.

A hand landed on my shoulder. "River, hey, it's me."

I peeked up at my brother, concerned etched onto his face. "Why does it feel like bones are broken?"

Asher pressed his lips into a hard line. "Because they are."

"Fuck."

"Fuck indeed."

Asher explained what happened as best he could and I slid down onto the floor of my mind. I was happy to be alive, but man this was not what I planned for. Not to mention the fact that my bike was also completely ruined.

"You'll have to get a normal vehicle with four wheels now." Asher sat down in front of me.

"Hmm, I wouldn't go that far." I looked around me, this place I was in was familiar to me, but then again it wasn't. "Why do I recognize this somehow?" It was dimly lit and there was nothing around but there was something about this place I found myself in. Like it was once something completely different.

Asher slid his hand down his pants legs. "The medicine they gave you numbed you and your powers. I guess a safeguard. You mentally went to a place you've...created before. Now as an adult you don't make it so dark. That's my working theory."

"What?"

He dropped his head, shaking it. "After all your awful moments with dad, you'd go to sleep and you'd end up here. Back then, it was pitch black and every single time, I'd have to find you."

I tilted my head to the side, trying to think that far back. Anytime I'd think back to all the times my dad was horrible, the same room came to mind, but it was filled with light and a wave of calm enveloped me. I thought it was my own kind of coping mechanism for when I found myself back in those thoughts. Maybe I didn't create those things at all.

Asher was never a dictator, but he wasn't ever easy on me. He wanted me to be good at my powers, but he didn't care if I was the best. He wanted me to take care of myself but was fine if I made a few mistakes. He knew who I was and he didn't judge me for it. My happiness, my safety, those things were his top priority and whether it was my dad or even Riley, he would make sure to always look out for me.

"You've always been there, haven't you?"

Asher nodded. "At least now," he waved his hand around the space, "you know how to create your own light. Now it's just time that you woke yourself up."

I rubbed my hands together. "Asher, I don't think I tell you this enough, if ever, but thanks."

He let out a short laugh. "Don't mention it, but sometimes all I want is for you to listen to me. I know you can do things for yourself, but I can admit that sometimes when I look at you—" he got up from the floor and held his hand out to me. I took it, standing in front of him. "I see that same kid balled up in a corner because his dad didn't know how to fucking talk to him."

I took in a shaky breath, instantly remembering my dad's screams and him throwing me disgusted and unimpressed looks.

The next day I always felt better, I could move on as if nothing happened. I'd always thought I made that happen for myself.

"Alright, alright. I just want to wake up and see Riley and Grayson."

Asher gave me a pained look.

I pointed my finger at him. "I don't like that face."

My brother took a few steps back, placing a hand on his hip. "We get you out of here and I'll explain about Riley."

"No, you'll tell me now."

He closed his eyes, clearly annoyed. "I tell you now and you might sink deeper into this space due to stress. Let's wake you up, see how much physical therapy you'll need and make sure you're all good. Then I promise I will catch you up to speed." He held his hand out for me to shake.

His tone was clear and authoritative, but he was probably right. Emotions blend with any kind of magic whether it be in a good way or bad. I was ready to get out of the state I was in and open my eyes.

I grabbed his hand and shook it. "Fine. Let's wake me up."

Chocolate.PSD
Bar Mock-Up
Food Packaging Collection

48
RILEY

"Honey, what's going on?" My mom peeked out one of the windows before making her way back over to the couch. Even when she sat back down, she looked over her shoulder again.

"Mom, it's, uhm, fine. Please focus." I ran my hands down my braids, feeling anxious myself.

"Fine doesn't cut it Riley. You go from letting me in on things to having your friends try to explain different vital pieces of information. I know you don't have to tell me things, you can do what you want, but I thought after everything we had a better understanding."

I pinched the bridge of my nose. "We do, Mom."

"And you're pulling up to this house in a car I've never seen. Riley, if you sit here and confirm what Grayson told me…"

My mouth formed into an O and my mom let out an exasperated sigh. "Oh god, it's true isn't it?"

I fiddled with a string on my jeans. "Um, that car out there belongs to Chancellor Fowler."

She nearly choked on air, clutching at the fabric of the couch. "Riley!"

I held up my hands in defense. "He didn't kidnap me, okay? I'm trying to fix things, Mom. I'm staying with him to make things smoother for when this all ends."

"All ends? That's very ominous and I don't like it. You spend all this time trying to separate yourself from the man and then this happens."

I sighed. "I'm not spending the rest of my college career tiptoeing around him. He started this whole thing with dad and it will end with me. That's that."

She touched the end of one of my braids, letting the hair fall through her fingers. "Always so determined. Just like your dad. That man was obsessed with making things better, but unlike you, he wasn't giving me heart attacks while doing it."

I winced. "Sorry. I would have preferred not to have such a colorful family history."

She huffed, leaning back on the couch. "I do too. I would have preferred that you had not seen so much blood and death in such a short amount of time. You don't belong in a bubble, but no one deserves to go through the things you did."

I pressed my lips together. "Even though you said it a million times on the phone, you don't think I'm like him, right? What I did to Teresa, to Geena, and how easy it was. How there are things I regret, but there are also things I don't."

She grabbed my body and pulled me in closer to her, so that I could snuggle against her chest. "Honey, I think you are *nothing* like him. I can tell you how much of a good person you are, your friends can say it to your face a million times but unless you believe it yourself, nothing will change. How I see you might matter, but how you see yourself is something I can't help you with." She kissed the top of my head. "Erik always let other people try to tell him who he was and I don't think he ever got over it, so he embraced it. You are stronger than him because I think you know *exactly* who you are, Riley."

"I love you, Mom. And in all honesty, I'm scared."

"It's not too late to change your mind and just move back in here."

I laughed a little. "Pretty sure it is, but keep the offer open just in case things don't work out with the guys."

She planted more kisses on the top of my head. "How's River?"

I pressed my head further into her chest. "I'm waiting for Asher's message with an update. He was stable with a lot of broken things when I last saw him."

My mom rocked me back and forth. "Well maybe you can go and see—"

"I already asked. Apparently, I should have asked to see River and not you. It was one or the other. I wasn't aware that was how it worked, but apparently, he makes the rules up as he goes."

She hummed. "I'll go to the hospital and see him. I know Asher still has a job and whatever is going on with their father..." She squinted at me. "Don't tell me about because I'm already full on information for now."

"Okay, okay. Thanks, Mom."

"Well, you *can* tell me if there is something I should be made aware of when it comes to Professor St. James." She leaned back, letting me lift my head up.

I dropped my eyes down to the couch when I pulled away from her. "I think that's a conversation for a different time." I was happy for the reprieve from Chancellor Fowler talk, but I really wasn't interested in getting into this. Talking about my relationship with Asher would cause me to, more than likely, dive into my relationship with Grayson.

My mom was cool enough, but I wasn't sure she was *that* cool.

"How about I get some food in you then?" She eyed me suspiciously, kissing my cheek and getting off the couch.

Chocolate .PSD
Bar Mock-Up
Food Packaging Collection

Chocolate Bar Mock-Up
Food Packaging Collection

49
RILEY

It was odd having Chancellor Fowler come in and ask me about schoolwork as if I was a little kid. It was odd not having Asher as our instructor on Wednesday morning even though he'd told me that he was taking the day to be at the hospital with River. It was even weirder when Chancellor Fowler asked to spend time with me, so he brought me down to the basement.

The space wasn't cold and dank like the ones people thought about, but it was well lit and the temperature was comfortable. It was a large open space with a few storage bins scattered along the walls. He'd used this space to house the witches he'd gotten Grayson to snatch. The basement didn't look menacing but that didn't mean I couldn't feel the weird energy that it gave off.

"I thought it might be fun to see your skills."

I finally turned all the way around to face him again. "My skills?"

"Yes, the powers you inherited."

It felt like my ring was getting tighter on my finger. "I should actually be finishing up a paper…"

He huffed. "We both know you finished your homework hours ago, so that excuse won't work here."

I ran my hand along the back of my neck. "Okay, what do you want me to show you? I don't really do things just for fun."

He walked over to one of the bins and snapped the sides open, placing the lid on the ground. An object lifted up and hovered above the bin. I furrowed my eyebrows, opening my mouth to say something, but then whatever it was flew at my face.

I jumped to the side, barely dodging it. "What the fuck!?"

"Your reflexes are nice, but I'll need you to use your powers next time," he explained, using his magic to lift what looked like a soccer ball out of the bin.

I took my ring off, placing it in my pocket. His eyebrows lifted and then he launched the ball at me. I willed the ball to stay in place, inches from my face and then let it drop.

Chancellor Fowler said nothing, but repeated this 'game' of ours for a few more minutes. I stopped a tiny football from coming at me, but then I felt a jolt to my body that shoved me back. I lost my focus and the football kept flying, slamming into my shoulder.

"Hmph, what was that?"

"Do you really think you won't get hit with other things at the same time?" I felt another shove to my body and when I tried to push back, it wasn't working. My efforts were being refuted. He brought the objects that were strewn around me up and had them spin around my body.

Their constant motion was starting to make me nauseous. Chancellor Fowler yelled in my direction, "Make them stop."

I held onto my power, wanting them to cease their movements and be still. I felt the force of the objects, the will of gravity to keep them in place. I was about to feel triumphant when something pulled on my hair, a push against my back this time and then a sweep from under my feet that lifted me up and slammed me onto the ground.

"Fuck," I cursed, using my arms to shield myself when the objects started falling down on me.

"Do I need to encourage you to work harder? Do I need to bring your mother here to make you focus?" he threatened, his composure still calm.

I scrambled off the floor. "No! Is this how you spend time with someone?"

"I'm trying to help you, Riley." The tiny football swooped around my head and was in front of my face now. "Set it on fire, if you can, I mean."

"I don't want to."

"I didn't ask if you wanted to, I asked you to do it."

I rolled my eyes and focused on the ball. My skin felt that heat that melted into my veins and sparked at my fingertips. One little flame erupted from the football and then another. Each tiny flame molded into each other and then the whole thing was on fire. I blinked, pleased with myself.

"Nice, keep it up and keep focus." I flicked my eyes to him when he lifted the other objects again. "Now all of them."

I moved my eyes over each thing and tried to focus my fire on them. One would light and then another. They bobbed up and down, their heat licking at my skin with how close they were. Chancellor Fowler spun them around, the fire forming a circle around me as it inched closer and closer.

I tried to duck away but it was like he had used his power to keep me in place. "Let me go! Stop!"

"Do it yourself, Riley! I was able to do things like this at age twelve."

He was getting a kick out of this, and all I could think was how this was the worst bonding time in all of history. The flames kept moving in and I swore if they got any closer, they would singe my skin.

"Stop!" I yelled as I kept trying to push them away. I tried to use my own heat to subdue the flames in front of me.

"Aw, I'm sure that's what your little telepath tried to tell his father before he crashed into a tree." Chancellor Fowler's voice was mocking and it cut deep.

I balled my hands into fists and scowled at him. "I said fucking stop!" Every single object halted, their flames growing bigger as they curved into a direct arrow pointing at Chancellor Fowler. He didn't look alarmed, but more so impressed.

They flew in his direction, the objects disintegrating and turning into one big ball of fire. Right before it reached him, he snuffed it out, whipping his hand towards the golden red flames and making them disappear. There were two more in its wake that I conceived myself. Two more that he wasn't expecting.

He used his hands to block them, backing up and I used my telekinesis to move one of the empty bins behind him. He tripped, but right before he hit the ground, I kept him elevated so that I could slam his body against the wall.

I was about to pick him up again, when one of the bins that was still very full came at me, knocking me off my feet. My head hit the floor hard, and I grabbed the side of my face. A powerful force grabbed my throat and I couldn't breathe.

Chancellor Fowler shook off the debris from his clothes and ran a hand through his hair. He walked over to me while I choked and gasped for air. My lungs were on fire, but it wasn't from my lack of oxygen. They felt overheated and my skin started to sweat.

He bent down next to me, pulling my hands away from my throat. "Can you get yourself out of this?"

I pleaded with my eyes for him to make it stop. He tilted his head, watching me. After what felt like an eternity, he let up. I sucked in enough air, tears stinging the edges of my eyes.

"Emotions lead your powers just as much as you do. You showed that in the first half, clear as day. If I had been there to teach you, you would have been out of that in less than a minute, but sadly, I don't think you trust yourself. You have to be willing to let your powers save you in a time of crisis, and you don't trust them either." He patted my shoulder. "Off to your room."

I rubbed the front of my throat, swallowing painfully. I lifted my hand, palm up and a flame formed right there. I willed it to be bigger, to have more volume and it did just that. I closed my hand, taking the flame back within myself.

I cracked my neck, violently using my power to throw the bins against the walls. The plastic broke and the items within them scattered out all over the place. I wasn't cleaning that shit up.

I got back to my room and took out my phone, texting Corrin the address I'd managed to see when we'd driven back from my mom's. Tomorrow would be the last day I would see this place.

I looked out my window at the darkening sky and let my mind drift a bit. Beau came up and nuzzled my hand.

I don't like it here. I want to go home. He thought to me.

Soon, buddy. We'll be home soon.

He sneezed, shaking his head and jumping up to prop his front paws on the windowsill. *With River, Grayson and Asher?*

"Is that home to you?" I asked, scratching the side of his neck.

His tongue dropped out the side of his mouth and his tail wagged vigorously. I took that as a yes. I couldn't say I disagreed with him. I sighed, letting myself have one small thing that made me happy right now.

I let my mind search for what I wanted and hoped he would answer me back like he did last night. The sound of his voice in my head was better than any phone call.

Hi, gorgeous.

I smiled to myself. *How are you feeling?*

Better than before. I do enjoy this whole being able to read your mind thing.

I chuckled. *Don't get used to it. Remember the stipulations.*

Yes, yes, you demanding thing. How are you holding up there?

I took in my surroundings and then responded. *Fine, I guess. I'll be better when I'm back in bed with you guys.*

I do like the sound of that. You give me the go ahead when it's time and we'll back you. Always.

I chewed on my bottom lip. *What do the others think about it?*

Grayson and Asher?

Mhmm.

His deep laugh resonated through my mind. *They'll do whatever you want. Asher might grumble, but he'll do it. If he thought it was dumb then he'd just say that. Please trust yourself, gorgeous. Any sort of doubt and—*

I interrupted him. *And my powers will malfunction, yes, I am very aware.*

Or you could hurt more people than you want. You know what you want the end result to be so let that be the only thing you focus on. I just wish I could help more.

I placed my hand on the window, seeing car lights come through the trees. *You broke and shattered bones, mister. Bed and rest for you.*

Hmm...are you going to come give me a bath when this is all settled and done?

I felt heat creep in my cheeks. *This is not the thing I need to focus on, River.*

I'm giving you something to look forward to. And then we can all get in the bath and take turns making you feel like the most special girl in the entire world.

The car pulled in closer and then the lights turned off. Maybe it was time.

I look forward to so much pampering. Beau barked and I shushed him. *Are the guys with you?*

River was silent for a minute and then answered me. *All accounted for. Mateo is leading the pack there and Corrin and Ike were already headed up an hour ago. Maps doesn't bring up any real location, it's just a lot of woods, but I'm sure they'll be fine.*

I know that at least. When I tried to search it myself, it was like Chancellor Fowler's family liked to live with a lot of land but discreetly...if that made any fucking sense.

I think he's here. I thought back, hearing a car door slam and voices, but I couldn't make out who.

Okay, be careful and let me know when it's time.

I love you and I...love them, maybe just a little.

Another round of laughter. *I'll be sure to let them know.*

Chocolate Bar
Bar Mock-Up
Packaging Collection

50
RILEY

I crept out of my room with Beau on my heels. I went up the stairs and towards where I heard the two men speaking.

"I can't rush the moon, Oliver. The witches do it at a particular time and you will just have to stop throwing a fucking tantrum and wait. When this is over, I want nothing more to do with you. My daughter is in my hands, so your assistance will no longer be needed."

Oliver scoffed. "When I get what I'm owed, I'm out of your hair. You act as if I didn't help with Thomas's death, like I didn't help clean up your mess with that silly girl who died here, or even with your own mother. You forget that your daughter is intertwined with my sons, so I'm sure you'll be seeing me."

Chancellor Fowler tsked. "That may be true, but I implore you to be on your best behavior because if I find that my daughter is unhappy because you've decided to take your weak little frustration out on those boys, then you won't be a problem for anyone anymore.

Your mind control tricks don't scare me, Oliver, now sit down and stop talking. I need to think."

If Chancellor Fowler wasn't an obsessed, murderous insane person, I would value his words about how my happiness was of the utmost importance. My dad always wanted me to be happy, but he never monitored River to make sure I constantly had a smile on my face. This man wasn't my dad and he never would be. That ended tonight.

I softly walked backwards, checking my phone for the time. I took the stairs down to the first floor and near where the back entrance was. When I rounded the corner, two bodies were on the ground. I bent down to see if they were breathing, a sigh of relief leaving my lungs when I felt their warm breath against the back of my hand.

I wanted to rid myself of the two men upstairs, not anyone else. At least not at the moment. I straightened back up seeing that the back gate was melted down. I narrowed my eyes then my body stiffened when I felt pointed metal at my back.

I swiftly turned around, using my powers to send whoever it was back. I heard a collective 'oof'.

"Get off me," I heard someone hiss.

"Corrin?" I whispered, the moon starting to let light into the dark hallway. Corrin and Ike blinked back at me, righting themselves from their collision.

"Who else would it be?" She rolled her eyes. "Did you think we were going to ditch you?"

I opened and closed my mouth, knowing that if I answered honestly, she would punch me in the arm. Beau jumped up on his hind legs and she caught him. He licked at her face, his tail whipping the dust around.

"Did you just throttle me into my own sister?" Ike stretched his neck, his voice getting louder.

I shushed him. "Sorry. Do you have a dagger?"

He smiled brightly. "Made it myself—"

"And yes, he is very proud." Corrin tilted her chin towards the opening to the outside. "Mateo and Jade just need some kind of signal, like a very cool, very lowkey fireball?"

I gave her a small smile and nodded, noticing the moon getting higher. "Right on time it looks like."

Ike pointed to himself. "Hey, that was me. I did the math, I looked at the weather and when the moon would set..."

Beau let out a heavy sigh. I felt a weird sensation along my skin. I ran my hand along my chest and it bothered me that I didn't know where it was coming from.

"It's the moon gathering. Whether you're there or not, you feel it. You may not lovingly accept Celica, but it is a part of you," Corrin explained. "It's a perfect indicator that says it's actually time."

When we got to the top of the stairs I looked over at Beau. "Stay here."

He cocked his head to the side, annoyed. *But...*

"No. Stay." I knew if I needed him, truly needed him, he would follow. I would never forgive myself if something happened to him when we were so close. I bent down to look him straight in his big, caring eyes. *You help the wolves if they need it and then you come find me.*

Beau licked my face, dipping his head down quickly and then looked back up at me.

I focused on the next staircase, hearing their voices again. The sound of groaning filled my ears. I got closer to the door, slowly pushing it open to see Chancellor Fowler at the window and raking his nails down the glass.

Oliver sat on the couch with a drink in his hand, watching.

The moon's light beamed inside the room and illuminated the chancellor as if he was absorbing it into himself. I didn't know how this all worked, but the way his shoulders were high and his fingers were curled, it didn't look like the ends justified the means.

I needed to focus on one thing. I zeroed in on the back of his head and felt my power rise to the top. I pulled his head back with all the strength I had and slammed it against the window. Oliver

I got up and went over to the window, seeing the car that had brought me here still settled in its parking spot outside the house. My phone buzzed and I checked the screen. It was a text from Asher.

ASHER
He's awake. Grayson's heading here now.

Surprisingly attached to the text was a picture. It was of Asher and River.

We would be okay. Just a little longer.

jumped up, surprise taking over his face as he looked around. There was a splatter of blood on the window, but Chancellor Fowler whirled around and used his magic to rip the door off its hinges.

I stumbled inside, the twins behind me.

"You." Oliver snarled at me.

"What is the meaning of this?!" Chancellor Fowler pressed a hand to his head, more blood coming from the wound.

He started to walk towards me, but I swatted my hand forward, sending him flying backwards and hitting the mantle at the fireplace. The back of his head connected with the brick and the sound it made had my shoulders tensing up. Corrin grabbed the dagger from Ike's hands and rushed over to Chancellor Fowler.

"You will not take this away from me, you little bitch." Oliver started to run over to me, but I stopped him, creating a blow to his knees which sent him toppling over. Ike took the metal from the doorknob and manipulated it into throwing knives. He held his ground as I kept Oliver distracted. I peeked over his shoulder and Chancellor Fowler was still out, his head slumped over. Corrin hovered over him, prepared for if he spontaneously did anything.

River's dad lifted his head up, but his eyes were on Ike. Ike's eyes widened and his body turned so that instead of facing Oliver, he was looking at me.

"Riley, I don't know what's happening." He sounded scared and he lifted his arm, his new weapons aimed at me.

"Ike, you don't want to do that." I looked over at Oliver who had a sinister smile on his face. "Stop it right now!"

"You won't let me have what I want, Erik Fowler doesn't get what he wants!" Oliver shouted, right as Corrin tucked the dagger under her arm and tackled her brother. Ike released the knives seconds before he hit the ground.

I turned my head the minute I willed them to move away from me and towards Oliver, feeling the sting of a small cut on my cheek. Oliver had dived out of the way and Chancellor Fowler was starting to stir. I did my best to create a quick fire in my hand and threw it out the broken window, hoping that would alert the others.

"Riley, people are coming," Corrin warned, but her face left my vision when I was grabbed and thrown down to the ground.

The girl I'd recognized from before, the one who basically dehydrated Grayson, barged into the room but before she could make any moves, Corrin turned around and kicked her in the stomach, sending her flying into the door at the other end of the room. The girl shook her head and pushed away from the door, staring right at Corrin, who started to wobble on her feet and cough. She was doing the same thing to her as she did with Grayson.

"Cor!" Ike gripped the metal dagger he'd made and slashed at the girl. He struck her shoulder and she hissed. He started to bring the edge of the dagger over to her neck, then he started coughing as well, but he kept trying to strike her even if the blows weren't as harsh or lethal.

I tried to get up but Oliver climbed on top of me, putting his hands around my throat. He brought my head up and then slammed it back onto the ground. I let my fire out, burning his forearms and anywhere else I could reach but he didn't seem to care.

He squeezed his hands tighter and I couldn't get my mind to give me the strength to push him off me. Multiple loud howls sounded throughout the room and I knew my fire had hit.

Black spots were encapsulating my vision as I thrashed and burned Oliver's flesh. Oxygen hadn't completely left my head so that I could do one thing. I found the mind I needed and gave him the go ahead.

The house shook and the sound of wood breaking and menacing growls was closer than I thought.

"That is my daughter, you insufferable shit." Chancellor Fowler had blood pouring down the front of his head and he stepped up behind Oliver. All at once, Oliver released my neck when he bent backwards at an unhealthy angle. I heard a crack and then some more, and those cracks were sharp and quick.

I coughed violently, watching as Oliver slumped over and a shadow was in my vision. A shadow that swirled in place, eventually dissipating and revealing Asher and Grayson. Grayson saw me, but then looked over at Corrin and Ike, swiftly moving over to the girl harming them.

"This is for the last time." Grayson moved his shadows over her body and covered her eyes. He pulled her away from them and flung her out the open door. The sound of her body thumping down the stairs echoing. He started to send shadows all around this room, likely planning to cover it in darkness and get me out.

He was knocked off his feet by an invisible force and catapulted into Asher, who reached out to steady them both before they fell over. Chancellor Fowler let out a harsh, annoyed groan as he focused his gaze on them.

Asher ran over to me, ignoring his father's body. Chancellor Fowler ignited the ground around us and Asher backed up, trying to look through the flames. I heard the crash of Mateo and Jade barging in and nearly taking an entire wall with them. The screams they'd left in their wake had ceased. Even through the massive flames, I could see my familiar, my Beau, between both Mateo and Jade. His teeth were bared, but he looked so tired.

Chancellor Fowler yanked me up by my neck and I let my legs dangle, trying to wiggle free.

"Where is she?!" Grayson yelled.

"She's in there! Can you get through?" Asher answered back.

"I can try!" Grayson confirmed and his shadow landed in the ring of fire, but Chancellor Fowler instantly grabbed his throat.

"I am having a moment with my daughter!" Grayson's body was thrown back through the fire, landing on the other side with Asher. He dropped me back on the ground and I tried to catch myself, feeling the pain vibrate through my legs. "I could give you everything, but you do this! You ruin everything you could have!"

My throat was sore from Oliver's hands but it didn't bother me. I didn't care. I used my magic and made the flames higher and he looked around.

"You want to be a disobedient child, Riley? Let's take a walk down memory lane." He brought his hand up slightly and all the glass pieces from the broken window ripped away from their place and stood at attention. He flicked his hand and the jagged pieces tore through Asher's side, Grayson was able to shadow out of the way, but another piece hit Corrin in the face and two sliced Ike's leg.

"STOP IT!"

"Why?! You don't like the privileges I've given you, the future you could have!?"

I didn't realize what he was doing until I heard Corrin screaming my name. Chancellor Fowler was dragging her over to the window.

I used my magic to try to pull her back, but he pushed back. My mind was exhausted, but I kept going. Corrin tried to squirm away but his hold on her was too strong. Asher was bleeding from his side but he grabbed her and tried to yank her back. Grayson's shadows tried to bring her in, hoping that would get her out, but she was planted firmly in Chancellor Fowler's hold.

"Let go of my sister!" Ike held onto his metal dagger, running over to them just to get tripped up by Chancellor Fowler and thrown back. The chancellor moved his desk with ease, and pinned Ike against the wall.

Mateo and Jade whined as Chancellor Fowler put pressure on their minds. I heard other wails from beyond the room and saw Beau trying to get to me. His own head was being forced down, but his eyes never left me.

Mom. Mom, make it stop.

He limped forward, a long cut displayed his side and he winced with each amount of pressure the chancellor was adding to his head. He kept moving towards me and my body started to vibrate. The wolves chomped at the air, the room collapsing from their jolts.

"You can fix this, Riley. You can just be my obedient daughter and we can put this all behind us."

I could feel sweat everywhere and it wasn't just from the heat that surrounded us. It was my mind working and reworking. I wanted to help relieve the wolves of their agony, I wanted to pull Ike from his entrapment, I wanted to help Corrin and Beau and everyone else, but it was all so much. This wasn't fair. I should have just shut up and did what I was told.

But that wasn't me.

You are stronger than him because I think you know exactly who you are, Riley.

My powers were amazing, and I couldn't wait to explore them on my own time. Right now wasn't that time.

I blinked over to him. "I'm sorry that I disappointed you. I'm so sorry I never listened to you."

His eyes turned soft, like I knew they would. He reached out to touch my cheek.

"I'm sorry that I ever made you think I was your daughter." I grabbed his hand and yanked it back, hearing the bones crack. He yelled, his magic temporarily releasing his holds. I held onto his arm, bringing my knee up and connecting it between his legs. He wheezed, dropping to his knees.

He willed some of the fire to wrap around my wrists, burning my skin and I screamed at the pain. "I am your father. You. Will. Listen. To. Me." The words came out through his teeth.

The pain was ruthless but I didn't fight against it. I wasn't a regular human. The fire could hurt but it was also at this moment my salvation. I pressed my lips together through the pain and I embraced the rings of fire around my wrists. The wisps of flames moved around my skin, burning the hairs on my arms, but eventually melting into my skin.

It felt like added heat to the burning sensation that was already settled at my very core.

Chancellor Fowler shook his head, scowling at me as he tried to get his bearings but I wouldn't let him. He used his powers to force me across the short distance over to me, but I willed myself to stop.

The power he was using to try to yank me over was heavy and I was straining to stand my ground. I watched as the last of the flames retreated from my wrists and I eased up my resistance. My body sailed towards him, but I kicked out my foot, hitting him in the stomach hard enough to hear ribs pop and crack.

I let my telekinesis roughly bring his face up towards me and I slammed his head down, letting the flames he'd created to enclose us, burn the top of his head. I forced him up with my powers, tilting his head back. "You are *not* my father." Blood trickled down the front of his face, coating his lips, his teeth. It dripped on the ground around me and I had no desire to black out or to let the red liquid deter me from what I needed to do.

I cinched my hand around his throat and applied pressure, hearing him gasp for air and forcibly opening his mouth. I collected the fire that was around us into my hand, feeling his pull to stop my hand but it was weak and almost like he was pleading with me, wanting me to let him in.

I smirked and dropped the fireball into his mouth, forcing his lips closed. His throat turned red and blisters popped up in various places. Smoke came from his mouth when he could finally open it, and he clawed at his throat when I let him go.

He reached for me and I leaped back, seeing Corrin running from the window and to my side. "Is he...?" Mateo's large wolf form towered over us, letting small growls leave his throat. The sound of wood scraping against wood sounded in my ears and I watched Ike shift the desk that had him pinned, away from his body.

My heart thundered loudly in my chest. "Not yet." Beau shook off his body, his cut still leaking blood, but he limped over to Chancellor Fowler's body, licking his chops and very viciously diving into the chancellor's neck. He ripped skin and tore through tendons. His tail wagged happily the entire time and when he was done, he came over to me and sat down. Blood coated his face, but it almost looked like he was smiling.

Good boy. You're a very good boy. I thought to him, tears collecting in my eyes.

Jade's howling got my focus again and she nodded at me, using her large paws to shuffle Ike and the others out. Grayson and Asher both grabbed me and we followed after the wolves. Blood soaked the walls as we ran down the hallway. Bodies of people I'd never met littered the ground.

I stopped when I saw one I knew. She had a large claw-like gash in her neck that followed down her chest. "Lena?"

Blood gurgled out of her throat. She coughed but managed to say something to me. "You couldn't just do what he said, could you?" She spat blood at my feet and I felt a tug on my arm, along with hearing a protective growl from Beau.

"You chose to side with a monster," I said, my feet shuffling backwards when Asher pulled me harder.

We all got a few feet from the door and Mateo quickly got behind Asher, who leaned against him as he grabbed his stomach. I walked up to him and placed my hand over his wound. "What do we do now?" he asked, looking to me for answers. Grayson threaded his fingers through my own and patiently waited for my reply.

I turned my head and looked back at the house. My nose turned up and I let fire erupt in my hands. I tossed it at the house, watching as the wood was slowly enveloped in flames and I watched my legacy burn.

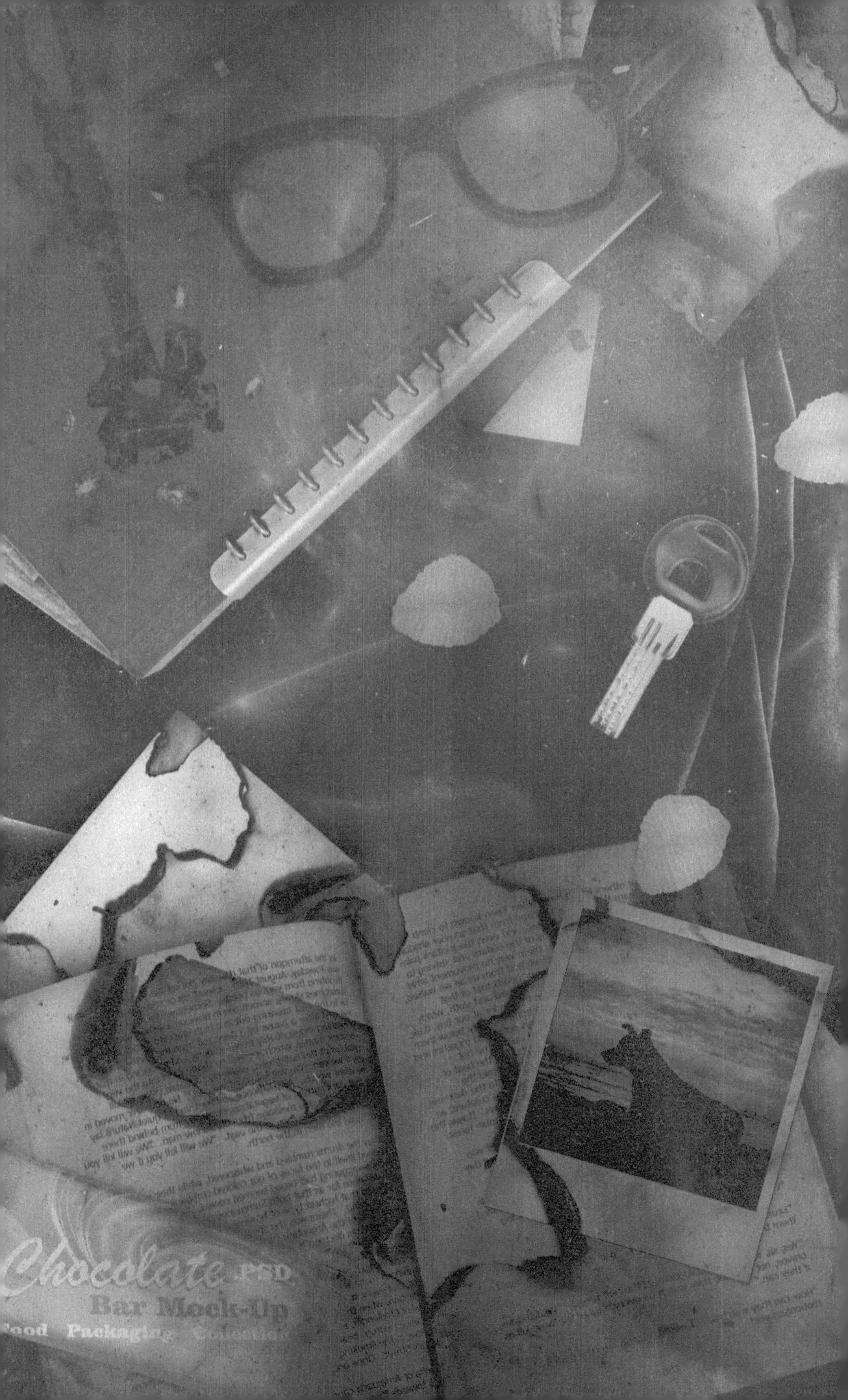
Chocolate .PSD
Bar Mock-Up
Packaging

51

RILEY

"You picked what we watched last time," Grayson whined, stealing the remote from River's hand.

"I am the injured one here. I had surgery and everything, so hand it over." River held his hand out.

I watched them argue from the kitchen, while Asher set our food up in cute little trays.

I considered the comfortable bliss we had settled into and how we'd gotten here. I thought back to what happened after we'd left that burning house with no idea how the future would play out. Ike had called 911 from the car and we all crossed our fingers that we didn't have to explain more than we needed to. The minute we got out of the general area, I wanted to go see River. I'd jumped out of the car, likely while it was still moving, and scared the nurse at her station when I asked to see my boyfriend. I was covered in mild burns and probably some blood, but I didn't care.

He'd winced when I hugged him as hard as I could, giving him the biggest kiss I could muster and told him it was done. I'd admitted I was scared for the future. I got into his hospital bed, being careful about his injuries, and cuddled into him. Grayson had texted later saying that the hospital wouldn't let Asher just meander around while he was bleeding out of his side, so they were going to patch him up first.

I'd passed on school the next few days after it happened and when the news got out about the massacre that happened at the Chancellor's house, it was all over social media. The school had tried to clean it up in their very fancy, but also very vague email, but people embellished. The house was nothing more than ash and rubble when the pictures on the news cycles started popping up.

Then there were the long theories where people connected him and his mother. Maybe someone had a vendetta against him? Maybe they pissed off the wrong people? I rolled my eyes at every single stupid word. They would find a new chancellor that had nothing to fucking do with me and that had my shoulders easing. Celica would be my only connection to him, but that would stay within my circle. Our own little secret that we all would happily keep. They would have to yet again find someone to fill my dad's job as well, hopefully someone worthy of the job.

Corrin checked on me frequently, along with Jade and everyone else. By checked on, I meant she came over and sat in bed with me while she made the boys do something else. Grayson would read with me, but I knew his eyes were also watching, making sure I didn't need anything. Asher doted on River, well, we all did, but I told him not to worry about me and that I didn't regret what I did.

River and Asher had to console their mother when she heard her husband was lost in that fire. River was much nicer to her than his brother, since Asher would blatantly state that 'she never came around when her son was in the fucking hospital'. She claimed she never knew about that, which, knowing their dad, that wouldn't surprise me. Asher said that she would be fine, there was enough money to keep her comfortable in that house and he would hire help for her if she needed it. And he did so in the most begrudging tone, admitting that he was glad she was out from under his thumb.

The story sent our parents off the deep end and things were just now settling down. Grayson spent a few days at his parent's house and I'd brought my mom over to Corrin's house, smiling while I watched them chat about their headache-inducing daughters. I'd been scolded and damn near had to sign a contract stating that I would check in with my mom twice a week for the next year. I'd just laughed, grateful that she didn't want all the details. I had started to explain but then she'd stopped me halfway through and told me that I should leave all the heroic acrobatics to the female characters in my books.

She'd mentioned therapy, for the both of us, and I didn't decline her offer. I'd gone ahead and started my research on female psychiatrists, since I was very done with men trying to tell me how to feel.

Beau jumped up onto the counter, sniffing and leaning towards the tray of food.

"Back off. You literally have food." Asher pointed to the dog bowl in the corner.

I plucked a plain chip out of the bowl and fed it to him. Beau happily munched away, giving Asher a smug look and jumping down. The scar on his side was still visible, but it had healed nicely. Corrin had healed what she could before we'd taken him to the emergency vet.

"You spoil him," Asher scolded, shaking his head.

"He deserves it, don't you buddy?" I got down and scratched Beau around the ears.

I love you very much. I told him privately.

I love you too, Mom.

I straightened up and walked over to Asher. "How are you feeling?"

"I told you yesterday, I'm fine."

"I ask all of you the same thing, so don't snap at me for caring."

He sighed. "Sorry. I'm good. You've put a lot of things on hiatus because of injuries." He leaned down to get closer to my face.

"Have I?" I asked innocently.

"You have, little liar, and while we all appreciate that, maybe we could talk about easing back into a routine."

I snorted, taking a pretzel from the bowl and popping it into my mouth. "A routine? Are you trying to have routine sex with me, *sir*? So romantic." My tone was overflowing with sarcasm.

He groaned. "River already said he was fine with watching."

"What?!"

"After we all talked about it of course." He winked at me which was so out of character I almost started laughing. "If you need more time, that's okay too. I know you might not be totally okay at the moment, so just say the word and whatever you want is yours....well, within reason."

Grayson walked up and snagged a tiny pretzel from one of the bowls. He looked from me to Asher. "Ah, did he tell you what we talked about?"

"You guys are ridiculous."

"*Aking sinta*, if it's too soon, we can—"

I pushed my hand over his mouth. "Yes, I know."

A knock came at the door and I walked over to open it, seeing Corrin and Mateo standing there. Mateo held two cases of beer in each of their hands. "*Buenas noches!* We brought drinks!"

"Oh hell yeah!" Grayson shrugged past me, grabbing one of the cases and ushering Mateo inside. I rolled my eyes and gave Corrin a hug before letting her through the threshold.

"Wait, Jade and Ike are back there. We also brought Beau friends to play with." Corrin clapped her hands and went to go say hi, while Jade and Ike came in behind her. Jax strutted inside, never giving Beau a second glance and Ted flew around the living room, eventually perching himself on top of the TV.

"Is that a fucking bird?" Asher said, stopping when he noticed Ted and then took all of us in.

"Yes, it is." I kissed his cheek.

River had his leg propped up on the coffee table and his arm was in its sling, but he made it work so I could adjust snuggling into him. Asher tucked himself in on the other side of River, while Grayson happily sat on my other side. Mateo took the other chair with Corrin in their lap while Jade and Ike sat on the floor, attempting not to scarf down most of the food.

Beau sat on the floor next to Jade, but never too far away from me, tucking his head into her lap.

"Are you happy, gorgeous?" River asked as he nuzzled the side of my face, kissing my temple.

I played with my nose ring and thought about that. I was happy because I was safe. I'd done scary things and made mistakes. I'd lost people I cared about and did some things I'll never be able to take back. We would go back to Mystic Riegan and I could fully decide if Celica was something I wanted. I was a witch before I even knew about the coven and I'd be a witch long after I graduated. My dad had loved that school despite its many, many flaws.

And now maybe I could learn to love it too.

"I'm home. So yes, I'm very happy."

EPILOGUE
RILEY

I kicked my feet as I sat on the counter, glancing up from my book to watch Grayson move around the kitchen. I dug inside the bag of candy gummies that sat next to me, pulling out a few and putting them in my mouth. Grayson had decided that since school was out for Thanksgiving break and after everything we'd been through, he was going to show off his 'cooking' skills. He'd claimed that he'd watched his mom make chicken adobo enough times that he could recreate it with no issues. The moment I'd walked into the kitchen and saw the raw chicken thighs, garlic, soy sauce and everything else, my mouth started to water. This couldn't be so bad.

I looked back down to find my place again when I heard a swift *fuck* and a splat. I put my book down, looking past my feet to see a chicken thigh laying on the floor, oil splattered around it. I moved my eyes up to Grayson, who was holding a pair of tongs and saying what I assumed was mumbled curse words in Tagalog under his breath. The telltale sound of Beau's paws hit my ears and I knew he was headed to the free food.

Not for you, buddy. I thought to him, I saw him peek around the counter, giving me sad eyes.

He looked away and towards the piece of chicken.

Beau. No. I scolded. He huffed and laid down on the ground, his head between his paws. He was so dramatic.

Grayson reached down and picked up the food, getting supplies from under the sink and cleaning up the mess in record time. He gave me a look over his shoulder. "You say nothing."

I was about to pick up my book again but stopped. "I haven't said anything this whole time."

"I know you're thinking about it."

I narrowed my eyes. "Okay, give me your best River and tell me what I'm thinking."

He finished washing his hands and attempted to go back to tending to his browning chicken thighs. "You are thinking, 'No Grayson, we should have just ordered in and made our lives easier, but you had to go and try to impress everyone by showing them one of your many skills that also happens to make you incredibly sexy.'"

I giggled, kicking my feet some more. "Oh, yes that was exactly what I was thinking, especially the last part."

He went over to a cabinet and got a large plate and placed it next to the pot he had the food in. He turned around and wiggled in between my legs, placing his hands on my thighs. His fingertips grazed the bottom of my shorts. "Is that right?"

I held in a smile, nodding. He kissed me, taking my bottom lip between his teeth. I let out a small whimper and his hands squeezed my thighs. I hooked my ankles together behind his back, keeping him close to me. His hands found their way to my waistband and I pulled away a tiny bit.

"I don't think Asher would be very happy if you had his house smelling like burnt chicken." I tapped his lips with my index finger.

He groaned, moving away from me. "Not only are your beautiful, *aking sinta*, but you are also right."

I picked my book back up. "As per usual." I plucked another gummy from the bag.

"You'll ruin your appetite, and you won't get to know the true deliciousness of chicken adobo. Hand them over." He pointed to my snacks and held his hand out.

I smirked at him. "No way. You take these away and I'll tell you what happens at the end of the book." I waved the book I was reading in his face.

He gave me shocked look. "That is diabolical but fine, you brat."

"Love you too." It was odd saying that out loud, but the first time we'd said it to each other was just as natural as this current moment.

Asher was at a late faculty meeting and it had just been me, him and River. We were all tired and sweaty, but no one was ready to get up and take a shower yet. River had whispered he loved me in my ear and wrapped his arm around me, but then Grayson cleared his throat and turned my face so that I could look at him. He'd looked into my eyes and said it. Three words followed by my name and then River grumbled 'it's about time' which caused Grayson to take the pillow behind his head and smack him with it.

A pillow fight that turned into one of the main reasons I'd started stretching every day in the morning.

Grayson started plating the chicken and then adding things to the empty pot. "Did the St. James brothers tell you when they would be back?"

I grabbed my phone from my pocket, checking the time. "Probably in the next thirty minutes or so."

I was happy to know Asher and River were spending more time together. I coaxed River into thinking about talking to someone about his dad, after therapy was going so well with me and my mom, but his condition was that he would go if Asher went. It took us only a week to break him down, but in the end Asher was always going to do what was in River's best interest.... not to mention he knew it would make me happy.

They had a session this afternoon and had told me to text them if whatever Grayson ended up making looked suspicious and they should pick something up for dinner. I trusted my shadow wielder, but I'd decided to remain in the kitchen instead of up in River's room, just in case.

The smell of different seasonings and herbs filled my nostrils and my stomach grumbled.

Grayson winked at me over his shoulder. "Don't worry. You'll get fed soon."

RIVER CRUSHED HIS NAPKIN AND THREW IT ON HIS PLATE. "NOW THAT WAS A meal."

Asher placed his silverware on his plate and got up. "I have to admit, you did good, shadow wielder." He placed our empty plates on top of his and went to the sink.

Grayson smiled proudly. "Please let my mom know I did her proud."

I leaned over his chair and kissed his cheek. I snuck around Asher to the fridge.

"What are you doing, gorgeous?" River asked, coming up behind me.

I pulled out a yellow cake with buttercream icing, the words happy birthday were written on top in black. I tilted the cake so River could see.

Asher raised an eyebrow at us when we both looked at him. "What the fuck are you two looking at?" Grayson sidled up next to him, his shit-eating grin appearing when he realized I was holding the cake.

I rolled my lips together, walking over to Asher. "Well, you said that you didn't want us to do anything obnoxious for your birthday, so we stayed in and just really didn't celebrate last week. You actually worked most of the day which was highly annoying. I took it upon myself to get you a belated birthday cake." I placed the cake on the counter, popping the plastic top off.

Asher slowly moved his eyes to all of us. "And you two knew about this?"

"Come on, big brother. You only turn thirty-four once and even your stubborn ass deserves a fucking cake." River pointed to the sugar filled dessert. "Besides, our girl got it for you, so I'm pretty sure you'll eat it just fine."

I batted my eyelashes innocently. "You wouldn't say no to me, would you?"

Asher scoffed. "Yes, I actually would, And I have."

I cocked my head to the side, eyeing the cake. "Hmm, okay. Sure." I stuck my finger into the icing at the top, scooping some of it up. All of them watched me carefully. "You don't really deserve this cake now, do you?" I stuck my tongue out, licking my finger and focusing all my attention on my grumpy professor.

We'd made it through the rest of this semester without getting caught and I was very proud of that. He was so put together in class, but as tough and stoic as he wanted to be, Asher was always the one texting me to come to his office for a teacher/student meeting. Meetings that included riding him while he sat in his desk chair or the newest one consisted of making me sit across from him and play with myself while he watched and used his dream magic to make me come so hard I nearly went blind.

Asher's mouth dropped open as he watched me suck my finger. I removed it with a pop and sighed as if nothing had happened.

"Holy fuck," Grayson said, running a hand through his hair. "I've never been more turned on by icing in my whole life."

"Well played, gorgeous," River complimented, placing his hand at my waist and leaning down to nuzzle into my neck. "You know not to rile up Professor St. James unless you intend to be screaming for the rest of the night."

I looked at Asher, licking my lips to get whatever remnants of the icing was there. "I'm well aware. Isn't that right, *sir*?"

Asher stalked over to me, gripping my chin. "You didn't get me a birthday present this year."

"You said you didn't want any," I said, trying not to rub my thighs together.

"I changed my mind." He let go of my chin and went down to my waist band, unbuttoning my shorts and yanking them, along with my panties, down my legs. He never took his eyes off me when he spoke to River. "Keep her steady."

I didn't know what he was talking about until he got down on his knees, grabbing my legs and putting them over his shoulders. River pressed his body to my back and held my middle, keeping me balanced. Grayson came up to next to me, looking down along with me as Asher buried his face in my pussy.

I let out a moan, squirming and tensing my thighs. River held onto me, leaning into my face. "Stay still, gorgeous. We got you."

Asher's tongue rolled over my clit and I gasped. The sound was captured by Grayson's mouth colliding with mine. River pulled me tighter against him, moving his hands up my shirt so he could move my bra cups down and toy with my nipples. I whimpered against Grayson's mouth, our tongues moving together. Asher lapped at my center, digging his fingers into my thighs as he drove his tongue further inside of me. He sucked my clit into his mouth and I all but screamed into Grayson's welcoming mouth. I was getting hotter and sweat was collecting on my forehead from the feeling of River's fingers pulling at my tight nipples and the hands and mouths that were everywhere. My powers boiled within me and I searched for that balance I was still learning to find.

"Let's not destroy the kitchen, hmm? You can come without making a fucking mess, can't you gorgeous?" River smiled against my ear.

I nodded lazily, feeling the orgasm start to happen. My thighs tightened around Asher's head and I came loudly. My toes curled and a sensation of pleasure flooded down my spine. Asher removed my shaky legs from his shoulders, straightening up. He bent down and kissed me hard, letting me taste myself on his lips. Asher put his hand around my throat and pulled me away, saying against my swollen lips, "Take her to the living room."

River gave his brother a salute and my vision was turned upside down when he picked me up and put me over his shoulder.

"River, put me down!" I playfully shouted, hitting his back with my fists. He'd taken physical therapy seriously and although he felt some pain doing certain activities, he worked hard to be able to maintain all the things he did before.

My boyfriend slapped my ass. "As you wish." He tossed me onto the couch, but before I could scramble away, he got on top of me, sliding his hand down between my legs and rubbing his fingers over where I was still wet. I stifled a moan, automatically opening up more for him.

"Someone's fucking needy." River pushed two of his fingers inside of me and I closed my eyes, biting my bottom lip. "That pretty cunt is making a mess all over my hand." He removed his fingers and held them out for Grayson. My shadow wielder opened his mouth and moaned around River's fingers, savoring my taste.

I pressed my lips together, reaching out and rubbing the front of Grayson's pants. He laughed, swatting my hand away. "Ask nicely, *aking sinta.*"

"Be a good boy and give me your cock," I said between breaths, while River kissed up stomach, lifting up my shirt and swirling his tongue around my nipples.

"Demanding thing, aren't you? You won't be so talkative when that fucking mouth is full." Asher grabbed his shirt from behind and tugged it off. He removed his glasses, placing them on the coffee table. He moved between Grayson and River and hauled me off the couch and placed me on my knees, facing him.

Asher undid his belt, sliding his pants down and his cock jutted out. He stroked his dick, running the head along my lips. I opened my mouth and flattened my tongue, tasting him. I swirled my tongue around his crown and then sucked him back down.

"I know you can go further than that, little liar. Gag on my dick." He held the back of my head and forced me to take more of him. I choked, but didn't tell him to stop. He hit the back of my throat and I breathed through my nose, wanting more. He pulled my head back and I coughed, tears running down the corners of my eyes. "You want me to fuck you while they take turns filling that slutty mouth of yours?"

My lower lip trembled as my pussy throbbed with need. I could feel my arousal slipping down my inner thighs. "Y-yes."

Asher pressed his forehead to mine. "Yes, what?"

"Yes, sir."

"Say it again."

"Yes, sir. Yes, sir," I said a little louder.

He hooked his arms under my mine and lifted me up, turning me around so we could go to the couch. I was met with River and Grayson engaged in a kiss that made my mouth water. Grayson had his hand wrapped tightly around River's cock, the metal of his Jacob's ladder piercing sparkling in the overhead living room light.

They caught sight of us and moved to the other side of the couch, watching as Asher bent me over and placed my knees on the cushions. He moved my legs further apart to the point where I felt a burning sensation in my muscles. Grayson gently grabbed my shirt, pulling it over my head, while River unclasped my bra.

"Ah, that's better. Now we can appreciate all of you. You and that sexy body that's all ours." River sighed in contentment as his green eyes scanned my naked body. They both removed their shirts, giving me an eyeful of sweaty torsos and abs. Grayson ran the head of his cock along my lips and I stuck my tongue out licking the pre cum from the tip. His brow furrowed but his eyes held a desire there.

Asher's hand went between my legs and my eyes rolled back.

"You're a dripping mess. Beg me to fuck you like the needy little slut you are." He nudged two of his fingers inside, curling them. I moaned and pushed my ass back needing more.

His fingers fucked me harder, the sound of how wet I was echoing through the living room. "Y-yes, please sir, fuck me."

"Oh gorgeous, that's not what he said." River caressed my chin, while Grayson let his shadows move over my hands and arms.

"Fuck, please sir, fuck me like the needy slut that I a-am." I stuttered on the last word when Asher pulled his fingers out and spanked my pussy. I dug my nails into the fabric of the couch when he pushed inside of me.

Asher grabbed my hips and pounded into me. "Is this what you wanted, little liar? You want me to use this pussy until you're begging me to stop?"

I couldn't move my hands because Grayson used his shadows to keep them where they were. River moved my braids out of my face, not phased by the sound of his brother's pelvis slapping against my skin. It shouldn't have since this has happened at least five times in the last month.

"Open that pretty mouth, gorgeous," he instructed, holding his cock out for me.

I opened up for him and he filled my mouth. My tongue ran over his piercing, my eyes finding Grayson's. He stroked his dick, watching me suck his best friend off. His hand flew over his shaft and he licked his lips, enjoying every minute of the show in front of him.

My noises were muffled around River's cock and Asher didn't let up. His rhythm and thrusts were brutal, hitting me deeper. River popped out of my mouth and backed up, letting Grayson take his place in my mouth.

"Come for me, Riley. Choke my cock with that wet little cunt." Asher moved one of his hands to my clit and pinched. A shockwave vibrated through my body, allowing Grayson to push even further into my throat.

Asher spanked me and pulled out. He yanked me up, keeping me flush to his body while River jumped over the couch and sat down. My boyfriend reached for me, adjusting my legs so I straddled him. My arousal dripped onto his thigh and he chuckled. I rubbed myself against his hard dick, his piercing causing me to stifle a moan.

"Be so fucking loud when you ride my cock, baby. We all want to hear you scream." River grabbed his shaft, angling it right at my entrance and guided me down.

"Oh fuck," I moaned, moving my body back and forth. He grabbed my hips, helping me keep my rhythm. I threw my head back, pressing my hands against his chest.

Grayson came up from the back of the couch and I opened my mouth, inviting his cock into my mouth. River moved his hands to my ass and squeezed. "That's it, gorgeous. Bounce on my dick like a good girl."

Grayson's shadows came out and trapped my hands behind my back. He flexed his hips so I gagged on him. He pulled his cock out and I took in a breath. I bounced up and down, reveling in the way River watched me. "Your cock feels so good."

"Yeah? It feels good? It makes you want to come? Especially when I play with your pretty clit." He thumbed my sensitive bundle of nerves and my breathing stuttered. I found Asher's eyes and pleaded towards him with my own.

"Kiss me." My voice was demanding, but I wouldn't apologize.

"Or what?" Asher taunted.

I groaned while my orgasm built. River held my hips and lifted his own, slamming his cock up into me and I nearly bit my tongue as I cried out. Asher came and grabbed the back of my head, pressing his lips to mine. He pulled away the minute I came so that I could scream out my climax. I slumped against River, feeling spent, but then my body was shifted off of River and moved to one side of the couch.

I faced the couch arm, my knees planted into the cushions and my arms over the side. Grayson came up behind me, arching my back and lifting my ass up. "Are you tired, *aking sinta*?"

Asher stood in front of me, his thick, hard cock, in my vision. I licked my lips eagerly. "N-no."

"You're going to be able to come one more time? Let me fuck that tight cunt," Grayson slid a finger down my wet slit and I shivered. His shadows roamed down my body and rubbed against my clit. I whimpered and Asher dragged his thumb down my bottom lip.

"He's going to fill you up, gorgeous and I'm going to fill his mouth. And he's going to swallow every drop, aren't you?" I looked over my shoulder to see River tug Grayson's hair, kissing him and licking his cheek.

"Don't I always?" Grayson snarked back.

"Good fucking boy. Make her feel good and don't stop until she comes." River let go of his hair and starting moving his hand over his cock.

I brought my lips towards Asher's dick and circled my tongue around the tip. He hissed out in pleasure, running his hand down my braids. "Answer the question, Riley. Can you give us one more?"

I nodded, moving my ass back to connect with Grayson's dick.

"Oh, the pretty slut is so eager," Asher said the words through his gritted teeth and leaned down to speak against my lips. "Fuck, what is it about you, hm?"

"I think you like my attitude, *sir*." I pecked his lips before he could retreat. "In fact, I think you *love* it." I bit my lower lip when Grayson drove his cock inside of me. I snuck a look behind me to see him perfectly bobbing back and forth along River's cock while continuing to fuck me hard.

River held onto the back of the couch, while he fucked Grayson's mouth. I could have watched them the entire night, but my head was turned around and Asher plunged his dick into my mouth. Grayson's thrusts pushed me further down Asher's shaft and his shadows tweaked my nipples.

Grayson's cock hit my sweet spot and stars started to shine

behind my eyes. There was a different kind of euphoria along with it. One that only a person with dream magic could create. I moved my hand along the arm of the couch and found where his hand was. I sent warm, fire like sensations through Asher's body and he groaned.

"Take it all, Riley," Asher said, thrusting into my mouth erratically before coming down my throat. I licked him clean, swallowing before he backed away. He kept up that feeling in my subconscious, that feeling like I was having an out of body experience filled with pleasure.

I heard a sharp grunt and then a groan of relief behind me.

"Fuck, that's a good boy." River slipped out of Grayson's mouth, catching his breath.

I found my boyfriend's mind and let him into my thoughts. *Fuck, I love you.*

River gave me that smile that showed off his dimples, taking Asher's spot in front of me. His brother settled in the other chair, watching Grayson fuck me. River bent down and kissed me. "Come for us, Riley. And then we'll take care of you."

"Yes, yes, yes," I yelled out in a response but also because I was coming so hard, I thought I might cry. Grayson kept up his thrusts until his climax came shortly after mine. He rubbed my back, delicately pulling out of me. I feel onto the couch, feeling like I could fall asleep right then and there.

"All of that over a cake?" I asked, my voice muffled in the couch cushion.

Asher's deep laugh filled my ears. "You started it with your tempting icing on the finger maneuver."

Grayson ran a hand down his chest. "Can we actually eat the cake now?"

"You're thinking of food right now?" Asher questioned, rolling his eyes.

"Eh, I mean we all could use a sugar boost after this," River pointed out, kneeling down and coming face to face with me. "Are you hungry, gorgeous? We can clean you up and then feed you cake."

I gave him a soft smile and that's all he needed. River went to pick me up, but Asher grabbed his glasses from the table and got in front of him, lifting me up bridal style and cradling me to his chest. "Start getting the cake together, I'll clean her up."

"We usually do that...are you sure you know how, Asher?" Grayson asked, wincing when Asher threw him a death glare.

"I promise she'll be just as immaculate as she always is when we come back downstairs. Go help my brother with the fucking cake."

Grayson shut his mouth and jogged to the kitchen. I didn't speak on the fact that Asher just said I was immaculate, but I would let that sentence replay in my head for weeks to come. I rested my head on his shoulder as he took me upstairs to his master bathroom.

"Happy belated birthday, *sir*," I said, giggling a little.

Asher placed a gentle kiss to the side of my head. "I do love your attitude."

I turned my face so I could kiss him fully. "I know."

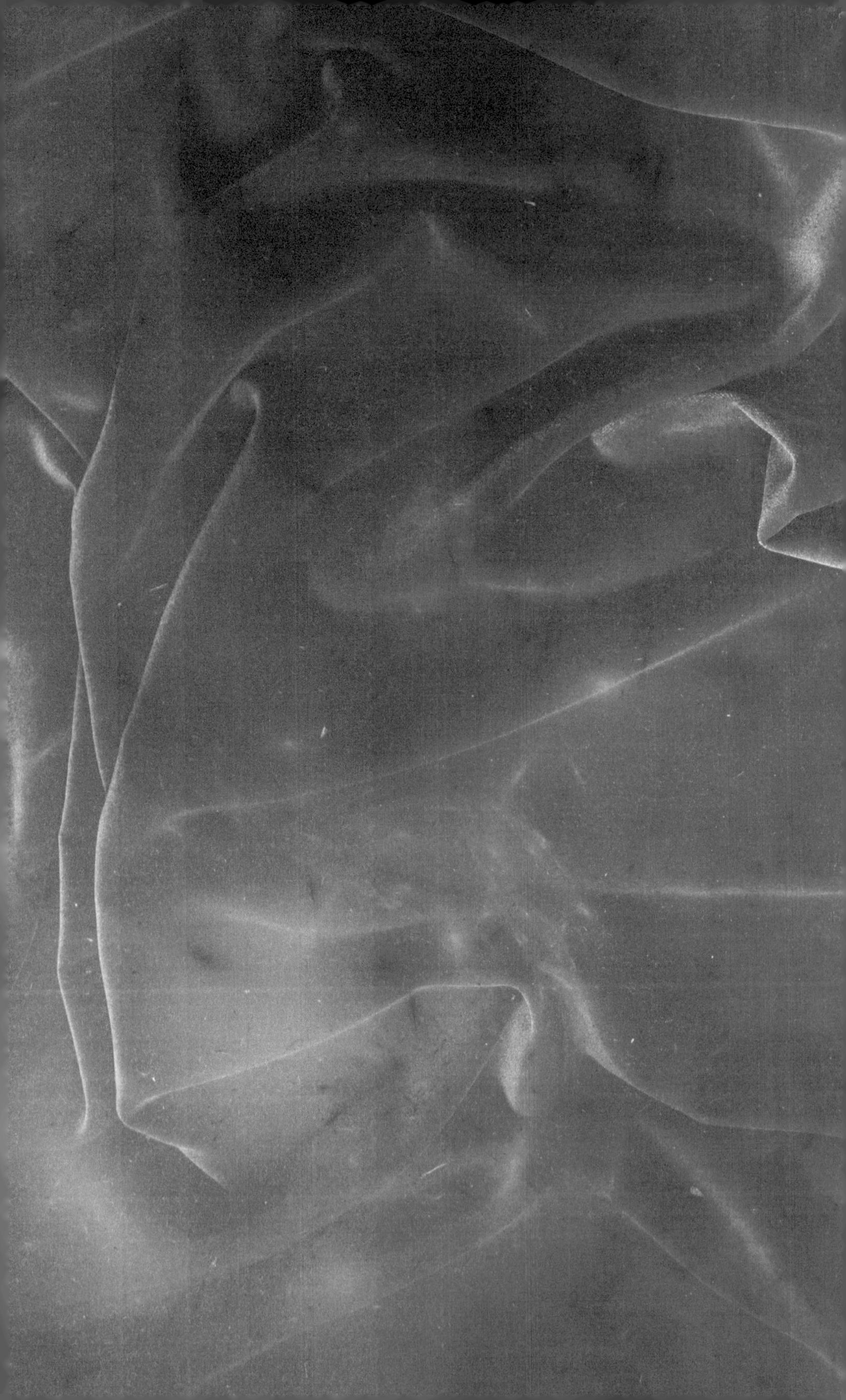

ACKNOWLEDGMENTS

Duet complete. Wow. To say I've finished two series is an incredible thing. This was so different than what I'm used to, but this was probably one of the easiest things I've written. I got to explore so many new things while writing this duet and I'll take everything I've learned into whatever I write next. I think more why choose will be in my future, believe me.

To my husband, thank you for supporting me in everything I do and making sure I eat when I'm on a deadline.

To my mom, thank you for always being there and being the gold standard for moms around the world.

To my sensitivity readers, Aurora and Marylife...thank you for the translation help. It means the world to me that you were apart of this duet.

To Jenny and Gabby, thank you for reading this story ahead of time and giving me all the unhinged thoughts. I adore you to pieces.

To my editor, Brittany, you are simply the best.

To all my readers, thank you for loving ALID so much and choosing to finish out this duet with me. This why choose wouldn't be much of a success without you.

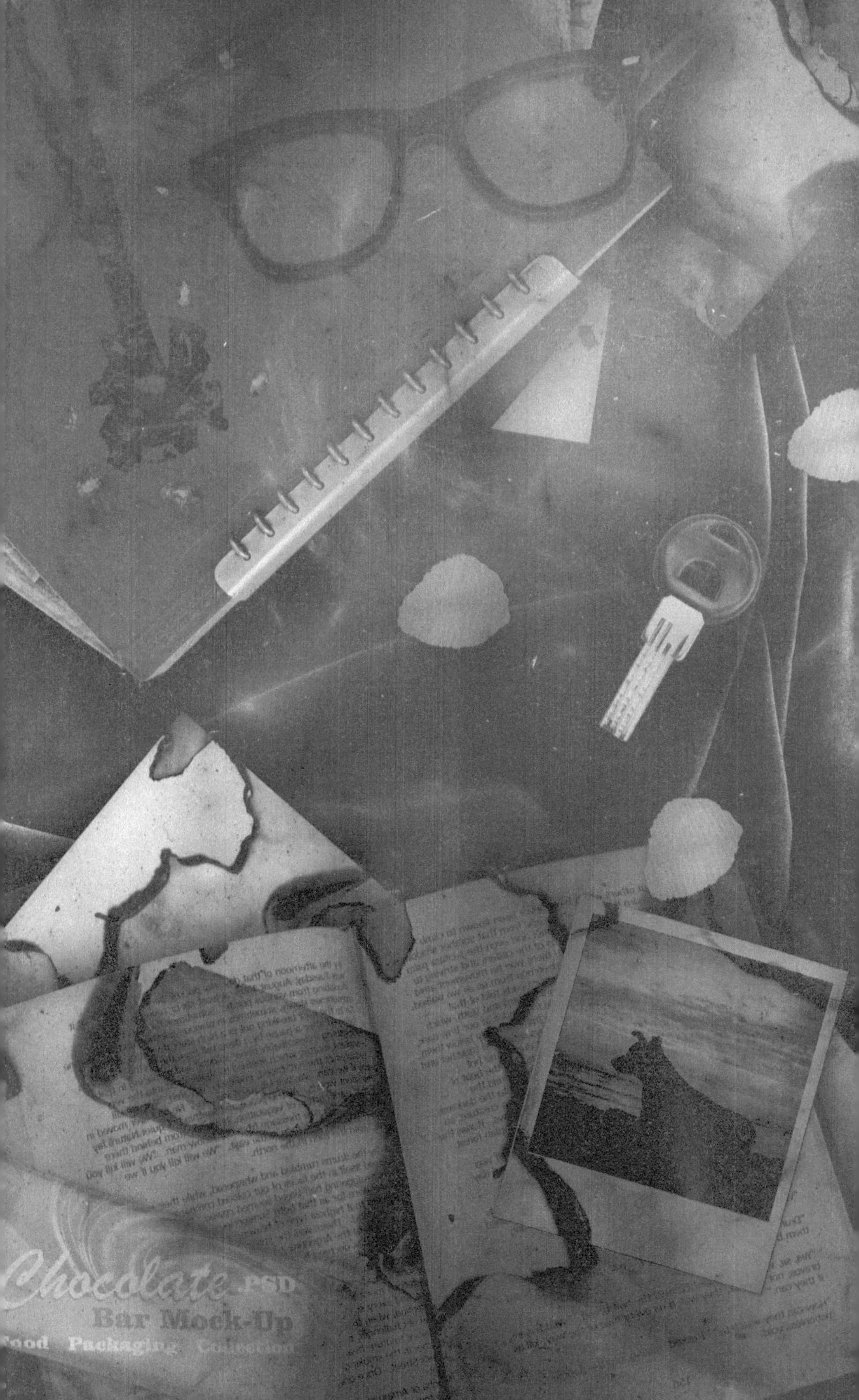
Chocolate .PSD
Bar Mock-Up
Food Packaging Collection

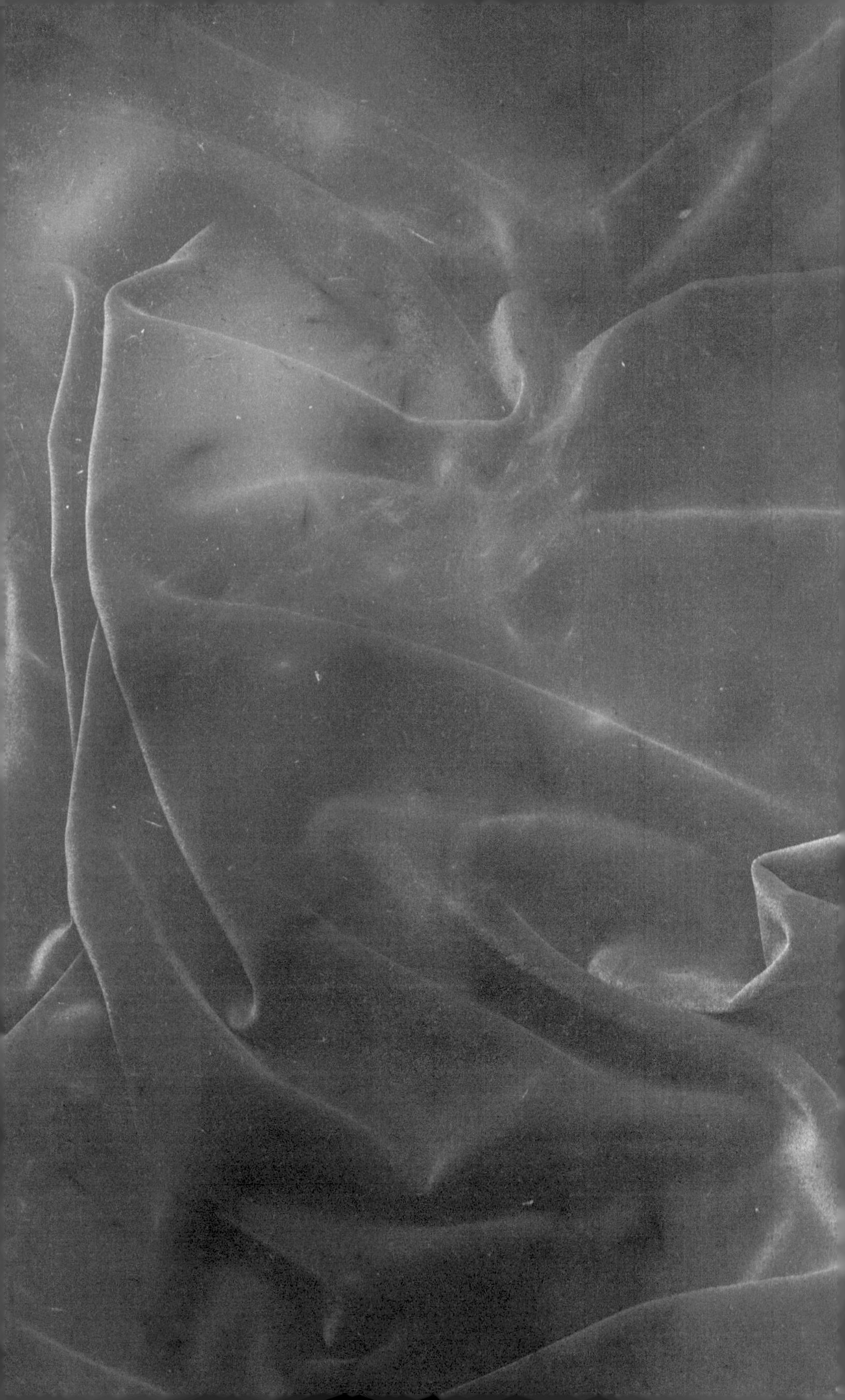

ABOUT
THE AUTHOR

Allie Shante was born and raised in Georgia and graduated from Georgia State University with a biology degree. While science was fun, books have always been a part of her heart and writing right up there with it. After writing and never finishing any of the books she started, she buckled down years later to finish a novel she never actually expected to write, let alone finish.

When she's not reading and writing confident females and stubborn men, she enjoys being an overprotective dog mom and crushing escape rooms with her husband.

Check out her out at: www.authorallieshante.com

Follow Allie on Instagram: @allieshantewrites

Follow Allie on Tik Tok: @allieshantewrites

instagram.com/allieshantewrites

tiktok.com/@allieshantewrites